# BREACH of TRUST

**Center Point
Large Print**

**This Large Print Book carries the
Seal of Approval of N.A.V.H.**

## Call of Duty
### Book #1

# BREACH of TRUST

## DiAnn Mills

CENTER POINT PUBLISHING
THORNDIKE, MAINE

This Center Point Large Print edition
is published in the year 2009 by arrangement with
Tyndale House Publishers, Inc.

The text of this Large Print edition is unabridged.
In other aspects, this book may vary
from the original edition.
Printed in the United States of America.
Set in 16-point Times New Roman type.

ISBN: 978-1-60285-508-3

Library of Congress Cataloging-in-Publication Data

Mills, DiAnn.
  Breach of trust / DiAnn Mills.
    p. cm.
  ISBN 978-1-60285-508-3 (library binding : alk. paper)
 1. Undercover operations--Fiction. 2. Intelligence service--Fiction.
  3. Large type books. I. Title.

PS3613.I567B74 2009b
813'.6--dc22

2009011475

*To Dr. Dennis Hensley for his wisdom, dedication, and generous contributions to the writing world.*

*Do not be deceived: God cannot be mocked.*
*A man reaps what he sows.*

GALATIANS 6:7

*Many thanks to all who made this book possible:
Beau Egert, Louise Gouge, Mona Hodgson,
Maryanne Keeling, Roberta Morgan,
Tom Morrisey, and David Staton.*

# CHAPTER 1

LIBRARIAN PAIGE ROGERS had survived more exciting days dodging bullets to protect her country. Given a choice, she'd rather be battling assassins than collecting overdue fines. For that matter, running down terrorists had a lot more appeal than running down lost books. Oh, the regrets of life—woven with guilt, get-over-its, and move-ons. But do-overs were impossible, and the adventures of her life were now shelved alphabetically under fiction.

*Time to reel in my pitiful attitude and get to work.* Paige stepped onto her front porch with what she needed for a full workday at the library. Already, perspiration dotted her face, a reminder of the rising temperatures. Before locking the door behind her, she scanned the front yard and surveyed the opposite side of the dusty road, where chestnut-colored quarter horses grazed on sparse grass. Torrid heat and no rain, as though she stood on African soil. But here, nothing out of the ordinary drew her attention. Just the way she liked it. Needed it.

Sliding into her sporty yet fuel-efficient car, she felt for the Beretta Px4 under the seat. The past could rear its ugly head without warning. Boy Scouts might be prepared; Girl Scouts were trained. The radio blared out the twang of a guitar and the misery of a man who'd lost his sweetheart to a rodeo star. Paige laughed at the irony of it all.

She zipped down the road, her tires crunching the grasshoppers that littered the way before her. In the rearview mirror, she saw birds perched on a barbed wire fence and a few defiant wildflowers. They held on to their roots in the sun-baked dirt the way she clutched hope. The radio continued to croon out one tune after another all the way into the small town of Split Creek, Oklahoma, ten klicks from nowhere.

After parking her car in the designated spot in front of the library, Paige hoisted her tote bag onto her shoulder and grabbed a book about Oklahoma history and another by C. S. Lewis. The latter had kept her up all night, helping her make some sense out of the sordid events of her past. She scraped the grasshoppers from her shoes and onto the curb. The pests were everywhere this time of year. Reminded her of a few gadflies she'd been forced to trust overseas. She'd swept the crusty hoppers off her porch at home and the entrance to the library as she'd done with the shadow makers of the past. But nothing could wipe the nightmares from her internal hard drive.

Her gaze swept the quiet business district with an awareness of how life could change in the blink of an eye. A small landscaping of yellow marigolds and sapphire petunias stretched toward the sky in front of the newly renovated, one-hundred-year-old courthouse. Its high pillars supported a piece of local history . . . and the secrets of the best of families. Business owners unlocked their stores and exchanged morning greetings. Paige recognized most of the dated cars and dusty pickups, but a black Town Car with tinted glass and an Oklahoma license plate parked on the right side of the courthouse caught her attention.

Why would someone sporting a luxury car want to venture into Split Creek, population 1,500? The lazy little town didn't offer much more than a few antique stores, a small library, a beauty shop, Dixie's Donuts, a Piggly Wiggly, four churches—including one First Baptist and one South First Baptist, each at opposite ends of town, one First Methodist, and a holiness tabernacle right beside Denim's Restaurant. She wanted to believe it was an early visitor to the courthouse. Maybe someone lost. But those thoughts soon gave way to curiosity and a twist of suspicion.

With a smile intended to be more appealing than a Fourth of July storefront, she crossed the street to subtly investigate the out-of-place vehicle. Some habits never changed.

Junior Shafer, who owned and operated a nearby antique store, stooped to arrange his outside treasures. Actually, Paige rarely saw an antique on display, just junk and old Avon bottles. "Mornin', Mr. Shafer. Looks like another scorcher."

"Mornin'. Yep, this heat keeps the customers

11

away." The balding man slowly stood and massaged his back. "Maybe I'll advertise free air-conditioning and folks will stop in."

"Whatever works." She stole a quick glance at the Town Car and memorized the license plate number. No driver. "Looks like you have a visitor." She pointed to the car.

Mr. Shafer narrowed his eyes and squinted. "Nah, that's probably Eleanor's son from Tulsa. He's helping her paint the beauty shop. She said he had a new car. The boy must be doing fine in the insurance business."

"Now that's a good son."

Mr. Shafer lifted his chin, then rubbed it. "Uh, you know, Paige . . . he ain't married."

"And I'm not looking." She'd never be in the market for a husband. Life had grown too complicated to consider such an undertaking, even if it did sound enticing.

"A pretty little lady like you should be tending to babies, not books."

"Ah, but books don't grow up or talk back."

He shook his head and unlocked his store.

"I have a slice of peach pie for you." Paige reached inside her tote bag and carefully brought out a plastic container. "I baked it around six this morning. It's fresh."

He turned back around. A slow grin spread from one generous ear to the other. "You're right. You don't need to go off and get married. I might not get my pies." He did his familiar shoulder jig. "Thank you, sweet girl." He reached for the pie with both hands as though it were the most precious thing he'd ever been offered.

The door squeaked open at Shear Perfection.

"Mornin', Eleanor," Mr. Shafer said. "I see your son's car. Glad he's helping you with the paintin'."

"That's not my son's." Miss Eleanor crossed the street, shielding her eyes from the steadily rising sun. "He isn't coming till the weekend."

Paige's nerve endings registered alert. "Won't that be wonderful for you?" She took another passing glance at the vehicle. "I wonder who's driving that fancy car? Too early for courthouse business."

"Somebody with money." Mr. Shafer lifted the plastic lid off the freshly baked pie and inhaled deeply. "Can't wait till lunch."

"Mercy, old man, you're already rounder than my dear-departed mama's potbelly stove." Eleanor's blue hair sparkled in the sunlight as though she'd added glitter to her hairspray.

"You're just jealous. If you weren't a diabetic, you'd be stealing my pie. Paige here knows how to keep a man happy."

One block down, a man carrying a camera emerged from between one of Mr. Shafer's many antique competitors and the barbershop. He lifted it as if to snap a picture of the barbershop. Paige swung her attention back to her friends. *He could be the real thing.* She hoped so and forced down any precursors of fear.

"What's he taking pictures of?" Eleanor paused. "I'm going to ask." Determination etched her wrinkled face. She squared her shoulders and marched toward the stranger as though she represented the whole town.

*Good, Eleanor. I'll head back and let you do the recon work.*

Eleanor and the stranger stood too far away for Paige to read their lips, but at least while the two talked, the man couldn't take pictures. A few moments later, the stranger laughed much too loud. Eleanor reached out and shook his hand, then walked back.

Paige focused on Mr. Shafer. She picked up a watering can leaning precariously against a rotted-bottom chair. "Is this a new addition?"

"Nah. It was inside. I just brought it out yesterday."

From the corner of her eye, she saw the stranger stare at them. Medium height. Narrow shoulders. Italian-cut clothes. Couldn't see the type of camera. The stranger walked their way, shoulders arched and rigid. Unless he was a pro, she'd have him sized up in thirty seconds, and then she'd go about her day—relieved.

Mr. Shafer lifted his gaze toward Eleanor. "Who's your friend?"

"Jason Stevens, a photographer looking for some

homespun pictures about small towns in Oklahoma."

*The way he's dressed?* Paige's heart pounded. She replaced the watering can. "Did he say for what magazine?"

"Didn't ask. Why don't you? He wants to take a few shots of us standing in front of our businesses." Eleanor beckoned to Stevens. "Come on over and meet my friends. Paige here wonders what magazine you work for."

The man continued to smile—perfect teeth, perfect smile. "It's for a newspaper, the *Oklahoman*." He stuck out his hand. "Mornin', folks. I bet you'd like your picture in the magazine insert." His camera rested in the crook of his right hand, a new Nikon with fast lenses, perhaps a D90 or D200. No dents or sign of use. Who was this guy? He wasn't any more a photographer than Eleanor or Mr. Shafer.

*Have you used that piece of equipment before today?*

"Welcome to Split Creek," Paige said. "I'll pass on the picture, though. I'm not photogenic, but you have a beautiful day to photograph our town." She turned and started across the street to the library.

"Of course you're photogenic," Eleanor called. "No one wants to see a couple of old fuddy-duddies like us, but you'd make front-page news."

"You two are the center of attention. I'm the dull

librarian." Paige continued to move rapidly across the street.

"Wait a minute," Stevens said.

"Sorry. I need to open the library."

"Come on back, sweet girl. There's no one waiting to get in," Mr. Shafer said.

She lifted her hand and waved backward. Guilt nipped at her heels for leaving them with Stevens, but she had more at stake than they did. "See you two later. Nice meeting you, Mr. Stevens."

She unlocked the old building that had once been a bank but now served as the town library. It oozed with character—beige and black marble floors, rich oaken walls, tall ceilings with intricately carved stone, and a huge crystal chandelier the size of a wagon wheel. The areas where tellers once met with customers now served as cozy reading nooks, and a huge, round, brass-trimmed vault—minus the door—held children's books. The windows still even had a few iron bars. If only the town had high-speed Internet access. They'd been promised that modernization for months.

For a precious moment, she relaxed and breathed in the sights and smells. Bless dear Andrew Carnegie for his vision to establish public libraries. Because of his philanthropy, Paige had a sanctuary. From the creaking sounds of antiquity to the time-worn smell of books and yellowed magazines, she had quiet companions that took her to the edge of experience but not the horror of reality.

In a small converted kitchen behind a vaulted door in the rear corner, Paige placed a peanut butter, bacon, and mayo sandwich in the fridge. Reaching down farther into her tote, she wrapped her fingers around a package of Reese's Pieces. Those she'd stash in her desk drawer. The rest of the peach pie sat on the backseat of her car. She'd retrieve it once Stevens moved down the street, preferably out of town.

If he worked for Daniel Keary, her life was about to change—and not for the better. She shook off the chills racing up her arms. *I can handle whatever it is.* Snatching up her tote bag, she closed the kitchen door behind her. With the election nearly three months away, Stevens could be one of Keary's men sent to make sure she still understood her boundaries. Regret took a stab at her heart, but there was nothing she could do about Keary's popularity. She'd tried and failed against a force too powerful for her at the time. But her prayers for truth continued.

Her sensible shoes clicked against the floor en route to the front window. Standing to the side, she peered out through the blinds to the sun-laden street for a glimpse of Stevens. He continued to take pictures. Mr. Shafer would most likely give him a tour of the town, beginning with his store and the history of every item strewn across it. The so-called photographer from the *Oklahoman* entered the antique shop.

*That'll bore him to tears and chase him out of town.*

Paige went through the morning ritual of checking the drop box for returned books, of which there were six. She changed the dates on the date-due stamps and stacked the books to be shelved in her arms. The seasoned citizens of Split Creek representing the local book club would arrive any minute, as regular as their morning's constitutional. For an hour and a half they'd discuss the merits of their current novel, everything from the characters to the plot. Today they couldn't storm the shores of the library too soon for Paige.

As if on cue, Miss Alma bustled through the door—her purse slung loosely from her shoulder, her foil-wrapped banana nut bread in one hand and two books in the other.

"Good morning, Miss Alma," Paige said. "Do you need some help?"

"No thanks. If I loosen my hold on one thing, everything else will fall."

A picture of PoliGrip hit Paige's mind. "Well, you're the first today."

Miss Betty sashayed in, a true Southern belle dressed in her Sunday best, complete with a pillbox hat. "Miss Paige, may I brew a pot of decaf coffee?" she asked.

"Yes, ma'am. It's waiting for you." Oh, how she loved these precious people.

Within moments the rest of Split Creek's Senior Book Club arrived. Paige waved at Reverend Bateson, and as usual, Miss Eleanor and Mr. Shafer were bickering about something.

"At least we agree that Daniel Keary should be our next governor," Miss Eleanor said.

At the mention of that name, Paige thought she'd be physically ill. Keary was running on an Independent ticket, and she didn't care if a Democrat or a Republican pulled in the votes. Anyone but Keary.

"I have banana bread," Miss Alma said. "But don't be picking up a book with crumbs on your fingers."

"We know," several echoed.

Paige appreciated the comic relief. The rest of the members placed chairs in a circle beneath the massive chandelier while Paige checked in their books.

The library door opened again, and Jason Stevens walked in with his camera. The sight of him erased the pleasantries she'd been enjoying with the book club members. He made his way to the circulation desk and stood at the swinging door, trapping her inside.

Hadn't she just swept the bugs off the steps of the library?

"Since you won't let me take your picture outside, I thought I'd snap a few in here. Wow—" his gaze took in the expanse of the building—"this *was* a bank." His brilliant whites would have melted most women's resolve.

Paige approached the swinging door. "No pictures, please. They always turn out looking really bad."

"How about lunch?"

"Are you coming on to me?" Disgust curdled her insides.

He waved his free hand in front of his face. The man knew just when to utilize a dimple on his left cheek. "I'm simply looking for a story to go along with my photos. This library is charming, fascinating, and so are you."

Revulsion for the dimple-faced city boy had now moved into the fast lane. "Miss Alma, I'll help you arrange the chairs."

"Nonsense." Miss Alma shook her blue-gray head. "You help this young man. Those old people can do something besides stand around and complain about their gout and bursitis."

Any other time, Paige would have laughed at the remark. But not today.

"Looks like they have everything under control." The low, seductive tone of Stevens's voice invited a slap in the face.

"I suggest you visit with a few other business owners for your newspaper's needs," she said.

"I'm very disappointed."

"You'll get over it."

"Can't we talk?" He leaned over the swinging door.

"You can leave, or I can call the sheriff. Your choice." She picked up the phone on her desk and met his gaze with a stare down.

"So much for sweet, small-town girls." He tossed her his best dejected look. Obviously he wasn't accustomed to the word *no*.

Her reflexes remained catlike thanks to tai chi workouts still done at home behind drawn curtains. With minimal effort, she could dislocate a shoulder or crash the kneecap of an opponent twice her weight. Such skills were not a part of the job description for most small-town USA librarians, but then again most of them didn't have a working knowledge of Korean, Angolan Portuguese, Swahili, and Russian. The ability to decipher codes, a mastery of disguise, and a knack for using a paper clip to open locks . . . not to mention a past that needed to stay buried. She had to resist the urge to toss Stevens out on his ear. *Calm down.*

"I'm sorry we don't have the book you wanted. I'm sure one of the branches in Oklahoma City can help you."

A silent challenge crested in his gray eyes, and she met it with her own defiance.

Stevens walked to the door and turned, carrying his camera the way patrons carried books. "Know what? This town would be a great place to hide out a CIA operative."

# CHAPTER 2

PAIGE WATCHED the Town Car pull away from the curb and head west to where she hoped Stevens would meet up with I-35 and drive north to Oklahoma City and never return. So Keary had sent him. Why? She hadn't interfered in his campaign for Oklahoma's governorship. Neither did she intend to get involved in any of his political aspirations. An ache rose and swirled inside her, helpless in a deadly storm.

"What a strange comment." Miss Alma shifted her banana bread to the other arm. "A mite early in the morning for someone to be drinking or doing any of those other things that boggle a person's mind. Imagine CIA people living here."

Paige had hoped no one had heard Stevens's final remark. "He's supposed to be a photographer from Oklahoma City. Said he was taking pictures of our town for a magazine. Frankly I didn't like the way he looked or talked. In fact—" Paige still had the phone in her hand. The incessant beeping reminded her she hadn't disconnected it—"I'm calling Sheriff George to have him run a license plate check on him."

"Smart girl." Miss Alma turned her good ear to Paige. "He could be some crook. Or worse yet, he could be one of those real estate developers who wants to turn our town into a mall or build a fancy subdivision. My goodness, he could have been at the courthouse for that very reason. I sure would like to know. We could petition and stop him. Ever seen that movie *Chinatown* with Jack Nicholson?"

Paige lifted a brow and hid her amusement. "I think that was about water rights between two states."

"Don't think it couldn't happen here," Miss Alma said. "Outsiders. Nothing but trouble. Make that call to the sheriff. Good thinking."

"I'll find out and get back with you." Paige dialed the sheriff's number and waited for Lucy to get George on the line. "Mornin', George. Had a little incident as I got to the library this morning."

"Anything I need to get involved in?"

"A guy was here taking pictures up and down the street. Claimed to work for the *Oklahoman*, but I have yet to see a newspaper photographer who could afford a Town Car and a hand-tailored suit. I didn't care for his attitude either. Anyway, I jotted down his license plate number."

"Might be a land speculator," George said. "Ever see that movie *Chinatown* with Charlton Heston?"

"Jack Nicholson." Paige willed her body to relax and gave him the plate number. "I'll be here the rest of the morning."

"I'll call you back as soon as I have something." She envisioned the tall, lean sheriff squinting as he scribbled the plate number. His friendship offered a benefit that came only from small-town living, but she feared what he could learn about her.

"Thanks, George. It's probably nothing, but his obnoxious behavior bothered me."

"No problem, little lady."

She replaced the receiver on the cradle. Some things she missed, like technology. She could still hack into systems with the best of them. For now, however, it would be best if she made the book club members comfortable and waited for George's call.

After the book club cleaned up and a grand total of two patrons returned and checked out books, the clock inched toward noon. Her peanut butter sandwich had begun to call her name, but she waited. A few moments later, the Split Creek High School football coach pushed his way through the double doors of the library.

"Goodness, Miles, you must be knee-deep in two-a-day practices."

"How can you tell?"

"Sunburned face, dirt streaks on your Eskimo Joe T-shirt, and the smell."

Miles grimaced. "I own up to it all."

She allowed herself one moment to appreciate the man who, under different circumstances, might have captured her heart. "How's the team looking this year?"

"Good. They're working hard. First scrimmage is a week from tomorrow on our field. That'll give us an idea of how we're shaping up before our first game after Labor Day."

"I'll be there."

"It'll be sold out."

"Scrimmages are free."

"But we're good." His sun-bleached hair, highlighted in a way many women paid big bucks for, caught her attention. No man should be that good-looking—inside and out.

"What's on your mind?"

"It's Thursday." His gold and brown eyes held the mischievousness of a little boy. "I just wondered what flavor of pie today."

"Peach. I think there are two pieces left. A couple of the book club folks discovered my Thursday pie-baking ritual and actually retrieved the container from my car."

"What will I do when school starts?" Miles asked.

The way he looked at her made her dizzy, and she turned to straighten the papers on her desk. The phone had not rung all morning. "Don't know. I suppose I could hide a slice or two until after school."

"Perfect. Can I request some of those chocolate chip cookies, the ones with peanut butter?"

"Oh, you can request anything you want. Not sure if you'll get them or not."

"What about that white cake you make with the coconut?"

"Italian cream cake? That's reserved for when you win a game."

"And what about the carrot cake?"

She pointed her finger at him. "That's for those poor boys when they lose a game." *Watch it. You're flirting too much.*

He stretched his hands to the ceiling. "It's all good! When are you going to let me take you for a ride on my Harley?"

"Thanks, Miles, but I have a theory that people have only so much luck in life, and I've already stretched mine to the limit. Keep your Harley. I'll stick with my sensible, economic car . . . and seat belts."

He wrinkled his forehead. "Stretched your luck how?"

"I'll get your pie." She walked toward the kitchen, and with each step, she pushed his presence into the no-feel arena.

His culinary requests amused her when she considered her real skills—the ones she couldn't use.

"Dinner?" His voice called after her.

Paige shook her head. "No, Miles. Just friends."

When she returned with the pie, he gave her a look of mock defeat. "I don't bite except during a full moon."

"I know who you are and not a finer man walks this earth. I'm simply not interested in a relationship."

"I'm not giving up."

"Maybe baking for you is all I can ever do."

He moistened his lips. "I'll take whatever you can give."

Resolve, commitment, and an obligation bannered across her mind. The shrill ring of the phone helped her to back away from him.

"Hey, Paige," George said. "I ran the license plate number."

Her pulse sped past the safety zone. "And did I overreact?"

He chuckled, a deep rumble that resembled the man's good humor. "Most likely so. His name's Jason Stevens. I'm sure he meant no harm."

"I see, but what about his taking pictures for the *Oklahoman*?"

"I have no idea. He could've seen a pretty girl and wanted to impress her. I think you can toss your concern."

But she couldn't. She knew too much. "But he *is* from Oklahoma City?"

"You sure make my job hard." George paused. Knowing him, he was contemplating protocol. "Yes, he's from Oklahoma City, but you didn't hear it from me."

So Keary wanted her to know he still held the reins. "Thanks. I appreciate this. The next Stephen Bly Western that comes in will be put on hold until you can check it out."

"Thanks, and don't hesitate to call me if this guy shows up again."

She hung up the phone. Later at home, she'd look into Jason Stevens when she had computer access and no one around to interrupt her.

"Everything okay?" Miles lifted his face to the fan to cool off.

"Sure. Better finish your pie."

He twisted his head and quirked a brow, but she ignored him. He had tweaked her emotions on more than one occasion. She had to distance herself from involvement with him, possibly include a round of rudeness. Not a road she wanted to take, but she didn't have much choice. At the moment, Stevens held more importance than a high school football coach who pursued her like winning the state finals.

"Did you see me in the back row of church last week?" he asked.

"Since when did you stop attending First Methodist? I thought you loved the worship there."

"Oh, I do, but this certain librarian belongs to First Baptist North, and I'm trying to get her to notice me."

"When she's in church, she tries to keep her focus on God."

"I know. Realized that last Sunday morning. And I didn't mean to sound like Sunday mornings were a social hour."

"No problem."

He lifted the pie from her arms. "I'm outta here."

After Miles left and she was alone except for a

mother and three small children who were amazingly quiet, she loaded a cart with new books to shelve.

*Paige—what a name for a librarian.* Split Creek, Oklahoma, had become her home with its single zip code, dial-up Internet, and enough fried catfish to feed a Kenyan refugee camp. It was where she had to be.

If only Miles didn't tug at her heartstrings, the ones she'd vowed over seven years ago never again to tangle around anyone.

The afternoon dragged on with a trickle of patrons. She couldn't seem to shake the unsettling encounter with Stevens. Keary wanted something, but what?

As soon as the clock reached six, Savannah arrived. She attended college part-time, studying library science, and pulled the evening shift as her semester internship arrangement. Paige drove home, the 103-degree heat fueling the turmoil that simmered inside her. She felt under her seat and touched her Beretta.

Paige's little house on the edge of town usually gave her a sense of warmth and security. The quaint bungalow glistened with fresh white paint, and yellow lantanas bordered the sidewalk. Between the plague of grasshoppers and the drought, she'd had to replace the plants twice. Normally she stooped to admire a flower or snatch up a weed here and there before walking inside.

Not today. This evening, her home's charm had been swallowed up by derelicts from the past. She unlocked the door and paused in the shadowed doorway to complete a visual check. The earth-colored pillows were in place, and the pen on her antique desk still balanced precariously on the corner. She took a quick glance at her favorite painting above the redbrick fireplace—a pastoral scene with a farmer separating the sheep from the goats.

With urgency racing through her veins, she took long strides to her bedroom. No quick change into running clothes or rummaging through her sparse pieces of mail until she laid her suspicions to rest.

She powered on her PC and slowly connected to the Internet. *I hate dial-up.* Her search would take several hours. While waiting for connectivity, she fluffed up the beige and turquoise pillows on her bed and tugged on the uneven bed skirt. She threw a load of towels into the washer and poured a glass of iced green tea.

Finally she was able to google Jason Stevens in Oklahoma City. *Ah, an attorney who works for Hughes and Sullivan, the same firm as Daniel Keary. Might as well check out the entire site again.* She clicked the link and read the blurb about the large law firm established in 1910. H&S employed more than one hundred attorneys. They specialized in meeting the needs of the business community in a diversity of legal expertise. Lots of prestigious honors, nationwide respect and recognition. Gave back to the community and offered free seminars to keep the public informed of legal matters. The site looked impressive, and visitors could even sign up for a newsletter. A good place to work for either the rising or established attorney. Hughes and Sullivan looked so good that she expected an evangelistic statement to pop up. Keary would likely hide a pitchfork in the source code.

With a deep breath, she clicked on the list of attorneys. While she waited for the link to download, her bare foot tapped against the hardwood floor. One of her big toes had a huge missing chip of hot pink polish. She grabbed the bottle of polish to the right of her computer and whisked color over the sad-looking toenail.

Finally the screen listed the firm's attorneys in alphabetical order, and Jason Stevens's name and photo appeared. She clicked on his name. He'd been with the firm five years and graduated from an Ivy League school. She went back to the alphabetized list of attorneys and read through each name to see if she recognized any others. She didn't have a clue as to why Keary had sent Stevens to approach her today. Did he think she'd cause trouble this close to the election? If the good people of Oklahoma wanted Daniel Keary as their next governor, that was fine with her.

*No, it's not fine at all. I gave up on bringing him to justice.*

Her eyes fixed on Keary's name. She clicked on the link and saw his picture. A deadly smile with a blue hole of memories stared back at her. Phone, fax, and e-mail were listed below his impressive list of qualifications. She'd previously read the information, but she reviewed it again to jog her memory. Keary's bio highlighted his legal expertise, Cornell education, various awards and recognition, professional affiliations, former work as a CIA operative, and even community work. The site did everything but establish his sainthood.

Paige shivered. She thought of calling him and demanding to know the meaning of Stevens's visit. But the thought of hearing his voice made her skin crawl—and the problems that call could evoke . . .

A vivid nightmare forced its way into her thoughts—the explosion, the screams. The threats. Reality.

She stood back from the computer and looked around. Through the open window she smelled the dry grass and heard birds call out to the early evening. The clock on the mantel in the living room clicked in rhythm to time passing. She walked into the living room and out onto the front porch to stare at the neighbor's horses grazing near the fence. Here in the quiet of the country, she should feel contentment instead of the old restlessness. She'd hoped her new identity would root her in the traditions of small-town living. She'd changed the way she talked and lived. But only God promised security and protection for those she loved. *I'd hoped I was a forgotten number in a deleted file.*

Once seated back in front of her PC, she checked out the links that led to more information about Keary. The professional Web sites—the ones that used the latest technology to display his credentials—revealed how the man had retired from a distinguished career with the CIA and joined the law firm of H&S seven years ago. He served on a hospital board and advocated faith-based initiatives. He supported many charities and worthy causes.

From still another site, Paige learned of his political aspirations that had now become dialogue for Oklahoma media. His conservative views would split those who supported the Republican party and possibly appeal to some of the more conservative Democrats as well. It didn't help that scandals had erupted in both parties. Keary promised to heal the state's distrust in political leaders and work to improve education. He also advocated tax incentives to attract more oil companies to base their headquarters in Oklahoma since they'd lost some huge companies to the Houston area.

Satan in bodily form planned to rule the state Paige had come to love as her own. And she couldn't do a thing to stop the political travesty.

*What do you want from me now?*

Picking up her cell phone, she punched in the old yet familiar number. At the sound of the recorded message, she gave her code. Instantly she was connected.

"I need to talk to Greg Palmer."

As expected, the phone went dead. Continuous moments of wondering and remembering slid into the present. Every horror was as graphic as yesterday.

Angola 2002. The happenings crept over her: the coup, the botched mission, her apparent death along with four others.

Her cell phone rang, yanking her from the heat of the African sun and the fire of a country swimming in unrest and oil. Caller ID registered *Unavailable*.

"Paige Rogers."

"Mikaela, this is Palmer."

Hearing his voice evoked a mixture of fulfillment and failure. "Any new developments on Daniel Keary?"

"You're living in Oklahoma, and he's running for governor. You probably have more information about him than I do."

Her hopes plummeted. "You know what I mean."

"Keary is a conscientious man. I wish you'd take a look at his accomplishments and where he stands today on crucial issues."

"Nothing's changed. You can spit and buff his name all you want, but he's a murderer."

"Look, Mikaela, put this vendetta against Keary behind you and come back on board. We can use you."

"Not likely. The only 'company' I need now is my books and magazines." She disconnected the call, then slipped into her running clothes. Physically working off the pressure and the zillion questions racing through her mind always helped to sort it all out. *Pray through the turmoil. . . . Forgive. . . . Give it all to God.* She'd been trying to do that for more than seven years.

After all, Mikaela Olsson had died in a desperate effort to protect those she loved. And Paige Rogers was a marionette who supposedly danced under Keary's strings. She slammed the front door and broke into a full run, hoping to distance herself from her worries, her past, and her day's worth of pent-up stress. But somehow she knew it wouldn't happen.

# CHAPTER 3

THE EPITOME OF SUCCESS is power, not a bank account or a feature in *Forbes*—those are side benefits. Success is measured by how many people snap to attention when power walks onto the stage. I should know. I've spent most of my life making sure nothing gets in my way. And each step has been worth the price.

"Daddy, I can't sleep."

I shift my gaze from the computer screen and blink at my pajama-clad son in the doorway. The spreadsheet made me dizzy, and I'd drifted off into analyzing the last few months of my campaign. "Hey, bud. What seems to be the problem?"

His bare feet clap against the hardwood floor, and he snuggles against me. I shove aside my irritation and pull him onto my lap.

"If I could watch the new VeggieTales movie one more time, I could fall asleep."

"Before Mommy gets home?" I ask.

He nods.

Where is his mother when I need her? My love for her has long since died, but her usefulness hasn't.

"Let's get that movie going again."

"Thanks, Daddy. I love you."

I ruffle his black hair and smile into his slanted eyes. A good kid, likeable, despite the fact that nothing about him resembles me. "And I love you."

# CHAPTER 4

MILES LAIRD SPED his Harley over the country road, kicking up dirt and stones the way a tornado tossed buildings and trees. The engine's rumble pounded out sweet music while the feel of the powerful machine drumming against his thighs offered a sense of control over the stress of the day. This machine was his baby. He'd taken an older model and worked on it in his spare time, always anticipating the next piece of chrome.

The wind cooled his face, and the approaching sunset in brilliant gold and orange radiated a beauty that most folks took for granted. Not Miles. Every day was a bonus. He swerved to miss a coiled copperhead—breathtaking but deadly, reminding him of life.

He shook his head at the grasshopper remains littered across the road. The lack of green on both sides indicated they'd eaten well this summer before meeting their demise. Random summer fires had raged over the countryside, scorching the pastures and leaving the woodlands charred black. Soon they'd have rain. At least that's what the weather forecasters were saying. Miles forecast more hope than rain.

"Paige Rogers, sometimes I wish I'd never met you." He shouted his words to no one but the dead grasshoppers and the copperhead in his rearview mirror. He refused to admit to frustration, so he coated his emotions with a "try harder" approach. But why? The woman clearly wasn't interested, or so she said.

Depending on his mood, Miles rode either his Appaloosa gelding or his Harley to unwind. Tonight, he'd needed both, and he still couldn't get Paige Rogers off his mind. He needed to compartmentalize her into a section of his heart that said, "Let it be," but something about her continually drew him to the library and Paige's private world of books. Every time he'd thought he'd made progress toward more than a casual friendship, she would slide back into her emotional fortress. There she stood guard over her post like a marine sentry.

The same questions always probed his mind. What had happened to cause her to run at the mention of a relationship? No, she didn't just run; she grabbed the tail of a twister. Paige had said her parents were deceased, that she had no family. Okay, then why settle down in the middle of nowhere, unless she had something to fear—or hide? God knew why Paige kept her distance. Sure would be nice if He'd pass on a few clues.

Miles remembered when the Aubreys had learned their little girl had leukemia, and the family didn't have insurance. The area churches all rallied to raise money—everything from donations to an auction and bake sale. Paige had jumped in with two spoons and must have spent an entire weekend baking her specialties for the event.

Miles nodded at a farmer who whizzed by in his pickup, tossing bigger stones and gathering more dirt. Evening was approaching and he needed to go over football plays for next week. With the two-a-days and in-service, he'd eaten microwave meals until he could peel back the wrappers in his sleep. Oh, the affection for the game that kept him alive and restless. The district had assigned him an American history class to teach this year in addition to his regular civics classes, plus he was feeling a mountain of pressure to take the football team to play-offs and bring home the state trophy.

Praise God for Harleys and horses and the two-story farmhouse on a bit of heavenly acreage. But what about Paige? He was of a mind to ride over there and tell her he loved her and demand an explanation as to why she refused to go out with him. A moment later he admitted his impulsiveness would accomplish nothing more than further alienation. Maybe he should avoid her until his shattered heart recovered. Right. As if that were possible.

At the crest of a hill where spotted cattle and horses nibbled at burnt grass, Miles reversed direction and narrowed his sights on Split Creek and the elusive librarian. He rehearsed his speech as he slowed his speed about a half mile from the outskirts of town. He'd make up something to talk about, maybe this dreaded history class.

Miles crept through town. The sheriff had a vendetta against motorcycles, and Miles wasn't in the mood to get a ticket or a lecture. He'd never been to Paige's house before, but he'd passed it a hundred times. With the flowers and rocking chairs on the front porch, it looked like a little old lady lived there. But in no way did Paige resemble a seasoned citizen. Her figure, tanned skin, and huge light brown eyes that missed nothing denied any hint of aging.

He reached for a handful of courage like a sophomore's dream of varsity first-string. A visit unannounced might push the odds against him. Too late now, for he'd already stopped in front of her house. He flipped off the Harley's engine and hung his helmet on the handlebars. Glancing about, he expected to see a dog. A single, defenseless woman should have one to keep her company and let her know when someone arrived . . . like an uninvited football coach who had a crush on her.

On the left side of the porch a fern sat in the corner and a white rocker held a copy of *Time* magazine. To the right, an old milk can painted red, white, and blue rested beside an oak rocker.

When Paige didn't answer the door, he walked around back. Her parked car in front told him she couldn't have gone far, but she was nowhere in sight. Maybe she didn't want to be bothered. A mixture of disappointment and relief swept over him. He felt too much like a love-struck kid.

He wished he had a way to leave her a note but resigned himself to the fact that she didn't want to talk to him. As soon as his feet moved toward his Harley, he spotted the sheriff's car. It slowed and pulled up beside him. *Here it comes.*

"Where's your truck?" George's long face reminded Miles of a horse.

"Sittin' at home full of football equipment."

"Sure is safer than that deluxe lawn mower there."

Miles fought a moan. "Now, George, if you want to ride my bike, just say so and I'll let you."

"No thanks. I have a personal campaign to get them things off the road." He pointed to the house. "I need to talk to Paige."

"Don't think she's home." Miles shrugged. "She might be in the shower or taking a nap."

The sheriff grinned. "You sweet on her?"

Normally he liked George, but not when he probed like he was going after a festering splinter. "This is about lining up newspapers and periodicals for my students."

"Hmm. I'll swing by later after Naomi and I finish with a church meetin'. Paige's probably taking her nightly run."

*George knows more about her habits than I do.* Miles bade the sheriff good night and watched him head back into town. Once his Harley sang out its own rendition of freedom, he headed out a different road toward home. His mind played with the next day's football plays and the problems with his star quarterback who had barely passed ninth grade.

Nearly two miles from Paige's house, he spotted a thin woman in dark pants and a white T-shirt standing next to a man who was leaning against a black Town Car. Even in the darkening shadows, he could tell the woman was Paige. She pointed a finger at the man's chest, and he grabbed it.

That's when Miles pulled out the stops on chivalry and pulled over to save his lady.

The man, dressed like he owned a half-dozen Town Cars, released his hold and moved back.

"Hi, Miles." She strode toward him with a smile that he hadn't seen this side of his dreams. Her walk made him sweat. She wrapped her arms around his neck and kissed him hard. "When you didn't show, I decided to run alone."

He nearly fell off his he-man Harley, but he'd waited a long time for that moment. "Sorry about being late." Miles swung a glance at the stranger. "Is this guy bothering you?"

"No, he simply wanted directions." She turned back to the stranger. "Do you understand which way you're headed?" She still spoke more sweetly than Miles had ever heard. "Losing your way can cause you to wander for hours, maybe days."

The man stiffened. "I know where I'm going."

Miles had never considered himself a fool, and this conversation held more meaning than a rooster strolling into a henhouse.

Paige patted Miles's shoulder. She swung her

long leg over the bike behind him and reached around his waist. He was glad he'd been lifting weights with the boys. "It's getting too dark for me to be running. How about a ride home?"

"My thoughts exactly. I have steaks marinating for dinner."

"Wonderful."

"Paige," the stranger called, "I'd like a word with you alone."

*He knows her name? Is this an old boyfriend?* "Whatever you have to say to her can be said right here."

"That's right," she said.

"The word is out," the man said. "I've done my job."

Anger suddenly raced through Miles's veins. "Are you threatening her?"

"Listen, hayseed. Take your one-time girlfriend and your tricycle back into Hicksville." The man rounded his car and vanished behind tinted windows.

"Let's get you home." Miles memorized the car's license plate. "Are you all right?"

"I'm fine."

He wished he could see her face. "I take it you know him, but I do have the guy's license plate."

"I had George look it up earlier. Besides, I could have handled him."

He watched the car speed away with more questions rolling around in his head than football plays. "Independence is a trait, not a means of self-defense."

"Good one. Thanks for coming by when you did."

He started the engine and turned the bike around. "Can I have another one of those special hello kisses?"

She jabbed him in the side. "Probably not, but I'll consider it for the future." She paused. "Nice bike. A 1450 engine. Every time I see you, you've added something to the trim package."

"I thought you didn't know anything about bikes. What else are you hiding inside that pretty head of yours? If George sees you're not wearing a helmet, he's going to shoot us both."

"What would Split Creek do without its football coach?" She leaned in a bit closer to him.

"And what would the town do without its librarian?" Miles had never had this much fun with Paige. "By the way, our good sheriff stopped by your house."

"How do you know?" She raised her voice to be heard above the engine's noise.

"I was there looking for you. He said he'd be back later." There, he'd said it.

"Two of the town's most important men looking for me? Whatever for?"

His heart pounded out a stronger beat than the engine. "I have no clue about George. Me, I wanted to ask a favor."

"What kind?"

"I'm not planning to camp on your porch until you go out with me, if that's what you're thinking. I need a library favor."

"Help all the jocks pass your classes?"

*Sure would be nice if we could always talk like this.* "Nice thought. I wondered if you'd stock the *Wall Street Journal* and the *New York Times*. A lot of the kids don't have computers to access them online."

"Sure. As soon as we get DSL, I'll subscribe to them online. If we could come up with at least one more computer, the kids could work on projects there. Until then, I'll order hard copies."

"The high school doesn't have enough of them to go around either," he said. "When do you think the library will get another computer?"

"When folks donate their used ones. Maybe around Christmas."

Miles slowed to avoid a couple of potholes. In the lull of the engine's song, he turned to catch a quick glimpse of her face and take advantage of not having to yell. "I have another request. Could you help me compile a suggested reading list for my American history class? I have a few books in mind, but I want to expose them to a wide range of information."

"Will I receive any free football tickets for my hard work?"

He pretended annoyance and turned into her driveway. "I'll scrounge up a few."

She swung off the bike. "Thanks, Miles. All kidding aside, you were just where you needed to be this evening."

"Are you going to tell me what happened back there?"

"Wasn't important."

"The man called you by name."

"He could have heard it anywhere."

"I could help."

"You already have. In fact, I don't think that guy will ever show his face here again." Her seriousness replaced the lighthearted tone of less than a minute before.

"Don't you know by now I want to be your number one hero?"

She glanced beyond her home to the empty field beside it. "Don't you think if it were possible, I'd have planted myself on your doorstep a long time ago?"

"What's holding you back?"

"I can't go into it. Complications, many complications."

"Like that fellow back there?" How could he convince her that he could be trusted?

"Maybe."

Miles ventured closer to the edge, knowing he was risking their friendship. "My past stinks. I've done a lot of things that make me want to crawl into a hole," he said. "But life goes on, and all things are new in Christ. We can create the future we want."

She reached out and touched his face. "I can't." Her words were soft, tender, spoken with enough caring for him to understand that whatever held her back couldn't be altered.

"I'll wait," he said.

She removed her hand. "Don't. Nothing's going to change." Paige turned and walked up the steps to her door. "I'll work on that book list for you," she said, then disappeared.

# CHAPTER 5

PAIGE CLOSED THE DOOR and fought the urge to watch Miles ride away on his Harley. No point in encouraging him any more than she'd already done. No future in it either.

Leaning against the door, she listened to the motorcycle's perfectly tuned engine fade into the distance. With a sigh deep enough to sink a battleship, she flipped on the lamp on her desk and took in every detail of the living room. The plush rug beneath her feet contained no footprints. The blinds against the windows facing the road were in the precise position in which she'd left them. Sofa pillows held a set angle, and the mail that lay deliberately heaped onto the oak trunk in front of the sofa had not been touched. No debris from the fallen leaves was littered across the wooden floors.

In the kitchen, the white ruffled curtain that blew to the left when someone entered the back door still hung vertically. The rug strategically placed at the back door was angled just the way she'd left it. Inhaling deeply, she detected no other scents than the familiar ones that marked her home.

Fury kept the adrenaline pumping, as though she needed to run another five miles. Jason Stevens had all the credentials of a dressed-up weasel. Most likely Keary had hand-selected Stevens's image coach to instruct him in voice lessons with appropriate delivery. And that included rehearsals for the precise moment to smile, according to the gender of his target. All paid for by a murderer . . . a man whose ambitions had led to carnage.

*"Keary wants to meet with you. He'd like for you to work with him on the last few months of his campaign for governor."*

The request was an abomination. Obviously Keary was afraid she'd learned something new—something to slander his excellent reputation. Why had he made the request now, with the campaign near the finish line? That question had dogged her for the past several minutes.

"Tell Keary to leave me alone," she'd said. "I don't waste my time with lowlifes. He's the type who gives lawyers and politicians a slide downhill."

"He'll be very disappointed."

"I'm sure he'll be very successful without my participation. Ethics is not one of his specialties."

Not a muscle moved on Stevens's face. Not even

a blink. "I have no idea what you're talking about, but he said you'd be willing to help."

"Tell him I said no." That's when Miles had ridden up on his iron steed. She could have said a lot more. And now she wondered how Keary would respond to her refusal. That might not have been a clever move.

*I blew my cover. Miles knows I'm not who I claim to be.* Paige had gone to a lot of work to dissolve her identity. For what she hadn't been able to do on her own, she knew who to call. She'd secured a new Social Security number, a high school alma mater and college sorority, a Visa card, checking and savings accounts, 4-H blue ribbons, and a MySpace presence to usher in the fresh world of Paige Rogers. All trails of her previous life now led to a death certificate.

But apparently she'd grown rusty, and that was dangerous. Later she'd phone Miles and smooth things over.

Paige walked through her small two-bedroom bungalow and continued to look for anything out of place. But a pro knew how to cover his tracks. For the next two hours, she looked for bugs in all of the usual spots—and a few unusual ones. She began by taking her landline phone apart and ended up in the garage, even scooting under her car. The idea of being blown to bits in the morning when she headed for work didn't sit well either. Everything appeared fine, but her hyperalert state lingered.

George had suggested a German shepherd to keep the predators away and as good company, but she had no desire to sacrifice a good animal in the event of trouble. If professionals wanted to get to her badly enough, no fancy alarms, dead bolts, or watchdogs would stop them.

Hunger had assaulted her in the form of a headache and eventually led her to the refrigerator. She'd made a pot of chicken and corn chowder two nights ago, and she was almost hungry enough to eat it cold. While it warmed in the microwave, she wrapped her fingers around a fresh tomato and a cucumber on the windowsill and turned on the water to wash them. Taking a deep breath, she resumed the conversation she'd begun with her heavenly Father before Stevens had stopped his car in front of her earlier this evening.

The doorbell interrupted her before she got past "Holy Father, I'm in a mess, and I blew my cover." Caution ruled her senses. Her gaze moved to the top shelf of her pantry. Within seconds, she'd reached behind the extra bag of unbleached flour and the virgin olive oil and tucked her Beretta into the back of her running pants. She pulled her one-size-fits-all T-shirt over the heavy weapon.

The doorbell rang again.

"Coming." Paige knew better than to take a look through the peephole. Many an unsuspecting victim had lost an entire face that way. She slipped to the side window where she kept the blind at the perfect angle to view anyone at her doorstep.

Relieved, she snapped on the porch light and watched the mosquitoes dance around the bulb before opening the door. "Evening, George. Miles said you'd stopped by."

"Sorry about the hour. I wanted to take care of an important matter before the morning."

"Do you want to come in?" What else had Keary or Stevens done? Her heart thumped louder than the hunger pangs knocking against her stomach.

"No thanks. Naomi's in the car, and we need to get home."

Paige glanced at the car and waved. "I understand. So does Georgie need help with his homework?"

"He'd better have his homework done and be getting ready for bed." He leaned against the doorframe. "What haven't you told me about yourself?"

Her senses whipped into attention, while she focused on paralyzing her emotions. She shook her head with a smile. "I'm not following you."

"UPS truck pulled up to the library after you left. The driver wanted to leave his delivery with me like he always does with after-hours orders. He had six fancy computers all addressed to your attention."

"Me?"

George reached inside his shirt pocket and pulled

out a delivery slip. "See? Split Creek Library to the attention of Paige Rogers."

"Wonderful. We must have a generous benefactor."

"But look who they're from." George handed her the papers.

Paige scrutinized the address of the sender. *Daniel Keary.* Now he thought she could be bought for six computers? Reminded her of thirty pieces of silver. Appreciation for the new computers dissolved into guarded control.

"That's the fella who's runnin' for governor," George said, as if she didn't know. "Independent ticket."

"I've heard about him." *"Seen him at his worst"* fit better.

"Which brings me back to my original question. Are you holding out on us? related to a rich lawyer-turned-politician? I read the man used to work for the CIA. Do you have connections with Daniel Keary that the rest of us don't know about?" George grinned like it was all a big joke. Maybe it was, to him.

"Me? Split Creek's librarian?"

"Doesn't hurt to ask. He's going to be the next governor. You watch and see. Keary's a good man. Look at what he's done for Split Creek today."

George clearly thought it was all quite amusing. But Keary's deceit dipped in goodwill left Paige feeling helpless. She clinched her fists. "The library really needs the computers. But I admit I thought I had an outstanding speeding ticket or something."

"Aw, Naomi thought it would be fun to tease you about knowing Keary. Almost had you going there, didn't I? But I'm glad for the library, and I wanted to tell you myself."

"I'm glad you did. The patrons will love this." She crossed her arms over her chest. "And just in time for school."

"Yeah." He glanced about. "I'll get them computers carted to you in the morning. Sure am curious as to how Keary found out about us, but I can't imagine it has anything to do with you, little lady. Anyway, there are twelve boxes in all, what with the computers and monitors." He straightened. "Guess you can go on back to whatever you were doing before I interrupted your evening." He turned to leave, and she lingered in the doorway.

"Thanks for stopping by, George. Your visit made my whole day." *Or rather added more silt to the mud.*

"Naomi suggested having the kids from the library write Keary a thank-you note. It might get printed and stick Split Creek on the map."

*Oh, George, if only you knew* . . . The town had been on Keary's radar for the past seven years. "Good thought. I'll have the children work on it. Give Naomi my best." She closed the door and double-bolted it.

Thank goodness the day was nearly over. Her head pounded, and she still hadn't eaten.

The computer delivery frustrated every inch of her. Keary knew her well enough to know she'd never relinquish her disgust for him for six computers. She had no plans to move out of her safety zone to attempt to destroy his campaign. But why ease his conscience by assuring himself his secrets were safe? Her stomach knotted. Someday the truth would surface, but it wouldn't be she who'd expose him. She'd tried that once and failed.

Miles munched on a fried bologna sandwich and some stale chips. He couldn't bring himself to eat one more microwave he-man meal. He lifted the carton of milk and downed it. What exactly had happened tonight? The whole scene replayed in his mind. If he'd been under the influence, he'd swear the entire event with Paige and the guy on the road had been an illusion.

Paige had a few secrets, and he'd tripped onto one of them. Or maybe more than one. Obviously the guy tonight knew more about her than the whole town of Split Creek did.

Miles shook his head and glanced down at the football plays in his notebook. The Xs and Os all ran together. *Bad pun.* He needed to focus on important matters, not on a woman who insisted friendship was all she could offer.

During the summer he'd added a few new plays,

and he was anxious to try them at the scrimmage. His team needed a winning season—every coach's dream. They might make it this season. The returning players were above average, and he had his eyes on a sophomore, Walt Greywolf, a Chickasaw boy who ran like the wind. When that kid wrapped his massive hands around a football, nobody could take it away. Problem was, the boy needed to take the game and his grades more seriously. One of the questions was leadership. A quarterback led the team, and it had to be a guy who wouldn't crack under pressure. A little motivation and a whole lot of work could mean a full scholarship for Walt. A talk with him and his parents was in order.

His cell phone rang with the school's fight song blaring around the kitchen. Miles glanced at the caller ID.

"Hey, Paige. Need a bodyguard?"

"Not now. The fort is tied down securely. Just wanted to thank you for coming to my rescue tonight."

"No problem. It's what we cowboys do best." With the window raised in his kitchen, a chorus of katydids blended with the incessant pounding of his heart, as if he needed a drumroll to accompany her voice. "Do you want to talk about it?"

"A little."

"I'm listening." Hope had taken root once again.

"The jerk on the road tonight? Well, he's supposed to be a photographer from Oklahoma City doing a spread on small towns. He came into the library this morning and wanted to take my picture. I refused, and I guess he couldn't take no for an answer."

"I see."

"I'm really embarrassed about the way I acted. Can't believe the things I said to you and—"

"No reason to apologize. I'm just glad I could help."

"That wasn't me. And I'm still shaking from the motorcycle ride."

She'd ridden his bike like a pro, and the lie caused the pedestal he'd put her on to wobble a bit. "We could fix that by taking a few more. I even have an extra helmet to keep good old Sheriff George happy."

"Not a chance. Oh, he stopped by tonight."

"You've been a busy girl."

"Actually those computers for the library came sooner than we thought. We now have six more. I'll make a few calls in the morning and see if the process for high-speed Internet access can be sped up."

"Thanks. The students will appreciate an extra source for their research."

"They deserve all the help they can get. Anyway, you must be worn-out with football practice and getting ready for the new school year, so I'll let you go."

"Anything else I can help you with?"

"You could promise not to tell anyone I made a fool of myself tonight."

"Oh, I could be persuaded."

"What will it take?"

Another wobble. "Nothing, Paige. Your secret's safe with me. Sleep easy. You might want to talk to George about some pepper spray."

"Good idea."

Miles disconnected the call. What was Paige hiding? He'd spent years hiding a previous drug addiction—tap-dancing around the truth, making needless phone calls to ease relationships, and working on his skills as a people pleaser so no one would detect trouble. He didn't want to suspect Paige of leading a double life, but he had seen a woman tonight different from the librarian he'd known for the past two years. The woman tonight was in control and confident. She hadn't played a role to chase off a wannabe stalker. She *was* the role. Where did that leave him?

*Get a grip.* He'd been watching too many movies and reading too many books. This was small-town Oklahoma. Nothing exciting happened here beyond high school sports and an occasional twister.

# CHAPTER 6

PAIGE SANK into the stylist's chair and tugged out her ponytail holder as though she were yanking out the tangles of her past. She had an hour and a half until time to open the library and more things on her mind than she cared to list. "Do your magic, Voleta. It's been three weeks, and I see roots. Ugly white ones."

"Girlfriend, you're obsessed with your roots." Voleta dug her blueberry fingertips into the top of Paige's hair. "All of my other clients wait four to six weeks for their color."

"They don't have premature white like me."

"I wouldn't know." Voleta picked up the small plastic box on her workstation that contained her clients' information. "You've never let your roots grow out long enough for me to really tell."

"It's a condition I inherited from my mother. At age twenty-five, I turned completely gray, then white." *Will I ever be able to tell the truth about anything?*

"For women like you, I am thankful. Keeps the rent paid." Voleta thumbed through the box and withdrew an index card that held Paige's color formula. "Can I talk you into some highlights? It sure would make a great difference." She gestured around Paige's face. "You'd look ten years younger. Not that you aren't gorgeous now."

"No thanks. I'm happy with the brown. Reminds me of dark, rich coffee. But you can trim a little off the ends so it rests on my shoulders."

"Got it. You know I'm not gonna give up on the highlights. I'm all about making my clients walking billboards, making them look younger and all."

"So, it's all about you then?"

"Darlin', it's always about me. Grab a magazine. I need a minute to mix up your color." Voleta headed for the supply room, her flip-flops slapping against her heels, and her back revealing a butterfly tattoo that peeked above her jeans. "I saw the sheriff at the doughnut shop this morning," she called over her shoulder. "He was laughing about his and Naomi's joke on you last night."

Paige grimaced. *The joke that hit closer to home than anyone here can ever find out.* She thumbed through a back issue of *Modern Bride*. She tossed it aside and picked up a current issue of *Farm Journal.* "You mean about the computer delivery?" The last thing Paige wanted to discuss.

"Yeah. Told me he was worried you might be upset with him."

She had been too relieved by the fact that George hadn't actually stumbled onto her secret to be angry. "If George had been anyone else, I would've pitched a fit. But I've pulled my share of pranks on him too."

"I remember when you told him a letter had

arrived at the library for him from one of those TV game shows."

"He's never forgotten it, so I guess we're even."

Voleta appeared from the supply closet. "Anyway, congrats on those new computers. It's a perk for our little town." She set her bottles on the edge of the sink. "I'll hush now and mix your color. If I'm not careful, you'll have purple hair."

Paige stared into the mirror of Eleanor's Shear Perfection. How many folks had George told that story to? She didn't mind being the butt of a joke, but linking her to Daniel Keary was another matter. Usually she counted on this time with Voleta to relax her and talk about girlie things. This morning she was coiled and ready to strike.

Keary was duping these people—these kind people. He was buying them gifts with his blood money. All so they'd vote for him, and she'd forget what he'd done. She shivered at his deceit—ached to bring him to a stop. The folks of Split Creek had opened their hearts to her. They were strong, real, a slice of America that she believed in. Until now she'd done nothing while he'd run his campaign, spewing the typical rah-rah promises and showing up at community-wide barbecues that people from the Bible Belt rallied to faithfully.

"Sure you don't want those highlights?"

Paige snapped out of her reverie. "Next year on my birthday."

"July it is. Here's another topic for you."

*Actually it's November.* "Is it up for discussion?"

"Get rid of the library talk. This is me, your pal." Voleta walked toward her, stirring a small plastic bowl of walnut brown color. "Eleanor said Miles was at your church last week."

"I have no idea, but he did say something about it. And your point?"

"Are you going to let him slip right through your fingers? He's a huge catch."

Paige closed her eyes. Miles talk only reminded her of what would never happen. "Voleta, he's a sweet guy, but I'm not interested."

"If you don't watch out, you're going to end up an old maid. Girlfriend, are you reading the *Farm Journal*? You scare me."

"I'm thirty-three, and there are worse things than being an old maid." She tossed the magazine aside and eased out of her comfy sandals, letting them fall to the floor.

"Don't you want babies?"

The idea cut deep. "I'd be a lousy mother. You know, I'd always have my head stuck in a book."

Voleta set the color bowl on the counter and pulled out a bright orange styling cloth to Velcro around Paige's neck. "I think you're gun-shy—afraid of Miles and afraid of motherhood. Honestly, I've never met a more caring person. You take better care of other folks than you do yourself. Give the man a chance. I think you two would be a perfect match."

Paige seized control of her emotions before Voleta saw her flinch at the word *gun-shy*. If Voleta only knew how true her words were. Another life, another context, but all the more validation that women like her weren't fashioned for rocking chairs, diaper changings, and PTA meetings.

If Miles hadn't already attached himself to her heart, Paige could counter Voleta's comments more easily. "Ever wonder why he isn't married?"

Voleta picked up a comb. "You mean Miles? Probably waiting for the perfect woman."

"There's your answer. I'd drive him crazy."

The phone rang before Voleta could list her countless reasons why Paige should welcome Miles into her life.

"Uh-huh. Yeah. Just a sec. She's right here." Voleta handed Paige the phone and mouthed, "It's a guy."

Paige figured it was George, still concerned that he'd offended her, but the moment the man's ultra-friendly, ultrasweet voice assaulted her ears, images of the past chilled her.

He had someone watching her. She stood from the styling chair and walked outside.

"You hurt my feelings," Keary said. "I thought you'd want to work on my campaign. It's nearing the finish line, and I can pay well for a hard worker."

"Think again."

"A woman of your talents shouldn't be wasting away in a library."

"That's none of your business. What do you want, anyway? I haven't bothered you."

"Cooperation, for starters."

*I've kept my end of the bargain and lost everything I ever cherished.* "Give me one reason why, because I don't understand the sudden interest."

"You have skills my campaign needs."

She had seen his "skills" in action and had no desire to be associated with him or anyone connected to him ever again. Once had soured her for good. "Forget it."

"We have a deal, remember?"

"And you won't risk doing a thing to damage your campaign." She disconnected the call but suspected that Keary wasn't finished with her. Judging by the amount of time and energy he'd expended on her behalf in the past two days, something had happened to shake him up. But what? And who was watching her every move?

Taking a deep breath to settle the anger, she stepped back into current time, walked inside, and set the phone on Voleta's station.

"Who made you mad?" Voleta stood back and placed her hands on her hips. "I've never seen you that upset."

"A jerk who doesn't deserve my repeating his name."

Miles wiped the sweat from his face with the back of his hand. Ninety-eight degrees and the kids were in full pads. "Keep drinking water," he called out. "We have a scrimmage a week from tonight, and it'll be as hot then as now. Maybe hotter."

He studied each of his players. Good kids. Most of them. Two of them would flunk out the first six weeks, and four others needed to keep their noses clean. Then there was Walt, his Chickasaw Wonder. Miles would personally tutor that kid and tuck him into bed every night if it would keep him in the game.

"Listen up." He gestured the boys to the side-lines. "We're going over the new plays again. First, though, we're going to talk about grades. Need I remind you that school starts Monday?"

Moans rose like a dust storm.

"This is a no-pass, no-play team. Grades are your number one priority. Those of you who have played before know I don't kiss up to teachers. You might think football is life now, but when you have a family to feed, you'll need a career. I'll stay on you about grades just like I stay on you about learning plays and perfecting your skills. Any problems with your schoolwork, I'll help you find tutors and be talking to your parents."

"Is that a threat or a promise?" One of the boys snickered.

"Both. Those of you who are taking history and civics, I'll be your teacher. Be ready. I won't cut you any slack, but I'll be fair. The public library has six new computers and will soon have Internet access. If you start falling behind, I'll be the one tutoring you and assigning research papers." Several more moans. "All of you get some more water and then back on the field."

All but Walt made their way to the five-gallon water jugs. "You want to talk to me?" Miles asked.

Walt lifted his helmet and ran his fingers through sweat-drenched black hair. "Coach, my grades have never been real good in English and history."

"We'll work on it."

"I got a job on Tuesdays and Thursdays after practice."

"Then come early to school. I'll help you."

Walt glanced toward the players.

"What else?"

"Nothing. That's it." He walked toward the team.

Miles understood exactly what was going on with his players. Chris Dalton, a senior, wanted the starting quarterback position, not the dual positions of second-string quarterback and first-string receiver. Chris hadn't hidden his feelings about a Native American sophomore taking his place. Miles would let them settle the problem among themselves unless a fight broke out or the team suffered. Didn't help that Chris's dad, Ty, sat in the bleachers and held a position on the school board. Ty's constant insistence that Chris had better skills than Walt was driving Miles nuts.

He blew his whistle. "I want to see that play

again." Miles zeroed in on his quarterback and receiver.

Walt went back for a pass. He took a five-step drop and waited in the pocket for Chris. Crucial seconds sped by. No receiver. A senior linebacker sacked Walt hard. He got up by himself and shook off the tackle.

Miles clenched his jaw. He drew the line with Chris deliberately setting Walt up for a hit. If Chris couldn't put aside his personal vendetta, then he could be replaced with a receiver who understood how the game was to be played. Miles sensed someone beside him—Ty Dalton wearing a smirk. Miles steeled the impulse to toss good sportsmanship to the dry wind and send him back to the bleachers.

"Put Chris at quarterback." Dalton nudged him. "He'll get the job done. Hey, Coach, don't forget who I am."

Miles took a huge gulp of water and attempted to drown out the laughter coming from a few seniors on the sidelines. He wouldn't give Ty the pleasure of acknowledging his comment.

Shouts echoed from the field. He knew in an instant a fight had broken out, and he could bet who was throwing the punches. If this kept up, no one would need to worry about the state championship this year. His best players would be injured or thrown off the team. He jogged to the scene of the scuffle.

★ ★ ★

Much later that afternoon, Miles tossed football gear into the back of his pickup. He'd delivered a lecture to Chris and Walt that had echoed from the field house to the courthouse. He'd talked about teamwork, playing time, and what the consequences would be if they chose to fight again. Miles doubted his pep talk had done much good. Teenage boys with an overload of testosterone had their pride and their own creative ways of handling disputes.

Glancing at his watch, he decided to rush home and take a shower before making another appearance at the library. He'd pick up the latest Dean Koontz novel for the weekend along with his school requests so Paige wouldn't think he was coming on too strong—again. Oh, and he wanted to see those new computers.

Who was he trying to fool? One look at her and he'd forget the problems on the field. For an hour, anyway.

Twenty minutes before the library was scheduled to close, Miles strode in wearing clean jeans and a Split Creek High football coach T-shirt and smelling more like Dial soap than sweat and grime. Paige had a book cart parked in front of an aisle in the nonfiction area. She bent down with a book in her hand.

"Need some help putting those away?" Miles asked.

"No thanks. Thought that was you—sounded like your footsteps." She straightened and smiled.

His insides felt like apple butter. Her teeth were perfect, her tanned skin flawless. A few phrases from the Song of Solomon stretched across his mind. Her hair looked different today. Why couldn't he let it go? move on and leave Paige at the library?

"I know you're not here to see me. It's not pie day." Her eyes widened. "Must be the computers."

He'd forgotten to look.

She gestured to a long library table where six tabletop computers faced each other. "I have three of the new ones up and running. And today I was promised high-speed wireless Internet within a week."

He wove around the book cart to the oak table that held the new computers and monitors. They were beauties. The brand did everything but dance. He'd seen the commercials on TV. "Where did these come from?"

"A donation."

"Next time put in a good word for the football team. We could use some new equipment."

She pushed the empty cart beside the waist-high circulation desk. "Don't hold your breath."

*Whoa.* Where had that tone come from? "You're not happy?"

"Oh, I'm thrilled for the patrons."

He pulled his list of books from his pocket.

"These are the books for my students that I was telling you about."

Paige took the paper and headed for an aisle. How amazing that one woman could fill out a pair of jeans like a magazine model and still attract him to her keen mind. Not in that order, of course.

"Have you memorized every book here?"

"Oh, most of them. You forget I work with media material all day long."

He studied her for a moment. "Your hair looks nice. Did you get it cut?"

"Thanks. Got a trim."

Miles realized he was supposed to continue with witty comebacks, but he couldn't think of anything else to say.

"So . . . how was your day?" she asked.

"Okay, I guess." No point in boring her about his problems on the field. "I've been thinking about how to make this history class more interesting."

She piled two books into his arms. "And what did you come up with?"

"I want to make history come alive for these kids. Maybe role-play. Possibly ask them to rewrite a segment of history, then trace that outcome to the present. Lectures and tests don't make it for me."

"Me neither, and I like your idea of engaging them in role-play."

"I'm also thinking of incorporating a section of history about national security, everything from the FBI and the CIA to the development of Homeland Security."

Paige dropped a book, and he reached to help her.

"Do you think that will keep them interested in history?" he asked.

Before she could answer, the phone rang, and she excused herself. He piled the books on the circulation desk and seized the opportunity to examine one of the new computers. Let it never be said that Coach Miles Laird spent *all* of his spare time gawking at the town's librarian. Correction: after last night he'd learned she was more than a librarian. He glanced over the monitor and tilted his head to pick up some of Paige's one-sided conversation. From her responses, she didn't care for the caller.

"Don't send your dogs around here again."

Paige turned and carried the phone as far as the cord would allow. Why didn't the library update those things?

"I already said no. Come on back and pick them up. I refuse to owe you a thing."

Miles lowered his gaze. Unhappy about the new computers? Why? The library had needed this kind of modern technology for ages. Most of the kids at the high school came from poorer families and couldn't afford computers except for used pieces of junk that had no memory. Several moments passed while he pretended interest in a software tutorial.

"Frankly I don't give a rip about what you do." She hung up and lingered a few moments at her desk. Experience with two sisters reminded Miles not to question a frustrated woman.

"The kids will get a lot of use out of these computers," he said when Paige returned.

"I'm glad." She picked up a children's book from the floor and walked toward the kids' section. "Can I get back with you about the items you need for school? What we don't have, I'll order."

"Sure. How about dinner? I hear the Methodists are having a fish fry."

"Not tonight, Miles. I'm really tired."

"I imagine so. Last night was a zinger."

She still didn't meet his gaze. Her cell phone rang several times.

"Aren't you going to answer that?"

"No. I'm talking to you. Patrons come first."

"Good to know. My ego just shot up a notch." He powered down the computer and noted the hour on the black-rimmed, round clock above the library's front door. "I'd better get going before you lock me in here."

"Ice cream."

"What?"

"How about treating me to the Dairy Whip?" She whirled around and leaned against the circulation counter.

He'd never understand women—especially this one. "I'm ready."

A few minutes later, with the library securely locked and his checked-out books on the front seat of his truck, they walked the two blocks to the Dairy Whip. Sweat once again formed on his temples.

"What's your poison?" he asked.

"A large vanilla waffle cone."

"I always drip those things all over me."

"You have to learn how to eat them. It's a skill, like throwing a football."

He deliberated whether to question her about what he'd overheard in the library, but she might need to talk. "Paige, what's wrong?"

"Nothing." She waved at a woman with two small children. "Can't a girl want ice cream on a Friday night?"

"The last time you asked me to treat you to a Dairy Whip was when the sheriff's wife was diagnosed with breast cancer, and the time before that was when those kids were driving back from a basketball game and a truck ran a stop sign and killed them."

She looked at him—no emotion, not even a blink. He didn't make it past the fifty-yard line when it came to reading her. "You're pretty good. But everything's fine."

"Do you want me to follow you home?"

"I want you to stop worrying about me." She nearly snapped with that one.

"Impossible." He stood in front of the order

window. "A large vanilla waffle cone for the lady and a chocolate milkshake for me." He paid and waited while the order was filled. A few moments later, he handed Paige her ice cream and watched her take a generous lick. "As I said before, it's impossible to not worry about you."

Without responding, she sat on a nearby plastic chair and focused on the young mom with the children. A little boy closed his eyes as he licked around a cone. Paige laughed.

Miles sat in a chair beside her, curious about her interest in the small boy. "I refuse to apologize for caring."

He caught a sadness in her light brown eyes. "We will never happen. This I can promise."

The children with their ice cream captured his attention.

"Why don't you ever try something different?" the older girl asked.

"I like vanilla. A lot," the little boy said.

The mother wiped a dribble of ice cream from the boy's chin. "There are wonderful flavors out there—like chocolate and strawberry."

"But, Mommy, I just like vanilla."

"One day you'll see what you've been missing."

# CHAPTER 7

THE NEXT MORNING Paige left her peaceful bungalow and drove to the interstate en route for Pradmore, where she faithfully subjected her body to a monthly car-wash tan. Mikaela Olsson had two shades of skin: pale and paler. But Paige Rogers kept her skin a golden color, even if it had to be sprayed on.

The burnt grass fit her dark mood while images of Keary haunted her—past and present. His reappearance in her life after all these years had shortened her temper and left her contemplating the idea of shortening his life span. Not exactly a Christian thought, but definitely honest. For certain, she'd never accept this charlatan gaining ground in popularity as Oklahoma's next governor.

Paige understood him well enough to know he wouldn't give up on his ludicrous demands for her to join his campaign. The man never took no for an answer. Unfortunately he had the power to persuade the most reluctant of objectors.

And therein lay her problem.

She'd done her best to bring Keary to justice a long time ago, and what did it get her? The world thought Mikaela Olsson was dead, a disgraced CIA operative who'd been killed in the line of duty. Paige couldn't do anything without proof, and that meant finding Rosa. But she'd disappeared into the throngs of Africa over seven years ago. Was she still alive and hiding with her children from Casimiro Figuiera or Keary?

Devastation again climbed to the top rung of Paige's emotional ladder. And as she stood there balancing regret and guilt with her hands tied behind her back, she remembered her parents were safe.

To make matters worse, a white Camry rode her bumper and not another vehicle appeared on either side of the interstate. She glanced into the rearview mirror again. The driver, who looked like a man, wore a baseball cap pulled down tightly on his forehead. Clown hair stuck out on both sides, reminding her of a truck driver strung out on NoDoz.

Paige sped up to seventy-five, then eighty, and the car tailed her like a magnet. She changed lanes, and the car swerved over behind her. *Oh, you have no idea who you're messing with.*

Paige's pulse raced into high gear as her foot pressed the accelerator. If the guy thought he'd succeeded in making her nervous, he'd better think a little harder. All he'd managed was to turn up her internal temperature. She changed lanes again while watching him in the mirror. The Camry swung behind her. This was not a good ole boy taking a break from picking turnips. She caught his attention, and he tipped his hat. Whether he was another one of Keary's thugs or just a jerk preying on a woman, he needed to know "defenseless" wasn't a part of her company file.

Paige clenched her fists and fought the urge to spin her car into a ninety-degree turn. The thought of killing the guy didn't sit well, especially if he wasn't the real thing. Taking the next exit eased her conscience. If the Camry followed her, she'd take a different approach.

Another mile sped by before an exit sign appeared. Paige flipped on the turn signal and slowed. So did the Camry. *So he wants to play.*

A stop sign planted in dead brush loomed at the bottom of the feeder. Before coming to a complete halt, she whipped her car left, zipped through the underpass, and turned down a country road with the Camry breathing down on her rear.

"I've had enough." Adrenaline flowed through every inch of her.

She whirled her car into a 180-degree turn in the middle of the road, sending the Camry squealing into the right ditch. She paused long enough to see the driver exit the car. From this distance, she didn't recognize the person, but she filed the image into her storage bank. Paige waved at the jean-clad driver and headed toward the expressway. This time she decided to take the back way into town.

All of this for a once-a-month, total-body, car-wash tan.

# CHAPTER 8

I WANT TO CALL her, tell her I've read about my contribution in the local paper, but I'd rather have her squirm. Timing is everything with Mikaela, and I'm waiting for the precise moment to unload her next assignment.

She won't dare refuse, since I hold all the aces.

# CHAPTER 9

MILES OPENED the door of the library on a warm Tuesday afternoon. The familiar musty scent of knowledge greeted him. As a boy, he'd spent hours wandering among the many adventures in his hometown library in Tennessee, peering inside to see if a journey called his name. He sailed the seas to *Treasure Island*, solved mysteries with the Hardy Boys, and rounded up the bad guys with Zane Grey and Louis L'Amour.

Miles gestured Walt inside. It was only the second day of school, and already Miles knew Walt needed help. The kid hadn't ventured into the library since he was in junior high—not because his parents hadn't encouraged him, but because books weren't cool. This morning, Walt had shown up at school forty-five minutes early to do homework. His math grades from last year were adequate, but his English and history studies needed a jump start. The slender kid, with shoulder muscles that spanned the doorway and hands that held a death grip on a football, hesitated before stepping inside.

Miles's gaze trailed to the circulation desk, where his favorite librarian pointed to a shelf of books for a little redheaded girl. Paige must have sensed his presence, for she glanced up and waved before returning her attention to the child.

*Love the smile. Hate the rejection.*

"We're going to find a couple of books and some online information this afternoon that will help you write your paper," Miles said and pointed Walt toward the computer table. "I think you'll find this less painful than my ground-kissing push-ups."

"Yes, sir."

Obviously Walt didn't find Miles's comments humorous. "Miss Rogers will help you with the reference material."

As if on cue, Paige pivoted and smiled. Miles's heartbeat thudded into overdrive, and his thoughts lingered on the one library adventure he'd most likely never encounter. He made his way to the desk with Walt close behind.

"Do you have time to give us a hand?" Miles asked.

"Of course. How about introducing me to your friend?"

Miles turned to Walt. "My star quarterback, Walt Greywolf."

She stuck out her hand, and Walt grasped it. "It's a pleasure. I know your coach is very proud of you."

"Thanks, ma'am. We try to keep him happy. Keeps the whip away."

Surprised at the dry wit, Miles focused on his Chickasaw Wonder with new admiration. "How come I don't see this side of you on the field?"

Walt blushed red. "You just don't hear it."

"He has you there, Coach. I never took you for a Simon Legree." A glint of flirtation sparkled in Paige's eyes.

"Who?" Walt asked.

Paige walked out from behind the circulation desk. "Simon Legree was a ruthless slave owner in the book *Uncle Tom's Cabin*," she said. "He liked to use a whip on the slaves. Are you sure you haven't read it?"

"I saw the movie *Catwoman*," Walt said. "I get your point."

"I saw that movie too, and I don't resemble either one of them—unless I'm pushed."

Paige laughed softly. "Okay, we'll not pick on the coach anymore." She gave Walt her attention. "How can I help you?"

The kid moistened his lips. "I'd like to use a computer. Gotta paper to write on Jim Thorpe."

"Take your pick of any of these. Need any instructions?"

"No, ma'am." Walt chose a computer on the far end and slid into a wooden chair.

"Very mannerly. A little shy," Paige said.

"Well, he just surprised me with his wit. The girls like him, but he fumbles his words."

"But not with a football?"

"Very funny. Actually he has a lot of talent and potential. Home life is solid, and he'd do much better in school if he'd only apply himself. The family's poor, which means he works part-time to help out financially. Doesn't have much free time for studying."

"From the looks of his left eye, football has a lot of his attention."

Miles reflected on his team's turmoil. "That wasn't from practice or a game."

Paige stole a glimpse at Walt. "Does his black eye have anything to do with your taking him under your wing?"

Miles seized the moment to lose himself in her eyes. "That obvious, huh?"

"I know you pretty well."

Miles glanced toward the boy. "He's a sophomore playing first-string quarterback."

"I could offer to take a look at his paper before he turns it in. Will he be writing it here?"

Miles leaned onto the desktop. "I have no idea, but I'll find out. Any help you could throw his way will be greatly appreciated." He couldn't even tend to business with Paige without his blood pressure rising to the point of needing medication.

"We've got a couple of books here about Jim Thorpe. I can find more info online. I'll pull something together before you leave."

"Thanks. I read in the paper that Daniel Keary donated the new computers."

A cold stare replaced the warm glow. "What of it?"

The sudden shift of mood caught Miles off guard until he remembered the phone call he'd overheard when she'd told someone to "pick them up."

"So you're not overly pleased about Daniel Keary's generous contribution?"

Paige smirked. "Don't look a gift horse in the mouth. But that doesn't apply to Trojan horses." She took a stack of books from a small boy and touched his cheek.

Miles studied Paige until the little boy said his good-byes. "Obviously you haven't jumped on the bandwagon to support Keary."

"Has it started to snow in July?"

"But he's conservative, stands for pro-life, wants to lower taxes, and he's a Christian. I read that he's served his country well too. The other guys are jokes."

"Even Lucifer was called 'morning star, son of the dawn.' Don't be suckered by the image, Coach."

"Hey, you know something I don't? He looks like a shoo-in."

"Whatever. You can nominate him for sainthood. I'm sure his office can supply the forms."

Miles was taken aback by her sarcasm. The woman he'd grown to know had never been vicious before. "Give me one plank of his platform that you disagree with. That's all I ask."

"You're right. Keary stands for good things. He's against abortion, wants to lower taxes, and supports faith-based initiatives, but a woman has a right to her own opinion."

"What is it that you dislike about this guy?"

Paige pulled a book from the shelf. "He shouldn't have had to give back his medals."

"Keary?"

"No," Paige said, walking away. "Jim Thorpe."

Miles chased after her, and she gave him two books on sports history. "The guys loved your Italian cream cake."

"Maybe I'll bake them another one to celebrate their first win."

"Tough team this coming Friday night. It's only a preseason game—a scrimmage. But the heat's on. You going to be there?"

"Wouldn't miss it. Voleta and I are working the concession stand the second half—more to help her count money than to sell snacks, so see if you can have the game all wrapped up by then."

"I'll do my best. How about hot chocolate and doughnuts afterward?"

"I suppose." Her attention was diverted to the

door. Eleanor and old Mr. Shafer shuffled into the library. The man's lined face reminded him of a walnut.

"There's your fan club," Miles whispered.

"Hush. Those are two of my best patrons."

"I agree. That old man watches me like he's your daddy."

She nodded. "Then behave."

He waved at the couple and anticipated their teasing. The two never failed to point out how he and Paige looked good together.

"There they are," Eleanor said. Her hair had a rather orange cast. Maybe she was supposed to blend in with the leaves this fall.

"The coach needs to take a cot at the library," Mr. Shafer said. "Oh, I forgot. He has his own house. A big one too."

"Have you seen it, Paige?" Eleanor asked. "He's remodeled it from top to bottom."

"No, ma'am." Paige pressed her lips together. No doubt to suppress a laugh. "I'm sure it's right out of *Southern Living*."

"When I did the plumbing, it was right out of a nightmare," Miles said.

Although he took part in the bantering, he couldn't seem to stop thinking about Paige's aversion to Daniel Keary. Miles had learned something new about her today, and of late those revelations needled at him like a case of the chiggers.

Miles and Walt exited the library with two books

and a half-dozen printed pages tucked under the kid's left arm.

"I'll take a look at these after work tonight and in the morning before school," Walt said. "Thanks for your help. I need to bring up my English grade."

"All I did was point you in the right direction." Miles touched the kid's shoulder. "I want to see you on the team and making progress in school."

"Yes, sir." Walt startled and frowned.

Miles glanced in the direction of the kid's gaze. Walt's fifteen-year-old dented car had a flat on its left front tire. "I'll help you with that." A minor irritation Miles could handle.

"Oh, I have plenty of time to change it, but I don't have a spare." Walt studied the area a moment more and nodded toward Miles's truck. "Someone tagged you, too."

Miles groaned. His front left tire sat squashed against the concrete, and in the heat, sweat already beaded across his brow, more from the rising irritation. "Not much chance of a coincidence, is there?"

"Nope."

"Don't suppose they left a calling card."

"No reason to. We both know who did this."

Miles chose not to dive into that comment. "Let's change my flat, and I'll take you to work. I'll help you deal with getting your tire fixed later."

"Like breaking a few heads?"

"That's what I'm afraid of. Let me help, Walt.

I'll talk to the sheriff after I get you to work. You're better and bigger than pranks and flying fists."

"Do me a favor and stay out of my business. It'll only make matters worse."

"Maybe this time, but not if there are any more incidents. I'll—"

"Look, Coach, you say that life is more than who gains yards on the field. I respect that and what you're trying to teach us. But, like, when someone doesn't play by the same rules, then you have to make up your own. You know? Maybe not today or tomorrow, but I'll find a way to get even."

# CHAPTER 10

PAIGE DROVE HOME from the library, exasperated with Miles's and Walt's flat tires. She imagined Ty Dalton had enjoyed a good laugh, since his garage was the only one in town to fix flats. As much as she'd like to shake some sense into a couple of teenage boys and a father who'd never gotten past Friday night lights, small-town problems were a whole lot easier to digest than international espionage. Especially with lowlifes like—

Her cell phone rang, and she snatched it out of the side pocket of her shoulder bag. The number registered *Unavailable*.

"Mikaela, I've learned a few things about Keary," Palmer said. "Can you talk?"

"No one in the car but me. What's up?"

"We've reopened his file."

Hope lifted a notch. "What happened?"

"You've heard about the oil deal he brokered in Angola?"

"WorldMarc Oil in Oklahoma City, a private company. Another one of Keary's brilliant political moves to bring revenue into the state. A big win for folks." She felt like she was standing in front of a junior high teacher reciting the day's assignment, except she had more passion for this topic.

"The drilling took place where a village and its people disappeared. It wasn't the first."

An old memory surfaced, one laden with the bodies of men, women, and children. "Keary paved the way for those in power, and they owed him. Any witnesses?"

"Not yet."

Same old story. "Operatives on the ground?"

"Yes. We need you back."

"Impossible. Keary threatened to kill my parents if I ever came out of hiding."

"Why didn't you tell me this before?"

"You weren't standing over me with a gun."

Palmer blew out an exasperated sigh. "I want to hear the whole story."

No one knew the *whole* story but God. The guilt, the shame . . . "Maybe someday, but not now."

"Come on back. We'll keep your parents safe."

Paige nearly ran a stop sign. "I have to think about it." *Pray about it.*

"What's there to think about?"

*If only you knew.* "There's a lot involved." She blinked and relied on her training to keep the tears away.

"Sounds like a no-brainer to me. People have been killed, and it needs to end. You didn't try to prove it back then, but now we have a second chance."

"We?"

"Do you think you were the only one who questioned Keary's integrity?"

She gripped the steering wheel to keep from agreeing to whatever it took to bring Keary to justice. "I'll call you."

"When?"

"Soon."

"Think about this, church lady. Finding the proof we need will clear your record and give you your life back. We *will* prove Keary's role in the Angola incident, but if it doesn't happen until after the election, the repercussions could be global." Palmer wasn't blowing smoke. "I need to hear from you in the next twenty-four hours."

Paige slipped her phone back into her purse. She trembled. *Oh, God, what do I do? Keary can't get by with this again. He's got to be stopped. But do You want me involved with the CIA again? Will You protect Mom and Dad? What about the tactics needed to prove Keary's guilt?*

She turned into her driveway and switched off the ignition. The old voices slammed against her logic, the issues she'd never been able to resolve. The questions, doubts . . . and where God fit into the life of a CIA operative. If He fit at all.

Once she was inside her home and the visual check was completed, she wavered between getting online and researching WorldMarc Oil or falling flat on her face and begging God for direction.

How often had she wrestled with the moral dilemma of a Christian working for the CIA? She'd given up the life of an operative and lived a lie to keep her parents safe. But what about the innocent people who'd died in Angola? So many times she wondered if her decisions would have been different if she'd been a Christian then.

Keary was a murderer. He'd betrayed a team of operatives to assist a military coup, and now he was linked to killing innocent people again. Palmer had touched on the possible disastrous effects of the governor of Oklahoma brokering an oil deal that involved a scorched-earth policy.

Citizens would ask if other American-based oil companies had covered up the same type of practice. They would wonder if the government backed them. The world would announce how the U.S. condoned genocide in the name of oil and then secretly covered up its involvement. Americans already distrusted their elected officials. The free world would shake their fists in disgust, and enemies would gloat—an international investigation, skepticism, global unrest, riots, economic and financial ruin. Her thoughts might be exaggerated, but the canal of deceit often led to tragedy. Keary had to be stopped before being elected as Oklahoma's governor.

Paige slumped onto her sofa and clutched a pillow to her chest. She tried to pray, but the only words that came were *help me*. Once again she considered searching the Internet for details, but her legs refused to move. Palmer needed an answer in twenty-four hours. Doing nothing meant allowing Keary to continue. Her parents' lives were at stake. Rosa and her family could be found and disposed of.

And Nathan . . .

*Dear God, keep him safe.*

Shortly after midnight, she turned on her computer and waited for the dial-up to allow her access to more information about WorldMarc Oil and the drilling in Angola. A few years ago, the media had announced that Keary's law firm was brokering the deal due to Keary's international expertise. She guessed he'd been the one to approach WorldMarc and not the other way around. Most likely he'd invested in Angolan oil long before moving back to the States.

If only Rosa Ngoimgo had come forward with what she knew back then. But the widow had four children to rear, and she was afraid for her family. Better to let her husband's killer go free than for her remaining family to face Casimiro Figuiera's machete. Alone, it was Paige's word against Keary's that he had sent innocent people to their deaths. Rosa's oldest son was about nineteen now. He might know the truth . . . and he might not be afraid to speak up.

Paige stared into the computer screen, not seeing the information about WorldMarc Oil but picturing a young African boy. That boy was now a man. Paige had much to think about, much to consider. Twenty-four hours just wasn't enough time. She brought up her e-mail and quickly typed Palmer a message. He would have to wait for his answer until Sunday night.

## CHAPTER 11

JASON STEVENS SITS across from me in my office, my temporary office until after the election. He leans back in his chair, legs crossed, shoulders erect, confident—the way he's been trained.

"You said we needed to talk," I say, taking a sip of my black Starbucks, Rift Valley Blend.

"I learned something over the weekend."

"In D.C.?" Curiosity always piques my attention when Stevens returns from D.C.

"It's not good."

I lean in closer. "Tell me." Problems are like welcome mats, and the ones that resemble jigsaw puzzles are the most intriguing.

"The file has been reopened." Jason doesn't even blink. "I'm on top of it."

I laugh. So does he.

"This afternoon he asked Mikaela to come back on board."

This problem might take some time. "What did she say?"

"She had to think about it for a few days."

I settle back in my chair and stare at Jason, not looking at him but through him. He is doing a good job getting me the information from Palmer's assistant. I need to keep a step ahead of the CIA. So the company thinks they can shake me up just before the election. They have no more proof than before . . . unless they've found Rosa Ngoimgo.

I should have made sure Mikaela was dead that day. "We've got to find Rosa."

"We have men on the ground looking."

Jason's carefully calculated words deepen my irritation. "Then get more men and find her. Kill all of them." I lower my voice to barely above a whisper. "It will be worth it; trust me."

He nods. "What about Mikaela? Why don't you get rid of her?"

I don't want to tell him that's one option I don't have. Not yet anyway.

"Where is Zuriel? He hasn't answered his phone all day," I say.

"Vegas."

Worthless piece of baggage. I should get rid of him.

# CHAPTER 12

FRIDAY NIGHT FOOTBALL, even a scrimmage, cleared the streets of Split Creek. All residents who could walk, be carried, or be wheeled made their way to the outskirts of town, where past and present heroes and sassy cheerleaders assembled in the bleachers and along the fifty-yard line of the gridiron. Folks lived and breathed the bright lights, the artificial turf, the halftime shows, and the thrill of the game. The game was spoken of as reverently as the utterance of God on Sunday morning. Tonight the battle lines were drawn amid temperatures soaring into the nineties, but Paige didn't believe anyone paid any attention to the heat—except the fire emanating from the pigskin.

The *click-click* of a drum cadence signaled the entrance of the drill team, who waved flags of blue and gold as they led the high school band toward the field for pregame activities. As if on cue, the stage lit up. Paige's attention swung to the field house, where the Split Creek Bobcats would soon race in to a roar of cheers. She imagined Miles giving last-minute instructions and lots of "attaboys." He yelled from time to time, and his face could glisten in a mixture of sweat and tomato red, but he loved every one of his players—and the game. From her perch in the bleachers, she could rest assured that no one knew how her heart ached to invite him into her life.

*Who would have ever thought I'd be watching a high school football game and selling hot dogs and Cokes for the booster club?* And enjoying it, even if fumbles and touchdowns highlighted her week.

It sure beat dead bodies and the uncertainties of wondering who were the spies, who were the counterspies, and who was issuing orders. Right now she carried her car keys and a wallet. Back then she carried her wits and a phony ID. Right now she could relax for a few hours. Back then she counted on her senses to keep her alert.

She glanced at Voleta sitting beside her, such a quirky friend who brought lots of fun into Paige's life. *Sweet home Oklahoma.* This was the idyllic life, not the covert missions led by a man who ended up betraying her and so many others. Maybe Keary hadn't fooled everyone. Maybe only a few people.

Paige still believed in the values and dreams of America's founders. She understood the importance of keeping the nation's borders free from terrorists and assisting the impoverished nations of the world to achieve a democratic community—a safe and healthy place for children to laugh and learn.

Brunner had written "the necessary end sanctifies the necessary means." She hadn't made a decision to assist the CIA yet, or rather she hadn't heard from God.

She sickened at the evil Keary had orchestrated. God forgive her for thinking of murder, but the inclination clung to her like the threads of a spiderweb. If she accepted Palmer's invitation, she would risk having her parents learn the truth. How would they handle their daughter's background . . . and the fact that she wasn't really dead? Paige shivered. Her mom's heart may have worsened over the past years. Her dad had always been in excellent health, but age had surely brought on new problems. Her thoughts lingered a moment on Nathan. He too was buried under paperwork and another identity in Africa.

No matter how she looked at what she'd done to those she loved, doing nothing while Keary clawed his way up the political ladder was the greater wrong.

"I sure hope we win." Voleta's words interrupted her thoughts.

Back to Paige Rogers . . . for now. "Miles said this team is tough. Did you see their stats?"

"I remember they went to the last game in play-offs last year." Voleta wiggled her shoulders, whipping black hair with streaks of purple-red across her shoulders. "Are you two any closer to being cozy?"

"Cozy? Are you serious? Really, Voleta, you need a new agenda."

"But I've never been in a wedding."

"Try Eleanor and Mr. Shafer. Better yet, settle down and attend your own."

"Are you or are you not seeing him after the game?"

"For hot chocolate and doughnuts among a hundred other fans. That's not a wild game of pool and a six-pack of beer in a smoky bar. The whole conversation will be about the team and how they did tonight."

"You're simply too independent."

Sometimes Paige wished Voleta understood her. "I don't need a man to make me happy."

"They sure do help on a lonely night."

"I prefer a fluffy pillow and—"

The announcer interrupted, listing the opposing team's roster as the players made their grand entrance.

"The Warriors have arrived," Voleta whispered.

Moments later, Paige and Voleta rose to their feet to cheer the Bobcats of Split Creek High. Paige lifted binoculars to focus on Walt. One of his own team members pushed him, but Walt shrugged it off. Poor kid. She could teach him a few moves that would send those bullies to the ER. On the sidelines, Miles stood by himself. No doubt he was praying. That she understood—the only safe place to be.

Four minutes before halftime, she nudged Voleta. "We'd better get to the concession stand before the big rush."

The Bobcats were down six points, and they were on their own ten-yard line. "I hate to leave without seeing this play."

"So do I," Paige said. "But think about it. There's only one thing worse than losing at the half, and that's no one working the concession stand when the hungry masses descend for fuel. Sounds like mutiny if we bail out."

Voleta blew out a sigh. "I hate it when you make sense."

*Make sense?* If only Voleta knew. Paige excused herself as she passed a bald, middle-aged man who seemed to think he knew more about football than the coaches. His wife, equally eloquent, shouted at Miles. Even though Miles could handle himself, Paige longed to give the woman a heavy dose of sarcasm.

Paige's eyes were fixed on the play while anticipation for the Bobcats to take the lead left her breathless. As she moved onto the concrete step, someone slammed into her from behind. Struggling to keep her balance, Paige came down hard on her right ankle, nearly falling headfirst down the bleachers. She caught the metal railing, but the damage had already been done to her foot. Fiery pain forced a cry from her lips. She bit down hard, irritated at her inability to handle a twisted ankle. At least she hoped it was just a twisted ankle.

"I'm sorry. I'm sorry," said a freckle-faced boy of about eight or nine. "I tripped."

"It's all right." Paige peered up into his anxious face. She touched his hand and forced a smile. "Don't you worry about a thing."

"Paige, you all right?" Voleta asked, bending down to her. "Oh, sweetie, did you break anything?"

She hugged her right ankle, willing the pain to subside. "I'm fine. Give me a moment until the fire goes out."

A whistle blew. The fans bellowed their dissatisfaction.

"What happened?" Paige asked. "I need good news."

"Flag on the play and a penalty . . . on us."

Now she wanted to be a real girl and cry. "Rats. Help me to my post." She grabbed Voleta's arm and attempted to stand but nearly lost her balance again.

"You need an X-ray."

"And leave you alone at the concession stand? Not on your life. We're partners." Paige recognized Voleta's many talents, but math wasn't one of them. The booster club would go broke if she handled the money and the food alone tonight.

Four hours later, Paige hobbled out of Pradmore Hospital with her right ankle wrapped like a white sausage. It throbbed like she'd been attacked by a swarm of wasps, although it was only bruised and sprained. To make matters worse, the Bobcats had lost. She'd sat with her ankle propped with ice for over an hour until the game ended: Warriors 18, Bobcats 12. What a night of regret.

Once the bleachers had cleared, Voleta had insisted that Miles send a medic from the field house to take a look at Paige's ankle. The evening went farther downhill after that, stopping abruptly in the emergency room.

After a staunch refusal to exit the hospital in a wheelchair, Paige mentally calculated how many steps it would take to reach Miles's truck, which was parked at the entrance. Mastering crutches again would take a little practice.

"We should fill your prescription before leaving town," Miles said.

"It doesn't hurt," Paige said.

He opened his truck door. "If your ankle doesn't hurt, then why is your face all scrunched up?"

His attempt at humor soured her mood. "I don't need pain meds tonight. If my foot hurts tomorrow, then I'll get the prescription filled. Just drive me back to Split Creek and my car." Paige swung out the crutch and would have fallen again, but Miles grabbed her waist.

"And how are you planning to drive home from the field?"

"My left foot works the gas and the brake as well as my right." Paige squeezed the crutch to fight the incessant throb.

"Right. And what will be your excuse when you end up in a ditch along the way?" While she leaned on Voleta, Miles took the crutches and laid them on the truck bed. "Women can be so stubborn." He lifted her up into his arms as though she were sports equipment and deposited her onto the seat.

"I could have climbed in by myself." If her ankle didn't feel like someone had lit a match to it, she might have come up with something wittier. *Suck it up, girl. You've been hurt worse than this.*

"You two fussin' won't solve a thing," Voleta said, handing Paige her shoulder bag. "Miles, she needs something strong or she won't get a wink of sleep tonight."

"Oh, great." Paige blew out a sigh that added independence to the guilt. "You two act like I'm totally incapable of taking care of myself."

"That's obvious." Miles said, reaching onto the floorboard to remove a set of football pads. He tossed them into the truck bed along with the crutches. "The doctor said that same foot had been broken before. *Shattered* was the word he used. Calcium buildup around your foot. Ah, 'metal plate and pins.' Sounds like you've taken care of yourself just fine."

A mental picture of being tossed by the force of a bomb sprung to her mind. "I twisted it running."

"Running? Looks like you fell off a cliff. Now I understand why you wrap that thing when you jog."

"My secret's out."

"Why do I think you haven't told me the whole story?" Miles glanced at Voleta. "Are you heading home?"

"Yes. Call me if you need anything. Otherwise I'll check on her in the morning and bring some doughnuts for breakfast. We can get her car tomorrow. The ride back should give Paige time to talk about how she once broke her foot into a million pieces. The scars look like a road map." Voleta waved and walked away.

"I'll do my best." Miles swung his attention to Paige. "For the record, you are the most bull-headed woman that I've ever seen. Good thing you have such a good personality."

"Do I get the Miss Congeniality award?"

"I saw that movie, and Sandra Bullock was working undercover at the time."

*Oh, great.* "She still got the award."

Once Miles had the prescription filled, Paige expected him to grill her about her past foot injury during the forty-five-minute drive back to Split Creek. She'd taken the time to put together a fail-proof explanation, but he didn't say a word. Then she remembered, and the guilt assaulted her again.

"Sorry about the loss tonight. Hard-fought game."

"The boys were really bummed out by it."

"Like Walt?"

"Yeah. Bad enough that he blamed himself, but a few of the guys blamed him too. Timing is everything, and the receiver wasn't working with him."

"You should have been with your team instead of taking me to the hospital."

"I said all I could at the field house. Tomorrow morning I'll pay a visit to Walt and a couple of the other players. The season doesn't start until after Labor Day, and a preseason game doesn't ruin our chances to head into the play-offs."

"The Warriors may have gone to the play-offs every year, but that doesn't mean the Bobcats can't take the state trophy *this* year," she said, doing her best to concentrate on the conversation and not on her ankle.

"I like the way you think." His gaze lingered on her briefly before he turned back to the road.

She wished he didn't care so much. It made saying no that much harder. "You needed your rest tonight, not hauling me to the hospital."

"I have an ulterior motive—carrot cake after practice on Monday."

"I should have known." She rolled down the window. Perhaps a little fresh air would keep her mind off the pain and the effect of the man beside her. "Thanks for all you've done for me tonight. Voleta could have driven me to the hospital."

"Oh, really? We both know Voleta, and she could have run out of gas trying to find the ER."

Miles was right. Voleta had the want-to, just not always the how-to. "She has a good heart."

"Yes, ma'am. I won't grill you about your foot. At least not tonight."

"I broke it chasing a guy who put down my best friend."

Paige leaned back in the seat, wishing she were already home. The instant the doctor had requested an X-ray, she knew he'd see the damage of her previous injury. But she hadn't expected the doctor to mention her once-shattered foot. Why had she ever allowed Miles and Voleta to come into the examining room with her? Praise God that Miles hadn't questioned her about the ankle scars.

At least she hadn't been asked to remove her jeans. The scars running from her feet to her shoulder blades would have raised a few questions.

*What about the ones embedded in your heart?*

Miles yawned and palmed the steering wheel of his truck. Three hours' sleep last night, and he craved three times that much. However, he wouldn't have traded one minute with Paige to alleviate the sand in his eyes. Last night she'd needed him. She had been forced to depend on someone other than herself, and he was there to fill the bill. At times he believed his campaign to win Paige was on life support.

Her scarred foot had a history behind it, and one day he'd ask for the whole story. Must have been a nasty accident—painful, too. That could be why she was reluctant to get on his Harley or ride a horse.

He shook his head to dispel the intense need to head back home and sleep a few more hours. Whatever happened to the old days when he could stay up all night and do fine the whole next day? He wasn't getting old, at least not from his perspective. Maybe the aching in his body and the pounding in his head had more to do with paying a visit to Walt and Chris. Tempers had flared last night, and if Miles hadn't interceded, a fight would have broken out, and Walt would have had more than a black eye. Chris and his buds had a vendetta against the Chickasaw Wonder, and they didn't mind repeating history by having the whites attack the red man in superior numbers.

Miles pulled into the dirt driveway of the Greywolf home and scattered chickens in every direction. Miles noted the small house needed several coats of paint, but not a piece of trash or a weed met his eye. A black dog bounded up to the truck, barking and growling. The animal looked like a mixture of a shepherd and a rottweiler, and it sure looked mean. Normally Miles could befriend a dog, but this one jumped up on the truck door, snarling like it hadn't eaten in weeks.

"Matches, down!" A man whom Miles recognized as Walt's dad stood on the front porch. "Get on back up here and let the man get out of his truck."

Instantly the dog jumped back and hid his incisors. He hurried up to the dilapidated front porch.

"Now lie down until I tell you to get up."

Again the dog obeyed. Miles opened his truck door with one eye on the animal. With his body near exhaustion, his response time was slow, and he had enough problems for one day. "Thanks, Mr. Greywolf. I think I need a watchdog like that one."

"Oh, he's territorial all right."

"I sure could use him on the football field to keep the team in line."

Mr. Greywolf laughed. "From what I hear, you could use more than one."

Sympathy for the family took a firm hold. "Is Walt around?"

"Sure, Coach." The man lifted his hat and wiped the sweat from his lined brow. "Sure appreciate you helping out my son with the flat tire last week."

"Glad to help."

"Anyway, you caught Walt before he heads into town for work. Come on in and have some breakfast."

"Smells good, but no thanks. Got lots of players to visit this morning. If it's all right, I'd like to speak to your son out here." Miles made his way up the wooden steps to the porch and stuck out his hand. His stomach growled, or was it the dog? "Good to see you again. I won't be long with your boy."

Walt opened the squeaky screen door. He wore the dark pants and blue shirt uniform of the local grocery store chain about ten miles from Split Creek. The lack of eye contact didn't surprise Miles; he expected it. At least the kid no longer had a black eye and was in one piece. His dad nodded at Miles and brushed past his son and into the house.

"How you doing this morning?" Miles wouldn't want to be in the kid's shoes and facing the pressures of his world.

"How do you expect me to be, Coach? We lost. Everyone says it was my fault. I hesitated. Slow on reading the defense."

Miles fought the urge to give the same talk again that he'd delivered to the team at nine thirty last night. "I'm not happy about the loss either, but it wasn't all your doing."

"How do you figure?"

"You can't do your job if the rest of the team isn't doing theirs."

Walt jammed his hands into his pockets. "That's what you said last night."

"If you'd screwed up last night, I would have let you know then. The Warriors are tough, and the Bobcats weren't playing their best. Everyone was slow, maybe too confident after last season."

"Maybe. But I fumbled a few times."

"And our defense failed to block their offense."

Walt glanced to the left toward a barren pasture where a couple of cows lifted their heads as if listening to every word. "Maybe I should quit." Walt whispered his words, as though if he spoke them more audibly, he might have to follow through.

"What? And throw away a chance for a full scholarship?"

Walt shrugged and continued focusing his attention on the cows. "I can get a good ride at a number of universities. You know that."

"Sure, your Native American status will help with your college education. But a football scholarship on top of it means even more."

Maybe it was Walt's indifference. Maybe it was Miles's lack of sleep. Maybe it was Ty Dalton's constant reminder that his son was the team's only hope for a winning season, but Miles's headache intensified, and he chose to challenge the kid, not sympathize with him. "Look at me, Walt."

Walt slowly turned to Miles. Heartbreak seeped from the pores of the kid's tanned face. But something else was written in his eyes—a spark of hope.

"What is it that you want to do with your life?" Miles asked.

The kid appeared to contemplate the question. "Nothing ginormous. Maybe agricultural research. Soil analysis. Things like that to help farmers."

"A fine idea, and you can do it. Your grades are rising, and I'm sure the scouts are looking at your stats this year." Miles wished he could read the kid's thoughts. "Guys like Chris will always be in your life. And others who'll say you aren't good enough, smart enough, the right race, or anything else that has the potential to stop you from living out your dreams."

"That's easy for you to say. You spout out things like a preacher. I'm the one who's supposed to lead the team. How many times have you said it's a mental game?"

Miles fought to keep from stating how he viewed those who had an excuse for doing nothing with their lives. He should have slept before tackling this. "If you want to give up on yourself, fine. Just let me know now. I'm not wasting my time on a kid who has no guts. You have to want some things bad enough to fight for them—and not necessarily with your fists. That's where real life begins."

Walt scuffed at a loose stone. "Some days when a couple of the other players are all up in my grill, I don't think I can take one more hour. Then I tell myself that one day at a time is enough. I know Chris wanted my position right from the start. But he doesn't even know me. Just hates me." He shrugged. "Sure makes me wonder where God is in all of this."

"I've come to accept that there are things about Him we might never learn. Keep praying for guidance. That's all we can do. Let me know what I can do to help. Your parents support you. Your friends respect you. And your coach believes in you."

"My parents and friends aren't the problem. Neither are you."

"Outsmart, outplay, outthink them. But don't let them edge you into giving up."

Walt's shoulders lifted and fell. "All right. I never was a quitter. Don't really want to start now."

"Good. We're on the same team."

"Someday I'd like to make friends with Chris."

"Go for it."

"Might take a miracle." Walt snapped his fingers at Matches, who had edged mighty close to Miles's leg.

"Thanks. I have a feeling that dog would take my leg off and eat it for breakfast."

"Not if you made friends with him first."

Miles grinned. Score one for the Bobcats.

"Okay, Coach, I get your point."

# CHAPTER 13

"Take the next flight to D.C.," I say to Jason.

"Why? What have you learned?"

I squeeze the cell phone and take a moment to pinpoint my ire. Jason shouldn't question my orders, but then I'm the one who has taught him the value of probing every source of information.

"Listening to everything that goes on in Palmer's office isn't enough. He doesn't need a reason to suspect her. Keep her happy—and quiet."

Jason pauses in his typical analytical manner. "All right. She's married, and that's a plus for us. According to her, she can't divorce her husband. He makes good money. I'll let her know that my job is at stake if anyone finds out about our relationship."

"Rent an apartment. Let her furnish it. Keep it all hot."

He laughs. "Have you seen her?"

I've seen the photographs and feel sorry for her husband. "Enough to know this is an easy one. You can handle it."

# CHAPTER 14

PAIGE WOKE with her ankle throbbing in sync with her pulse. If she didn't know better, she'd swear her foot was broken again instead of sprained. Hadn't she paid her dues? The pain medication and a glass of water sat on her nightstand, and she didn't waste any time swallowing a pill. Closing her eyes, she lay back on the pillow and waited for the incessant aching in her ankle to ease.

Her attitude followed the same path as her outlook for the next six weeks or so. Patience had never been one of her admirable traits, and tolerance for wasting time ranked second. Her number one way to relieve stress was running—after wrapping her foot and sliding it into a shoe that had good ankle support. But running had been eliminated until her foot healed, which meant a trip to an orthopedic specialist and most likely physical therapy. The last time she'd injured her foot, she wasn't able to run for a year. Back then the doctor had told her she might never run again, but she'd worked hard and overcome the odds. How could she handle taking on an operative role with her foot in this condition? Maybe God had answered her prayer after all.

Keary would get a good chuckle out of her predicament. She couldn't run from him or anyone else by swinging a crutch.

She stared at the whirling ceiling fan above her, allowing her mind to swing into operative mode and pushing the overwhelming emotions into a remote part of her heart. Uninvited snapshots ushered in the afternoon her world's infrastructure collapsed. But she needed to once more rethink every detail, every word.

Over seven years ago, she'd given up on showing the world the real Daniel Keary. Back then she'd equated working for the CIA with picking up potatoes: she'd never get the dirt out from under her fingernails, and obviously Keary had picked up his share too. It took several weeks in Africa and her new life as a Christian for her to realize the problem was not with the CIA but with a man who had betrayed his country at the cost of many lives.

Why had Keary sold out? That was crucial in worming her way into his head and catching him in the action needed to put him away for good.

The mission had been going smoothly: the retrieval of Leandro Ngoimgo, a prominent figure in Angola who was on the hit list of an extremist rebel movement. Paige had worked with Keary and two other operatives—one on the ground in Angola—for several months, utilizing all-source intelligence. The plan was in place.

Leandro paced the floor of the concrete building, his forehead a mass of worry. He pulled his cell phone from his pocket and walked into an adjoining empty room. A few moments later, he cornered Keary.

"Rosa and the children are leaving separately."

Keary stepped away from a window. "I know you're concerned about this airlift, but once the helicopter arrives and all of you are safe, you'll feel better."

Leandro shook his head. "No, they will leave before me. I've made arrangements."

Rosa gasped and rose from her chair. "Don't do this thing. We want to stay with you."

"I know what's best." Leandro's words were firm. He took Rosa's hand and led her into the empty room. When they returned, he grasped the shoulders of his twelve-year-old son. "Gonsalvo, we need to talk before my men arrive."

"This is foolishness." Keary's face reddened. Rarely had Paige seen him angry.

"This is my family." Leandro's voice graveled low. "I know what's best."

"Where are you sending them?" Keary asked.

"That's my business."

As soon as Leandro had finished talking to Gonsalvo, a truck arrived and whisked off Rosa and the four children. The good-byes had been short and tearful.

Keary sent Paige outside to keep an eye on the building and to watch for any signs of trouble. A commotion caught her attention, and she took a few moments to try to chase off a group of children. One of them had a deflated soccer ball. He kicked it closer to her. *Great.* Potential firefights weren't a place for kids to play.

"Get out of here," she said in Angolan Portuguese. "Bad soldiers nearby." One of the boys looked her way and grinned. Beautiful white teeth.

Three military trucks approached, and she hid behind a rattletrap of a car while radioing Keary. Six soldiers in cammies poured out, each wearing a small arsenal, while drivers stayed with the vehicles.

"Do you want me to eliminate them?" Paige had a good vantage point—if the kids would stay away.

"Describe them."

Once she finished, he told her to head back inside. The Angolan soldiers were there to help in the transport. Puzzled, Paige studied the men. One of them looked like the coup leader, Casimiro Figuiera, but he turned his back before she could positively identify him.

The soldiers moved inside the building, leaving one to guard the door. Paige hesitated. In the torrid temps, chills raced up her arms. Unless the men had a good disguise, they were members of the rebel movement. The soldier guarding the door picked up his radio and contacted someone. Paige read *bomb* on his lips. She realized everyone inside would soon be dead. Shots from inside the building broke the afternoon's stillness. Keary and the soldiers bolted out the door and onto the trucks.

Instinctively she knew Keary had betrayed them. Paige remembered how the late afternoon sun had shadowed the vehicles and darkened the doorway. She rushed toward the back entrance of the building to warn those waiting inside, hoping they were still alive. The door was locked. She pumped several bullets into it until she could maneuver her hand to unlock it. Just as the door swung open, an explosion pitched her several feet from the building. Later she learned that everyone inside had been killed. Only she and Keary had survived.

The helicopter pilot who was to carry them all to safety found her and Keary lying together on the ground. He'd been shot in the arm, but she believed he'd inflicted the wound upon himself.

Paige had no memory of her rescue, only what she'd read in Keary's report. She was flown to a hospital in Luanda, then on to Nairobi. She suffered a concussion, along with a ruptured spleen and a broken arm. She required surgery to her foot and more than two hundred stitches trailing up her spine. Before she could expose Keary, he filed his own report, documenting her supposed mental breakdown during the mission—her failure to keep her team safe.

During her stay in the Nairobi hospital, an operative from Langley completed her debriefing. She denied any mental breakdown and relayed what had really happened during the botched mission. But in the end, it was her word against Keary's.

Keary phoned her in Nairobi with his demands. If she did not resign from the CIA and take on a new identity, Keary would kill her and her parents. He'd tell her when and how she'd resume the rest of her life. Helpless, Paige had no choice but to concede.

Before she was released from the hospital, Rosa Ngoimgo called her. Paige had no idea how the woman had located her since she was in the VIP wing of the hospital. And how the widow knew Paige had survived was still a mystery. Rosa's husband had told her that he suspected Keary had sold them out. Oh, to have heard what Leandro had said to his wife and son.

"Help me bring him to justice," Paige had said. "The CIA will protect you and your family."

"The way they protected my husband from Casimiro Figuiera and your traitor?"

Paige couldn't argue with her. "Where can I find you?"

"I can't tell you. I must protect my family. My call to you is for this: I don't blame you for my husband's death. I'm glad you're alive, but you must be in danger too."

Paige hesitated. "Yes, you're right."

"May God keep you safe. And I pray someday He will help you find a way to stop the killing."

Later Greg Palmer's objectivity had crushed her

hopes of keeping Keary under investigation. "I understand why you're resigning," he'd said.

"Wouldn't you if your file stated you'd sent innocent people to their deaths?"

"Yes, I would." He hesitated, and she clung to an inkling of justice. "Keary's been cleared of any wrongdoing. But he's been warned that if something happens to you, the file will be reopened."

"So meanwhile, he continues to betray our country." Apathy seeped into her words.

"Not exactly. He's furious with our questioning his documentation and has resigned to resume his law practice in Oklahoma."

Bitter and alone, Paige buried Mikaela Olsson just as Keary had ordered. The other unexpected complication gave her even more reason to follow his explicit instructions. She'd lived with the regret and the guilt of her survival every day.

Six months later, Paige left Africa with a new identity and a determination to never forget the treachery. Keary had ordered her to a small town in Oklahoma called Split Creek. There she was to take on the role of a librarian, a minor from her college days, and he would keep an eye on her from Oklahoma City.

Paige adjusted the ice pack on her foot and reached for the TV remote to find an old *I Love Lucy* rerun. She might be on Keary's radar, but he couldn't remove the hope or erase the truth. Someday he would slip and expose himself to the whole country. Couldn't she just wait for him to trip himself up? Did God really want her to risk all she loved and treasured?

With the remote still in her hand, images crossed her mind of those she held dear—Mom and Dad, Rosa, Miles, Voleta, the others of Split Creek, and Nathan. Her heart ached, and she trembled.

Promptly at noon, Miles pulled into the gravel driveway at Paige's house. He'd meant to get there sooner, but he ended up having breakfast with Walt and his family after all. Good people who had goals for their children and exceptional faith.

Snatching up a Sonic bag containing lunch for Paige and himself, he once more anticipated a nap before the day was over. Locking his truck, he made his way to her porch and knocked on the door.

"Come on in. I saw you drive up," she said from inside. "Not much to do here today but watch who speeds by."

He walked into the cool air-conditioning. "If I'd known that, I'd have ordered a parade."

She tossed him a teasing look with a half smile. That special look in her eyes kept his longing alive.

"What's for lunch?" she asked.

"The best Split Creek has to offer."

"That's a Sonic bag."

"You have a problem with that?" He studied her

bandaged foot propped on the sofa table. "First tell me how you're feeling."

"No pain, only the thrill of ice."

"I thought it was the chill of ice."

"Depends on what you're taking at the time."

"I think I'm going to enjoy the new you."

"Which is why I hate taking anything that reduces my reaction time." She tilted her head. "The bag doesn't look full enough for both of us."

"Were you expecting a grocery sack?"

"Sitting around high on pain meds makes a girl hungry."

"Point me in the direction of plates, and I'll get this feast spread out."

"To the left of the sink, second shelf. Anything else you need?"

"Nope. You sit right here. Close your eyes so I can surprise you."

Instantly she obeyed. Too bad he couldn't kiss her. He chuckled. With the effect of the pain pills, he might get by with it.

"What's so funny?"

"Nothing you'd find humorous." He took a peek at her on the sofa, looking far too appealing—even with no makeup. With her hair pulled back in a ponytail, she looked fresh, natural, and he'd better get the food on plates before he *did* kiss her.

With her eyes still closed, she lifted her chin. "I don't hear any plates rattling."

He whistled the last song he heard on the country

and western radio station—something about picking turnips and falling in love. Miles found the plates and arranged the food in what he referred to as a good presentation. He carried hers to the sofa and set it on the table. "Okay, your lunch is served, O injured one."

One glance and she rubbed her palms. "Yum. Grilled cheese, onion rings, and a lemon-berry slush. You remembered my favorites."

He could remember a lot more if she'd only allow him. "Only the best for the lady. How was your morning?"

"Hmm." She bit into her sandwich and chewed it slowly. "I made coffee, surfed the Internet and the TV, made more coffee, and talked to Voleta. Actually she came by with doughnuts. How about you?"

"Went to see Walt."

"Is he doing better?"

"I think so. He's in a tough spot any way you look at it, but I believe in him. His family supports all of their kids." He paused, thinking about his not-so-great visit with Chris and Ty Dalton and nixed telling Paige about that venture.

She nodded. "At the benefit catfish fry for the Aubrey girl, the Greywolfs helped Voleta and me more than any of the volunteers. Did you see Chris too?"

"Oh yeah. His parents blamed last night's loss on Walt and my poor judgment. Nothing I didn't expect."

119

"I'm sorry. But the season is just starting."

"That's what I keep telling myself."

"Oops. We didn't bless this. Why don't you pray, and while you're at it, ask God to bless the team?"

He removed his baseball cap and prayed for a multitude of things. When he finished, he took a bite of his burger and picked up a stack of DVDs. "Voleta?" he asked.

"How did you guess? The movie queen."

Miles thumbed through the stack, all suspense. "These aren't chick flicks. All of them are about the FBI, Secret Service, CIA, or border guards."

"She knows what I like."

He pulled out a season of *24*. "Mind if a tired coach watches this one with you?"

"I'd really like the company, but I don't want to—"

"You're not stopping me from anything. I'd rather be here with you than anywhere else." He raised a brow. "No negative comments please."

"Only because you brought me lunch and it's perfect. I suppose you have a chocolate shake." She reached for an onion ring.

He lifted the shake and nodded. "If you eat all of those, no one will want to kiss you."

"That's *my* defense line."

He saluted her and slipped the DVD from its case. He needed a diversion from the gorgeous woman beside him.

Paige pretended interest in the show, but she'd seen it before. Lived some of it too. And although the screen couldn't possibly bring the complete plot to the viewer's eye, it might pull off a realistic film. TV and movie producers always amazed her at what they got right about government security agencies and what they perceived as accurate information. Now and then a well-done episode caught her attention. But most of the time, the producers threw in tactics or technology that no one within intelligence had ever heard of or would consider using. Right now, she had difficulty doing much more than reining in her emotions wrapped around the man sitting beside her.

Her logical side said to chase him away, to say her ankle hurt or the pain meds had made her sleepy. She could think of lots of excuses for why Miles should go home. Lots more for why he should stay there. And the lines in his face and droopy eyes indicated his exhaustion. Then why didn't she send him packing? Was it the lure of the forbidden that kept her drawn to him?

She and Miles actually had much in common. They enjoyed sports, especially football and baseball. They shared much of the same likes and dislikes about food. Both were Christians. They valued teens and serving as good role models for them. But the big difference was her deceit in her identity and her shadowed past. Paige Rogers existed only on paper. Hollywood could do a reality show about her life and call it *The Ex-Survivor*.

She took a bite of her grilled cheese and snatched a glimpse of Miles from the corner of her eye. She couldn't marry him, which is what she suspected he eventually wanted. The problem was she cared for him, as ridiculous as it sounded. Still, the idea of sharing a life with Miles and bearing his children, no matter how far-fetched, reached deep down inside and caressed a need. *A wife. A mother.*

She remembered crawling up on her own mother's lap and listening to her read stories. They baked cookies together, and her mother, of Swedish descent, had introduced her to the art of preparing herring salad, ostkaka, and authentic apple cobbler. Mom had made her prom dress that was a knockoff of a New York designer original. Both parents had sent care packages when Paige was in college. And Dad . . . She missed his humor and his wisdom. They lived in a rural community in Wisconsin near a small town that reminded her a bit of Split Creek. A few times she'd phoned to hear the voice of whoever answered. It was always Mom, and it took all Paige's strength not to break down and tell her the truth.

Guilt over the lies squeezed her heart. She had nearly enough money in the bank to someday repay the insurance company for the generous check written to her parents. But a parent shouldn't have to bury a child.

She shouldn't be thinking about Miles or her parents while under the influence of painkillers. That was like going on a date and drinking, then wondering why poor decisions were made.

She attempted to concentrate on the show. Her focus should be on what to tell Palmer.

She blinked and her mind dulled. She willed the strange vision to evaporate, the one that swept across her memory without warning. But no, this was a key to her past. She needed to experience it and not block out what she didn't understand. Closing her eyes, she allowed the moment to unfold.

She was blinded by the sun, so bright that she wanted to turn her face, but she couldn't move. Heat engulfed her body. A furnace ignited every nerve ending. The muffled voice of a man captured her attention. *"Too bad she had to die. She's much too pretty to waste."*

"Are you okay?" Miles asked.

"A little tired." And she was, but not physically. The vision always ended with the garbled voice of a man she didn't recognize. It had to be from the bombing. When she found Rosa, Paige would ask her to help pull the pieces together.

"I can pause the show so you can rest," Miles said.

*My sweet man, I am not from your world. Won't*

*ever be.* "Probably a good idea. You look tired too."

"I am. Guess I should leave you alone and check back later."

She nodded. "If you will hand me my crutches, I'll make my way to bed."

"Need any help?"

"Ever worn a crutch?"

"Uh, I don't think so." Miles handed her the crutches. "I'll be back around six thirty with something more substantial and nutritious."

"Chicken soup?"

"Yeah, I can bring the cans and crackers if you have a can opener."

"Sounds tempting."

"Thanks for lunch."

Once more her conscience needled at her. She should have refused dinner, given him a good excuse to stay away. She should have done a lot of things differently. "Let me take a rain check. I'm really not doing well."

# CHAPTER 15

SUNDAY MORNING, Paige woke with a mixture of anticipation and dread. She'd told Palmer that she'd give him her decision tonight, and she'd been praying. Her mind had swung into a debate over right and wrong. She was not only asking God if she should resume her operative role but also giving Him a deadline for the answer. Not exactly the best approach to seeking His will.

Her ankle throbbed, but she refused any pain medication. Her head and heart needed to be open. Palmer had said her parents would be protected. He needed to know about Nathan, if he didn't already. And what about her foot?

Voleta arrived at noon with more Sonic and a spontaneous plan to watch movies all afternoon. Here it was a gorgeous day in August, and Paige was sitting with her leg propped up on the table in front of her sofa, munching fries. Much more of this, and she'd have to buy bigger clothes.

Paige closed her eyes and pondered the decision bearing down on her.

"I love romantic suspense." Voleta sighed as the credits rolled by at the end of the movie. "What more could a girl want except maybe a real hunk?"

"I thought you liked this new guy."

"Found out he was married. That's what I get for going to a casino, lookin' for a good time beside a slot machine." She tapped her chin. "Casinos and slot machines are eating up my tips and turning my love life into two cherries and one orange."

Paige smiled at her goofy friend; however, Voleta's dark hair, today streaked with copper and worn in pigtails, gave her more of a punk look than that of a grown woman in rural Oklahoma.

"You've told me before about home life being rough. So what was it like growing up?"

"That's a joke." Voleta shook her head.

"Why?"

"My folks had a love affair with the bottle—sort of a Dr. Jekyll and Mr. Hyde approach to life."

Now she understood Voleta's need to help others. "I'm sorry. Did you have any brothers or sisters?"

"Four older brothers. Do you want to know what they did to me when dear old Mom and Dad weren't using me as a punching bag?" Voleta glanced away and swiped at a tear.

"That's okay, unless you want to tell me."

"Not really. I went through the shrink thing."

If Paige could have stood, she'd have wrapped an arm around her friend. "I know we've been through this before, but I really think you should give God a chance."

"What about my hair, tattoos, and eyebrow piercings? And my lifestyle is not exactly the granola type." She picked up her glass of iced sangria and chinked the cubes. "I don't imagine your God approves of this either."

"He's more interested in your heart."

"Mine is filled with how to have fun, not avoid it."

Paige chose to let the conversation drop. It was always a challenge to know how to share her faith with Voleta without shoving it down her throat. *Lord, please show Voleta how much You love her.*

"How did your parents come up with the name Paige?"

Paige grinned. "Didn't I ever tell you? It was a compromise. My dad was a baseball fan, and Satchel Paige was one of his heroes. My mom was a schoolteacher. She thought if she named me Paige, I'd grow up with my head in books. It must have worked, because I don't play baseball, but I work at a library." That story had brewed while she lay in the Nairobi hospital.

"I think it's funny, like you were destiny. What's your middle name?"

"Turner. It's my mom's family name."

"Oh, nice," Voleta said. "My middle name is Marie."

Paige stared at her for a moment. "That was a joke, Voleta. No one would really name a kid Paige Turner."

Voleta paused a second. "Oh yeah. Ha! I got it."

"Elizabeth."

"I'm sorry?"

"Paige Elizabeth . . . my middle name. Why are you so curious about me anyway?"

"I like names. Got to admit mine is unusual. Voleta."

"Let me guess. Your dad drove a Volvo, and his family name is Loleta. So you became . . ."

Voleta's cell rang. She glanced at the caller ID. "I need to take this. Mind if I step outside?"

"No problem." Paige shook a finger at her. "If he's married, you don't need him. Like the kids say, he's sketchy."

Voleta stood and shrugged one shoulder before walking onto the front porch. She shut the door.

Paige had noted a quick dart of Voleta's eyes to the left when she normally cast her glance to the right, which indicated she was hiding something. One day Voleta would see that her social life would never satisfy the yearning in her soul. Paige reached for her glass of iced green tea with a dose of aloe vera. She willed the antioxidants to speed up the healing process. Even if it didn't do a thing, it tasted good.

Voleta came back inside and dropped her phone into her purse.

"That was short."

"It needed to be." Voleta offered no eye contact. "He had the nerve to say he'd like to continue seeing me and have a relationship with his wife too."

"I'm proud of you. Think about coming with me to church. The answers to life and its problems are there." Paige picked up the TV remote and pressed in channel 6. "Hope you don't mind if we catch the six o'clock news." She needed a dose of reality after the movie and happily-ever-after nonsense— along with learning that Voleta was hiding the details of her social life.

A dark-haired anchor wearing a much-too-low-cut blouse introduced the next story. "Now we're going to Jake Montoya at Oklahoma University Medical Center, where Daniel Keary and his family visited the hospitalized children."

*Oh, great. As if I wasn't already depressed enough.*

"That's right, Leah," the reporter said. "Daniel Keary, the man who is quickly rising in the polls as the candidate most likely to secure the office for Oklahoma's next governor, put aside his political ambitions today to allow charity to take precedence. Keary's dedication to critically ill children at Oklahoma University Medical Center began six years ago. Today his wife and five-year-old son joined him in making hospital rounds. Keary brought picture books that he and his wife read to the children."

"I really like this guy," Voleta said. "Even if he's a bit conservative, I can't find much not to like about him. Put him in a pair of jeans and a T-shirt, and he'd be hot."

Paige wanted to change the channel, but it was easier to find out what the saint of Oklahoma was up to rather than explain her dislike for him.

His actions didn't surprise Paige in the least. The videotape showed a small Asian boy handing a doll to a child who had no hair.

"Do you like coming with your daddy and mommy to the hospital?" the reporter asked the dark-haired little boy.

"Yes, sir. I like picking out toys for them and puzzles too. At home, we talk about the sick children."

Paige sank her teeth into her lip. Keary's tender

side for children was not an act. Nine years ago, while he and Paige were working in Russia, his first wife and their two children were killed in a tragic car accident. The vehicle had burst into flames, and his family had suffered through an agonizing death. If the man had one humane bone in his body, it was his passion for children. She'd thought more than once that the devastation of having his family destroyed might have been part of the reason he'd betrayed his country. The CIA used the acronym MICE to figure out what motivated traitors: money, ideology, compromise, ego, or a combination. For Keary, it was a complex combination of it all, and to outwit him, she'd need to put all of the pieces together—working from the outside in, just like Aristotle.

The camera flashed to Keary and an attractive woman. "Mrs. Keary, how often do you visit the children at the medical center?" the reporter asked.

"Once a week. Actually we'll visit anywhere there are hurting little ones." She smiled into the face of her husband, and he reached around her waist. "We met here when I was a nurse."

Paige wished she were wrong about him. His wife appeared devoted . . . and Keary had a child to help ease the pain of the two he'd lost.

More footage showed him and his family talking to a mother whose child suffered from cystic fibrosis. Again, Paige recognized genuine care and concern.

Voleta picked up her drink. "I know you don't like him, which I have no clue why. But he did contribute computers to the library, not only in our town but also all over the state. I actually helped Eleanor put up the campaign posters around town." Voleta pointed to the TV. "Any man with good abs who cares for kids has my vote."

"Something about him bothers me. He comes across as too good."

"He's a Christian, isn't he? That's supposed to make a person an outstanding citizen."

Paige forced a laugh. "Then why aren't you going with me to church?"

"I'm waiting a little while longer to see if my theories about religion pan out."

"And what are those?"

Voleta set her drink back on the coaster. "I'll let you know. Gotta run, kiddo. I'll return the DVDs on my way home."

After Voleta left, Paige reflected on the evening news. She wished she didn't know the truth about Keary. If he hadn't sent the team members in Angola to their deaths, she'd still be an operative today, employed by the company and putting her life on the line to protect the citizens of the U.S.—honest, hardworking people like the ones she'd grown to know and love in Split Creek. People like Mom and Dad, who had no idea what sacrifices others made to ensure their freedoms and no understanding that the ones who made those sacrifices did it willingly without thought of reward. Strange how she could long to be both people at the same time and have such a diversity of opinions that fluctuated with the time of day. No wonder her life was an epidemic of uncertainty.

This morning she'd received an e-mail from Keary's campaign headquarters with another request to help with his election. He must know his file had been reopened.

An eerie sensation nudged at her thoughts. She'd always prided herself on being in control of her emotions and actions. Even before coming to faith in Christ, she'd conducted herself in a manner that in her worldview was above reproach. Back then she represented her country and the CIA; now she represented Jesus.

Paige started to rise, felt the weight of her bandage and the incessant pain. She dropped back onto the sofa with new resolve. The answer had been there all along, and she didn't need a burning bush to get her attention. Picking up her cell phone, she dialed Palmer's number.

"I'm in," she said. "But I hurt my foot Friday night. Not much good on the ground."

"No problem. We want you right there in Split Creek. Let Keary think everything is normal."

"What about my parents?"

"That's taken care of."

She took a deep breath and noted her shaking hands. "I have something else to tell you." She hesitated, not wanting to get weepy. She'd been trained to put aside her feelings. "There's another problem." *Suck it up and tell him.* "I . . . have a child."

"Are you sure you want to tell me this?"

A dull ache persisted across the top of her head. "You probably know most of it. While I was in Nairobi, I had a baby, a son. And I gave him up for adoption."

"A woman missionary originally from North Carolina."

"Yes." Her mouth went dry, and her breathing accelerated. "I signed the papers as Paige Rogers." She glanced around the comforts of her living room. "He's Keary's son, and no one can ever learn the truth. For me to resume my former role, I must have all the paper trails destroyed that might lead Keary to Nathan."

"Let me get this straight. Keary doesn't know about his son. No clue, nothing."

"Correct." She swallowed the knot in her throat.

"Consider it done. I'm not at the office right now, but I'll take care of it personally tomorrow. No one will learn about it. And I'm real sorry."

"So am I." She massaged the back of her neck. *Move on.* "How quickly do I have security clearance?"

"How about now?"

"Good. First thing on my list is to find Rosa Ngoimgo."

"That's the Mikaela Olsson I remember."

Yet in the excitement and determination to utilize her training, to do what God required of her, she regretted putting those she loved in possible harm's way. Palmer was a good man, and he'd stand behind his word. For certain, once Keary discovered she was on the job again, he'd bring out both guns to keep her out of the equation. This must be what faith was all about.

# CHAPTER 16

AT EIGHT O'CLOCK on Monday night, Paige locked the library and closed the blinds. She breathed in the quiet beauty of twilight and remembered a time when she welcomed the darkness because it camouflaged who and what she'd become. Snatching up a bag of Reese's Pieces and her laptop, she limped to a chair in front of one of the computers and squeezed in to connect to the Internet. She had a hunch about Keary, or rather his wife, and searching out the information online here rather than grinding her teeth with dial-up at home was easier on her nerves.

Moments later, she had access to the site that showed her what she needed. Sheila Keary had been on staff at Oklahoma University Medical Center before she'd married Daniel and still volunteered there in the children's unit. Sheila's maiden name was Adamson, and her father was a shrewd banker—handy, if Keary ran short on funds. Sheila sat on the advisory board for Oklahoma City's professional businesswomen and also chaired a nonprofit organization that supplied grants for low-income women who desired to learn a trade. She had nothing suspicious in her background. If she hadn't figured out her husband's character by now, she'd learn about it soon enough.

Sheila's mother, Brenda Adamson, worked as an advocate for children's health care. That supported Keary's desire for children to grow up healthy and safe, his only good point. The Adamsons belonged to a large Southern Baptist church and generously supported missions. Squeaky clean. No ties to anything questionable. Keary may have married into a good family.

The Adamsons' son, Lucas, who was older than his sister, worked in government security. Paige slid her fingers into the open bag of candy and leaned back in the wooden chair. *Government security.* Lucas Adamson wasn't a familiar name.

Paige tried another site. Lucas Adamson had held a position in the Secret Service for the past ten years. Solid record. Currently on assignment in D.C. She'd ask Palmer about it. Chances are he'd already run a profile, especially if he'd been keeping track of Keary all these years.

Scooting back her chair, Paige retrieved her cell phone from her shoulder bag and punched in numbers. Everything she did seemed to take forever. Moments later, Palmer responded.

"I have a name for you," she said.

"When don't you?" He chuckled. Working with Palmer again had its perks.

"Lucas Adamson, Keary's brother-in-law. Anything I should know about him?"

"He's not a part of this, but I'll send you what we've learned."

"Thanks. What about his campaign manager?"

"Elizabeth Carlton Howard. Highly respected. She's a speechwriter. MA from Yale. Whistle clean. She helped Jon Weathers get elected to Congress. That guy was only thirty-three, no name recognition."

"I remember. Graduated from OU Law. Moderate Democrat. She also handled his campaign for the Senate. Weathers lost, but he was extremely more competitive than anyone would have ever thought."

"From all we've seen, she's strictly aboveboard. I'll send you the reports."

"Okay, now what about WorldMarc? What do you know there?"

"Looking to be bought by a big public company for about a hundred million. I'm sending you a photo and dossier of Joel Zuriel, who's been with the company since the start—about ten years. He's in his early forties, ambitious, and worked with Keary on the latest oil deal. In fact, the two worked on a diamond deal right after Keary resigned from the CIA."

"Angola diamonds?"

"Namibia. Zuriel's the man we're watching."

Paige opened Palmer's e-mail and read through Zuriel's information.

"He's single," Palmer said.

"Oh, and he likes a woman with a bandaged foot?"

"He's been known to step on a few."

"Bad pun, Palmer. Send me his info, and I'll work on this."

Immediately her thoughts sprang to Miles and her feelings for him. Then she focused on her faith. What she'd done in the past to obtain information from men would not happen again.

"Do you happen to have anything on Rosa?" she asked.

"Not yet. I'll let you know the moment we locate her."

"Thanks. I'll get back with you."

Paige deleted the call. For the next few minutes, she processed Palmer's information. All the work she'd done after the bombing in an effort to prove Keary guilty of treason might not have been wasted. However, she doubted if Keary had slipped in his eagerness to acquire the governor-ship. The weak spot most likely lay in his pursuit for power and the money needed to acquire it.

Taking a breath, she glanced around the empty

library. A haven of sorts, but now it was time to resume her calling. She believed in what she was doing and the CIA's covert work that protected Americans from those who slithered in and out of national and international borders.

Paige spent a few minutes investigating Elizabeth Howard with the information that Palmer had just sent. Nothing there either, just as he'd said. An attractive professional woman with a good social smile. She clicked on Joel Zuriel's intel report.

*Whoa. He's better-looking than Brad Pitt—but obviously not a humanitarian advocate for Africa.* His report held a little more complexity than Howard's. Zuriel's VP role at WorldMarc had obviously filled a few material needs. He collected red sports cars like he collected blood diamonds. A collection of photos showed him with exquisite women in a variety of social arenas. *Greedy in all things.*

Paige lingered on the pics to see if she recognized anyone before reading on. *Values appreciation and respect for his role at WorldMarc—cutthroat businessman, shrewd. Has collected a few enemies. A talker.*

Keary's connection to blood diamonds didn't surprise her. What she needed to learn more about was Zuriel.

*I shouldn't have given up. I should have stuck it out. . . .*

At ten o'clock, she turned off her laptop, assured that no one could turn it on without her fingerprint, PIN number, and three passwords to unlock the encryption. She slipped it into her tote bag and gathered up her belongings. Keary had done a good job in surrounding himself with reputable people. Except Joel Zuriel. Possibly the weak link. If she considered him a possibility, then Keary had already considered means of eliminating him.

She slipped her purse and tote bag over her shoulder, clutched her keys, and left the library. Instinct had always been a vital part of her survival, except for the months she'd been seduced by the charms of Daniel Keary. Tonight, beneath the warm temperatures of an August sky, she sensed trouble.

In the old days, Paige wouldn't have closed a door behind her without her fingers wrapped around a Smith 908 with its black matte finish. In the old days, she wouldn't have had the safety on. In the old days, her hands wouldn't have been occupied with two books and a plastic container that had earlier held her lunch. In the old days, she wouldn't have exposed herself on crutches. In the old days, she'd been Mikaela Olsson, CIA operative.

But tonight she was wearing two identities, and she was fully aware that Paige Rogers, the librarian with a bandaged foot, wasn't prepared for whatever lurked in the quiet blackness.

Years of training raced through her thoughts. Emotions intact and logic on the forefront. She slid her hand inside her shoulder bag, on the far side of her laptop, until she had the Smith 908 firmly in one hand and her keys in the other. As she pulled the weapon to the top of the bag, her fingers touched the trigger. Someone moved behind the left column of the courthouse across the street. Stalkers and hired assassins worked solo. That kept things tidy. Whoever was hiding across the street probably worked alone. She laid her bag and library books on the concrete and awkwardly stood.

Paige's car sat directly in front of her, about fifty feet from one of Split Creek's few streetlights. If her armpits hadn't been smashed against the crutches, she'd have attempted to make a run for her car. She needed a shield of defense. Using her remote, she shut off the vehicle's alarm and limped down the concrete steps toward it. Every nerve stood at alert.

A bullet whistled past her shoulder. The sound of a library window's shattering glass destroyed her delusion about Split Creek's peaceful existence. She dropped to the sparse dried grass between the sidewalk and the street where her car was parked. The scent of earth mingled with the stench of an unscrupulous man. Pros miss on purpose or toy with their prey like a cat. Amateurs try and usually miss. Which was this?

Another bullet cut through the air above her head. Paige tightened her grip on her weapon and crawled across the bristly ground, moving away from the streetlight. The shooter hid in the landscaping of the courthouse. She wished she had the same good fortune. A magnolia tree stood about twenty feet away.

"If you want to talk to me, you have my attention." If Keary knew his file had been reopened, then he had nothing to lose by killing her. But would he risk the election?

A third bullet responded.

"I hope you're getting paid well for this, cowboy. Your little rodeo show is going to bring the sheriff here in a matter of minutes."

Nothing. Not even a wisp of the breeze.

"What do you want? Let me guess. You don't like my politics. Oh, I know. You're upset about an overdue fine?" From her position on the ground, she scanned the darkness. The figure behind the column slithered back and disappeared. *Coward.*

A few moments later, the distinct rumble of a motorcycle reverberated in the night air. Its engine sounded like the pipes on Miles's Harley. She'd recognize that engine's purr anywhere. Why was he riding through town? Unless . . .

"Are you still out there? Obviously you don't have the guts to state why you're firing at me. Lousy aim, too."

Paige listened until the motorcycle disappeared

down the street and toward Miles's twenty-acre plot, complete with horses, a truck, and a Harley. Suspicions pounded into her brain. She waited a few more moments to be sure the motorcycle had carried away the shooter. Doubt attached its barbs to her logic like a parasite. Trust paid a high price, and she couldn't let go of those who had betrayed her in the past.

She crept back to the top of the steps and reached for her cell phone tucked inside her shoulder bag. In the light, she saw a hole in her bag. Thank goodness, it hadn't pierced her laptop. Whoever had been shooting at her had deliberately sunk a bullet through her bag to prove they *could* have killed her. *Cat and mouse.* She punched in the numbers to Miles's phone and waited until the groggy coach answered on the third ring.

"I'm sorry to call so late," Paige said.

"That's all right. I hit the hay early tonight. You okay?"

Relieved that Miles couldn't possibly have been the shooter, she scrambled to divert the conversation. "One of your players told me Chris didn't have a good practice. Then one of the cheerleaders said he had the flu." That part was true.

"Physically he's fine. Between you and me, the kid's an emotional wreck about something. I'd like to think his conscience is getting to him about the way he's treating Walt." He yawned. "Might be some problems at home too."

"Anything I can do to help?"

"How do you feel about checking on his mom? Heard some gossip that I don't want to repeat."

"Consider it done. She usually stops by the library on Wednesday afternoons. Is that soon enough?"

"Perfect. Thanks."

"Go back to sleep. I'm calling it a night myself."

Paige dropped her cell phone into her shoulder bag and crawled back to her crutches. She gathered up the two library books. One was a James Patterson novel. She didn't need to read about suspense in a novel. She'd lived all the suspense she needed.

Relief that Miles wasn't a part of Keary's ruse gave her a moment of peace. Now she needed to notify George about the shooting before she drove home. Within seconds, she had the town's sheriff on the phone.

"George, had a little trouble at the library. Someone's shot out a window."

"While you were there? Were you hurt?"

"I'm fine. Just a lot of broken glass. Is this Split Creek's first drive-by?"

"Very funny. Probably some kids out with their daddy's gun. High on booze or drugs. I have an idea who's responsible."

"This town needs more men like you."

"Did you see the car?"

"No." Paige glanced about. Dirt covered her hands, khakis, and shirt. She didn't want to tell him that she'd been outside the library when the shooting occurred. He'd find out soon enough. "Are you headed this way?"

"I'm walking out the door. You must be scared out of your wits."

"A little."

She listened to the door squeak, then shut, at George's house. "Stay inside the library until I get there," he said. "Then I want to know why you were working late."

"Sure. And I was cleaning up from the high school kids. George, don't use your siren. I don't want any attention over this."

"Why's that?" His car door slammed shut.

"Well, I was thinking that whoever did this is planning on bragging to their buds about scaring the local librarian."

"I see."

"So, if you don't make a fuss, they risked getting caught for nothing."

"Makes sense, Paige. Have you ever thought about going into law enforcement?"

She studied the outline of her automatic and nearly laughed. "I don't like firearms, and I'm afraid of my own shadow."

"Say, fellow officer, how are we going to explain the hole in the window?"

George was working on keeping her on the line. Sweet guy, but she'd been through a lot more than the wannabe desperado tonight.

"I can call someone from Pradmore to replace the glass in the morning," Paige said.

"Excellent idea. Now, tell me again why you don't want the word to get out?"

Paige stuffed her pistol back inside her shoulder bag and unlocked the library door. She shoved it open gently so George wouldn't hear. "I think it was kids, like you said. Probably thinking they could make a name for themselves by shaking up our town."

"And you'd like me to conduct a quiet investigation?"

"I have a personal reason, George. I think those kids saw me, and I don't want them sitting on my front porch thinking I identified them."

"That's true. You go on ahead and call the glass company in Pradmore in the mornin', and I'll do my detective work in private."

"Thanks, George." She saw his car whip around the corner. "Hey, I see you."

"What are you doing outside the library?"

"That's where I was when the window was shot out."

"Those kids and I are going to dance all the way to jail. There you are on crutches and trying to work, bless your heart. And now this. You could have been hurt bad."

*If you had any idea* . . . "But I wasn't."

For the next twenty minutes, George asked questions, wrote up the report, and shone his flashlight up and down the street. He found the bullet inside the library that was fired through the window, but Paige didn't have an opportunity to see the type. After all, librarians weren't typically ammunition experts, and George didn't offer any information. She attempted to clean up the slivers of glass, but George took the broom away from her and finished the job. Keary's game playing had her mad enough to drive to Oklahoma City and pay him a visit. A little confrontation on his own turf might cause him to loosen up a bit. An added bonus would be to see Stevens.

Her cell phone rang. Why give Keary the satisfaction of gloating over his latest escapade? The phone continued to ring and curiosity got the best of her. She checked the caller ID. It was Voleta, a diversion Paige could use.

"Hey, what's going on?" Paige studied a piece of glass on the circulation desk. "Dave Letterman not appealing to you tonight?"

Voleta sobbed. "My electric bill is overdue, and I owe Eleanor for my workstation."

"Did you put back money each week from your check and hide your tips like we talked about?"

"Yes." Voleta sniffed. "And I paid my cell phone bill on time."

"Then you don't have a problem—unless you went shopping and spent it all."

"Not this time. I have my tips in a jar, and I deposited my checks."

"Wonderful. No need to panic. You've been—"

"Would you stop by in the morning and help me write out the checks and balance my checkbook?"

*What next?* Weariness tore at her. "Sure, but soon you're going to have to handle your finances by yourself. Did you sign up for that math class at the junior college?"

"No. I decided to take a computer class instead. Paige, you're the best friend I've ever had. How about a free manicure on the Friday morning before I do your hair? I have some fabulous new shades for fall, great oranges and browns."

"Sure. Glad I can help. And let's wait on the manicure. I'd rather have a pedicure after my foot heals. I'll look at those new fab colors in the morning, 'cause I'm ready for a change from the hot pink."

"Seven o'clock too early? It sure would help me out."

"I'll be there." Paige waved at George, who stood at the door. She dropped her phone into the pocket of her khakis and limped his way.

"Let's lock up and go home, little lady," George said. "I think you've had enough excitement for one night."

"Probably for the next year. Sure glad you were at the other end of my phone when I needed you."

His tense look softened. "I'll follow you home and make sure you're safe inside."

*Oh, I think I can take care of myself.* "Thanks, George. That would be great. What would the people of this town do without you to keep them safe?"

"Oh, some other old ex-marine like me would come along and do a better job."

She locked up the library for the second time that evening. No more sixth sense feelings weighed the air. No flying bullets or rumbling motorcycles. The danger had dissipated . . . for now.

# CHAPTER 17

MILES PICKED UP a large coffee at the doughnut shop and headed to his truck. He swung a glance toward Eleanor's beauty shop. Yep, there was Paige's car. She stepped out and hobbled to the rear door to pull out her crutches. She sure could do great things with a pair of crutches.

"Ever think of asking for help?" he asked.

"Only when I need it."

"I should have known. You're out early." He pointed to her foot. "How's the monster?"

"Still wrapped like a sausage."

"Could've fooled me. Don't you have an appointment with the orthopedic doctor in Pradmore today?"

"Did you take notes last Friday night? I nearly forgot the appointment."

"Had to. You were a bit incoherent."

She wrinkled her nose at him. "I'm headed there right after Voleta and I visit over some coffee."

"She *is* driving."

"Hey, Coach, I'm an independent gal. My left foot works just fine."

"Oh, so you're ambidextrous with your hands and your feet?"

"Absolutely."

"Does Sheriff George know that?"

"You sure do ask a lot of questions so early in the morning. Is this a quiz?"

"Pop type. The kind that can make or break your grade." He smiled into the face he'd grown to love. How he loved her wit. How he loved every inch of her. "I wish you'd get someone to drive you to Pradmore. Driving into town is risky enough."

She tilted her head. "Tell you what, I'll ask Voleta when she has her first appointment."

"Thanks. Can I call you later to see how you're doing?"

"Are you sure you don't have something better to do?"

He heard the question, but her words were soft. "I can fit it in."

Her gaze lingered on him a moment. She did care, if only a little. A woman like Paige didn't take advantage of a guy. She was sincere. She didn't see how beautiful she was inside and out.

*I'm worse than a lovesick kid.*

Paige stepped into the Shear Perfection beauty salon and glanced about the neon orange and yellow shop for Eleanor or Voleta. A floor-to-ceiling palm tree hovered over a display hyping some kind of cream that was supposed to do a better job of erasing wrinkles than Botox. Beside that was a chrome chair and a glass-topped table with more nail polish colors than The Home Depot had house paints.

Voleta stuck her head out of an open closet. "Be right there, sugar."

Paige allowed her mind to swing from the man who sent delicious shivers through her body to hip-hop Voleta. She emerged from the closet carrying a huge mug of steaming coffee that had a picture of a yawning cat in a nightshirt. The rich, nutty scent wafted through the room, reminding Paige that she should have stopped at the doughnut shop. But how could she manage hot coffee and the cumbersome crutches?

"Wish I'd taken the time to brew some coffee," Paige said. "Can't seem to wake up this morning."

Voleta's eyes widened, drawing Paige's attention to the eye shadow that matched the orange and yellow decor. "Remember, I said I'd get you some. So I got you a cup before I filled mine." She pointed to a large to-go cup at her workstation. "And a chocolate peanut butter doughnut."

"Wonderful. Just what I need this morning. Thanks." She glanced around. "Is Eleanor running late?"

"She overslept and asked me to take care of her client this morning."

There went her driver to Pradmore. "Is she not feeling well?"

Voleta shook her head. "She and Mr. Shafer played games with the senior citizens group last night. My guess is she partied too late."

"I'll have to ask her about that. Those two sure are the odd couple."

"They're trying to make it work." Voleta giggled as she walked to her chair and picked up the to-go coffee. "Have a seat, sweetie. I'm sorry to have bothered you about my checkbook, especially with your foot and all."

"No problem. I do have a ten o'clock appointment with an orthopedic doctor in Pradmore."

"A what?"

"Bone doctor."

"Oh. I see." Voleta's eyes widened, and her eye shadow lifted like half-moons. "You're not driving there, are you?"

Paige laughed at the dramatics. "Yes. I do fine with my left foot." *Here we go again. . . .*

"I don't think so." Voleta whirled around and picked up the phone. She propped her hand on one hip and dialed. "Thelma? This is Voleta. Eleanor's running late this morning, and I need to run Paige Rogers—you know, the librarian—to the doctor. Can we reschedule for this afternoon? . . . Yeah, she's right here. I'm taking her to the orthodontist in Pradmore. . . . What? Yeah, she might have broken her foot."

Paige turned her head to keep from laughing. Voleta tried hard, really hard.

An hour later, after Voleta's checkbook had been balanced and bills had been paid, Paige climbed into Voleta's slightly battered car. Actually it looked like a war zone and smelled like greasy fries and banana peels. But Paige had her ride to the doctor, which meant she could swallow half a pain pill. Now if only it would kick into gear.

"You look awful," Voleta said.

"Gee, thanks, girlfriend." Paige closed her eyes.

"No, I mean, you look like you haven't been sleeping."

Last night had a lot to do with that aspect of her life. Good old George had decided to call the glass company with a lot of "pressure" to make sure the library window was replaced first thing this morning. Thank goodness neither Miles nor Voleta had noticed—she hoped. "My foot's a real pain."

Voleta laughed.


The orthopedic specialist pointed out a slight fracture in the X-rays and chose to cast Paige's foot. "Four weeks," the doctor had said. "Considering your past injuries to this foot, I want to eliminate any future surgeries—and keep you off of it."

Delays and more delays postponed when she could begin physical therapy and run again. At least now she could wear a boot-type cast and pitch the crutches. But even though she had mobility, it was severely limited, leaving her irritated and tired just thinking about the work that needed to be done regarding Keary.

Her stomach rumbled. The thought of a peanut butter and mayonnaise sandwich rolled around her head, but since she couldn't exercise, calories would have to be cut in half. What a sacrifice.

"Thanks for being my taxi," Paige said, once they were on the road again.

"Hey, you'd do the same for me. I just feel bad I didn't see that kid running down the bleacher steps."

"As clumsy as I am, it probably wouldn't have made any difference."

While Voleta stopped at the beauty supply store in Pradmore, Paige phoned Palmer.

"I'm fitted into a boot cast for four weeks. Not the prescription for an operative, but I'll make it work."

Palmer blew out a sigh. "This slows you with Zuriel."

"Four weeks from today, I'll be on the road to Oklahoma City."

"We're cutting it close."

Ouch, but true. "My concern is his living long enough to tell me anything. I know that he and Keary have been working together in oil and diamonds since 2001, but Keary has this thing about usefulness taking precedence over life."

"My point. The photos of what was left of those

villages and the dead bodies before Keary and Zuriel got involved in the oil show are the connection to WorldMarc. We need the link before November 3."

Voleta opened the car door.

"Okay, Miles, I'll let you know if I need anything." Paige erased the call and slipped the phone into her purse. She glanced down at the royal blue cast, thankful her foot no longer hurt but resenting the time required for it to heal.

*How can I speed up this investigation?*

# CHAPTER 18

THURSDAY MORNING, Paige listened to the members of the book club debate the literary merit of their selected read. Why seasoned citizens would choose a chick-lit book about a twentysomething heroine for their discussion was beyond her. Mr. Shafer claimed to like the story, and Eleanor blushed and agreed. Reverend Bateson had already given his diatribe about fiction being an abomination to the Lord, which threw the whole group into a heated discussion about Jesus teaching through parables.

Paige loved these people—their spunk, their courage, their love for each other, and the years of wisdom that contributed to their wit. She respected their commitment to their community and their country. If she had one prayer for them, it was that they would hold on tightly to their ideals. The unresolved betrayal with Keary had left her cynical. A cynical Christian . . . that didn't make sense. It sounded like an oxymoron, but nevertheless it was true in her case.

As soon as the book club left, she planned to do a little research with her laptop. The duo of Keary and Zuriel needed more work, and how far up the ladder was Jason Stevens?

"This apple pie is the best ever," Miss Alma said. Today she wore a red bow in her nearly blue hair. "Is that caramel I taste?"

"Yes, ma'am." Back to Paige's world.

"And I bet that caramel is homemade."

Paige settled into her librarian mode. "You're forcing me to be honest. It's the bite-size pieces that you have to unwrap."

"Don't tell anyone else," said a gentlemen whose few white hairs stood straight up above his ears like whiskers on a cat. "Spoils your image."

The library phone rang before Paige could respond.

"Good morning, Mikaela. How's Oklahoma's number one librarian?"

*Keary.* "Outstanding." What a way to spoil the morning.

"I could use you in the campaign."

She turned her back to the book club folks. "Knowledge of human nature is the beginning and end of political education."

"Very good. But I'll keep asking until you change your mind."

"By then the election will be over."

"And I'll be leading the state."

*Not if I can stop you.* "I really have things to do."

"I understand. Hey, I have a question for you. I heard there are fires in northern Wisconsin. I'd sure hate to think your parents might be caught in one of those, especially in view of your mother's heart condition."

Paige felt the color drain from her face. Had Mom's heart problem grown worse? "If anything happens to either of them, I'll . . ."

"What? Try to prove I'm not an upstanding citizen? You tried that before, remember? Didn't work. Now I'm offering you a chance to make up to me for your lies."

*He is delusional.* "Why do you care if I support you or not?"

"It's a matter of principle. Besides, you already have the answer. By the way, you can't possibly be happy playing with books in that hick town. And what do you see in the football coach?"

"Integrity. Morals. Honesty. A few things you don't have."

Keary's sneer used to amuse her. How could she ever have found this man appealing? "You have far more talents than any of those people realize. Come on board, Mikaela. I'll make it worth your while."

"Not interested." She replaced the phone on the desk, fighting the urge to throw it across the room. Instead, she took a breath so deep that it made her chest ache. She walked to the nearest computer and searched for *Wisconsin fires*. Nothing. His call to scare her had worked. Concern for her parents wrapped alarm around her heart. In the whole scheme of things, could the CIA protect those she loved from a seasoned operative?

"Sweet girl, are you all right?" Mr. Shafer asked from across the room. "You look a little pale."

"Oh, I'm fine." She limped toward the group.

"I thought your foot might be bothering you." Mr. Shafer took the award for the most caring man in town—except for Miles.

"Oh, I didn't sleep well last night. Drank coffee too late in the evening."

"At least you can still have the real stuff," Mr. Shafer said. "When you get to my age, the doctor tries to cut off caffeine."

Paige wished she could enjoy her favorite people, but her job took priority. She excused herself to make another call outside the library.

"Palmer, my parents have been threatened."

"Your parents are fully protected. They have a new hired hand."

She exhaled while keeping a calm demeanor, professionalism in her chosen career as Mikaela Olsson. "I just know what he's capable of."

"And soon everyone will know the truth."

"Right. You can't teach a crab to walk straight. I don't care about me. It's my parents. Remember one of the dead operatives was Keary's own cousin."

"I know. I mourned his death as much as I grieved your decision to resign."

"I'm driving to Oklahoma City tomorrow. I want a face-to-face with him. See if I can draw him out of his safety net."

"Be careful. He knows all the ways to eliminate you."

"I'll take my chances." She erased the call history from her phone and focused her gaze on Ginny Dalton, who was walking toward the library with several books tucked in her arms. Paige called out a greeting. "I missed you yesterday."

"And I owe a fine." Ginny's words were cheery, but her eyes were red.

"If you have Internet access at home, you can take care of renewing books yourself. I'll show you."

Ginny, a tall, pleasant-looking woman with lots of freckles, opened the library door for Paige. "I like coming here. It's peaceful and the world inside of books is . . ." She stopped and replaced her dour look with a smile as artificial as most of the book club members' teeth.

"Are you okay?"

"Sure. Just tired. Ty's working a lot of late hours." Ginny placed her books on the return portion of the circulation desk.

"We have three new fiction titles."

"I think I want a nonfiction this time." Ginny's gaze darted about, obviously to make sure none of the book club members were nearby. She then focused her attention on Paige. "Marriage and relationships. I trust you'll keep that to yourself."

"Do you need to talk?"

Ginny touched Paige's arm. "If there is anyone in this town whom I can trust, it's you. But for right now, helping me find a couple of books is all I need."

No one would trust her if they knew the truth. And at times, Paige had to fight for a glimpse of it. Too many times it seemed the world was a mass of gray—no color and no light.

Thursday before lunch, Miles finished grading the last history test. Part of the students' work was an essay about Coronado's exploration of Oklahoma. Their dislike of writing couldn't be any stronger than his loathing of reading and grading their work. But now he'd graded the last of them, and a couple of the essays were well researched. His office door squeaked open, and Chris stood in the doorway.

"Hey, Coach, got a minute?"

Chris's tone held more respect than he'd heard in a long time. Maybe this was the beginning of real teamwork, especially after last Friday's loss. The kid's eyes held a sparkle that Miles hadn't seen in weeks.

"Sure." Miles gestured to the chair in front of his desk. "Your grades okay?"

"English had me a little nervous, but Miss Rogers at the library helped me write a paper. Thanks for asking her to give me a hand. My dad tried to pay her, but she wouldn't take it."

"I'm not surprised. What can I do for you?"

Chris rubbed his pant legs and slid into the chair. "I got a call last night from one of OU's coaches."

"That's great. Which one?"

"Coach Netterfield."

Miles tilted back in his chair. "He's a good man. Dedicated to his players and the game. What did he say?"

"Said he was following my stats, and, like, I looked good. Said I needed more playing time to meet their qualifications for OU ball."

"That's odd. Two years ago, one of our boys was recruited as a junior, got hurt the first game of his senior year, and couldn't play the rest of the season. OU still brought him on with a full scholarship."

"Well, Coach Netterfield said they were looking for a star quarterback."

*That doesn't sound like Netterfield—a defense coach checking out an offensive player—or any coach worth his grit.* "Anything else?"

Chris shrugged. "Not really."

"Strange, he hasn't called me."

"Maybe he will." Chris glanced toward the window behind Miles and beyond to the football field. "That must be it."

"Must be what?"

"Uh, nothing. So can I get more playing time, Coach?"

Miles worked at rephrasing his thoughts about egotistical football players. Of course Chris had a good teacher when it came to a lack of good sportsmanship. "As quarterback?"

"Well, yeah."

Miles studied the boy in front of him. He did a good job playing receiver when he wasn't nursing his wounds about Walt, and he did fine as a backup for Walt. "You're a good player in your current position, and any college would be proud to have you. Why a defense coach called you for an offense position raises a few questions in my mind."

Chris stiffened. "I was hoping this would make a difference."

"I'm the coach here, son."

Chris stood. "My dad talked to him too."

Miles didn't want to waste a moment's breath discussing Ty Dalton. "I'll contact Netterfield tomorrow."

Chris's eyes widened. "No. Don't do that."

"Why?" *So you lied. Should have done your homework on who coaches offense at OU.*

"Just wait until he calls you."

"Why wouldn't you want me to help you with a scholarship?"

Chris shifted from foot to foot. "He asked me and my dad to keep it to ourselves."

"Then Netterfield wasn't the man who called."

"Forget it."

Once Chris left the office, Miles stood to see if he headed to the lockers before practice. Chris and his buds had made life miserable for Walt, often cornering him. That needed to stop, along with stories about OU coaches. He snatched up the phone and called Brad Netterfield.

"Hey, Brad, I hear you phoned one of my players last night."

Moments later, Miles replaced his phone. Netterfield hadn't contacted Chris last night or any other night. Would Ty have put Chris up to this, or was this something Chris had put together?

*Okay, Lord, I need a little help here. How do I get this team to work together?*

During lunch, Paige powered up her laptop and checked e-mail before logging on to secure sites. A message from Bobbie Landerson snatched her attention, and she quickly clicked on it.

*Paige, we need to talk. Call me as soon as you can.*

# CHAPTER 19

I REALIZED RECENTLY that I know little about the months Mikaela spent in Kenya before returning to the States. She was in the Nairobi hospital for two months, but the other four months might lead to people, relationships, things I need to know.

That's Zuriel's department.

And he's late.

Again.

I pick up my phone and wait for him to get on the line.

"Where are you?" I curse. I'd rather have my fingers around his throat.

"I'm heading to the elevator. Got in a few hours ago from Vegas."

Ten minutes later, he sits across from my desk. Hungover. Alcohol seems to gush from the pores of his skin. I am tired of dealing with him.

"Where did Mikaela go after she left the hospital in Nairobi?"

Zuriel rubs the back of his neck. "You called me for that? We're talking seven years ago."

I ease back in my chair and allow the fury to slowly dissipate. "She has the power to potentially bring down the CIA on us. My file has been reopened, and your name is slapped with mine on every page. Is that enough?"

Zuriel says nothing while he stares at me. I see a glimpse of the old Zuriel, the calculating man who measured his words like a miser weighs gold. "She lived in an apartment."

"Who did she see? Where did she go?"

"I have the address."

"What name did she use?"

"I don't remember, but I think Paige Rogers."

"I need to know it all. Get on it now."

Zuriel's face reddens. "Who do you think you are? Without me, you wouldn't be where you are today."

The clichéd threat strengthens my resolve to eliminate him. I change my tactics. "This is not about any of your abilities. This is about staying two steps ahead of the investigation. Joel, I need for you to do what you do best—keeping this team together."

# CHAPTER 20

BY THE TIME Paige had a free moment to make a private phone call, it was six o'clock and Bobbie would have been in bed hours ago. Savannah, the library intern, had this Friday off from school, so Paige asked her to work. The sooner she faced Keary the better, and she could phone Bobbie along the way.

At home, Paige pulled her mail from her mailbox, a task she always performed with caution. However, if anyone wanted to plant a bomb, they'd handle that at her front door. She leafed through the few pieces of junk mail until she saw a newsletter from Hope Abound International, the missionary organization that sponsored Bobbie, Nathan's adoptive mother. Paige had supported another missionary with the organization since moving to Split Creek, partly so that she could receive the monthly updates. She also supported missionaries from three other agencies . . . just in case someone got too curious about her philanthropy and started poking around.

She slipped her forefinger under the seal, breaking the skin. Drops of blood rushed down her finger. Clenching the bleeding finger against her palm, she used her left hand to open the newsletter. She scanned the contents until her attention fell on Bobbie's name under prayer requests.

Bobbie Landerson in the Rift Valley area of Kenya has been diagnosed with stage four pancreatic cancer. As she spends her final days in a Nairobi hospital, please pray for this courageous woman who has devoted her life to bringing the gospel to others.

Paige gasped, and the newsletter fluttered from her fingertips to the ground. *Stage four pancreatic cancer?* Bobbie Landerson was full of energy and excitement—a picture of health that mirrored her missionary zeal. The prayer request must be for someone else. That was it. A mistake. Paige bent to pick up the newsletter, but it had disappeared. Slipping her shoulder bag to the ground with the rest of the mail, Paige groped around the flower beds. The more she searched, the more the lump in her throat thickened. Finally, with dirt-smeared fingertips, she touched the newsletter beneath blossom-filled marigolds.

The prayer request read the same. Bobbie, the woman who had led Paige to Christ and adopted Nathan, was dying. Hot, stinging tears blinded her vision, and her stomach churned. This was why Bobbie had sent the e-mail. If only Paige could talk to her now, but the hospital would not allow a call to go through at such a late hour.

*Oh, dear God, not Bobbie. Must she go when she has so much to give others?* A pang of conviction twisted in Paige's heart. Selfish as her thoughts

166

may be, Nathan did not have a mother without Bobbie. Her baby boy. Her dear friend.

Paige gathered up her belongings and limped to unlock her home—her sanctuary that could not ease the thought of losing Bobbie. Paige longed to be in Nairobi with her. Paige could read to Bobbie, as the missionary had once done for her. Once inside, she sat on her sofa until darkness surrounded her, holding the newsletter and reliving those months in Africa when she hadn't known what to do and desperately needed a friend. It was Bobbie who listened to her frustration and anger. It was Bobbie who held her when she cried. It was Bobbie who knelt on the floor beside her and taught her how to pray. It was Bobbie who coached her through Nathan's birth. And it was Bobbie who had opened her arms and her heart to Nathan. The tears dried on Paige's face. She prayed and cried some more. Hours later, when exhaustion finally overtook her, Paige crawled into bed.

After a sleepless night woven with memories and nightmares, Paige dressed before dawn for the trip to Oklahoma City. Snatching up her cell phone, she phoned the Nairobi hospital and waited for Bobbie's sweet voice.

"Hi, Paige. You received my e-mail." Her weak voice tugged at Paige.

"I did. How are you feeling?"

Bobbie laughed softly. "You must have received the newsletter. I tried to get to you first."

"What can I do to help? How can I pray?" Paige wanted to ask about Nathan, but her emotions teetered near the edge for both of them.

"Oh, Paige. I don't know what to do about our son."

*Our son.* She swiped at a tear. "How good of you to refer to him that way."

"I remember the day you left Africa—the tears and the grief in leaving him behind. But we have a problem." Bobbie took a deep breath. "I'm sorry. Just weak. I . . . I have no living relatives, nowhere for Nathan to go. How soon can you be here?"

Paige trembled and sank onto her bed. Her mind whirled with what Bobbie had implied. Bring Nathan to the U.S.? Subject him to the dangers and secrets of her life? What kind of life was that for a child? Worse yet, what if Keary learned the truth about his son?

"Say something," Bobbie managed. "I know I've dropped a bomb, but what choice is there?"

*God, help me. I don't know what to say or do.* Paige refused to allow tears to disrupt the conversation. "You've loved Nathan and provided a home for him when I could do nothing. For that I will always be grateful."

"And you allowed me to be a mother, a real mother. It was a sacrifice for you and a treasure for me."

Paige snatched up a tissue and dabbed her face. "Everything is so complicated."

"I've prayed about this, and I think God wants you to take him."

Paige longed to trust God, but the ache in her heart was true fear. Was this a leap of faith? She wanted to believe that having Nathan back was part of God's plan. Still her heart hammered against her chest.

"Paige?"

"I'll be there on the next flight out." She spoke before she could think about it another minute.

"Are you sure? I don't mean to be a burden."

"I will never be able to take your place with him, but I will do my best."

"My dear friend, please hurry. I have little time left."

Paige disconnected the call and continued to sit on her bed. With the shadows of night lifting to dawn, she shed one tear after another for Bobbie, for Nathan, and for the evil of Daniel Keary. Her reason for bringing Keary to justice now escalated. He would never be a part of Nathan's life, or she'd die trying to prevent it.

An hour later, after making travel arrangements to Nairobi and talking with Palmer about arrangements for Nathan, she showered and dressed for the trip to Oklahoma City. She slid her left foot into a Croc shoe, one of a pink pair that she'd bought to wear while her foot healed. Voleta had been with her at the time of the purchase, encouraging her to escape from her traditional box to a bright world of color and fashion. But as Paige studied the popular but not necessarily classy shoe, she wished she'd chosen something else. With a shake of her head, she dispelled her misgivings about her footwear and backed her car out of the driveway. She needed to focus on all the reasons why she was speeding toward the interstate en route to Daniel Keary's office.

Nearly eight years after coming to Oklahoma, and just when she thought she'd left her old world behind, a call to duty, responsibility, and a nudging in her prayer life had her populating the database of those striving to keep America free from those who threatened its freedom.

*I'm certainly sounding noble.* But it felt good—satisfying an intrinsic call to her life purpose. She no longer had a desire to spend the rest of her life checking books in and out of the library and baking pies on Thursday mornings. Neither could she stand by and do nothing while the citizens of Oklahoma voted in politically corrupt leadership. Had her views changed because of her devotion to God and to her son, or had her priorities changed because she knew instinctively that no one but God could protect her loved ones? Paige paused a moment to theorize her convictions. Actually she believed in what she was doing because God had opened her eyes to truth and the meaning of real love.

Even though Bobbie's news had only begun to

sink in, she found part of her was excited about the unexpected possibility of being a real mother to Nathan. Another part of her realized she didn't know the first thing about mothering. Odd how she felt confident in her role as a CIA operative and scared to death of parenthood. Maybe her son would be better off being adopted by someone else. That thought had shadowed her enthusiasm for bringing Nathan home. Was she being selfish? Definitely something to pray about.

Another problem was that she really cared for Miles. No point in debating that fact any longer. Her emotions had played a wild trick on her, and she'd sunk so deep that it would take a forklift to pull her out. Listening to his passion about each player on his team, the students in his class, his firmly rooted faith, and even football, she could no longer deny the depth and solidity of him.

However, once Keary was exposed, Miles would most likely deny his heart, realizing he could never trust her again, especially when he learned about Nathan. And how could she blame Miles? She'd abandoned personal relationships before, as though the men in her life had expiration dates stamped on their foreheads. But her feelings for Miles were undeniably bittersweet, reminding her of Tennyson's famous words: "Better to have loved and lost than never to have loved at all."

A truck passed her on the right shoulder, nearly shoving her into the car on her left. Paige glanced in the rearview mirror for the umpteenth time to make sure she wasn't being followed. Not since she'd run the Camry off the road weeks before had she detected anyone on her tail. But her adversary was adept at keeping his presence unnoticed. The truck driver carrying diesel fuel or the cowboy in the F-350 hauling a horse trailer or even the student driver gripping the wheel nervously could be working for Keary. After all, she'd worn disguises like a fourth-grader on Halloween.

Were there many CIA operatives who were Christian? She didn't know of any, but faith wasn't exactly the topic of discussion when being briefed about a mission or seeking cover in the heat of a firefight. Would she ever have the answers to how God viewed the world of spies and counterspies? The assassinations and the lies were completed in the name of national interest.

Could she slip back into the life of Mikaela Olsson? Did she really want to, or did she simply miss the excitement that a librarian's job failed to supply? What if . . . ? What if Miles and she could have a life together? What if he thought of her and Nathan as a package deal? Would that make a difference? Was it possible to be an operative, a wife, and a mother? The whole question of how God considered the CIA hit her again—as it did on a regular basis. The Israelites had used spies when they were about to enter the Promised Land. God had led them to a woman who had helped them within that ancient city doomed for destruction. What was that woman's name? . . . Rahab. Yes, she'd been a woman of questionable character, until God scooped her out of the way of eternal death and placed her onto the way of life. Sort of like Paige.

She reflected a moment more on her philosophical mode when she needed to be putting together the responses to all of the questions Keary would pitch at her like fastballs at the World Series. Either that or praying. Both were on the table.

Palmer already had an operative planted in Keary's campaign team. And chances were that Keary knew he was under the scrutiny of the world's largest intelligence force. He knew how to cover his tracks and where to find the people to do his dirty work.

If Paige threatened Keary, he would not hesitate to have her arrested. Neither would he relinquish the pressure for her to saddle up and join his trail ride to Oklahoma City. She glanced up at the skies and saw a blue gray cloud in the east. Maybe there was a little hope for rain in this desert.

"God, You know him better than I do. I need a little help here."

Keary believed that only the strong survived, and those who didn't subscribe to his esoteric views deserved whatever happened to them. He'd murdered before, and he would again. She had to give him credit because he was right about the

American people being tired of buying from China when goods could be made here. Last Christmas half the toys made in China had to be recalled. What the citizens didn't realize was Keary had no problem encouraging a position of harmony with the Arab world and divesting oil from those countries in Africa where a scorched-earth policy paved the way for American businesses to make a bundle.

Paige had heard and read enough of his policies to understand his call for Americans to remember when they were happy—a false nostalgia. Big business supported Keary. Evangelical leaders supported Keary. She knew the process, the philosophy, of some spy schools: begin by convincing the public about small inconsistencies in values, then build them up until they accepted the evil ones. Hitler had done a fine job of it, and Keary had always been a student of that dictator.

Once Paige made it to Oklahoma City, she found the law offices of Hughes and Sullivan housed in a black glass building. *Quite fitting.* She pulled into the underground parking and snatched up a ticket as the machine spit one out from the gate. Fat chance of H&S validating her parking, but the thought made her laugh and lifted the heaviness from the ordeal ahead of her.

She rode the elevator up to the tenth floor. In an instant, she was Mikaela Olsson. Odd, it was the first time she'd ever worked a file with a prayer. The elevator doors opened to opulence—everything from the plush carpet to the stylish contemporary furnishings and the original paintings framed on the walls. It was rich. It was tasteful. The offices were laid out in a semicircle, which allowed the various pieces of artwork to be displayed aesthetically.

Paige wound around a pale green corridor to where a young woman who resembled the current cover model for *Vogue* met her at the doorway of a reception office.

"May I help you?" The young woman's smile did not flow into her words. Perhaps Paige's pink Croc, boot cast, and wide-leg jeans detracted from her appearance.

"I'd like to see Daniel Keary, please."

"Do you have an appointment?"

"No, but I'm sure if you give him my name, he will see me."

"Do you represent a charity organization, because if you do—"

"I have business with Mr. Keary. If you'd kindly tell him that Paige Rogers is here to discuss business, he will arrange time in his busy schedule to speak with me."

Miss Magazine Cover stiffened. "I will escort you to our waiting area while I contact Mr. Keary." She turned abruptly and swiveled down the hall in her stilettos.

Paige concentrated on her upcoming conversation with Keary. She seated herself in a contemporary symmetrical chair. Copies of *Money*, *Forbes*, *Economist*, and *Golf Digest* lay on a glass-topped table. She picked up a recent copy of *Forbes* and thumbed through it.

Within ten minutes, the young woman reappeared. "Mr. Keary will see you now. I'll take you to his office." Her cool and condescending tone amused Paige.

"Thank you." Paige had replayed the various scenarios of this meeting with Keary. She was in character; she was herself.

Keary stood from behind his massive desk, a combination of glass and wood. Not a single sheet of paper on his desk. Not a smudge either. "Good afternoon, Miss Rogers. Come in and sit down." He nodded to the young woman. "Please close the door when you leave."

Paige slid into a chair where she could watch who entered Keary's office. An old habit she had no intention of breaking.

Keary folded his hands on his desk. Already he'd taken on the bearing of a governor. "Shall I bring out the champagne?"

"Alcohol numbs the brain."

"I can remember when that didn't matter when it came to us."

"I grew up."

"Then enlighten me," he said with a smirk.

She stared into his hazel eyes, issuing a silent challenge. "I'm tired of your game-playing."

"I don't play games. I play for keeps."

"I've noticed."

"But I haven't gotten your attention enough to persuade you to work on my campaign."

"The election's in two months. I imagine you've paid plenty of willing supporters to carry on in that area. Or are you offering me a job in your administration?" Her gaze moved around the room. She was certain their conversation was being recorded. "I'm assuming your political aspirations exceed that of governorship."

"I'm qualified."

"Depends on who is viewing your list of personal achievements and current loyalties."

"Point well taken. I have close associations in Washington. It's only a matter of time before this country experiences new leadership."

"Your venality disgusts me."

"I have my ethics," Keary said.

"Ethics? Oh, that's rich. Your definition of ethics is what brings the ultimate good to you."

The sneer that greeted her said she'd spoken the truth. A brief moment of triumph gave her the confidence she needed.

"What brings you here today?" he asked.

"To tell you to leave me alone. I will never support you. So call off your hired guns."

Keary leaned across the desk. "I'd think you would have learned by now that I always win. Check the polls on Election Day."

Paige leaned toward him. "I have the same skills as you do."

"But not the same tactics. Look at the record. I'm smarter, and I'm still holding all of the aces."

"The big difference is I learned from my mistakes."

"Don't think you've learned a thing."

Paige stood. "Leave me alone, Keary. Don't touch my parents, my friends, anyone I know. This stops here. All of it. The company knows where I am. If I end up dead, you're the first one on their calling card. My parents end up hurt, and I release your past to the media. My rear's covered with anything you might try to pull. I've had a lot of years to think about it."

He clenched his fist. Lines tightened around his eyes.

*He knows about the investigation.*

"Accidents happen."

"I'll remember that." She adjusted her shoulder bag—devoid of her gun—and exited Keary's office and the building of Hughes and Sullivan. She'd won this round whether he acknowledged it or not.

Once in her car, she phoned Palmer. "The mouse took the cheese."

# CHAPTER 21

PAIGE LANDED in Nairobi at 7 p.m. on Saturday. After picking up a rental car and checking into Nairobi International Youth Hostel, within walking distance from the hospital, she hobbled in to see Bobbie. Stupid cast.

As soon as Paige entered the room, Bobbie opened her eyes. A Bible lay on her chest, and a lamp cast a lambent glow about her. The large woman had been reduced to a frail figure, a reality that Paige had anticipated but was not fully prepared to see.

"I've been expecting you," Bobbie whispered and lifted her bare head.

"How are you feeling?" Paige leaned over the bed and touched her friend's cheek with a trembling hand.

"No pain, dear friend. For that I'm grateful. But I like to sleep." She smiled and eased back down onto the pillow.

Paige took her bony hand, the one not connected to an IV. "As well as I can remember, you never used to do much of that."

"I'm dreaming about heaven," Bobbie said.

"Remember when you read to me about heaven and how wonderful it would be? We talked about our mansions. You wanted a beach house next to the bluest sea with lots of shells, and I wanted a little house in the country with a front porch."

Bobbie's eyes were bright despite her rapidly failing health. "Oh, we did have good times, didn't we?" She moistened her lips. "We need to talk while I'm still coherent."

Paige started to protest, but Bobbie shook her head. And Paige knew the time was fleeting.

"What do we do about Nathan?" Bobbie's raspy voice and rattled breathing spoke of her nearing the end.

Paige blinked back the tears. Being here, at the hospital in Nairobi, brought back so many memories she'd tried to forget. She'd been transferred here when the hospital in Angola could not give her the care she needed. Luckily the Nairobi Hospital had a VIP wing, where patients could be treated confidentially. Paige was able to take on her new identity and try to make plans for an unknown future, all the while preparing to give birth to Daniel Keary's child and wondering how to protect the innocent child from his father.

She didn't know what she would have done had she not met Bobbie during those difficult days. Bobbie had been hospitalized as well, no doubt for something related to her current condition. But of course, being Bobbie, she'd never said much about it at the time. No, her concern had been for Paige— Paige's heart, Paige's baby, and most of all, Paige's soul. Her loving example had opened the door for Paige to come to faith in Christ. And when Nathan was born, Bobbie agreed to be his mother. She had never asked why Paige had to give him up for adoption. No condemnation, only love.

Paige shook her head and turned her attention to the present. Bobbie had asked her a question. About Nathan. "I'd still like the opportunity to be his mother, but . . ."

"I was hoping you hadn't changed your mind."

"I do wonder if he'd be better off with someone else."

"Do you love him?"

Tears welled in Paige's eyes. "Oh yes."

"You're a good woman, and I've never doubted your love for our boy. Now it's your turn." Bobbie paused as though to find the strength to continue. "I had the papers drawn up for you to take guardianship." She pointed to the nightstand. "They're inside, all ready for you to sign. If you'll call the number on the envelope, my lawyer can be here in a few minutes."

Paige lifted the manila envelope from the drawer. Could she do this—be a good mother to Nathan?

"Make the call. My lawyer is downstairs waiting. This is the way it's supposed to be."

"Okay." A moment later Paige replaced the receiver on the cradle. "I'll meet him downstairs on my way out. The words *thank you* are not enough, but they're the only ones I have. Where is Nathan now?"

"A missionary friend is keeping him for me. He and I will say our good-byes tomorrow morning. You can meet him then." Tears flowed down Bobbie's face. "I hate to leave him, but I know God has this all worked out."

Paige swallowed the devastation in her soul. "Indeed He does." She inhaled deeply to gather strength. "Bobbie, I can't be seen with Nathan here at the hospital. Can I visit him at your friend's home?"

"Is your life still in danger?"

Paige forced a smile. "I must keep Nathan safe from his father. Just a little while longer. Arrangements have been made for a couple to escort him to the States."

Bobbie closed her eyes. "I trust you."

Paige kissed her cheek. "We trust God. I love you, Bobbie."

After the two prayed, Paige revealed enough of herself to let Bobbie know that she was not involved in anything illegal or immoral. She had Nathan's address and would visit him tomorrow after he visited his mother for the last time.

The next afternoon, Paige drove to a shopping area, browsed, and purchased a candle in case someone was following her, then drove back to the hotel. Once in her room, she darkened her makeup and slipped into a black ankle-length skirt and a *hijab*. She stole down the back stairs of the hotel and out the back door, where she slid into a Lexus with two people, an African American man and a white woman.

"Raif and Anissa Wilkinson?" she said, once inside the tinted-window vehicle.

"Right," said the man, who was driving. "Do you have the address?"

Paige handed him the information Bobbie had given her the previous night. The alias names would not leave a trail. "If you could take a little time with Nathan, I'd appreciate it. He's going to be upset about leaving his mother."

"Sure thing." He glanced out the rear window. "I think we're clear."

Paige removed the Islamic dress and wiped off the dark makeup. She allowed her mind to dwell on Nathan—seeing him, touching him, hearing his voice. Who did he look like? Was he a sports fan, a reader, a good student? A flood of emotions swept over her, strangling her in one breath and churning her stomach in the next. CIA training had equipped her to endure pain, fake a polygraph, and secure information. But none of those things had prepared her to meet her son.

The car pulled up in front of a small house on the outskirts of Nairobi. The area looked less than desirable, but that was where missionaries worked—with the people in need.

She and the operatives exited the car. Digging her fingernails into her palms in an effort to settle her emotions, she stood in front of the door unable to take the next step. Raif took the lead and knocked. *Get a grip.*

The door opened, and a Kenyan woman appeared, carrying a baby and with a toddler tugging on her leg.

"Bobbie sent us," Paige said.

The woman's face hardened. "I don't agree with her sending Nathan to the States," she said in a clipped accent. "He needs to stay here with those who love his mother."

"I'm honoring her wishes." Paige didn't need to study her body language to note the animosity. "May I see Nathan?"

The woman shifted the baby to her other hip. "Who are these people?"

Paige could handle this part. "Raif and Anissa Wilkinson. And your name?"

"Rachel." She opened the door and Paige stepped into the unknown. She'd rather have stepped into a minefield. At least she knew how to handle that.

A young white boy sat on the floor with two other children. A scattering of building blocks, homemade, lay about them. A paralyzing chill moved through Paige's body.

"Nathan." Rachel knelt beside him, holding the baby against her chest. "This is the woman your mother told us about."

Nathan looked up. For an instant, time suspended while Paige caught her first glimpse of her dark-haired son. Her ears rang. A fire rose in her throat. She fought nausea. *My baby. My sweet son. How beautiful you are.* Her mind drifted back to when she had loved Daniel Keary, when she had respected his position at the CIA, when she'd memorized his every feature. She looked deep into blue eyes, icy blue. *My eyes.* But he had Daniel's mouth and thick, wavy hair. She willed herself to talk, to act, anything.

Modeling Rachel, she bent to Nathan's side. "I'm Paige, and I'm sorry about your mother."

Nathan nodded and clamped down on his lower lip. Paige remembered as a child, she used to do the same thing. With trembling hands she touched his face, as though he weren't real . . . a dream . . . a blessing she didn't deserve.

"You're going to take me to the States?" The Kenyan lilt of Nathan's voice nudged her with the years she'd missed.

Raif and Anissa knelt beside Paige and Nathan. Rachel scooted the other children out of the room.

"Actually my friends Mr. and Mrs. Wilkinson will take you."

"Hey, Nathan," Raif said. "I'm looking forward to the plane ride with you."

"Me too." Anissa's soft tone relayed her sympathy for the situation. "We can read books and watch movies."

Nathan stared at all of them. *Poor baby. We're all strangers.*

"I'll catch up with you once I finish my work." Paige realized once again she was failing him.

"And you're going to be my mommy?" Nathan swiped a tear.

"No one will ever replace your mommy. Like you, I love her, and I will do my very best to be your second mommy."

"Mommy is going to be with Jesus."

"I know." Tears fell over Paige's face. She wanted to pull him into her arms. Maybe later when he felt more comfortable.

"I want to stay here."

"I understand. Leaving your friends is very hard."

"Mommy said I must be brave."

"I can tell you are." Paige searched for something to ease his pain. "Would you like to take a ride with me?"

"In that big car?" Curiosity sparked in his eyes.

"Yes, just you and me."

He nodded. Raif fished in his pocket for the keys. A few moments later, Paige drove her son down a side street. What should she ask? What should she say? She wanted to know everything, but now wasn't the time.

"I may need you to help me be your second mommy." Paige turned to the little boy. "I want to do things like you're used to—like school."

"Mommy is my schoolteacher."

Homeschooled. That was a tough one. "Do you like it?"

He shrugged. "I've never been to a real one."

"What do you do in your mommy's school?"

"Read, do math. Science stuff. Lots of things. And I memorize Bible verses; then we talk about them."

Paige could do that part.

A shot rang out. She spun into operative mode. No doubt the car was bulletproof, but she didn't intend to take any chances.

"Nathan, listen to me, sweetheart. Unbuckle your seat belt and get down on the floor. Hold on to the seat belt and do not let go."

"Yes, ma'am."

Another shot bounced off the trunk of the car. Nathan scrambled to the floorboard.

*Keary, you monster! This is your son.* She stepped on the gas and whipped the car around two others in front of her. A glance in the rearview mirror showed a white SUV gaining ground. The tinted windows hid the occupants, but someone fired an automatic from the passenger side.

"You're going too fast." Nathan's high-pitched voice couldn't get to her now. She needed to work through this.

"It's okay, honey. I know how to drive."

Paige stepped on the gas, weaving through traffic. The SUV did not let up. Another bullet whizzed past, and from the clunk, she knew it had hit her door.

"We'll be safe soon," she said, taking a sharp turn to the left.

The SUV followed. They were heading into Kibera, the slum district. People loitered in the streets—children too. She slowed to a quick stop amid a crowd of people, all hammering the car for a handout. Good. They'd do the same for the SUV. She pulled Nathan from the floorboard and hobbled through the busy crowd, one hand firmly clasped in his and the other wrapped around her Smith 9 mm. They rounded a hut and squeezed between it and another. The lack of sanitation gagged her. She swung Nathan up into her arms and hurried on.

"Nathan," she heard a man call. "Nathan."

Paige caught her breath and swung her attention toward the voice.

"Isn't that Miss Bobbie's son?" The large man had one arm, and a scar zigzagged down his shirtless chest. But if he knew Bobbie . . .

"Mr. Charles?" Nathan pointed. "I know him."

Paige glanced behind her at a sea of black faces. "Sir, a couple of men are trying to rob us. They fired at our car."

He motioned. "Come; I'll keep you safe. God would want us to help you." He turned toward a group of men and shouted orders to stop anyone coming through.

*Thank You, Lord, for keeping my son safe.*

# CHAPTER 22

"WHAT DO YOU MEAN, you lost her?" I cannot fathom such incompetence.

"I was told she disappeared in Kibera with a kid," Zuriel's voice on the phone rises.

"What do you mean, disappeared? And what was she doing with a kid?" This doesn't make sense. Zuriel was supposed to follow Paige, hopefully to Rosa, and eliminate both of them. With the recent turmoil in Nairobi, it could easily be mistaken for an accident.

"She visited a Bobbie Landerson in the hospital, a woman dying of cancer. Then she—"

"I read the report." I give myself a moment to process what I've learned. She hasn't been seen with anyone who resembles Rosa. But why else would she be in Nairobi? "What I want to know is why she was with a kid. Who is he?"

"I have no idea, but I'm working on it. We found a picture of him in the car with some other woman. Don't know who she is. It might be his mother."

"Send it to me."

I hear Zuriel tap computer keys. "It's headed your way."

# CHAPTER 23

FRIDAY NIGHT after Labor Day, Miles watched the team warm up before the first district game of the season. Excitement seemed to radiate from the field. The rivalry between Chris and Walt had apparently smoothed over, or the two finally realized that unless they worked together, the Bobcats would not have a chance at state. Walt had taken a lot of abuse from Chris and his buds, and the dispute needed to end before Walt retaliated with a few of his own friends.

Miles sensed someone approaching him and swung his attention toward Ty Dalton. The man reminded Miles of a bull ready to charge. The local gossip from well-meaning church people and cafeteria talk indicated Ty Dalton intended for his son to play first-string quarterback, just like Ty had done at Split Creek High twenty-two years ago, or Miles would no longer have a job.

Dalton's eyes narrowed. "I need to point out a few things that need your attention."

A little tension was good for the soul, kept a man relying on God. Conflict, on the other hand, caused ulcers and heart attacks and kept a man grasping on to God with both hands. Miles preferred the easier route. He'd prayed about the possible confrontation with the school board in hopes he wouldn't lose his temper.

"Are your concerns as a fan, a father, or as president of the school board?"

"You sound antagonistic, Coach. Makes me wonder if you know what this is about."

Miles sensed his wannabe ulcer sending up a fire signal. "I take my job seriously, and anything that takes me away from practice takes me away from helping the boys be successful."

"Then I'll make this short. The school board wants to see Chris play first-string quarterback. OU is looking for a quarterback. One of the coaches—"

"Coach Netterfield never called you. I checked with him. Somebody played a rotten joke on Chris and you." Miles started to say that Dalton should have recognized a hoax call when he heard one—unless he'd made up the call.

"I don't believe you."

"Why don't you call Netterfield and verify it?"

"I will." Dalton inhaled deeply. "You won't be destroying my boy's chances to play college ball by using a dirt-poor Indian. The school board's waited through the scrimmages for you to put Chris where he—"

"Excuse me? And this is from the football coach. I was hired to train and equip young men to play a great game. I was hired to look at their skills and assign them to a position in which each player could excel and learn the value of teamwork. There is no clause that states the school board will dictate to me what player plays what position."

Dalton's nostrils flared. "You can be replaced. I thought you had more sense than this." He took in one of Chris's passes. "I warn you. I'm not the man to mess with."

The words fueled Miles's anger. "Don't threaten me. I have a game to coach." Without giving the man another look, Miles strode onto the field before he could explode and put on a show.

Miles paced the sidelines in front of his team. "You look good out there tonight. I see great plays, passes, and catches. Do you want to know why?"

"Teamwork." Walt's response led to many others echoing him.

Good. He was stepping into leading the team. "Right. I saw you play as athletes who put their personal agendas aside for the good of the team. Tonight we're up against the Mustangs, a team that tied the Warriors during a scrimmage. Anyone want to tell the rest of us what's going to happen?"

"We're not going to lose." Chris slowly stood from a kneeling position. "I don't want to feel like I did the night of the Warrior game."

"You're all winners—a notch above the other high school teams. If you look at the stats and what the papers are saying, we have a fantastic opportunity to take the team into the play-offs and bring home a trophy. Anyone interested?"

Cheers rose from the group. Miles raised his hands. "I'm willing to do whatever it takes. What about you?"

Nearly two weeks had passed since Paige had returned from Kenya. Raif and Anissa had taken Nathan with them the same night that Paige and Nathan had found refuge within Kibera. The investigation had taken a slow turn. Keary hadn't bothered her, but she hadn't turned up any new information. Every day that ticked by brought him closer to the election and kept her apart from Nathan. She questioned her motives in wanting her son. If selfishness caused her to place him in harm's way, then she needed to give him up to a couple who could keep him safe.

Her bright spot came in seeing Miles. Lately her thoughts had turned to a home with her two favorite men. It wouldn't happen, but she'd dream anyway.

Paige had worn the boot cast a little over two weeks, and she was ready to toss the clumsy, in-her-way encumbrance in the county dump.

She pasted a smile on her face and stared at the top of the stadium. The nosebleed section would be a great place to sit. She could observe the crowd while keeping track of yardage and touchdowns on the field. A mole was in Split Creek, and she'd never had much use for furry little creatures that lived underground—and were hard to get rid of. Wilhelm Busch said it much better:

*A gardener by the name of Knoll*
*Goes for a joyful garden stroll.*

*His joyfulness, however, sours:*
*A mole is digging up the flowers.*


"Girlfriend, where are you going?" Voleta called from behind her, panting like the two were climbing Mount Everest.

"To the top."

"Why?"

Paige turned to Voleta and grinned. "Because I can."

"You are the most stubborn woman I know."

"I've heard that before. This is good for you. Gets the blood pumping."

"You should know, Miss Run-a-Marathon. Have you forgotten what's attached to your right foot?"

"Absolutely not. Just keeping in shape."

"Don't forget our jobs at halftime."

"I haven't."

Once seated, she scanned the crowd, those who watched from the sidelines, and anyone else strolling about. Nathan would love this. She'd called him every day since he'd returned. This afternoon he'd cried for her, but as much as she wanted to see him, she couldn't risk it. Palmer had him placed at a safe house in Dallas. Oh, the two worlds she lived in. Tonight, despite the aggravation of the boot cast and her longing for Nathan, she felt the old enthusiasm for her job, the sense of purpose, and the excitement of being a part of the

CIA. Some might call her sentiments hokey, but she didn't.

An hour and a half lay ahead with good visibility before night settled in, and she intended to use every minute of daylight to scope out those lingering in the crowd—those who were not Split Creek fans but Daniel Keary fans. That person or persons would mix in with the crowd, pretending interest while keeping an eye on her. The inability to view their microexpressions issued a challenge, but one she welcomed. Just let the mole get a read on Paige the librarian. The adrenaline pumped faster into her veins while her exterior remained calm and interested in the battle about to begin on the field.

With a satisfied grin, she picked up her binoculars and focused briefly on Miles. Then she used them to search the crowd before focusing on the team.

"What are you grinning about?" Voleta asked. "Oh, I know. You're checking out the coach."

"Where did you get a ridiculous idea like that?"

Voleta pointed to an invisible line from Paige's nose to the field. "Now I know why you wanted to sit up here."

"I like to see the looks on the players' faces."

"Sure. Keep telling yourself that and before the season's over, you might believe it."

"Honestly there is nothing between us but friendship."

Voleta patted Paige's knee. "I may not be the smartest kid on the block, but I see in your eyes what you refuse to admit."

Paige locked onto Miles watching his boys practice. Life was full of *if only*s, and she understood the path ahead with Miles led to misery.

At halftime, the Bobcats and the Mustangs were tied. No pressure there. She and Voleta made it to the concession stand before the clock ran out. Paige zeroed in on a man and then a woman while answering the call for drinks, chips, hot dogs, and nachos. Using her phone, she snapped their pictures.

With less than one minute left in the fourth quarter and the score still tied, Paige picked up the binoculars and zeroed in on the tension etched across each player's face, especially Walt's. She swung the binoculars to Chris. His face was marked with the same determination. Out of curiosity, she focused on Ty Dalton, who stood behind the sidelines. From the way he set his jaw, anger and disgust were playing their own game. Why couldn't that man just let those kids play ball?

Chris leaped into the air and caught a pass from Walt, then took off down the field toward the Mustangs goal as if the field were on fire.

Paige sprang to her feet with the other Bobcat fans in a wild frenzy—clapping, screaming, whistling. Drumsticks clicked against the snares' rims. Trumpets and cornets blared the opening notes, and the band ripped the air with the school's fight song. The crowd thundered its applause in wild excitement, alerting anyone who hadn't been at the game that the hometown team had won. From the sidelines the remaining sweat-drenched players rushed onto the field to shake the hands of the opposing team members before whirling around to holler and hug each other. The scoreboard read Bobcats 12, Mustangs 6. Grand game. The Bobcats and their charming coach were headed to the top. She could feel it.

# CHAPTER 24

PAIGE PUNCHED HER PILLOW and rolled over to see the numbers on her clock glow 2:48. She'd spent last night rereading every online post she could find about Keary: where he stood on issues and what he'd accomplished at his law firm. Sometimes the obvious was the most concealed. Little had been accomplished this week, and the rising disappointment kept her head spinning. What a lousy operative. In the old days, she'd have been sitting on Zuriel's or Keary's lap to find out what she needed.

If she were Keary, with his incredible intelligence cocooned in a drive for money and power, how would she secure the office of governor of Oklahoma? How would she cover up the money earned from the diamonds in Namibia and the oil deal in Angola?

Paige reached up and snapped on the lamp. A notebook and pen lay beside the clock radio. Actually, two pens were there in case one evaporated. She propped her pillow behind her back and began to make side-by-side lists of Keary's strengths and weaknesses. On a second sheet, she made two columns listing his political views about popular issues locally and nationally and his views regarding U.S. foreign policy. On a third sheet, she listed his personal achievements and hobbies that had nothing to do with his past association with the company. Within those notes lay the one fatal mistake that proved his fallibility.

Paige started a fourth list of the clandestine missions in which she and Keary had worked together. She recalled in detail what occurred in the planning sessions, and the individual and group responsibilities, just as she'd done so many times before. Except this time, something might click and give her new insight into proving his guilt. She then linked the initials of the first names of those operatives who had worked with them, searching for a connection to tie this all together. From what she'd learned about Joel Zuriel and his habit of bragging about his business endeavors, he might let something slip. But she couldn't approach him until the doctor removed her boot cast.

Tucking the notebook into the zippered pouch of the turquoise and brown quilted Bible cover that Eleanor had made for her last Christmas, she threw back the sheet and blanket and sat on the side of the bed. Her Bible accompanied her everywhere, and someone would have to break her arm or kill her to get it. Besides, Keary's thugs would never think to look there.

At four o'clock she brewed a pot of coffee so strong that it would jolt like a rabbit punch. She grabbed a half-full bag of Reese's Pieces and alternated a candy with a sip of coffee. The coffee and sugar put her nerves on alert. If she didn't eat something substantial before the service, she'd be escorted out because she wouldn't be able to sit still.

For the next three hours, she drew lines and listed questions for Palmer. Rosa *had* to be found. At seven, she headed to the kitchen to drop a piece of whole-grain bread into the toaster and pull out a near-empty jar of raisin and cinnamon peanut butter. While the bread toasted, she peeled a banana and sliced it into manageable pieces—sort of how she tried to do life.

Her mind refused to end the brainstorming session, but she needed to focus her attention on church. Her duties with preschool Sunday school were on hold until the cast was removed. Hard to keep up with three-year-olds while hobbling on one foot. Instead, she greeted folks when they arrived for Sunday school and helped visitors find what they needed.

After reading Psalm 39 and 40 and noting she wasn't the only person in history who had been misunderstood and thought God had forsaken them, she tied a plastic bag over her cast and hurried through her shower. She cut her hair-drying time in half and gathered her shoulder-length hair into a ponytail. Leaning into a magnifying mirror, she applied concealer under her sleep-deprived eyes. Paige started. Tiny crow's feet extended from the corner of her left eye. Scary. Instantly she snatched up a regular mirror and was relieved to see that the lines were no longer visible.

With a mascara wand in hand, she stole a quick look at the clock. Miles would pick her up at eight thirty. They'd won their first game Friday night, and he'd be talking football all the way to the piano prelude. Escorting her to church was a courtesy on his part, not a date. *Who am I kidding?* He'd pursued her for nearly two years. . . .

Paige flinched and dropped her mascara wand into the basket of makeup in the sink. Could Miles be the informant? Her thoughts raced back to how he'd taken the relationship slowly right from the start—visiting her at the library, showing up at the same community events. And recently he'd started attending the same church. And the shooting at the library . . . At the time, she'd satisfied herself that he'd been home in bed. But that could have been a cover. The more she pondered the situation, the more plausible the suspicion seemed. Keary had the means to plant him and to train Miles about her cautious nature, plus all of the other things he knew about her.

The clock read 8:25. She snatched up the phone. "Palmer, I need a favor."

"When don't you? I thought you went to church on Sunday mornings."

She dismissed the momentary irritation. He had access to when her bathroom light flipped on in the dead of night. "This afternoon I'm going to send you a man's photo—Miles Laird. I want to know what turns up."

"He's clean, but I'll run another one. I was going to call you later. I have a possible locale on Rosa Ngoimgo—South Africa."

Even with the caffeine and sugar overload, her body relaxed. "Good. I want to be the one to contact her when you get something definite. I appreciate this."

Relieved, she limped to her nightstand to gather up her Bible. Miles's truck spit gravel in the driveway, and her heart longed to see him, and yet she feared what she might learn. She loved a man who could be betraying her, as though she'd been tricked into a covert operation in which she was the only one on the team.

★ ★ ★

"Good sermon today." Miles opened the truck door for Paige and helped her climb in before she denied needing any assistance.

Finally the heat that had beaten down on them all summer had diminished. To him, it seemed like the birds sang a little sweeter this morning, too. Or could it be the worship service shared with Paige had made his Sunday a little more special?

"I like the way your pastor applies the Bible to everyday life." Miles leaned against the open truck door.

"And today he used football as an object lesson."

"Did he? I hadn't noticed." Miles drank in the beauty of the woman who had stolen his heart.

She glanced at him from the corner of her eye.

"Okay, so I noticed the mention of the game. And you don't think I paid attention? Well, lady, he said that just how we love the Bobcats whether they win or lose is how God feels about us. The point was relationships."

"Very good. I'll put a gold star by your name." Paige grinned and tilted her head. "What made you stop attending the Methodist church?"

"The truth is I was saved in a Baptist church, but my parents are Methodists."

"But why switch now?"

He rubbed his chin. How forthcoming should he be when he and God were still discussing the move? "I'd been considering a change for quite a while. It wasn't about denominational differences. The decision had to do with where I believed God wanted me to serve. And I'd be a liar if I didn't admit seeing you on Sunday mornings was a bonus."

"Not sure if the latter is a theological argument."

"Ouch. My relationship with God is the most important part of my life. Having you there is an added perk." He dwelled a moment on his caring for her and his hope for her one day to feel the same about him.

"Good. Now I feel better." She yawned.

"What? Am I boring you?"

"I woke up early this morning and couldn't go back to sleep. Hey, I have an idea. Instead of eating out today, let's stop at the Piggly Wiggly and cook at my place."

"What about your foot?"

"Cooking is done with the hands and the brain, not the feet."

"Sold. One day I'd like for you to see my place."

"Is it a bachelor's domain?"

Miles squinted, thinking through each room. "Parts of it."

"Maybe next time." Her lack of enthusiasm threatened his hopes, but that was Paige.

Once inside his truck, she tapped him on the shoulder. "Give me your best smile."

Paige held her fancy phone, the one with all the bells and whistles, and aimed it at him. She clicked his photo and then showed him the result.

"What made you snap my picture?"

"Darts for charity. Or I could use it as blackmail. Can we do it again? This time stick out your tongue. You can flash it when the guys on the team aren't listening."

He shook his head. "Better go after what pitiful amount of money I have now before I get fired."

"Forget that craziness. You're the best coach Split Creek could ever have. The school board is being bullied."

"Thanks for building up my ego."

"Anytime." She flashed him a magazine-cover smile.

He turned the corner for the Piggly Wiggly. What a great day. Good worship. Good woman. And soon, a good lunch.

At one time, Paige had used whatever means she deemed necessary to persuade others to talk, including her feminine wiles in a predominantly male-dominated world. But inviting Miles for lunch made her feel like scum. However, he wouldn't be the first man who appeared to be Mr. Nice Guy while trading U.S. secrets for a fortune. Besides, the cozy atmosphere of her bungalow offered the opportunity to take pictures with her digital camera and send them to Palmer. What a sick joke if she discovered Keary had planted Miles in Split Creek to spy on her. She'd rather think he was honest . . . sincere . . . her knight on a shining Harley.

Her heart wasn't supposed to get involved. What a combination: a CIA operative who had a background of alleged mental instability and a secret child, and a high school football coach who longed to take his team to state. But were they so different? In many ways, Miles reminded her of how she felt about her country and the determination to preserve freedom. Sometimes she thought about being Miles's wife and living barefoot and pregnant with him and Nathan in Split Creek. The high school football coach and the librarian. She wondered what it would be like to pay her parents a visit with a bunch of kids and a doting husband. Impossible, but oh so alluring.

Miles dropped the paring knife into the sink. Not once had he complained about peeling potatoes. What a trouper. Each time her conscience scolded her about lunch preparations, she shoved away the guilt.

"You sure are quiet." Miles proceeded to hack away another perfectly good potato.

She cringed at the amount of potato flesh that was whittled off into the sink. "I'm observing your expertise in the kitchen." She picked up her camera. "In fact, here is one more shot."

Miles moaned. "The last one posing beside your

pink mixer nearly did me in. And if my team sees any of these, I'm toast."

"The one I like the best is your scowl at the sink full of potatoes."

"I've counted eight of those babies. We'll have enough left for me to feed my entire team."

"Oh, I plan to send them home with you as part of a care package."

"More like 'I really care you had to peel all of them.'"

He laughed, and she joined him. Even though loving Miles was forbidden, even though she'd allowed it to happen, even though she'd end up breaking his heart and the whole mess would end up breaking hers, she still cherished every minute with him.

*I can pretend I'm normal for a little while.* "How are your parents doing?"

"Good. I talk to them at least once a week."

"You're a good son."

"Not always." His tone plummeted.

Paige prodded for more information. "I can't imagine your being anything but a model of perfection."

"I played games until I found the Lord."

"That makes two of us." She crossed her arms and leaned back against the table, facing him. "Do you want to talk about it?"

"I might slip off my pedestal."

"I don't think so."

He rinsed the potato—several times. "The possibility of losing my job isn't a pleasant topic either. Both are harsh."

"I'm really sorry about what's happening at school."

"Oh, that's life. Can't run a play unless you're prepared to get tackled." He hesitated as though he questioned telling her what burdened his mind. "Did you ever read Voltaire's *Candide*?"

She startled. "I live in a library. I read everything."

"Then you know what I mean about this not being a perfect world. One fewer evil act does make the world a little better, and hopefully, one more good act makes life a little better for someone." He picked up another potato. "My trials right now are insignificant compared to the atrocities going on in the world."

"You certainly are philosophical this afternoon." She snatched up a dirty dish towel and pulled a clean one from the drawer.

"Ah, I bet you thought the only things football coaches think about are the next plays." He sliced away a generous hunk of peel and potato. "And most times I fit right there, with about as much intellect as the contents of a pigskin." He paused and lifted his hand. "Or potato skins, as the case may be."

"I think you have more depth than most people give you credit for. I don't think you've ever told me how you came to be a coach," she said.

He seemed to reconsider his offer to tell the story. "I came to Split Creek four years ago from Knoxville, ready to make a difference in kids' lives. Before then, I worked in the corporate world with a big addiction to football."

"What kind of work did you do?"

"Owned my own computer security company."

"Wow. I'm impressed." She hoped her internal alarm system didn't skyrocket with the new tidbit of information. "What kind of clients did you have?"

"Mostly government contracts."

Alarm sounded louder than a tornado siren. "What swayed your decision to enter the world of education and be a coach?"

"My brother overdosed. Died. And I needed a change." He continued to peel a potato. "There's more to the story. His death was my fault. He watched me in my younger days drink myself into oblivion and use every drug out there. Eventually God grabbed hold of me, and I cleaned myself up. But my little brother modeled his behavior after what he'd seen me do. All the talking, pleading, and following him around to keep him away from substance abuse did nothing to convince him of changing his path." Turmoil twisted on Miles's face. And Paige understood how the ugliness of life could stain everything a person attempted to do.

"In time, his drug of choice, cocaine, isolated

him from his family, and he flunked out of college. Then one night after his girlfriend broke up with him, he snorted too much and killed himself."

Paige took his hand—wet and gritty. Oh, how she wanted her suspicions about him to be wrong. "I can't think of anything more painful than taking the blame for someone's death. But, Miles, your brother made his own choices, including not to accept the help you offered. I'm sure you did all you could do."

"It's easy for me to counsel someone with the same problem and give the same advice. But forgiving myself was another matter."

"God wants you to live in freedom." Her own words echoed in her mind. Like Miles, she could give advice but not believe it applied to her. She wanted so much more for Nathan. She and Miles had more in common than she had realized.

"I know. He and I have had a few lengthy talks about it. Time will tell. But now you know what motivates me to help kids."

She squeezed the hand resting in hers. "Where would we be without God to help us over the rocks?"

"Lost and miserable, sweet lady. And probably bleeding."

"I remember what life was like without Him, and I don't want to ever live without my faith again."

"I agree. I simply need to live my life as a man of integrity. Truth and honesty mean more to me than being a people pleaser or collecting a steady paycheck." His shoulders lifted and fell. "Enough of this serious stuff. If I lose my job, do you suppose I can work at the library shelving books?"

"People might talk."

"They already do."

"Then by all means. I could use the help."

His arm brushed against hers as she bent to check on a chocolate pecan pie. Despite the heat from the 350-degree oven, she shivered. Surely Miles didn't work for Keary. Truth yanked her into reality. Computer security, government contracts . . . and Keary liked kids, too.

# CHAPTER 25

I CAN'T STOP STARING at the picture of the little boy and the woman. Her name is Bobbie Landerson, a missionary who works with displaced people in Kibera. She is suffering through the last days of cancer. Her son's name is Nathan, but she's never been married. Myriad questions pour from my brain. Why was he with Mikaela? Could the woman be a link to Rosa Ngoimgo?

And yet, it is the picture of the boy that haunts me. My sources indicate he was born while Mikaela lived in Nairobi.

If Mikaela knows his mother, she may have been there at the birth.

My heart hammers against my chest. My mouth goes dry. . . . He looks like my childhood photos . . . but his eyes are Mikaela's. Is it possible? Could the boy be mine?

I must find out. If Nathan is my son, no one will keep him from me. No one.

## CHAPTER 26

UNTIL TODAY, Mondays had never been Miles's favorite day of the week. "Attitude" said it all. If he could skip over Monday and slide into Tuesday, he'd be one happy man. However, he'd never confessed his aversion, because a Christian man was supposed to find joy in the Lord and not in his circumstances. Hogwash. The whole town probably stayed clear of their grumpy coach on Mondays. When he focused on the spiritual side of it, he bet there were plenty of days when the apostle Peter wanted to lay a fist alongside one of the other disciples' jaws. And Paul had gotten frustrated with John Mark's immaturity about running back to his mama when the missionary journey got rough.

So continued Miles's justification to feel perfectly righteous and somewhat of a bear on Mondays. But today the edge had tipped to the well-behaved side, downright jovial, all because of

Friday's game. Congratulations and greetings from teachers and students made the day a little easier to wade through. His body didn't ache with the overwhelming load of teaching and coaching, and he didn't feel one bit guilty about the seconds and thirds of fried chicken, mashed potatoes, Caesar salad, cornbread, and green beans with a touch of dill he'd eaten after church yesterday with Paige. Once the food was cooked, they'd filled their plates and enjoyed the cooler temps outside. Admittedly so, being in her presence felt like a jolt of electricity.

In truth, the chicken, combined with Paige's chocolate pecan pie, had lain a little heavy on his stomach, so this morning he worked out hard to turn all that fat and sugar into muscle. Today he planned to start eating healthier. Oops. Not today. Paige had sent home a ton of leftovers.

Miles sucked in his gut and continued down the hall and out the side door to the field house. Being around all of these teenage boys was raising his testosterone level and making him more aware of the male competition.

Every time he allowed his mind to wander, it slipped back to yesterday with his favorite lady. She did appear a little preoccupied, though. He sighed. If only he could break through the barriers surrounding her heart. It hadn't happened yet. Whoever had hurt her had done a devastating job.

At one point he thought she might open up, but

212

as quickly as he'd seen the light of hope, she'd slammed the door again. He'd told her about his brother. But all his story did was garner sympathy, not an outpouring of who and what comprised the town's librarian.

Several months ago, Paige had told him she'd been reared by an aunt who had died when Paige was in high school. She had no one left. The folks of Split Creek were her family. At the time, Miles believed she hadn't told him the whole story, but he didn't want to bombard her with questions. Now the temptation to quiz her surfaced again.

Once inside his office, he closed the door and dropped into his chair. With a deep breath, he reached into his pocket and pulled out his wallet, where a slip of wrinkled paper held Paige's Social Security number. She'd given it to the nurse in the ER the night she'd broken her ankle, and he'd memorized it until he'd gotten home and jotted it down. Bafflement was getting the best of him. Whenever he considered one of her peculiar mannerisms or her reluctance to talk about her past, he thought about researching the numbers. Other times he chided himself for thinking about invading her privacy. He'd been watching too many movies.

But his former position as owner of a computer security company allowed him access into unique files. Maybe it was a sixth sense. Maybe it was God's revelation. Or maybe it was a driving curiosity. Miles had no logical reason to doubt anything she'd ever said, but the notion that something wasn't quite right persisted like a mosquito bite on his big toe.

He pulled his personal laptop from his briefcase and glanced around, as though someone stood outside his glass wall watching his every move. The last time he'd used his computer technology expertise, it had been in the confines of the sixth floor of an office building. This time he ventured into an area that rode the fence of legality. Rubbing his hands, he reminded himself of the vast amount of information about everyone floating in cyberspace. One simply needed to know how to retrieve it.

After logging on to the school's Internet system, he tapped into a secured site and keyed in his password where he could obtain a wagonload of information—or trouble. His fingers refused to type in the nine numbers. He wanted to be wrong. He wanted to spend the rest of the day berating himself for being a jerk, for ever considering that the woman he loved had concealed secrets about her past. For several seconds he daydreamed about her and the life he one day hoped they would share. But if he didn't follow through with this search, he'd spend another sleepless night. Miles typed in Paige's Social Security number, clicked Enter, and then stuffed the slip of paper back into his wallet.

While he waited for the intel to download, he

nearly opted out of the program. *I don't need to do this, checking up on Paige as though she's involved in something illegal or immoral.*

A moment later, information about Paige Rogers lit up the screen like the scoreboard of a losing game. Miles stared at the report while his emotions spun nearly out of control. Her Social Security number was a fake. Her name was a fake. Paige Rogers didn't exist except on the forms she'd given to the nurse in ER.

He snatched his cell phone from the desk, ready to confront her with his findings. What would he say? "Excuse me, but I decided to do a security check on you. Can you tell me why you've lied to everyone in Split Creek?" Taking a deep breath, Miles relaxed his fingers around his phone and placed it back on his desk. With what he'd told her about his background in government security, she had to know it was only a matter of time before he learned the truth.

If a credit card company or her employer or any of a hundred other sources had done the research, they'd find her a solid taxpaying citizen. But this secured site told it all. Miles slammed his fist into his palm. The truth stared back at him as though mocking his feelings for her. He'd rather have been in the dark. Time—he needed time to think this through.

He stood and faced the window. Every muscle in his body tensed, and he stretched to rid himself of the anger that mounted each time he realized she'd lied to him—and the whole town.

*Who are you? And why are you hiding out in Split Creek? Dear Lord, who have I fallen in love with? And You have this all planned out? How about a little insight here?*

Paige's favorite day of the week, other than Sunday, was Monday. She loved the challenge of a new week and making a list of all she needed to accomplish. UPS had delivered two cases of new books to process. Whether cataloging a fiction title and properly assigning its topics and descriptions or seeking out the correct Dewey decimal number for a nonfiction book, she looked forward to the process—like a puzzle. Books—she loved the smell of them, the touch, the adventure and knowledge on each page.

Yet this Monday her natural enthusiasm waned as she waited for Palmer to report his findings about Miles. By eleven o'clock, impatience attacked every nerve in her body. With the library empty, she punched in the numbers on her cell.

"Palmer, do you have anything on file with the name and photos I sent to you yesterday?"

"I expected your call."

"Those are fighting words."

"Imagining you squirm is more fun."

"Twelve years we've known each other, and you haven't changed a bit."

"I have to keep my sense of humor or this job would destroy me. But in response to your question—" his voice took on a sober tone—"Miles Laird is clean, just like I said. Everything he told you is true. Regarding his computer security business, he still has access to some secured sites."

"Can he pull up falsified information?"

"Sure. Have you given him reason to access a secured site?"

Paige shifted from irritation to the many times she'd covered up her past. "His only question is why I don't support Keary for governor. Had you investigated him before I got involved with the company again?"

"Of course. You know as much about him as we do."

"That was omitted on my original paperwork." She laughed in an attempt to soothe her own tension. "But I won't hold that against you."

"How kind. Should have a location for Rosa today or tomorrow."

"Thanks, and I appreciate this."


Hours later, the dilemma with Keary continued to roll around in her head. Paige paced her living room searching for answers. She rubbed the chill bumps on her arms—the chill of understanding, like a little girl attempting to jump rope and missing the rhythm until one day her body responds to the beat.

Keary wouldn't stop at becoming governor. He was much too ambitious for that. For certain, he had his sights set on the presidency. His last speech had been dynamic. He'd called for unity among all faiths in raising educational standards in Oklahoma. His passion for children's health care rang with sincerity. And his pro-life zeal had earned new support among the Judeo-Christian citizens. Paige fought the churning in her stomach. Keary collected more votes each time he opened his front door.

Reality shook her. Behind closed doors, she could hear him talking about how the country should be run. As president, he'd call in his global chips, and then—look out, America. No longer would we be giving away billions of dollars to countries that would always have the poor and needy. The U.S. would have oil in all the corners of the world where the current administration didn't want to tread. Who cared about slave labor when America needed oil? Besides, Keary knew how to hide things.

She simply had to stir through each phase of Keary's habits and associates until the truth surfaced like rich cream. The possibilities swirled in her head. She headed to her bedroom for the notebook concealed in her Bible that contained her thoughts and observations about Daniel Keary.

When successful in bringing Keary to justice, she'd lose all she'd gained in Split Creek, including Miles. He wasn't the type of man to understand deceit, which was exactly what she'd used. Media attention would expose Keary and her association with the company. Nathan could not, would not grow up here. Small towns were unforgiving, and children were judged for the mistakes of their parents. This home, her new life built on the ashes of her past, would be gone.

Perhaps she'd resign for good from the CIA. She didn't want anyone else nurturing her child. Again she deliberated whether her son should be adopted by a couple who didn't work in espionage.

Her phone rang, interrupting her musings. The call was from the safe house. Alarm shoved away all thoughts but Nathan.

Paige recognized Anissa's voice. "I need to talk to you about Nathan," she said.

"What's the problem?"

"He's not adjusting well to his new surroundings. I mean, he's stuck here in an older neighborhood with no kids. We can't let him out of our sight. He can't find the picture of him and his mother, and he's crying for his mother—and you."

"Visiting him is too dangerous. I'm afraid of being followed." The near catastrophe in Kenya had proven her adversary's strength. "I'll add e-mails to my daily calls. See if I can get him to open up. I'll ask him about his picture. I know he had it with him in the car." She hesitated. He *did* have that photo in the car.

"Paige?"

"Nathan had the photograph with him when we took off together in Nairobi." She wanted to throw something. "That means Keary could have gotten hold of the picture."

Paige disconnected the call. Her precious son was miserable. Keary might have the lost photo. Maybe Rachel in Nairobi had been right. She should have left Nathan there, where he would have been safe with people he knew and loved.

# CHAPTER 27

PAIGE POLISHED the top of the library's return counter with a dusting cloth and a sprinkling of lemon oil. Now to keep anyone from piling books on the damp area until she had time to rub in the polish. This afternoon the library was quiet, with students on computers and other patrons reading. She bent to put away the oil and cloth.

"Miss Rogers?"

She snapped back up. Chris stood alone, weariness tugging at his eyes and a ragged Bobcats T-shirt hanging from his shoulders. "Hi. How can I help you?"

"English is killing me again. Gotta write another paper and put together a PowerPoint."

She smiled at his pitiful frown, but he obviously wasn't amused. "I'm sorry. What's the topic this time?"

"I'm supposed to compare the characters in *Night* by Elie Wiesel to the guys who built Israel. I talked to my grandpa, but he didn't know much about either one."

"Have you read Wiesel's book?"

"Yeah. It was hard reading about all that stuff."

"Sounds like your teacher is trying to instill values while you learn how to organize your thoughts on paper."

"Whatever. You should have read the book."

"I have. It makes you appreciate our country."

Chris slumped. "You'll help me?"

"Might cost you one hundred push-ups." He smelled like he'd done five hundred.

"Might be easier."

Paige searched the library's software program that linked Elie Wiesel's book with similar information. "How's your mother?"

"Okay, I guess. Dad's working late hours."

She'd heard plenty of rumors about his parents not getting along. But most couples had a tiff now and then. *Tiff? I've become entrenched in Southern terminology.* "Sometimes jobs demand more of us than we're ready to give."

"Unless you don't want to come home."

She wasn't about to delve any deeper into Ty Dalton. No wonder Chris couldn't get along with Walt Greywolf. "Have you started your paper?"

"All I've done is name the file and type the title page."

"Do you have any thoughts about it?"

"Some. Everything seems to jumble together." He lifted his laptop from his backpack. "My girlfriend says I'm not organized."

"We can fix that too. Give me a moment to help a girl at one of the computers."

A few moments later, Paige pulled a chair beside Chris. He peered into the laptop screen, and his brow furrowed.

"Tell me what impressed you the most about *Night*."

Chris blew out a sigh. "That whole holocaust thing—sometimes I think it didn't really happen, you know? Creeps me out. Like, how could the world let a sketchy guy do all that killing? No way. I mean, I couldn't have gone through that kind of stuff. Maybe it would've been better just to, you know, not really live. Not really make it through. It's totally whacked."

Chris's interpretation hit a sensitive nerve. "I agree. It was a group of people gone mad in a world that didn't want to get involved."

"Like a sick world."

*Okay, God, I get the message.* "It does seem that way. Have you read anything about the courageous people who formed Israel?"

"Not yet. Thought I could find something online and in a book. You know, I can't respect people who let innocent people die. How do they sleep?"

What a confirmation for what she was trying to

do. "Let's look at a few of the library's resources, and then we'll talk about your paper." She walked to the wall of books in the 900 Dewey decimal section to pull two volumes about the history of ancient Israel and how the country was reunited after World War II. She laid them beside Chris's laptop.

He glanced at the titles. "How could so many people stand by and do nothing while the Jews were killed? Man, were they cowards?"

"The cowardice of noninvolvement." She studied his young face and hoped the world of tomorrow would be better than what her generation had given him.

An hour later, she walked by Chris to see if he was making progress. The boy stared into the computer screen at a map of Angola. Curious, she touched his shoulder.

"That doesn't look like a map of Israel."

Chris cringed. "I was getting kinda tired and decided to look around."

"Why Angola?"

"My dad worked there."

Cymbals clanged in her brain. *How did we miss that?* "Doing what?"

"Oil driller for WorldMarc."

Paige's pulse doubled. "When was this?"

"About five years ago."

*After I came to Split Creek.* "I bet you're glad he's home with you now."

223

"He made lots of money there. But he wanted to be home with me and my mom. That's why he quit and bought the mechanic's garage."

"Family's more important than money."

"That's what my mom says."

Paige patted him on the shoulder. His tone left more unsaid than said. She suspected the troubles at the Dalton house weighed on his mind and left him confused. Compound that with the pressures of school and football and the rivalry with Walt, and that led to one hurting teen.

*He worked for WorldMarc during the same time as Keary's involvement with oil.* Now she had something else to do. Dalton could possibly be the mole. Possibly a witness to what had happened to the missing villagers. She'd see what she could find once the library closed tonight and she could power up her laptop in privacy.

Friday afternoon Miles paced the classroom while his students finished a reading assignment. Part of him said to confront Paige about her deceit, and the other part told him to wait until he'd had more time to pray about it. What he wanted to do didn't sound very God-honoring. But . . . she might have a good reason to keep her identity unknown. A bad relationship in which she had to run for her life or a past that needed to be kept there. He thought back over the many times Paige had said the two of them couldn't be together, as though she had no control of the situation. He glanced out the window. Yeah, he'd let it ride for a little while.

The bell rang, and he opened the door from his history classroom to the hallway to dismiss his students. He chuckled. *Eager* couldn't begin to describe teens leaving class on Friday afternoon and the anticipation of the second football game of the season.

Some of the teachers let it be known that Miles's habit of greeting students before and after class was a bit old-fashioned, but he knew personal contact created a bond between student and teacher. For some, this was the only positive moment of the day. Perhaps he and his younger brother might have made different choices if someone within the education system had reached out to them. Too many kids led separate lives at home and at school. Miles's goal was to try to bridge the gap.

Once the last student exited the room, Miles caught a glimpse of Principal O'Connor standing across the hall. Another visit Miles had been expecting.

O'Connor gave a tight smile. "Isn't this your free period?"

"Yes, but I do have a student coming by in about fifteen minutes." Miles stared into O'Connor's eyes, but the man quickly looked into the classroom as though interested in a map of 1750 America.

"This won't take long," O'Connor said.

Miles gestured him inside, but he kept the door open. "What can I do for you?"

O'Connor walked to the wall of windows and took a deep breath. "Dalton is the president of the school board."

"And I'm the team's coach."

"He's threatening to dismiss you."

"On what grounds? The team's record? Check the paper's sports column. We're slated to head toward state this year." *Easy. Losing your temper won't solve a thing.* "My record for the past four years is spotless, Mr. O'Connor. I'll give you the same answer I gave Dalton. I have never bowed, nor will I ever bow, to threats. We have a great team this year with great kids playing positions in which they excel. Chris will continue to play receiver, and Walt will continue as quarterback."

"Your refusal means things could get ugly."

"Then let them. I'd rather be fired than cower to the school board's unreasonable demands."

"I like you, Coach. The kids respect you on and off the field, but my hands are tied."

"But mine aren't, and my conscience is clear." Miles reached out to shake O'Connor's hand to prove his point. A fire truck raced by, grabbing both men's attention.

"I'm not taking sides, just relaying what's going on."

"Then neither of us has anything to worry about." Miles stared into the lined face of the man who was nearing retirement. This conversation and what he'd learned about Paige called for a chocolate milkshake to ease his ulcer. Probably two.

# CHAPTER 28

I GLANCE AT my watch and pick up the phone. Mikaela needs a little pressure. I want her in Oklahoma City for more reasons than I care to list. Leaning back in my chair, I punch in her number.

"Good afternoon, Mikaela. And how are things in Split Creek?"

"Cut the pleasantries. What do you want?"

"Hostile, aren't we?"

"Unless you have something to say, I'm hanging up."

"Oh, I have plenty to say, but for the moment you might want to check out the fire on Lower Bottom Road. I hear a friend of yours is losing his barn. How regretful, especially with his horses."

I end the call. This should cause her to take notice of me.

# CHAPTER 29

MILES STOOD BACK and watched his barn turn into ashes. Not a thing he could do about it, but it made him sick. He'd built the barn himself for his horses and equipment. He even had an office there. Thankfully no one had been hurt and the firefighters had gotten his horses and some of the tack out before the blaze took over. A neighbor came by and transported the horses to his own farm, and another came by and offered his condolences. Most likely the heat had ignited dry grass, and it spread to the barn, but the firefighters had extinguished the fire before it spread to his house.

What a way to end the week. The last thing he wanted to do tonight was focus on a football game.

"Six, five, four, three, two, one." The scoreboard buzzed like an agitated swarm of bees.

"Bobcats 20, Pirates 6."

Miles trotted across the field to shake hands with the Pirates' coaches, then walked back to the sidelines to watch his boys celebrate the win. They were high-fiving and hollering about the "ginormous" plays. He crossed his arms over his chest as though someone might notice how he'd puffed up like a Thanksgiving turkey. What a high. His players had worked hard tonight, and their commitment had paid off. God had blessed them—

overlooking the rivalry, the occasional cursing, and how their coach often had to bite his tongue to keep from losing his temper. Miles scanned the defeated team—the slumped shoulders and grim looks. Poor kids. Why couldn't both teams share in the sweetness of victory? He understood the meaning of healthy competition and the life lessons learned from winning and losing, but he wished more for both sides.

And for a moment, he forgot about the fire.

Miles might have the community's support, but he didn't have the school board's—well, not the president's anyway. The other members didn't seem to have a problem with good old Prez Ty dictating how they should vote, but they might find the guts to do otherwise after tonight's game. How many coaches had been fired for having a winning season? The irony of it all. Ty Dalton emerged from the crowd and stood next to a French horn player who finished up the last notes of the fight song. Obviously Dalton itched to get to his son, which wasn't a bad thing. But if Dalton would keep his nose out of his son's business, Chris and Walt might have a chance at friendship.

Miles caught a glimpse of Paige leaning against the wall of the concession stand. She raised both hands to the dark sky in response to the win and limped his way.

He'd have preferred a kiss, but extra sprinkles on the doughnuts and an extra marshmallow in the hot chocolate would have to do. *Great. I've turned into a woman, using chocolate to pacify my wounded heart.*

"Congratulations." Once Paige walked closer, the field lights shone like diamond chips in her eyes. "The team looked terrific, thanks to a dedicated coach." She pointed to the binoculars dangling from her wrist. "I actually saw Chris and Walt talking to each other. Made me cry."

"They'll be all right. Hurt feelings are always hard to deal with, especially when you're young." He gazed at his boys. "I feel like I'm a daddy to each one of those boys. Hey, I appreciate the call about the fire."

Pain etched her face. "I'm so sorry. I know how much you take pride in your home."

She seemed to grieve as much as he did. "What we need is rain to stop the fires. At least no one was hurt. Guess I'd better do the coach thing before one of them gets the bright idea of carrying me around on their shoulders like they did a few weeks ago."

"You looked good, even if you don't like the accolades."

"Hey, Coach," a voice shouted from across the field.

"Better get over there," Paige said. "I'll meet you at Denim's Kitchen once I'm finished at the field house."

Miles sensed his emotions heading into overdrive. He jogged toward his boys, his team, his pride and joy, no matter how clichéd it sounded. A whirring sound caught his attention. Glancing up into a star-studded sky, he caught sight of the Channel 6 helicopter flying low. As it descended, it occurred to him that the game tonight capturing Oklahoma City TV news might slam a big dent in Ty Dalton's plans to have him fired.

A few moments later, the helicopter landed on the field. Miles straightened his shoulders and marched toward three men—the sports newscaster for Channel 6, a cameraman, and a third man. Miles startled. It was Daniel Keary. Smart man to mix a high school football victory with his campaign for governor.

Keary stooped as he exited the copter wearing a smile wide enough to break into a chorus of "Oklahoma."

"Welcome to Split Creek football." Miles reached out to grasp the muscular man's hand. The camera rolled. *Sweet.*

"Congratulations on your win tonight."

"Thanks. The boys played a great game."

"A dynamic coach is always behind a winning team. Do you mind if I offer my congratulations to the boys?" Keary's relaxed smile confirmed the candidate's charisma.

"I'd be honored. I was just heading their way."

"Can't resist an opportunity to encourage young people. We were flying around reporting on the area games when we heard you'd won. Sure you don't mind?"

"Not at all. Welcome it."

By this time, the boys were enthralled at the sight of the Channel 6 copter. They crowded around the sports anchor while the cameraman videotaped the celebration. None of the players tossed Keary a second look. On Monday, Miles planned to address his students' lack of awareness of current state affairs.

"We have a special guest with us tonight," the anchor said. "Daniel Keary, who is way ahead in the polls for governor in November's election, has asked to join us in congratulating a win for the Bobcats of Split Creek High School." The camera flashed to Keary shaking hands with the football team.

Keary waved away the cheers. "Please, guys. This is your night. I just want to congratulate you on a job well done. I believe in youth. You are our future, and I want to encourage you in any way I can to see our state and nation grow. You are tonight's champs and tomorrow's leaders." Keary gave another smile, a slow lingering one that evoked humility and sincerity.

*Spoken like a true politician, but a good one.*

"Thanks for the computers," one of the boys said.

*He just got three points added to his six weeks' grade.*

"You're welcome. I'm always ready to help." Keary stepped away and mingled with fans while Miles complimented the team on working together for a win.

Walking back to the field house several minutes later, he looked for Paige by the concession stand. Keary hovered over her. He adjusted his jacket and lifted his chin. Whatever had transpired between them must have upset Paige, because she stiffened and made her way toward the parking lot. She'd indicated her dislike for him on more than one occasion, but rudeness wasn't a part of her character. Did Paige's aversion go deeper? He wished he knew more about her. Right now the green side of envy had taken over.

Saturday morning Paige woke at three thirty, wide-eyed and unable to go back to sleep. Her mind refused to unravel. In the darkness with the hum of the ceiling fan and the steady click of the living room mantel clock, thoughts of Keary and how to beat him at his own game pounded in her brain. He'd displayed the audacity of an agitated rattler by approaching her after the game last night—and after the call about Miles's fire.

"I could use you in Oklahoma City." He had leaned into her, forcing her to take a step back.

"Head back to your kennel, Keary. There's nothing I can do to challenge your illustrious career. You have this election wrapped up like a Christmas package."

"You and I both know you're on the CIA payroll again. That's a bit dangerous, don't you think?"

"Not at all. You'll be the first one arrested if anything happens to my parents. The fire today proved you're out of control."

Paige studied his every move, when he breathed and how he emphasized his words. If evil was the absence of good, then Daniel Keary could be the poster child for corruption in politics.

"It's all about control. I heard about your trip to Nairobi. Too bad about your friend's cancer."

"The good seem to die young."

"Touché. You know, my wife and I are planning another adoption. Possibly another boy. What do you think about that?"

While fear for Nathan enveloped her, she kept her emotions in check. "Your wife must not know you very well."

"I admit you were better." He smirked.

"She'll learn the truth."

"Today was a little warning about what will happen if you try anything to jeopardize this election. Don't underestimate me. When I want something, I get it."

"Heard it all before." Paige shifted her shoulder purse and whirled around to her car, leaving Keary standing in the glory of his own shadow.

In the darkness, Paige replayed the conversation.

It all fit into a vicious puzzle; she simply had to find the right pieces—or rather the right witnesses. And it had to be completed before Keary's leeches found Nathan. No point in telling herself he didn't know something about the boy, but how much?

She was certain now that Ty Dalton was the mole. He'd worked for WorldMarc on the first crew that entered Angola right after the oil deal. According to Palmer, Dalton quit fourteen months later. Odd for a man who'd worked offshore oil for twenty-two years. He could have decided to make a living at home to be near Chris and Ginny, or he could have seen something that sickened him. Would he have told his wife? Could he have been a part of the murders? Paige knew Ginny Dalton well enough that she thought she could dig a little deeper.

With last night's confrontation with Keary fresh and biting, questions became prayers and prayers became journeys down a road filled with regrets. As much as Paige hesitated to relive those nightmares, she'd go there again if it led to Keary's capture. In fact, she'd park on each moment until he was arrested.

# CHAPTER 30

IN THE EARLY HOURS before dawn, I pace my study, searching for answers to the problems robbing me of sleep. The governorship has been so ingrained in me that the thought of losing has never crept in. I have my aspirations in Washington; that has never changed. My plans are flawless, and I know how to get the job done. What complicates my life now is Ty Dalton, Mikaela Olsson, and Joel Zuriel.

At the moment, Zuriel is at the top of the list. I've given him power to handle other matters while I've been busy launching my career. And now I learn he placed Mikaela in the same town as Ty Dalton. Zuriel's defense echoes louder with each passing moment.

"It was a way to keep an eye on both of them," Zuriel told me.

"You think? What about the two comparing notes?"

"Impossible. Dalton's scared, and he has the personality of a roach."

"I'm tired of your botched jobs."

Zuriel stood from the chair in my office. "You owe me." He headed to the door. "I have things to do, and listening to your whining is not one of them."

I can't kill Mikaela or Ty Dalton. The CIA would connect those dots. But earlier today I made arrangements with Stevens to eliminate Zuriel. Two million dollars' worth of diamonds are missing, and I know where they went. And everything is in motion for him to take the fall for the oil deals.

# CHAPTER 31

PAIGE LIMPED to the outside book drop to gather up returned items. With school in session, the box was stuffed, mostly with books from homeschool moms. What normally took her five minutes and one trip had stretched to twenty minutes and three trips. She looked across the street, expecting to see Keary or Stevens or Dalton spying on her. A crazy thought. Or was it?

Miss Eleanor and Mr. Shafer waved from an old church pew sitting in front of Mr. Shafer's antique store. Those two sure were cozy to be arguing all the time. Paige waved, and Mr. Shafer rose from the bench with Miss Eleanor. As they made their way across the street to her, she thanked God for such good friends. No matter how low she felt—or how lonely—they perked up her day. A twinge of remorse twisted in the pit of her stomach. Oh, to see Mom and Dad one more time. But that might never happen, and she'd find what she needed from the dear seasoned citizens of Split Creek.

"Good afternoon," Paige called. "Are you coming to see this crip hobble around the library?"

"I am. Don't know about this old man beside me," Miss Eleanor said. She must have tried a new hair color, because her tight curls were a little pink, or maybe it was the orange lipstick and grass-green eye shadow that gave her a unique look. Voleta must have been experimenting again. "My next appointment is not for another hour."

"And I locked the door at the store." Mr. Shafer rubbed his hands together. "Where do we start?"

Paige confirmed her love for them. "You two are just the dearest folks in town. I'm nearly caught up, but you could help me bring in the rest of these books."

The couple gathered armfuls and brought the last mound of media items inside.

"I heard that one of our school board members was having an affair." Miss Eleanor leaned against the open door of the library. "But I didn't hear who."

"*An Affair to Remember*?" Mr. Shafer asked. "I saw that movie. Pat Boone and Ann Margaret."

"Turn up your hearing aid," Miss Eleanor fairly shouted. "That was Cary Grant and Deborah Kerr."

"What car? I'm so tired of those whippersnappers racing up and down the street."

Miss Eleanor tossed Paige an exasperated look. She hid her amusement.

"As soon as I check these in, I'll be taking off the rest of the afternoon to have my cast removed," Paige said.

"You're not going by yourself, are you?" Miss Eleanor planted her hands on her hips.

"No. Driving with my left foot is not hard, but Miles is taking me. His assistant is handling practice today."

"One of us could have driven you." Mr. Shafer furrowed his wiry brows, intensifying the lines in his leathered face. "No point in Miles taking off from practice, unless you can talk some sense into his thick head."

"Miles? What about?"

"Why he's not starting Chris Dalton as quarterback. That boy is a senior, and his daddy's on the school board."

Paige swallowed a harsh retort. "From what I've seen, Chris does a fine job as receiver."

Mr. Shafer leaned in closer. "But he wants to play first-string quarterback like his daddy did. Chris is more mature than a sophomore kid. He's built like his daddy and has the same skills. Sweet girl, someone needs to set him straight about Split Creek tradition."

"I don't believe in pleasing daddies."

Miss Eleanor gasped.

"Look, I don't mean to be disrespectful, but I

value Miles's judgment on and off the field."

"But he wasn't born here." Mr. Shafer lifted his whiskery chin. "You have to know how folks expect things done."

Paige sensed the heat rising up her neck. "But you sang his praises when the team had good seasons. They've just gotten started and only lost one scrimmage." She shoved down the other remarks threatening to bubble up her throat. "Help me understand. Is the problem about Chris's desire to play quarterback or Miles's standing up to his principles? Of course, the boy playing quarterback is Chickasaw."

"Now, Paige, you've let this hurt foot of yours get you all riled up," Miss Eleanor said. "We'll talk about something else."

"Yes, maybe we should. I don't want to say anything I'd regret to two people I love."

"Whew." Mr. Shafer smiled. "Leave it up to the school board to make those decisions. That's what those folks are there for."

Paige glanced up at the glittering chandelier as she put Miles's situation into perspective. No wonder he downed chocolate shakes to ease his ulcer. Paige blinked. Immediately she was transported back to the heat and the blinding sun that sparkled in her eyes. Her body refused to move, and all she could hear was the muffled voice of a man. *"Too bad she had to die. She's much too pretty to waste."*

★ ★ ★

For the present, Miles could shove aside what he knew about Paige. He could drive her to Pradmore, tease her about having two feet again, and continue this surface-type, superficial relationship. He'd gone over a hundred different scenarios as to why she lived in Split Creek under an assumed name, but none of them made sense. Her perfume wafted around the truck, making him more angry than appreciative of the woman beside him—the woman he loved, the woman with no name.

"You're quiet," she said after several minutes. "Everything okay?"

*Not really.* "Just have a few things on my mind."

"Do you need to talk about them?"

Her question nearly brought him to the boiling point. "I'll talk about mine when you talk about yours."

"What do you mean?"

"Problems and secrets. Everybody's got them." He was going to alienate her at this rate. "I'm sorry. Two of my players are flunking. Ty Dalton's becoming a real pain. Chris and Walt aren't getting along any better, and the fire marshal suspects arson."

She looked at him oddly. "Arson? Who would do such a thing?"

"There's a suspect."

"Is there evidence enough to make an arrest?"

He studied her face for a moment. Nothing about

her revealed deceit. This really wasn't about Ty Dalton possibly burning his barn. He hated the thought of a man being that upset about high school football to even consider it. Miles pulled off to the side of the road, his emotions spinning like a kid's top. "Paige, do you have any feelings for me?"

"Is that the real reason you're bummed out?" She glanced behind them as a car sped by, full tilt on the horn. "Your hormones nearly got us killed."

"Cut the sarcasm and answer my question . . . please."

"We're . . . well, obviously we're good friends." She tugged on her gold sweater, then rubbed her palms. "There are things about me that you don't know. Things that would cause you to despise me. Things that are bad."

"Just answer my question; don't give me a list of all of the reasons we can't be together."

She kept her attention on the stone shoulder of the road.

"Look at me, please."

When she slowly lifted her light brown eyes to him, he knew without a doubt that she cared. But he had to hear her say it.

"If it were were possible, I'd tell you those words for the rest of my life," she said, barely above a whisper.

Silence seemed to echo about the cab. "So it's not the lack of love; it's the lack of trust. Odd. I thought the two went together." He put the truck into drive and slowly drove back onto the road. "I would like to protect you for the rest of my life."

"And I would like the same—if it were possible."

Miles had his answer. Who or what had happened to keep her from him?

# CHAPTER 32

ON WEDNESDAY MORNING, with the stress of Friday's game nipping at his heels, Miles's ulcer burned like someone had lit a match to his stomach. To make matters worse, he'd developed a fresh case of hives in places he couldn't scratch. If the Bobcats won this week, they'd have three wins. This year's team was the best he'd ever coached, and he believed they could tackle the whole state. In the meantime, his insides reacted as though he'd drunk the water in Mexico—laced with jalapeños.

Ty Dalton hadn't given up on having Miles removed from his coaching position, but his argument was fast losing credibility. And Miles hadn't found any answers as to why Paige wasn't Paige. Asking her about her false identity meant confessing to how he'd obtained her Social Security number. So, who was deceiving whom—or was it who was deceiving who? English had never been his shining apple. He continued to wrestle with what to do about Paige, knowing he had to find out the truth, no matter what the cost.

And then there was the growing suspicion of the fire marshal and the sheriff that his barn had been deliberately set on fire. Ty Dalton's name had been mentioned more than once, but Ginny claimed she was with him at the garage that night.

Chris lagged behind after third-period history. He shifted from one foot to the other, and perspiration formed on his forehead. "Can we talk, Coach?"

"Sure. What's the problem? You sick?"

The teen closed the door. He moistened his lips—twice. "I . . . I wanted to tell you what I told my dad last night. It's kinda important, and I . . . I think you should know."

Miles sat on the corner of his desk. Did this mean the revenge against Walt was over? "Okay. You have my full attention. This is my free planning period."

"I don't want to play college ball. I've thought about it a lot and, like, I can't do it. My back hurts all the time, and four more years of football isn't what I want to do."

"Have you been to a doctor?"

"Remember when I was in that car wreck a year ago? Well, I totaled my car and walked away from it, but my back didn't heal right."

"I'm sorry, Chris. I had no idea."

He shrugged. "Yeah, I fake it when I'm on the field. But my dad is real mad."

"I think I understand." Miles saw the torment in Chris's eyes, the pain inflicted by the scars of time. "Chris, he loves you. Wants the best. And telling your dad about not wanting to play college ball took a lot of guts."

"He read me the riot act: letting everyone down . . . passing up the golden ticket . . . not fulfilling my potential."

"You'll be good at whatever you set your mind to. I'll pray your dad supports you."

"Thanks. He and Mom haven't been . . ." Chris paused. "Never mind."

Miles read into what Chris didn't say about his parents. The gossip in the teacher's lounge had a steady hum. Ty Dalton had gotten into an argument with his wife after last week's game, and Sheriff George's deputy had to settle him down. "Life doesn't always make sense, but it does work out, even when we're confused."

Chris took in a deep breath. "I'm sorry for the fights and junk I caused. All about a game I didn't really want to play and a position I stunk at. I know my dad can be cold, and it probably isn't over with." He shrugged. "Still don't care for Walt. Just being honest."

"Being honest can be tough—either with your parents or admitting you don't get along with another player. Walt's a good kid. If you'd give him a chance, you two could be friends." Miles shook Chris's hand. "You're a good man."

"Thanks. No one's ever called me a man before."

"Glad I'm the first. Can you handle the pain of finishing out the season?"

"Sure. I want to. I wouldn't quit in the middle of the season, no matter how I felt."

"I'm counting on you to let me know when you're hurting."

"I'll think about it."

Miles understood male pride. He'd have to keep an eye on Chris. Miles wished he had the same confidence in every aspect of his life as he did with coaching. His focus twisted and turned from the problem with Paige, to his school responsibilities, to the school board, and to trying to figure out what in the world God was up to with all of it.


Paige tapped her credit card on the counter to let the cashier know she was ready to pay for her gas. She despised technology that didn't work—like a gas pump with a broken credit card scanner. Having to come inside the gas station to pay was an irritation she didn't need right now. As if irritation ever arrived at a good time.

"I see you got rid of that cast." A bald man wearing a dirty T-shirt stood beside her.

She recognized the self-proclaimed coach and referee who sat beside her and Voleta at the games. She glanced down at her foot stuffed into a tennis shoe. "Thought I was going to have to wear it forever."

He pointed to the cigarettes behind the clerk. "Pack of Marlboros, please." Then he glanced back at Paige. "I understand. The kid and your friend were real upset."

"Well, it's all over with, and my ankle is nearly good as new."

"Glad to hear it. Say, your coach friend sure is doing a fine job with our boys this year."

"Thanks. I'll be sure to tell him." And this was from the guy who trashed every coach and player on the field.

He smiled his good-bye and waddled off to his truck, carrying a twelve-pack of Bud Light in one hand and a gallon of milk and a banana in the other. At least he was balanced on the food pyramid.

She laughed despite the mess of her life. Paige slipped back into her car and headed toward Oklahoma City, where Palmer had arranged a car rental. It had been a long time since she'd worked in disguise, and she was looking forward to Mikaela Olsson stepping into a role. This was a good time to call Nathan. She soon had him on the line.

"Hi, sweetie, this is Paige."

"Hi. Miss Paige, when are you coming to see me?" The despair in the boy's voice shook her to the core.

"Soon. I'm working very hard to finish this job."

"Are we going to live with Mr. Raif and Miss Anissa?"

"No, someplace different. Someplace all our own. Are you still having bad dreams?"

Silence.

"Nathan?"

"Yes, ma'am. I miss my mommy."

*And I so much want to be there for you.* "Is the special lady talking to you about those dreams?"

"Yes, ma'am, but I'd rather talk to you."

Paige reveled in the fact that Nathan had formed an attachment to her so quickly, but danger often did that. "Are some of the dreams about our fast car ride?"

"Yes, ma'am." He started to cry. "I want to see you."

Paige's heart sank to the ground. "Let me see if I can arrange it."

After talking to Anissa, Paige learned that Nathan's counselor had suggested an antidepressant to help him, along with the counseling. Paige didn't want to medicate her baby, but he'd been through so much and the counseling alone was not ending his nightmares. She must believe that God would soon end her precious son's nighttime trauma.

Once at the Will Rogers airport in Oklahoma City, she picked up a rental car—a silver BMW convertible—and drove to a hotel downtown, where she checked in under an assumed name. Inside the trunk of the rental were a change of clothes and a few other items she'd need for tonight. She read through Zuriel's dossier one more time to make sure she had it all memorized: his vulnerabilities and the characteristics she would use to gather information. He liked women with reddish hair and green eyes. That she could do. And tonight she'd wear real big-girl shoes and not one tennis shoe or a pink croc.

Zuriel's choice of entertainment on Wednesday nights was a piano bar on the third floor of the hotel. Paige imagined his type would much prefer some of the hot spots that she once frequented in other parts of the world, everywhere from New York to Singapore.

After a quick shower, she removed her light brown colored contacts and replaced them with emerald green ones. The wig—auburn with lighter highlights—lay about her shoulders in curls. Layers of eye shadow, three coats of black-black mascara, and a deep shade of copper lipstick with lots of gloss, and she was ready to slip into her dress—short, black, and snug.

Paige took a head-to-toe look at herself in the full-length mirror. Her ankle still felt a little weak. Good thing her work tonight would be sitting and not on her feet. She laughed at the ridiculous image before her, one guaranteed to entice and lure Joel Zuriel into spilling his guts in anticipation of personal entertainment. After inserting a small bug into her bra, she wrapped her fingers around her room key and slipped it into a tiny black bag that held nothing but a twenty-dollar bill. Too much was riding on this clandestine event to risk carrying anything personal.

*God, I've never done anything like this with You. I feel a little strange—this walking the thin line between right and wrong.*

Her cell phone rang.

"He's there," the woman said.

Paige pasted on a charming smile and adopted the walk of a woman on the prowl before heading to the elevator. As soon as she stepped onto the third floor, her senses went into overdrive—operative mode. Ten people gathered around tables circling the piano, and two sat at the bar. A suited man played "Hey Jude," but it didn't sound like the original Beatles' version. At a table in the middle of all that was happening, which wasn't much, sat a couple—Joel Zuriel and a blonde. Paige strolled by his table on her way to the bar and bumped his shoulder.

"Excuse me." She moistened her lips and smiled.

She slid onto a padded barstool that faced the blonde's back and crossed her legs. Two seconds later the Latino bartender, a young man who was too good-looking for his own good, asked for her order. "Grey Goose, please, and on the rocks."

The piano player finished his tune and began a Whitney Houston song—"I Will Always Love You." Paige turned slightly to view the piano and watch Zuriel from her peripheral vision. Sensing his attention, she touched her hair and briefly glanced his way. Ten minutes later, Zuriel made his way to the bar beside her. He'd loosened the top button of his white silk shirt, and his gray tailored suit had a West Coast cut. He placed his order and waited.

"Are you alone?" he whispered.

"Depends."

"Working?"

"On what?" She cast her gaze toward the piano. "I'm relaxing."

"Need some company?"

Paige nodded toward the blonde's back. "You're occupied."

"Things can change."

She shrugged. "That's up to you."

"What's your name?"

"Eva."

"I'm Joel."

Zuriel gathered up his drinks and walked back to his table. He picked up the blonde's hand and kissed her cheek. Tilting his head, he said something and offered a sad smile. A moment later, the two left. Paige lifted her drink from the bar and headed to the entrance.

"Leaving us so early?" the bartender asked.

"I'll be right back. Do I need to pay you now?"

"Are you staying here?"

He was interested too. "Yes."

"No problem."

Paige gave him her best smile before swishing into the hallway and the lady's room. Inside she dumped her drink and filled the glass with water. Then she resumed her perch on the barstool and flirted with the bartender.

In less than twenty minutes, Zuriel touched her shoulder. She inhaled his cologne, rich and woodsy. If she *had* been a woman on the prowl, he'd have definitely captured her attention. But she knew nothing but oil and diamonds ran through his veins.

"How about a table?" he asked.

Paige swung around to face him and pasted on her best bring-it-on look. "Sure. All I want to do tonight is talk. Okay?" She arched her back. "Been a rough week, and I still have a full day tomorrow."

He lifted his palms and took a step backward. "Fine with me. I've had a hard week too."

Where had she heard that voice? "Maybe we can help each other relax."

"I'm sure of it."

At a remote table, Zuriel sat across from her and began with the right lead-in. "Tell me why your week's been rough."

"I'm a sales rep for a diamond company, and I haven't met my quota." Paige crossed her legs and noted that his gaze traveled from her toes to her thighs. *Good.*

He frowned. "I'm sorry."

"I thought with the holidays coming up, I'd reach a bonus, but . . ." She took a sip of her wannabe Grey Goose and leaned toward him. A memory from an obscure part of her mind struggled to surface. "Never mind. I always make my quota. And I will again."

"Sounds like you have the stuff that makes for a successful businesswoman. You certainly have what I'd look for."

She read straight through his concerned tone. "Thanks. I'd like to think so. What keeps you afloat?"

His eyes sparkled, even in the dim lighting. "I'm in oil. VP for WorldMarc."

"I've heard of them. They're about to go public, right?" She kept her voice husky and low.

"Right, and we're going to make a ton of money."

*At the expense of whose blood?* "So what's your role there?"

He picked up his glass and swirled his drink. She noted the showy diamond ring on his right hand. A snapshot of *something* flickered again in her mind. The ring . . . where had she seen that ring and heard his voice?

"Oh, my." She gasped and leaned forward. "Before you tell me about your job, can I see your ring?"

He held out his hand. Paige touched his ring but found herself repulsed at the thought of touching his skin. *Come on, girl. You can do this.*

"Yes, you *are* in the diamond business." Zuriel chuckled. "I have a few investments in them myself."

"Really." Paige widened her eyes and deliberately touched her tongue to her lower lip. *Buy it, baby.*

"Overseas. Africa, actually." He took a sip of his drink. "You have beautiful hair and eyes."

"Thanks. So you've traveled to Africa?" She brushed across his ring finger, knowing that hand had sent far too many people to their deaths, and rested in the thought that his arrogance would send him to prison, where pretty boys were the target.

"Yes. Strictly business. Oil and diamonds."

"I'm impressed." She pulled her hand back into her lap.

"You should be."

*Don't make me sick.*

"WorldMarc would be nothing without my contacts. The CEO consults me before he makes any moves. I actually put them in a position to go public with my latest oil deal in Angola."

Paige lifted her chest. "So, are you an attorney too?"

He offered a half smile and leaned in to her. "No, but I'm tight with Daniel Keary."

"The guy who's running for governor?"

"The same."

She lifted the corners of her mouth. "You must be indispensable to your company."

"I'd like to think so." Seduction oozed from every muscle bent in her direction.

She propped her hand under her chin. "Tell me more. I like what I see—a man who knows how to run the show."

"Trust me. I know how to make it all happen."

Paige already knew his expertise. "I could use some tips, especially when it comes to diamonds. I'm not even wearing any." She touched her neck with her left hand, then slid it across the table.

"That could change." He lightly stroked her fingers. Paige slowly withdrew her hand and reached for her drink.

"I'm interested." She met his gaze. "Which came first, the oil or the diamonds?"

"Oil. I invested in the diamonds while scouting out a drilling sight."

"I bet nothing gets in your way." She lured him in with every syllable.

"Not when I want something."

She laughed softly. "Tell me how you became acquainted with Daniel Keary."

"He approached me about brokering a deal in Angola. We traveled over there long before the deal was finalized. You know, paved the way, so to speak."

*You murderer. I know how Keary operates.*

"Then we worked together about a year ago on another site."

"I hope he remembers you when he's elected,"

she said. "This state owes you, since you initiated the oil deal."

"Yeah, Keary and I made the maiden voyage." Zuriel nodded. "And he will take care of me. Has no choice. Say, enough of this. Why don't you and I—"

Paige managed a pout. "No, Joel. I . . . I broke up with a guy a couple of weeks ago, and I don't want to get involved again so soon."

"Are you sure? Maybe all you need is a change."

She sighed. "I'm tempted. I haven't met a nice guy with a head on his shoulders for a long time. But I . . . don't think so."

"I understand. A woman as attractive as you must run into a lot of jerks. Can I see you again? tomorrow?"

She reached across the table and brushed her finger across the top of his hand. "I'm staying here at the hotel."

"Sounds like a plan."

"Great. I need to head to my room. Still got to meet my quota." She opened her purse for the twenty.

"I've got it," he said.

"I don't like to owe people." *And you are at the bottom of the list.*

"Consider it a beginning."

She forced a promising gaze into her eyes. "I already do."

Paige stood and made her way to the elevators. She had what she'd come for and had no intentions of sticking around. Inside her room, she changed clothes and resumed the identity of Paige Rogers, librarian. Palmer would be pleased with what she'd extracted from Zuriel. Within the hour, she was en route to the airport to return the car and drive back to Split Creek. And as always, she wrestled with tonight and how God viewed it. Uncertainty slammed against her heart. How could God be a part of deceit? Could she continue to take Him with her on missions like this? Of course He'd be there. What was she thinking?

*God, I need answers. First I'm convinced this is what You want me to do; then I feel like I've let You down.*

A thought rooted in her mind: she was a soldier. And just as in the military, some things needed to be done to protect the masses. People had been murdered. More were in line if she didn't succeed. She had the skills and contacts others lacked in this kind of mission while . . .

Paige gasped. The ring . . . the voice in her flashback. It was Zuriel. He'd been with Keary after the bombing when she'd been blown from the building.

Paige exited the interstate a few miles from Split Creek. It had been a long night, and even though her mind shuffled through the cards of all that surrounded Keary, she needed sleep. Her cell phone rang. *Who could be calling at this hour?*

"Good morning, Mikaela. Hope I didn't wake you."

*What a nightcap.* "Actually you did. What do you want, Keary?"

"I have sad news to report. Your friend Bobbie just died."

"And you called to tell me that?"

"She had help—you know, with the suffering and all."

Paige's car veered right and onto the shoulder. She gripped the steering wheel and swung it back onto the road. Not another vehicle was in sight. Only blackness.

"You killed Bobbie?" Loathing caused her to shiver, and she struggled to keep what little composure still remained.

"Why would you think that? I'm simply reporting what I was told."

"Soon your bag of tricks is going to explode in your face. And you're going to pay for all you've done." She bit her tongue to keep from saying more.

An oncoming car approached from a distance, its headlights growing brighter as it drew closer. Just like the truth. She ended the call and stretched her back. A few minutes later, she confirmed Bobbie's death with the hospital in Nairobi. Bobbie had lived longer than anyone had expected, but Paige still wasn't ready for the news. With tears streaming down her face, she prayed for wisdom in what lay ahead. The more she thought about her friend, the more she realized the unlikelihood that Keary had had a hand in Bobbie's death. He was no doubt fishing for a reaction from Paige. And she'd given him one that clearly showed her anger.

This madness needed to end soon.

# CHAPTER 33

THURSDAY MORNING while driving to the library, Paige called Palmer. She needed to break the news of Bobbie's death to Nathan, and not over the phone.

"Don't even think about it," Palmer said. "It's too risky. If Keary had someone follow you in Nairobi, you can be sure it will happen again."

"I managed fine while en route to see Zuriel, but I was extremely careful." Frustration oozed from Paige's voice—even if Palmer was right. "I can't bear for Nathan to learn about his mother from anyone but me."

"Didn't he tell her good-bye in Nairobi?" When she didn't respond, he cleared his throat. "In his mind, she's already gone."

And Paige had to admit, Palmer spoke the truth.

When Split Creek High won Friday night's game, bringing its record to 3 and 0, Miles told Paige that he deserved a trip to the Gilcrease Museum in Tulsa.

By midafternoon Saturday, Paige had gained a rich appreciation for the culture and beginnings of Oklahoma. Someday she'd bring Nathan here and let him explore all the learning possibilities for kids. She observed Miles as he stopped to admire another one of Frederic Remington's bronze sculptures. This one sported a bronco and its rider, one of many on display at the Gilcrease. So intent was his study that she doubted he sensed her scrutiny. His grasp of Oklahoma history spoke of more than textbook interest, but his appreciation of the arts and biographical knowledge about the artists surprised her. He had a lot to offer the kids at Split Creek: his experience in the business world, his faith, and his commitment to expanding their educational perspective.

Paige tapped her finger to her lips and studied a painting near where Miles stood, but that gesture failed to suppress her growing attraction for the man before her. He peered more closely at the horse. The depth of his wide-set eyes revealed his intellect. If she wasn't careful, he'd catch on to her soon. What a relief to learn from Palmer that Miles had no connection to Keary. And after her visit with Zuriel and the recorded conversation, along with realizing the source of her flashbacks, the company could do a little more digging.

Miles moved to the other side of the sculpture, his back to her. Those massive shoulder muscles would give any man doubts about crossing him.

Did he know martial arts? A curiosity on her part. Maybe she'd ask.

He tossed a glance over his shoulder. "Are you checking me out?"

"For what?"

"Aw, I think you are."

When he turned to face her, she feigned interest in the sculpture. "You misinterpreted my admiration for this sculpture for something else way out in left field."

"Right."

They'd talked about this trip on previous occasions but had never scheduled a time. She'd given her consent, as long as he understood it wouldn't be a date. But her involuntary actions were making it look like one. "So, you're a Remington fan."

"Muzzleloaders, ammunition, and knives."

"A devout fan."

"I like Remington's bronzes and his paintings. Over the years I've developed a respect for the West's history and how Remington captures it."

"This is an incredible museum," she said. "Thanks for asking me along."

"I agree. Before we leave, I'd like to stop at the gift shop."

"You?"

"Watch it, lady. A man does have to get in touch with his feminine side at least once in his life. I'm looking for Remington's *Mountain Man* or *Outlaw*."

The two walked toward the gift shop. Miles took her hand, and she allowed it. *I wonder what he'd think of me if he knew about Wednesday night.* Another reason why this so-called relationship would have a bad ending.

"I just learned something new about you."

"Wish I could say the same thing, Miss Mysterious."

"I'm the cowgirl from west of nowhere."

"I understand. But I'm trying to get to know you better. What brought you to Split Creek? Bigger cities have libraries with greater career potential."

"I like small towns—the close-knit community and the way everyone looks out for each other."

"Some say that can be a deterrent when the whole town knows your business."

She touched his shoulder with her finger. "Then you and I have to make sure no one has anything to talk about. Besides, you have enough going against you right now with Ty Dalton's attempts to boot you out of a job."

"Oh, he isn't going to convince the school board to get rid of me. One of the other members said no one was paying attention to his ravings. The winning season pours ice water all over Dalton's plans. But we were talking about you."

"That's a dead topic."

They walked into the gift shop. "You know, relationships are built on time and trust," he said. "I understand caution and even skepticism. But I'm asking you to give me a chance."

"I wish I could be the woman you want . . . need." Paige despised keeping a constant guard on her emotions. *Lord, will things ever change?*

"Can I help you?" asked a woman behind the counter.

*Probably not.*

Miles watched Chris hesitate in reaching up for a pass from Walt. The ball slipped through his fingers. A safety nailed Chris, and a linebacker smacked into Walt. Third time in the afternoon's practice. Chris's head wasn't in the game—yesterday or today. His back might be giving him problems, which meant he needed to be off the field. Chris stood and shook off the tackle, then headed back for the next play. He massaged his neck. Report cards weren't due, and Chris and his girlfriend were inseparable. What was bothering him?

Miles had a stake in Chris's life, and he'd been praying for all of his players since before the season had opened. The blessings he asked for them had nothing to do with how they performed on the football field but how they played life.

Once the boys left the locker room after practice, Miles found Chris standing at the door of his office. His stooped shoulders and hands stuffed into his jean pockets said something more than a couple of bad practices was bothering him.

Miles unlocked his office door and gestured inside. "Have a seat."

Chris pulled the single chair away from the desk as though proximity mattered in the conversation. He dropped his duffel bag and backpack on the floor. Rather than comment, Miles propped himself on the corner of his desk, his usual perch.

"Sorry about practice the last two days."

"Why don't you tell me what's wrong? Your back? Grades? Girlfriend?"

"None of those things."

*Must be home.* "Something has you bummed out."

"Not sure I can talk about it."

"Do you want to?" The truth probably settled somewhere in the vicinity of the Daltons' failing marriage, Chris's choice of college, and the barn burning.

Chris's eyes darted about the room. "I haven't told anyone."

"You're safe with me. The only time I'd ever reveal anything a student told me is if that student planned to harm himself or someone else. If you need to get something off your mind, I'm listening."

Chris glanced down at his hands. "It's about my dad and mom."

Miles despised what marital problems did to kids.

"I found out something on Saturday night that

makes me sick." Chris raised his head and blinked once, then again. "He said he'd been working late at the garage, but I hadn't noticed a lot of cars sitting around. When I saw Mom crying, I told her I needed to see one of the guys about football practice. Instead, I went to see Dad. Find out if he could be home more for Mom." Chris shrugged. "But he wasn't there."

"And you're wondering where he was?"

"Oh, I know. One of the guys at school had said his mom works nights at the motel out on the interstate near the casino. She'd seen Dad coming in the back door with some woman."

"That could be nothing more than gossip, or your friend's mother could have been mistaken."

Chris shook his head. "I drove there to see for myself. His car was parked in back, and I waited until he came out . . . with her."

"Did he see you?"

"Yeah. I was real mad. They came out hanging on each other, you know, like they'd had a party or something. They were kissin', and he patted her butt. I got out of my truck and hollered at him, and she ran back inside the motel. Didn't even see her face. I asked him if this was his idea of working late." Chris swiped at a tear.

"I'm sorry."

"He told me what he did was not my business. And he reminded me that my truck could disappear if I didn't watch what I was saying. I handed him the keys. Told him I'd walk home. Dad said I was stupid and gave the keys back to me. Told me to keep my mouth shut." Chris pounded his fist into his hand. "I hate him, Coach."

"No, you don't. Only those people we love have the power to hurt us."

Tears poured from Chris's eyes, and all the blinking couldn't stop the flow. "I didn't tell Mom. Couldn't. Shoot, she probably already knows."

Chris and Miles sat in silence. If and when the kid wanted to say more, the door would be wide open. In the meantime, Miles offered silent support.

"Dad moved out. Probably living with that . . . never mind." Chris stood and faced the glass window to the empty lockers. "Mom's better off without him. I told her that. She wants him to come back. Asked me to pray for him. But I told her I couldn't." He stared into the locker room area. "That's it, Coach. I'll do better at practice. I know all of us have to work together to win."

"I'm more concerned about you. Why don't you stop in to see me every day either during my free period or after practice?"

"Um . . . I can do that." Chris continued to stare out the window.

"Look at me, son, not the lockers."

Chris turned and wiped his wet cheeks with the sleeve of his shirt.

"Don't be ashamed of your tears. When I'm mad

at someone or something, I try to focus on the positive things about them."

"Yeah, like my dad is nothing but scum. But my mom needs me now." Chris reached for the door. "Thanks, Coach, and I may take you up on your offer."

After Chris left, Miles prayed for the Dalton family. Betrayal did a good job of breaking up families, and sometimes those hurt by it never recovered.

# CHAPTER 34

WITH FIVE WEEKS until election day, I'm beating down the campaign trail. That part comes easy. The more people I speak to, the more excitement bursts in my veins. What takes up needless energy is covering up the whole Angolan deal nearly eight years ago. Since the election appears to have all of my attention, the CIA won't take a second look at my getting rid of Zuriel. Stevens has arranged a private plane accident in Angola while Zuriel checks on WorldMarc investments. Neat and clean.

I still have to deal with what Dalton might have learned while working for WorldMarc. Thanks to Stevens, medical records indicate Dalton has type 2 diabetes, and that could play easily into another accident. Having those two out of the way will ease my mind. Mikaela, however, has me frustrated. The company might overlook Zuriel and Dalton, but they'll never close my file if she ends up dead.

Stevens promises to have Nathan Landerson's investigation completed by next week. "You'll be pleased."

"Are you telling me he's my son?" That means more than the election.

Stevens chuckles. "Give me a few more days."

Everything will change with that confirmation. Everything.

# CHAPTER 35

PAIGE PUNCHED in the phone number to Rosa Ngoimgo in South Africa. An operative on the ground there had located her but had not initiated contact. Rosa had been a cautious woman, and Paige had been specific about no one approaching her. The phone rang three times. A woman answered.

"Rosa, this is Mikaela Olsson. Do you remember me?" Paige asked in Angolan Portuguese.

Several seconds passed.

"Rosa?"

"Yes, Mikaela. How did you find me?"

"It took years. I'm working on bringing Daniel Keary to justice."

"He's a murderer."

"And he's been involved in killing more African people. This time for oil."

"Thank you for telling me this."

"I still need your help, Rosa. Your testimony about what happened will put him in prison for the rest of his life."

"He or Casimiro Figuiera would have my family killed."

Paige heard someone in the background ask who she was talking to.

"It is not your concern," Rosa said to the person.

"Is that one of your children?"

"It's Gonsalvo. He's a man now, but he hasn't forgotten what his father told him about Daniel Keary's betrayal."

"Wouldn't he want the man who orchestrated his father's murder to be brought to justice?" Hope rose in Paige. Keary could be arrested with either Rosa's or Gonsalvo's testimony.

"Not if it meant his family was in danger. I'm sorry. I cannot help you. It's a nightmare that I want to forget."

"I understand. It's a nightmare for me too. But think about the other men, women, and children who have died because of Keary. He has to be stopped."

"Didn't he threaten your parents?"

"Yes, I have good people protecting them. They could protect you and your family too."

"Not in Africa. No one is safe here. No one can be trusted but family. You should kill him yourself, Mikaela."

Paige took a deep breath. She'd shared that sentiment more than once. "Will you take my phone number in case you change your mind?"

Rosa took the number, giving Paige a few moments to form the right words to convince her to testify. "Can I call you again?"

"No. I have chosen to forget yesterday and to live for today."

Paige clung to her last resort. "Oh, Rosa, if I could finally find you, don't you think Keary can too?"

"Please don't call me again."

Tuesday evening, Miles laid his Bible and devotional on his nightstand and switched off the reading light. Some folks preferred mornings to get close to God, but he preferred the end of the day. He could drift off to sleep with Scripture or prayers rolling around in his head and sleep like an old man chasing his nightly meds with a bit of wine. Tonight a phrase from his devotional echoed throughout his mind until he closed his eyes to discern what God was saying to him. *"Truth is seen in what it does and whom it seeks."*

One of the situations that had hit the top of this evening's prayer list was about Chris's stumbling onto his dad's affair. Ty Dalton's behavior had irresponsibility and deceit tattooed all over it. And even with all Dalton had done, he still had the audacity to call Principal O'Connor yesterday and state his continued efforts to dismiss Miles from his coaching responsibilities. Chris had excelled in every game at his current position. Not once had the kid complained about his back injury. Ty Dalton needed a reality check before he lost everything that had once had meaning in his life—his wife and son.

*I have no business judging Ty Dalton, considering my own dirty laundry. Lord, how do You love us miserable creatures?*

The information Miles had uncovered about Paige yanked at his heart. Who was she? What was she doing in Split Creek under an assumed name, and was she in danger? He'd observed her for the past couple of years, first simply admiring her and then seriously "crushing," as the kids would say. *Truth is seen in what it does.* Paige's morals—the way she dressed, the words she spoke, the unselfish deeds she performed for others—embodied what Miles believed was truth.

*And whom it seeks.* What was she looking for? Without a doubt, she sought God, but how did she justify the deceit? Was she running or hiding . . . or both? She did seek truth; he was sure of it. One glance at her on Sunday mornings would convince a die-hard atheist that God existed. But how could Paige represent Jesus and lie about who she was?

Miles had not forgotten the confrontation that August evening with the guy in the Town Car who knew Paige by name. Men dressed in three-piece suits don't visit librarians in the middle of the road to talk about books. And what about the night Daniel Keary landed in the Channel 6 News helicopter on the football field to congratulate the Split Creek Bobcats on their win? Whatever Keary had said to her had made her furious. Her stiffened shoulders had revealed her sentiments louder than the band's earsplitting fight song.

Both Keary and the driver of the Town Car had some kind of a relationship with a woman who'd lied about her identity. They knew something about Paige that Miles didn't, and he didn't intend to stop until he uncovered her secret. Not because he wanted to expose her deception to the community, but because he'd fallen in love with her.

*Truth is seen in what it does and whom it seeks.*

In less than ten minutes, Miles's players would rush the field to play the fourth game of the season. A mixture of excitement and nervousness crackled in the air. He took the time to capture each boy's attention, to silently let him know that his coach valued and cared for him far beyond his skills on the field.

"Remember to respect each other and the opposing team members, to abide by the rules, and to be safe." Miles anchored his hands on his hips. "I'm so proud of you that I could shout it out for the whole town on the courthouse steps. Who wants to join me?"

Cheers rose from Split Creek's varsity football team. Five minutes later, the team burst onto the field through a banner of blue and gold with the cheerleaders turning cartwheels and the team's Bobcat mascot dancing alongside the girls. The crowd rose to its feet and cheered. The band saluted the team with raised instruments and a blaring fight song. Even the stars seemed to twinkle a little brighter as if to welcome the best football team the town had seen in ten years. What a grand night for football.

The Bobcats and the Eagles held each other scoreless the first quarter. Miles paced up and down the sidelines. His players were assuming too much. Although the Eagles had a record of zero and three, it didn't mean they were pushovers.

"What are you doing out there, Walt? Get your head back in the game. Chris was wide open." Miles sensed his ulcer kicking the pit of his stomach. They weren't hitting on all cylinders. Walt was missing too many passes, and Chris seemed to be two steps behind the Eagles' linebacker. The defense was playing like girls. The offense looked like ballet dancers.

273

Miles knew exactly where Paige sat in the stands—third row, fifth seat. From the fifty-yard line, he could swivel on his heels and see her face. She'd been a bit preoccupied since she had her cast removed, as though something had snatched up her attention. Tonight he needed to see an encouraging face before he lost his temper. Some of the comments from the crowd weren't worth repeating.

Ty Dalton trotted up beside him. "Put Chris where he belongs. Now."

Miles fought the urge to ask him where he was living. "When I want your advice, I'll ask for it."

"Too bad about your barn."

Now Miles wanted to lay a fist alongside his jaw.

With twenty seconds left in the half, the Eagles' quarterback ran for a second TD—0–13. The clock buzzed, and Miles pointed his team toward the field house. He refused to blow his stack like an irrational jerk who thought the whole game was all about him. Besides that, he didn't want to make a spectacle of himself. Miles felt sorry for the team, but sympathy never instilled confidence.

"Some of you thought we had this game wrapped up," Miles said. "That's a cocky attitude. That's not the attitude of winners, and you *are* winners."

"We look like fools out there," Walt said. "I let that ball slip right through my fingers too many times."

A couple of the other players bemoaned their mistakes.

Miles held up his hand for them to stop. "Hey, guys, what's in your heart? Play this game for what it means to you. Not for mommies and daddies and girlfriends watching your every move through binoculars. How you play tonight is a reflection of how you play life—one yard gain at a time. Believe in what you can achieve."

Once the halftime show had ended and both bands had marched into the stands, Chris and Walt led the team back onto the field with shouts that sounded more like war cries. Miles saw in the players' eyes what he hadn't seen before—determination. The third quarter started slow, or maybe it only seemed that way to Miles, who was anxious to get some yardage.

Four minutes into the third quarter, Walt broke free. Good timing gave him a race down the field. He sailed over the goal line for a TD, and the crowd roared. Miles started to call his players in before attempting to score another point but changed his mind. His boys could do it. The kicker backed up. He raced toward the ball. It soared over the goalpost.

The fans cheered louder. Miles's squeaky team had responded to the halftime tune-up. When the clock ran out at the end of the fourth quarter, the scoreboard flashed 20–13. The Bobcats had finished with another win.

# CHAPTER 36

PAIGE SEARCHED the blackness around her house and garage as Miles pulled his truck into her gravel driveway and turned off the ignition. Darkness could be a friend or foe, depending on who held the edge—as the shooting at the library had proved. Her weapons lay inside the house, where they did her no good. Some women had a favorite necklace or ring, and leaving home without their jewelry made them feel naked. Paige felt the same about her preferred gun, but the scanners at the football field protested against firearms.

Miles's face reminded her of a little boy who had gotten a pony for Christmas. And who could blame him? With the team's 4 and 0 stats, the Bobcats were on their way to the play-offs and the state championship. The celebration tonight had lasted long after everyone's curfew, but no one had wanted the excitement to end.

"Is that grin permanently etched on your face?" Paige asked.

He tapped his fingers on the steering wheel. "Set in stone. I shouldn't be surprised at how the team pulled things together. I mean, they started off tonight badly, but they rallied at the half. Paige, I'm really proud of those boys. They've worked their butts off this season. Walt and Chris are actually getting along."

Paige stared into the face of the man she should

discourage and whose company she should avoid. But she couldn't.

"Paige is smitten," Miss Eleanor at Shear Perfection had said.

"He's crazy about you," Voleta had said on more than one occasion.

So where did this lead? To her living a double life forever? To pretending her life with the CIA wasn't back in the swing of things? No point in debating the truth of where it all would end. She also had Nathan to think about.

"Where are you?" Miles asked.

"Thinking that it's one thirty and past bedtime, but I'm as wound up as you are. Would you like to come inside for a cup of coffee and a slice of apple crumb pie?"

"I'm wide awake." He relaxed against the truck seat while holding her gaze. His body language had nothing to do with pie.

A pleasant shiver coursed through her, accompanied by a carnal ache that she forced back down into the part of her that she must resist. "Do not say what you're thinking, or you might get your face slapped. Your victory tonight ended on the field. One cup of decaf and a piece of pie, then I'm chasing you home."

"How do you manage to read people so well? Special training in library science?"

She reached for the door handle. "Years of practice."

"I could use that technique when I'm on the field. Reading the opposing coaches sounds good. What about reading lips? Can you manage that feat too?"

"If I confessed to reading lips, then I'd lose all of my fun."

The two made their way across the yard to the porch. She rubbed her arms to ward off the night's chill. The falling temperatures might bring a frost by morning. The familiar complaint of the second step and the warm glow of the porch light had come to symbolize everything she'd grown to cherish: the squeaking rockers, the patriotic milk can that still gave her hope for her country, the ivy that trailed off the end of the porch and rooted in the flower bed beneath it. This was her haven, and Miles had come to fit into the whole idyllic picture. He meant much more than a cowboy or a coach or a knight on a Harley. Perhaps her time had come. Perhaps God had something else planned for her life other than hiding out in small-town USA and attempting to fight Daniel Keary, and He walked beside her. If only there was an answer to the inner turmoil about Miles and Nathan.

"Hey." Miles took her hand. "We have another reason to stretch out this party. We haven't officially celebrated the removal of your cast."

"Hallelujah. Let's raise the flag and climb the pole."

"I'm glad for you." He squeezed her hand. "Remember the evenin' when I rescued you on my Harley?"

"Maybe. Why?"

"If you will recall, that evening you let me kiss you."

"I don't remember it happening in quite the same way." She allowed her vulnerability to take over. "I kissed you."

"I kissed you back."

Her heart thumped like a cornered rabbit, over-powering all the reasons why kissing Miles was asking for trouble. "I remember needing a diversion from a two-legged pest."

Miles's shoulders lifted. "Are you sure there wasn't more to it?"

"Sure enough not to resist a second time." Paige should have stopped right there. Should have stopped any more thoughts of what was racing through her mind. Should have left Miles sitting in the truck. But she'd been more in control back when she ran from camouflaged soldiers with AK-47s slung over their shoulders.

Miles wrapped his arms around her waist and drew her to him. She'd noticed the muscles in his massive arms at the museum, even imagined being held by them. This place reminded her of something she didn't feel she deserved . . . and yet desperately wanted.

His head lowered, and his lips brushed across

hers, hesitant. He paused as though he savored every moment. She certainly did. *Tomorrow I'll hate myself for this. But right now, I want this moment never to end.*

The kiss deepened. She circled her arms around his neck while her senses melted into oblivion. The clean scent lingering after his shower, the embrace of the man she loved, the taste of his lips upon hers, and the chorus of insects singing along with the rhythm of her heart told her it was right. Suspended in time, her heart confirmed what her mind wanted to deny.

When the moment was over, he held her even tighter. She didn't dare mouth the words. Perhaps she never could.

"Paige, I . . ." Miles's deep-throated voice cracked.

The sound of his voice snatched her back to reality. She'd broken her own code, cracked the wall of her resolve. "I know. You want a cup of coffee and a slice of pie."

She separated herself from the moment and blinked before staring into his deep pools of brown with their flecks of gold. She'd always prided herself on being in control of her emotions—for control was power, and power kept her alive. But this was different. He'd touched the part of her that had nothing to do with national security.

"Actually, pie and coffee were the farthest things

from my mind. But filling my stomach might keep my hands busy."

"Can you behave yourself?"

His features softened, and his finger traced the side of her face. "We must. There is no other option."

And she knew exactly what he meant. For above all things, Miles was a man of integrity. Paige slipped her hand into her bag and drew out the house key. Willing her heightened senses to still, she unlocked the door and snapped on the light. Her gaze swept around the room, taking in the pen on the corner of the desk, the mail, the exact position of the sofa pillows. Satisfied, she walked into the kitchen and turned on the lights there. The kitchen curtain was slanted to the left.

Someone had been in her house.

From the moment Paige strode into the kitchen, Miles could tell something about her had changed. She stiffened. Her face hardened. Wariness replaced the passion he'd experienced moments before. Did she have second thoughts about their kiss, or did she regret asking him inside?

He'd never been able to read her very well until tonight on the porch. There she'd been open, sensual, and for the first time Miles had seen in her eyes what he wanted to believe nestled in her heart. He was a man, for heaven's sake. What had happened?

"Paige, what's wrong?"

She motioned for him to stay in the living room. "Someone has been here. May still be."

From his stance near the front door, he saw her reach high into a cabinet and pull out a Beretta, a heavy weapon for a lady. He held his breath. She wasn't having any problems handling it.

"Whoa." Startled, Miles watched her aim it with both hands at an invisible target down the hallway. This was the woman who used a bogus name and Social Security number. "Is that thing necessary?"

"I've had lessons."

"Why not let me check out the house?"

"Hush, Miles."

Her tone implied a command, not a request, so he obeyed. Perhaps his compliance came with a twinge of fear that she might turn the gun on him. Ridiculous, but true. Once she'd calmed down, he'd issue a heavy dose of caution about gun safety. But Paige stood before him composed and in control. Incredibly strange for a librarian—but maybe not for a librarian with a fake ID.

"I have a few things to do before I make coffee," she said with her back to him. "Stay put unless I call for you."

"I'm your backup."

"I don't need a Tonto."

That toppled his ego. "Doesn't matter."

Paige blew out an exasperated sigh. "I'm in no mood to argue. Stay behind me."

Miles followed her down the hall. She explored each room in the small, two-bedroom house, haphazardly dumping clothes from dresser drawers and pulling out items from the closets. She ripped the blankets and sheets from her bed and piled them in a heap on the floor. She lifted the mattress, refusing Miles's help, and bent to her knees to search beneath the bed.

"Do you want me to move the dresser?"

"Nothing's been touched there."

How did she know that? Miles swallowed hard. She *did* watch all of those suspense movies about government security organizations and crime fighters. Could she be delusional? But she'd swept the rooms as though she knew exactly what she was doing.

He stood in the doorway of her bedroom and saw her shoulder bag—with a burnt hole. "I have questions. Beginning with why does it look like there's a bullet hole in your leather bag."

"I was ready for a change." She shut a closet door and walked toward him, pointing the automatic at the ceiling. "Ask anything you want after I'm finished. But don't expect any answers." She motioned him out of her way and walked into the living room, peering into every corner. Snapping on a table lamp, she grasped it and peered up into the chimney. Next she flipped over the cushions on the sofa and chair. Her attention settled on a small desk by the front door and the landline phone there. A moment later, she took the phone apart. Seemingly satisfied with the manner in which it operated, she snapped the phone back together and examined the wall jack.

He might as well play along with her game. "Are you bugged?"

"Not here, anyway." She righted the little box and snapped it back into place. "I need to check the garage."

The quiet librarian had once again thrown him into a tailspin. Were there some mental issues involved with her living under an assumed name? "I'm going with you."

She studied him. Not really seeing him, as though her thoughts had taken precedence over reality. "All right, but you have to follow my instructions. No questions. Understand?"

"Why all this secrecy? If your house has been broken into, then we need to call George. He's trained to handle these kinds of things."

Paige spun to face him. "I have the gun."

He gasped. No one had ever threatened him with a weapon before.

"I need your word that you will never tell George or anyone else about this."

"Why?"

"Promise me." Her voice rose.

No point arguing with a determined woman. "Okay. Let's go."

With the Beretta in her left hand, she walked

back into the kitchen and reached for the door leading to the garage.

"Do you know how to use that thing? I know you said you'd had lessons, but you're making me nervous." The hammering of his pulse cemented his gut reaction.

She flung open the door. "You're in better hands with me than George." The garage light clicked on. She appeared to inhale every detail. Miles stood in the doorway and watched her move from one corner to another, mesmerized by the transformation of the woman he thought he knew into someone who acted like a professional. *Professional what?*

"Don't touch my car. In fact, I'd feel better if you cleared about one hundred feet from the house."

"Not on your life."

"It might be yours."

"Surely you don't think someone has been tampering with your car. You haven't even proved anyone's been in your house."

"Yes, I have." She tucked the Beretta inside the back of her jeans and lifted the car's hood. She studied the engine.

"Need some help?"

She ignored him. Scars splayed from below the waist of her jeans up to the back of her knit top, beneath which the markings disappeared. "Jerks," she said.

"Can we stop playing cops now?"

"Not until I deactivate this bomb."

Miles caught his breath. "That isn't funny."

"Neither is getting blown to pieces." For the first time since they entered the garage, she stared straight into his face. "For the last time, I'm asking you to step outside."

He squared his shoulders. "Forget it. When this is over, I want an explanation."

Ignoring him, she retrieved a pair of wire clippers from a toolbox. He stood over her, stubborn enough to call her bluff and curious enough to see if she spoke the truth. Paige pointed inside the hood to a small brick of yellowish claylike substance that held two wires running to a detonator cap. Duct tape held the brick in place.

His mouth went dry, and his heart seemed to pound in his throat. "It's attached to the starter solenoid. Who would do this?"

"You wouldn't believe me if I told you."

"Don't you think it's time to call the authorities?"

She studied the brick. One of the wires was yellow, the other green. He'd watched enough movies to know the wire's color supposedly meant something, like snipping the wrong one could activate the bomb.

"No one to call," she said.

"I'm assuming you know which one of those wires to cut."

She chuckled. "Does that bother you? Coach, it

doesn't matter which one. It's a simple circuit." She clipped the green one, then lifted the blasting cap from the clay brick.

Until Paige held the bomb in her hands, Miles had not attempted to relax. His doubts about her abilities lifted like the fog on a chilly morning.

"If this was an amateur job, then it would have been a pipe bomb." She examined the brick from every angle before laying it on the workbench. "There are different types of bombs depending on the materials available."

"I want to know about this one and who planted it."

"Don't think so." She studied the room again, then the ceiling and floor.

"Refusing to tell me the truth doesn't cut it. Is it *can't* tell me or *won't*? For that matter, who are you, and who would try to kill you?"

She slowly turned to face him, wearing a dispassionate look he'd seen more than a few times in the past. A spark of pain registered in her eyes, but it quickly vanished. She squared her shoulders. "Like I said before, you cannot ever tell anyone about this—the bomb or what I did to deactivate it."

"Are you involved in something illegal?"

"Depends on whose side you're on."

Never again would he view Paige as a helpless woman. "Should I be worried?"

"Not unless you plan to tell someone about tonight."

"Are you threatening me?"

"Warning you." Paige shook her head. "I . . . care too much to allow you to get involved. These people play for keeps."

Miles had waited a long time to hear the words, and he had no reason to doubt her feelings. However, the evening's events made no sense. Someone had tried to kill her, and he'd watched her deactivate a bomb. Part of him was numb, still processing it all. The rest of him floated through a surreal world. He placed his hands on her shoulders. "I can't help you if I don't know the problem."

"No deal. This is my project."

Miles opened his mouth to speak, but she touched his lips. "No more questions."

"I know your name and Social Security number are false. I memorized it that night at the hospital."

"You did a search on me?" Admiration flashed in her eyes, but he also saw something else. Was it fear or apprehension? "Guess I can't blame you," she said. "What did you learn?"

"Only that Paige Rogers with the Social you're using doesn't exist. Are you going to tell me what's going on, or do I have to search more on my own? You know I have computer access to secured files."

"Is that legal?"

"You're one to ask me about what's legal?"

Her eyes narrowed. "You'd better leave, Miles."

"Why? You can keep secrets, but I can't? We have feelings for each other, whether you want to admit it or not. I have no clue what any of this is about. But you're in danger, and I want to help. If I'm wrong and you're some notorious crime figure hiding out in small-town Oklahoma, then the joke's on me."

She rubbed her palms. "Bonnie and Clyde died in a shoot-out."

"Can't you talk to me straight? If you're in trouble with the law, we can deal with it. What I want is the truth."

"I have to finish in the garage."

"Fine. I have no place to go." Frustration seeped through his voice, and he didn't know how to stop it.

"I can't explain this. But I promise you that I'm not involved with anything illegal. Can we let it stand for now?"

"Are you in the Witness Protection Program?"

"You've been watching too many movies again."

"I'm assuming this is why you've kept your distance from me."

Miles saw a spark of emotion. He opened his arms, and she hesitated before stepping into his embrace. He held her close, noting she didn't tremble like when he'd kissed her. How could a woman tear her house apart and discover a bomb in her car without a quiver?

"Paige, or whatever your name is, one day soon I want every detail."

"It's muddy . . . bloody."

"I can handle it. Would my access to secured files be of use to you?"

"You don't have any access I don't already have."

"Are you involved in government security?"

"You're asking questions." She laid her head against his chest. "This started out as a celebration of your win."

"All right. I'll keep my questions for another day. You do your thing in the garage, and I'll make the coffee."

Miles ground the decaf beans while his mind whirled in time with the grinder. The clock on the microwave flashed 2:30. Anybody heading down the road past her house and seeing his truck would think he was spending the night. Great for the librarian's and coach's reputations. He reached into an open bag of Reese's Pieces on the kitchen counter and pulled one out. What was he doing at this time of the morning making coffee and munching on candy as though everything was normal?

If Paige hadn't done anything illegal, then she must be involved with law enforcement in some way. An old friend could help him with fingerprint identification. Guilt spilled over him. He'd rather she'd tell him her story, but then he'd wonder if it was the truth.

# CHAPTER 37

PAIGE'S SLEEP-FILLED MIND sent off an alarm. Her cell phone rang again. This time she snatched it up.

"Mikaela Olsson?" The man's voice held a distinct African accent—Angolan Portuguese.

"Who's calling?" she asked in the same language while switching on the light.

"Gonsalvo Ngoimgo."

*I need good news.* "How can I help you?"

"I believe I can help you. I want my father's murderer brought to justice."

She attempted to keep her rising hope in check. "You're willing to testify to what your father told you?"

"Yes, and I will convince my mother to do the same. My father told me that another American was working with Daniel Keary."

"Did he give a name?"

"No. Not sure my father knew either."

"Have you told anyone else about your decision?"

"Only my mother. She's frightened. Casimiro Figuiera is a key figure in the Angolan government."

"Not all killers are brought to justice."

"I will deal with him myself . . . and take care of my family."

"Be careful," Paige said. "Vengeance is an awful

burden. I'll make a call now for you and your family's protection."

"I want this to end," Gonsalvo said. "My mother said others have died because of Daniel Keary."

"Men, women, and children—over oil."

"Oil and blood are the same."

"Thank you, Gonsalvo. You will be contacted shortly by people you can trust."

Paige disconnected the call. Fully awake, she wiped the tears streaming down her cheeks. She didn't know if they were tears of sadness or joy or both. Gonsalvo's testimony could very well be discarded due to his age at the time of the killings, but not Rosa's. *But not Rosa's. . . .*

On Friday morning, Paige stepped into Shear Perfection, into the world of neon orange and yellow where a woman experienced an opportunity to enhance her beauty. Or so Miss Eleanor always claimed. Paige carried a casserole dish filled with hot apple strudel for her friends and their clients.

"You are right on time." Voleta held out a cup of coffee for Paige. "I've been thinking about your apple dessert since I woke this morning."

"Great. 'Cause there's enough for an army." Paige set the dish on the appointment desk and took the offered coffee. Steam swirled from the cup, as though Voleta had poured it just when she saw Paige exit her car.

"My fingers are itching for highlights."

"Use them on the next willing client."

"I thought you might want a little extra appeal for the carnival this weekend." Voleta inhaled the cinnamon and sugar.

"Carnies add all the color I need."

"Morning, sweet girl," Miss Eleanor called from the back room. "Has it been three weeks already?"

"Not yet. I brought by some apple strudel."

"That's what I'm smelling. Wonderful! My sugar level is okay, so I'm diving in. Say, you and Miles sure look good together."

"Yes, ma'am. He's a good friend."

While Paige served up the strudel, Ginny Dalton walked in. Her clothes hung on her like the scarecrow mounted at the town square. Her once-startling blue eyes held the pain of hurt and betrayal.

Miss Eleanor left the closet and wrapped her arm around Ginny's shoulder. "Honey, how about a cup of coffee?"

Ginny's shoulders lifted and fell. "I'm not so sure I could keep it down."

"Paige has one of her specialties here." Voleta pointed with a gloved finger to the appointment desk.

Ginny shook her head. "Thanks, but my stomach is really upset. Not sure why I'm here."

Voleta stiffened. "That husband of yours is lame. He has no business hurting you like that."

"If I'd been a better wife, he'd—"

"Don't you dare go blaming yourself, honey," Miss Eleanor said. "He'll get tired of his new toy and come on back to you."

"He's changed so much since he came back from Angola. I told him if he misses it, to go back. But now he has something to keep him here."

"You don't need him." Voleta furiously wiped around her workstation. "Good men are rare as hens' teeth."

Paige studied the women around her—Ginny hurting and Miss Eleanor and Voleta doing their best to comfort her. Today would not be the day Paige sucked out more agony from Ginny by asking her about Ty's stint in Angola.

Miss Eleanor and Ginny talked in whispers while Voleta and Paige chatted about the weekend. Paige ached for Ty's wife. The depression in Chris's voice had been hard enough that day in the library, but Ty's betrayal of Ginny cut even deeper. How would Miles feel when it came his turn to learn the truth about the one he loved?

Miles brushed down his Appaloosa gelding. He'd raced the magnificent animal across the fields behind where his barn once stood, and the gelding had glistened with sweat. The insurance company was dragging its heels with the mention of arson. With a nip in the air and the thrill of winning the fifth game in the season, Miles couldn't concentrate on anything except last night's win and riding his favorite horse. His boys had played like college athletes. Well, okay, not exactly, but they sure had looked good. Five more games in the season, and Split Creek's Bobcats would be heading into play-offs for the state title in 2A football. Ah, he could see the trophy in the school's display window now. Sweet.

"Yahoo." Miles's horse flinched. "Sorry, Puma. Got a little carried away there."

He checked his watch. He was supposed to pick up Paige at eleven for an afternoon at the carnival. What a weekend—a winning team and a date with his best girl. He finished with Puma and hurried inside his two-story farmhouse to shower. Someday he'd sure like to fill up this house with kids. Especially if their mother was Paige.

The house had been rewired, the plumbing updated, the hardwood floors refinished, the wood-work stripped, a new kitchen installed with those fancy granite countertops, and a ton of other updates. Much of the work he'd done himself. And, as with most older homes, each time he finished one project, another caught his attention. Too often he wanted to invite Paige to supper so she could see the house for herself. With the fall chill, he could build a fire. . . . But tongues would wag as soon as she set foot inside the front door. Of course, he had been to her house a few times, and tongues had been wagging for a long time. *Admit it, old man. You're nervous about her seeing the house.*

Another thought occurred to him. He could have a party—one to celebrate a play-off win. Everyone could bring something to eat. Miles could call it a "Bobcat Bash." Paige might even help him. He had no clue about decorating—except to have a football in the center of the table.

The thought of Paige and a possible life with her had hit a concrete wall. Miles didn't even know her real name, who she was, or why she was keeping her life a mystery. So why did he continue to see her at every opportunity? Wasn't he setting himself up for a crash that had the potential of shaking him as badly as his brother's death?

Paige marveled at the small children skipping several feet beyond their parents, excitement evident in their sparkling eyes. Innocence. If only adults could shield them from the ugliness of the world's reality.

A glance down the crowded midway almost convinced her that she could be happy living in Split Creek for the rest of her days, where the only concerns were a lack of rainfall and a bad football year. Nathan could attend the local school, get involved with the children's group at church. It didn't hurt to dream, did it?

She monitored the crowd, looking for the person or persons who had instructions to make her life miserable and were paid by the soon-to-be governor of Oklahoma. She noted a man in his thirties wearing an OU sweatshirt and munching on peanuts; another man around fifty years old, wearing high-dollar boots, stood by the caramel apple wagon; and a woman about forty years old wearing jeans and a rhinestone necklace moved down the midway and seemed to take interest in every booth. All fit the profile.

Up ahead she spotted Miss Eleanor and Mr. Shafer. He slipped his hand around hers, and the two exchanged looks that had "heading to the altar" written all over them. Music from the carousel stirred up feelings of nostalgia, and a long line of children waited for their turn on the ride. A few entwined couples ambled by, sharing a smile, a single bag of popcorn, or glances meant only for each other. Carnivals always attracted children and lovers—no matter what the age. And there she stood among all of them, a CIA operative determined to keep the nation secure.

Paige stole a look at Miles beside her. How long could she continue this charade? She inwardly grimaced. If he really wanted to know who she was, he could find out. He'd been on to her since the night Keary had arranged for the C-4 bomb to be wired to her car. What she couldn't figure out was why Miles hadn't grilled her about her identity. Unless he already knew.

Shouts of "Step this way!" broke into her thoughts. "Win the little lady a teddy bear."

"Popcorn. Hot, buttered popcorn!"

She inhaled the delicious aroma.

Creaks and groans followed by squeals from the Ferris wheel reminded her of growing up in Wisconsin. Before they left the carnival this afternoon, she'd ask Miles for a ride. As a girl, she'd loved seeing the world below from the top of a Ferris wheel.

"Funnel cakes right here!"

A banshee shrieked from the spook house, followed by a laugh that would wake the dead.

"Have your palms read by Ma'am Rozella. Discover your future!"

No thanks. She'd rather not know.

"Are you ready for some cotton candy?" Miles asked once they stood in front of the pastel pink and green sugary clouds.

"Disgusting. Reminds me of sugared hair."

His eyes widened. "Since when have you eaten sugared hair?"

"Probably kindergarten, but let's not go there." She spotted another concessions stand. "I'd love some chili fries with lots of jalapeños."

"My kind of woman," Miles said. "Will this be before or after the Ferris wheel and flying saucer?"

"Before. Makes the ride more exciting. Nothing like living on the edge."

"Yeah, hanging over the side and puking our guts out."

She'd hung on to a cliff once. "Not me. I love it."

Miles stopped in front of the firing range, where a row of yellow ducks paddled across a moving target. "What do you think?"

"You'll get beat."

"Want to bet?"

"Sure. You name it."

"A day trip on my Harley."

She wiggled her shoulders. "That won't ever happen. How about another day trip in your truck? This time to the Bartlesville Museum."

His mouth dipped lower than a cowboy's handlebar mustache. "It will happen on my Harley because I now have more incentive. Have you forgotten who has walked away with first place three years in a row at the county's shooting match?"

But he hadn't seen the stats in her file. "That's because you weren't up against me."

Miles pulled his wallet from his jeans pocket and handed money for a round of tickets to the rail-thin vendor. Paige studied the six rifles laid vertically before her and selected one.

"The sight's off on this one," Paige said and picked up another one. "Rats, this one's off too." Probably how the carnival made its money. She slid Miles a silent challenge. "We'll need to leave early the day of the Bartlesville trip. Don't forget I love breakfast on the road."

"My bike can manage early breakfast any day of the week."

A twinge of warning pricked at her conscience. She should let him beat her. Play the librarian role. With a sigh she reminded herself he'd already seen a side of her that butted against Miss Dixie of Southern Charm, America. She lifted the rifle and took out three ducks in a row.

"Very impressive," Miles said. "I'm all for healthy competition."

"By the time we're done here, you'll be calling *me* coach."

Miles leaned on one leg and stuck his thumbs in his belt loops. "I think you'll be begging me for lessons." He picked up the nearest rifle. A moment later, he knocked off three ducks in a row. Swinging his attention toward her with superiority oozing from his pores, he laid the rifle back with the others. "I'll grant you a tie."

"No way." She'd ease into beating him.

Five rounds later and twenty dollars of Miles's hard-earned money in the hand of the vendor, Paige walked away with an armful of novelties, which she gave to a family with three small children. "Didn't mean to hurt your feelings," she said to Miles.

"Oh, it's all a part of my research."

Her pulse accelerated into overdrive. "Research about what?"

He leaned closer and planted a quick kiss on her cheek. "About the real Paige Rogers. Is she faster than a speeding bullet? prettier than any belle of the South? It's a bird. It's a plane. It's Super Librarian!"

She saw herself flying over Split Creek with a red cape and a book tucked under her arm. She bit back the laughter. "Can't you accept the fact that I'm a woman of varied interests?"

"And spoil my fun?"

A scream pierced the air. Then another—and neither of them were sounds of excitement. Instinctively Paige raced in the direction of the sound, toward a house of mirrors, where a crowd had started to gather.

"We need help!" a male shouted.

"There's a kid down!" another voice called.

Paige reached for her gun in her new shoulder bag, but logic stopped her from drawing it. The problem could be a fight, something that security had already broken up. Miles called her name, but she ignored him. She pushed her way through the crowd, her hand itching for the gun she could not grasp. A young man lay facedown in the dirt. Blood spurted from his right thigh and formed a crimson pool, a sight from the past she'd seen far too often. Recognition of the mass of black hair and Bobcat sweatshirt sent a flurry of grief and regret to the core of her heart.

*Oh, God, no.* Paige bent to his side. "Walt."

"My leg," Walt whispered and squeezed his eyes shut.

She turned him enough to see he'd been shot in

the femoral artery. Without intervention, he'd soon bleed out.

Miles touched her shoulder. "Call for an ambulance, and I'll tie a tourniquet on his leg."

She ripped off the sweatshirt tied around her shoulders and tossed it at him.

They exchanged a brief look while he twisted the arms of the sweatshirt. A carny handed him a wrench for the tourniquet. Paige retrieved her cell from her purse and punched in 911 while scanning the crowd. Later she'd work through her anger. A teenage girl with raven-colored hair stood above her sobbing. Paige had seen her at the library with Walt.

A teenage boy reached out to comfort the girl. A father yanked his child out of the way of the horror. A mother shielded her daughter's eyes.

"Please, stay back," Paige said. "An ambulance is on the way." She sifted through the sea of faces for the shooter.

"Anyone see what happened here?" Miles's voice thundered around her as he finished tying the tourniquet around Walt's leg.

No one responded.

"Paige." She recognized Voleta's voice beside her. "What's happened?" Terror seared her face. "Oh no. It's Walt."

"Help will be here soon." The two men and the woman whom she'd seen earlier were not around. Paige wished she'd snapped their pictures, but she'd memorized the way they'd walked and looked.

"How bad is he? There's so much blood." Voleta stared at him, her face growing pale.

Paige grabbed Voleta's shoulders and swung her around. "Don't look at him. I can't take care of both of you."

"Okay. What can I do?"

"See if his parents are here. Don't scare them. Just bring them to Walt before the ambulance arrives."

Voleta hesitated and chanced another look at Walt.

Paige had no patience for weakness. "If you can't help, then stay out of the way."

The sobbing girl, who was one of Walt's friends, fell to her knees. "He was teasing me about the way I laugh. And then he grabbed his leg and fell."

"Did you hear the gun?" Paige asked.

"No. Nothing," the girl said.

Amateurs didn't use silencers. Who could stoop this low? A chill raced alongside her thoughts. Ty Dalton? Would he now add attempted murder to suspected arson? She didn't read Chris into this . . . unless he was provoked by his dad.

# CHAPTER 38

PAIGE PACED the tan and brown tiled hallway outside the surgical waiting room. She ached for Walt's family in a way that left her physically ill. A sixteen-year-old kid battled for his life in emergency surgery. Anger and grief fused with a lust for revenge against whoever had pulled the trigger. The question she hadn't been able to answer was why someone had found it necessary to shoot—maybe kill—Walt. But Ty Dalton kept rising to the top of the list. Maybe he'd gone nuts with this thing about Chris playing quarterback. Or maybe Chris *hadn't* been able to take the pressure at home anymore and lost it. Nothing in her reservoir of possible explanations made sense.

She still suspected Ty of being the mole, and that meant he could have a silencer. She shoved away the thoughts about Chris, wanting to believe he was a good kid trying to figure out where he fit in the world. From what Miles had said about Chris's back and not wanting to play college ball, Paige doubted his involvement. But she wanted to know where the Dalton men were at the time of the shooting.

If Dalton worked for Keary and had decided to venture off on his own personal vendetta, Keary would be furious. *Welcome to the no-spin zone.*

Walt's parents sat to the right of Miles. Mrs.

Greywolf wept silently. The couple held hands with rosary beads dangling from their union. Two small boys and a girl swung their legs back and forth in their chairs. The children were too young to understand that their brother lay close to death. Paige watched Miles's eyes move from the grieving parents to the doors of the emergency room. He'd divided his time between the kids and Walt's parents. Everyone waited for the doctor to step through the outer doors.

Walt's dad cleared his throat and swiped at a tear rolling down his dark cheek. He wore a tarnished WWJD bracelet on his left hand. Paige stared at the bracelet, allowing Jesus' sacrifice to sink deep inside her.

About a dozen other kids had taken residence in a corner, talking, crying, praying. Chris and his mother stood with them. Parents and two pastors and a priest from the community offered hope and attempted to answer questions. Maybe she should pose her own questions to the pastors about God allowing this to happen. But those righteous people wouldn't want to hear her thoughts about retribution. She glanced at her watch. Palmer needed to be notified about this latest incident, especially if Ty was involved.

What if it were Nathan fighting for his life? She remembered the car chase through the streets of Nairobi with bullets flying at her and Nathan. Desperation and a desire to land a death punch to

Keary had stayed with her for days—even now. Palmer used to say she was a human black widow. And that was before she had a son. She had to find a way to see him. Counseling wasn't going well. And no wonder. His mother had died, he was surrounded by strangers, and the woman who'd said she'd be his second mommy had deserted him.

Paige walked to the window of the waiting room and stared out at the late afternoon sun. What a blessing to enjoy comfortable daytime temperatures before the cold days of winter settled on the drought-ridden land. She turned her attention to the anguished people and saw Miles had made his way to her side. The sadness surrounding the waiting room and her concern for Nathan and all those she held dear had taken its toll. She wanted to tell him about herself. She needed a friend. And although company protocol frowned on what she was about to do, her heart overruled it.

"The mercury dropped."

"Why don't you tell me what you're thinking?"

She wrestled with what she could say and what was classified information. "I ache for Walt and his family." She glanced away. "I ache for things I can't change."

"Talk to me, Paige. Don't carry whatever it is alone. I've wanted to help all along, and since the car bomb . . ."

She walked out to the hallway by the elevators

and turned to face him. "Julius Caesar didn't see it coming."

"Would it have made any difference?"

"Depends on his advisers. Once you said the time would come when I'd tell you the truth. Can we take a walk?"

He pressed the elevator's down button. They rode in silence as though she suspected the walls to contain untraceable wires. Miles smiled. The muscles in his face showed his sincerity. The light in his eyes emitted his love. Was she being selfish in wanting to confide in him, knowing he could be the next target? He'd earned her trust and her love, but that didn't equate with losing his life.

"Don't change your mind about telling me," he said.

She'd lost some of her ability to remain stoic. "You're getting good."

"Not good enough."

Outside the hospital a slight wind blew through her hair. She rubbed the chill bumps from her arms and questioned whether the cool breeze was the early evening temperature or her icy heart. Miles slipped off his jacket and laid it across her shoulders. Her bloodstained sweatshirt was somewhere with Walt. The ER doctor had said the tourniquet had saved the boy's life, but the loss of blood had caused his blood pressure to dip dangerously low. *It could have been Nathan.*

To the west, the sun had started its descent in

chalky shades of yellow and orange. Miles deserved to know the underlying factors of why she'd chosen to live an alias life and how the past and present connected to Daniel Keary. Palmer would have her skin for this, but right now it didn't matter. Her emotions wavered between sobbing on Miles's chest and driving to Dallas to hold her son. Both choices were selfish, but she couldn't help herself.

*I need help here, God. I need You.*

She hoisted her shoulder bag and made her way to the prayer garden adjacent to the parking lot. A manicured lawn and flower beds created an atmosphere of peace. She walked the perimeter of the garden and then stopped at a small waterfall and dipped her fingers into the cool water. Pennies lay in the bottom, as though desperate people had cast one last hope for whatever plagued their hearts. Prayers hadn't worked. Noninvolvement hadn't worked. Neither had logic or reason.

When Paige saw no one was standing nearby, she walked to the end of a sidewalk where an empty bench offered privacy. She finished forming what she could reveal. Operatives always had stories to back up stories to back up stories. But this was an exception. This was the man she loved, and although she couldn't tell him all of the truth, she could tell some.

"This goes much deeper than my false ID. You don't know me at all."

He hesitated. "You might be right."

A car drove by. A family turned into the parking lot.

"This stays with us," Paige said. "Even a well-read librarian can't defuse a bomb and be a crack shot with a rifle."

"Unless her older brother is in Special Forces," Miles said as though attempting to lighten the tension.

"You're not as far off as you might think." Paige eyed him closely. "I used to work for the CIA in field operations. My last assignment was in Africa. Angola, to be exact."

Miles pulled back in obvious amazement. "The CIA? You? Like spies and satellites and terrorism? You were part of that? You're kidding me, right?"

Paige ignored his disbelief. He'd either believe her or not. "I've tried to outrun my past, but sometimes our sins find us out. Or at least *somebody's* sins. My last mission was a total bust. One of our team members sold us all out. He and I were the only two who survived, but I couldn't rat him out because I'd been injured and was in and out of consciousness for days. While I was down, the turncoat filed a report saying I had cracked under the strain of field duty and was mentally unstable. I filed my own report, but neither of us had a witness."

"You? Ridiculous," Miles said. "Did you demand a psych eval?"

"Inconclusive since I'd been trained to combat those kinds of tests. To make matters worse, he gave me orders to disappear and promised that if I ever attempted to bring up the allegations again, he'd kill my parents. At that point, my parents believed I was working in international business. So it wasn't difficult to fake my death. I quit the CIA with more anger and resentment than anyone should ever have."

"Oh, Paige." He pressed his lips together and shook his head.

"Don't feel sorry for me." She snapped her response. "I chose that world." She took a breath and plunged ahead. "Anyway, I changed my name, my looks, and all those things necessary to start life all over again. My former team leader knew I had a minor in library science and arranged for me to live in Split Creek, where he could keep an eye on me."

"The man lives here?"

She shook her head and realized she'd ventured too far to change directions. *Oh, the different worlds of Miles Laird and Paige Rogers.* "He never bothered me until a few months ago—when his election for governor was only weeks away."

Miles grabbed the iron handle of the bench. "Daniel Keary?"

"That's him. I'm sure he's not the only corrupt politician in our country. Chew on this: his ambitions far exceed the governorship, and he has more charisma than a Pentecostal convention."

"And he sent that guy who stopped you on the road?"

"It all began again, even a threat to my parents if I didn't agree to help him with his campaign. I refused, then learned the CIA had reopened his file due to some questionable oil dealings."

"I see." Miles nodded. "If he could convince you to work for him, then your former accusations would look contrived, and the investigation might be canceled."

"Something like that. Miles, I wanted to tell you the truth about me when you explained to me about your brother. All I could think about was the pain I'd inflicted on my parents. How my death must have devastated them. More important, you saw me deactivate a bomb. What you know about me cannot leak out. And there's more. I agreed to come back on board with the CIA to prove Keary's guilt in exchange for my parents' protection." Paige stared into the pool of water containing the many pennies.

"Aren't there programs to protect your parents?"

"Who's the enemy? Keary was exonerated from any unlawful activity. His record was filled with outstanding service, and mine was tainted with accusations of mental incompetence. Keary was satisfied with the original result of the company's investigation. He'd secured the dead bolts on all the doors that would lead to the truth. But he didn't count on the CIA digging up new allegations."

Miles stiffened. "To think I planned to vote for him."

"So does most of Oklahoma."

"What can I do to help?"

"Nothing. You aren't getting any more involved than as my sounding board." She gave him a wry smile. "You can also pray that I don't lose it and kill Keary."

"You're serious?"

She didn't respond. Neither did she volunteer details about any of the things she'd already done in the name of national interest.

"Don't you know I love you?" Miles's words hinted of anger.

"Love is . . ."

A pickup truck pulled into the parking lot and parked. No one got out.

"Wait until this is over; then we can talk."

"That's fair."

She noted the license plate of the truck. Emotions could be put on hold—all of them. "I came to Split Creek with the resolve to push the past as far away as I could. I wasn't able to kill Keary for the same reason he couldn't eliminate me. The CIA would be all over it."

Miles looked away. "No wonder you didn't want to drag George into the car bomb situation."

"Don't underestimate George." She recalled the

shooting at the library. "He's a smart man. It won't take too long for him to start asking questions about the unusual things going on."

"Should you confide in him?" Miles asked.

"No." Paige shook her head. "Then he'd become a target. And Keary has mentioned you, so don't think you aren't already involved."

He swung his arm around the back of the bench. "I love you. I'm not afraid of Keary."

"Don't be stupid. You should get into your truck and drive as far away from me as you can." She braced herself against what she must do now. "I have a request."

"Name it."

"We need to stop seeing each other."

"Forget it."

"Listen to me, please." Paige touched his arm, and he looked back at her. "Your life is in jeopardy as long as we're together. I need your prayer support and willingness to let me lead. Folks need to believe we're no longer together."

"Like I can't play spy games?"

"You don't wear a muzzle when you play with the big dogs."

As much as Paige loved Miles, she had to chase him away. After all, she'd done quite well by herself for the past seven years. A life with him was a foolish fairy tale—a fantasy. At times she'd thought they could make it together, that the two of them could exist without him knowing the truth about her. But now that Nathan was in the picture, that was impossible. And as long as Keary was allowed to live free, every life she touched faced destruction. Faces of her parents, Nathan, Miles, Voleta—all those she loved passed through her mind.

"I can't stop you from refusing my company," Miles said. "Neither can you stop me from camping on your front porch. You can't go to George to file a restraining order because then you'd have to fabricate a reason to keep me out of your life." He leaned over and kissed her. "I'm a part of this, and I'm not deserting you."

Miles stood from the bench, his face reddened, and his breathing deepened.

Her gaze swung around. "What's wrong?"

"Ty Dalton worked in Angola for WorldMarc—little over five years ago. Chris told me about it. And that's the same company that Keary brokered oil deals with."

This was part of the story that she hadn't intended to discuss. "Could be a coincidence."

"I doubt it. Sheriff George asked me if I suspected a shooter," Miles continued. "I didn't think Ty would be low enough to shoot Walt any more than I thought he'd set fire to my barn." Miles studied her face. "George asked me about the silencer too."

"Part of his job is to ask questions." She scanned the parking lot, always looking, always listening.

"Split Creek High has some rough characters—other Chickasaw kids who might believe Walt's sold out to the other side by playing ball or other kids who might want Chris to play quarterback."

"My gut instinct is Ty Dalton," Miles said. "Have you checked him out? I mean, he could be involved with all of this." When she didn't respond, he jammed his hands into his jeans pockets. "Of course you have. I'm simply mouthing what you already know. I feel stupid."

"You are not stupid." Already regret had grabbed hold of her heart. "Miles, I've admitted to so much today. Let's go back inside and check on Walt."

He took her hand. "I may not have your skills and knowledge about how things are done at the CIA, but I'm still in this. I suggest if you're concerned about my welfare, then talk to your contact," Miles said. "I've been involved with your problem since the day you hitched a ride on the back of my Harley."

Paige focused on an SUV parked near the truck. "I think I'll spend a little time in the chapel."

He gazed at the parking lot. "I didn't see anyone get out of it either."

"You must have picked up a workbook."

"Who needs a workbook when a pro is teaching the class?"

# CHAPTER 39

I MEET STEVENS before my eight o'clock speaking engagement. I want a drink but nix that idea, considering the attendees tonight will be a bunch of Southern Baptists, like I'm supposed to be.

Stevens has a martini, but he isn't campaigning for governor. "I surprised myself with this one."

"And if you don't tell what's in your file, I'm going to kick your rear." I laugh, but inside I fear my hopes are about to be blown to bits.

"The first news is that Rosa Ngoimgo and her son are in the States in protective custody."

"That's right. And I've found out where," I say. "That problem will be taken care of tonight. Your little jewel in Palmer's office is priceless."

Stevens chuckles. "She's not little. In fact, she adds a new dimension, being fat."

"What about Nathan?" Raw emotion roots in me at the thought of having a son. Ever since the accident, all I've been able to think about is what I lost—children of my own flesh and blood.

"He's yours, Daniel. A woman in records who used to work in the VIP unit at the Nairobi hospital verified it all. She remembered that a white woman fitting Mikaela's description was hospitalized for two months about seven years ago. The same woman returned a few months later to give birth to a boy. I tracked down the family who'd been keeping Nathan while Bobbie Landerson was in the hospital. She said the boy was adopted, and recently Bobbie had legally given Mikaela guardianship. The woman also said the boy was somewhere in the States."

I can't breathe. I'm hot and cold at the same time. "The CIA has him."

"I'm already on it. Nothing yet."

I want a cigarette, and it's been five years since I gave them up. "Find him for me, Stevens, and you can name your price."

"I'm doing this for you." Stevens speaks soberly. "You've taught me things I would never have otherwise known."

Nathan. My son. Nothing else matters. Nothing. I'll begin arrangements tonight after the dinner.

# CHAPTER 40

SOMEWHERE IN MILES'S JUGGLING act between his male ego and his love for Paige, he'd made a commitment to help her expose Daniel Keary as a corrupt politician. A pledge that could get him killed. God would have to help him, because his skills in the defense coliseum were rather pathetic. Computer security and a lucky rifle shot didn't make him a gladiator for the CIA. But when Miles's brother had died, he'd vowed never to abandon anyone he loved again.

However, he'd be a liar if he didn't admit he'd doubted her every word since he'd learned about her false identity. Ex-CIA operative . . . As incredible as the explanation sounded, it made sense after all that had happened in Split Creek.

They walked back inside the hospital, and he escorted Paige to the chapel door. She was a strong woman wrestling with her faith and what God required of her. He wanted to draw her close to him but knew she'd resist. He'd seen love for him in her eyes, but right now those emotions were on hold.

"I'll be waiting upstairs."

She offered a thin-lipped smile and disappeared inside the wooden doors. Miles rode the elevator up to the surgical floor. The faint hum and the click of each passing floor reminded him of a slow heartbeat. He focused on Walt. The boy had dreams and goals, not a death wish. According to the doctors, Walt was clinging to life with the same tenacity that he lived each day. He had a fighting chance, and the Chickasaw Wonder never backed down from any worthy challenge.

Paige sat in the third row of pews in the small chapel. A cross was centered in an alcove in the front, illuminated by a hidden light in the ceiling. Lighted stained-glass windows bookended the sides of the room. One depicted Jesus kneeling in the garden of Gethsemane, and the other portrayed Jesus touching the eyes of a blind man.

Arching her shoulders, she swiped at a tear. Paige seldom wept; she believed in solving problems, not feeling victimized by them. But her world was burdened with helplessness and concern for others. *Dear Lord, let Walt live. Let this all end.*

Everything she believed in lay in a hospital room. Her past ideals. Her aspirations for mankind. Her belief that the world's youth were the inspiration for tomorrow. Her trust in the CIA. She recalled the agony on the faces of Mr. and Mrs. Greywolf as they attempted to console each other. Death was truly a formidable enemy. She tried to imagine the grief and bitterness of those who had lost loved ones over oil and diamonds in Africa. She remembered the intensity of her hate for Keary when Nathan was nearly killed.

Time ticked by for proving Keary's guilt. In a little over three weeks, the voters would crowd the polls to choose the next governor of Oklahoma. Rosa and Gonsalvo were safe somewhere in the States. Paige needed to talk to Ginny Dalton and see if Ty had confessed anything to her about Angola. All brought her closer to her dreams with Nathan. She pulled her cell from her purse and waited while Raif got him on the line.

"Hi, Miss Paige. When are you coming to see me?"

The sound of his voice nearly caused a meltdown. "I'm trying to work that out."

"That's what you always say. Remember when you said you were my second mommy?"

"Yes." She ached to be there with him.

"But how can you be my second mommy when you aren't here?"

Her stomach lurched. "I'll make this up to you as soon as I can. We'll do movies, spend a day at Lake Murray, buy you a bicycle, pick out a puppy, and—"

"I don't want those things. I just want you." His voice trembled.

"And you are what I want, more than anything. Honey, I have to go now. I'll call you tomorrow." That's when Paige realized that she'd give the last drop of her blood to keep him from Keary.

The door to the chapel opened, and Miles appeared. His shoulders drooped.

*Oh no. Oh, please, no.* She stood and walked toward him. Sorrow ripped through her, and he hadn't spoken a word.

"You need to know something before you head back to the waiting room." He reached out to draw her into his arms, and she willingly stepped into his embrace. "I'm sorry, honey. The doctor has called in the family to say their final good-byes."

Paige could not utter a word. Her throat stung, and her heart ached for Walt's family and all those who loved the dynamic young man. She wanted Nathan. She wanted her parents. It didn't matter that she was a grown woman; she needed her mommy and daddy. They were alive and living in Wisconsin. Would those she loved forgive her for what she'd done to them?

"A family should not lose a child." He drew her closer. "I refuse to give up."

Nathan. Always Nathan. "Not until he takes his last breath." Paige drew back and linked her fingers in his. "I'm trusting God in this."

Miles led her from the chapel to the surgical waiting room. She despised the minutes and hours with no answers. Walt's family had returned from saying good-bye, their eyes red with dark hollows carved beneath them. Their priest held their hands in each of his, a picture of love in time of sorrow.

In the last hour, the waiting room had flooded with more kids and parents. Paige glanced around the room and saw Voleta, Miss Eleanor, and Mr.

Shafer sandwiched in the crowd. Every member of the football team stood in the hallway and around the waiting room. George, Naomi, and Georgie had arrived shortly after the shooting and offered their support to the Greywolfs. The drone of muffled voices wafted over the crowd. How could anyone explain a senseless shooting? For that matter, how could anyone explain murder?

Her tears were gone, and the old, familiar, impassive anxiety had settled in her bones. She was becoming Mikaela, a transformation that she welcomed and feared, but one she couldn't deny.

Sunrise filtered in the solitary window. It was supposed to bring hope, but those around her saw only the blackness of night. *How much longer?*

"We should have news soon," Miles said. "I tell my kids that 90 percent of the journey is in the struggle. Walt has held on this long. Every hour he lives increases his chances of survival."

"Seems like every breath is a prayer," she said. Every prayer filled with a list of names that scrolled like movie credits.

A commotion rose in the hallway. Paige's attention flew to Mr. and Mrs. Greywolf and their priest. Cheering caught everyone's attention. The crowd laughed and cried at the same time.

"Walt's rallied," Mr. Greywolf shouted and waved his arms. "It's true. They're trying to wake him."

If Walt could fight, she could too. She must be

strong when it came to Nathan. As much as she wanted to see him, she had to wait. Keary, despite his need to keep his hands clean, had almost killed them before, and she would not let that happen again.

## CHAPTER 41

HOURS LATER, after a long nap and a hot shower, Paige drove to where the carnival had still continued to draw in swarms of people. She thought the carnival should have been closed after yesterday's shooting, but the sounds of happy people rang around her. Couples and children lined up for the merry-go-round, and children shouted for hot dogs and popcorn. They didn't seem to care that a sixteen-year-old boy lay in serious condition in the hospital.

Paige had phoned Miles just before leaving her house and learned that Walt was steadily improving. He'd awakened, talked to his parents, and then drifted back to sleep. Paige doubted many of Walt's friends had attended church today, since most of them had spent the night at the hospital. George had questioned most of the players, cheerleaders, Chris, and Walt's girlfriend. The kids who'd been with Walt had nothing to report, and Chris had been seen at Denim's for lunch with his mother. No arguments. No running into anyone who could have been an enemy.

Mr. and Mrs. Greywolf had a few suspicions, but nothing substantial. They didn't understand how anyone could do such a thing to their son. No clues equaled no motive, and that equaled no suspects.

Ty Dalton hadn't surfaced from under his rock. Paige checked her thoughts. *God is the ultimate judge, not me.*

A lot of this had to do with a personal stake in Walt and his family. She instantly reverted to her operative role—calculating, impassive, and alert. With Ty having a possible link to Keary, this whole thing could go deeper than a small-town shooting.

Now, as Paige sat in her parked car across the street from where the shooting had taken place, she studied the area and noted all of the places where the shooter could have been hiding. Perhaps a clue had been left behind.

Paige opened the door and grabbed her digital camera and shoulder bag. She assessed her surroundings, needing to be more than reasonably sure no one had followed her. Keary wasn't finished with her—and she wasn't ready to tuck him into the governor's mansion. Neither was she ready to explain why she'd driven to the crime scene. A burly man, dressed in clean jeans and a button-down shirt instead of a T-shirt, carried a tray of popcorn. Sloppy for one of Keary's people, but a possibility. She strode to the midway where Walt had been hit. Her head thundered with the questions of who and why.

The shooter had fired approximately twenty-five feet from Walt. That person had *been* in the crowd and staged himself as a family man or a woman playing the role of a mother . . . or a teen . . . or a booth vendor. She walked the twenty-five feet and mentally examined the events from when she'd first discovered the bleeding young man. If only she'd been there when Walt had taken the bullet.

Her cell phone rang, and a quick glimpse told her it was Palmer. She hadn't phoned him yet because she needed to investigate the crime scene.

"Your town hit state news," Palmer said.

"Yeah, a good kid too. No one's been arrested yet, but I have an idea."

"Ty Dalton?"

"You got it."

"That man does make the rounds. I have a bit of news for you." Palmer's tone wasn't celebrative.

"I'm ready."

"Had to move Rosa and Gonsalvo last night. Split Creek isn't the only spot that has a mole."

Paige kept her attention focused on those around her, making sure she kept her distance. "This smells worse than week-old garbage."

"And getting real personal," Palmer said.

"My parents are okay?"

"Yes. And Nathan has two of the finest operatives with him along with two others. Keary thinks he's a step ahead of us." Palmer didn't need to finish. She knew his sentiments about anyone sabotaging the work of the CIA.

"That will be his downfall," she said.

A police car eased in behind her vehicle. Paige cringed. "Gotta run. I have a situation here." She dropped her cell back into her purse.

George stepped out of his police car and waved, shoulders erect. She couldn't see his eyes. Long strides carried him her way.

"Hey, George."

"Paige." Flat. No warmth or kindness.

"Is there bad news about Walt?"

"He's holding his own, actually gaining a bit." He studied her a moment. "I figured you'd be here. I have a few questions. Some things don't make sense, and I need for you to explain them to me."

This did not have social call written on it. "Sure. I'll do whatever I can to help, but Miles and I didn't witness the shooting."

"I understand that." He leaned on one leg. "Split Creek's always been a quiet town until recently. It began when that fellow from Oklahoma City showed up—the one who works at the same law firm as Daniel Keary. You weren't happy to see him, but I overlooked it. Thought he was harmless, just pestering a pretty lady. I still find it odd that Keary contributed those computers. It's rare that politicians perform random acts of kindness. It's even rarer one would choose Split Creek." George paused. Paige recognized the grilling stare, and she assumed the stance.

"Then the library window was shot out during hours you should have been at home. Makes me question whether the shooter was aiming at the library window or you." George peered into her face. "Keary showed up after a football game, and you two exchanged a few heated words. I couldn't hear what y'all said, but from a distance, I could see you two weren't chummy."

"You must be stressed, George, because you're not making sense." She stood motionless, allowing her mind to focus on those methods that left her unreadable.

"I think I'm making good sense. Tell me why you're licensed for a Beretta Px4, a pretty hefty gun for a little lady. It's a military issue. Oh, and you have a Smith 9 mm automatic, too."

"I live by myself, and I'm not fond of watch-dogs."

"Who else knows you have those weapons?"

"I believe Miles has seen my Beretta."

"Where are those guns now?"

"The Beretta's in my car, and I have the Smith in my shoulder bag."

He pointed to her shoulder. "That one?"

"Yes." She handed him the bag. "Want to see it for yourself?"

"Not really." He handed the bag back to her

without searching it. "The bullets from the broken window and the one that hit Walt don't match either of those weapons."

Paige allowed horror to fill her face. "Do you suspect me of having something to do with what happened yesterday?"

He shook his head. "No, but I suspect you might know what *is* going on."

"I have no idea why anyone would want to hurt Walt." And that was the truth.

"A few lowlifes have come to mind, but nothing I can hang my hat on. I do wonder why a small-town librarian has the caliber of weapons that you find necessary to keep and carry. Our town is not a crossroads for criminals."

"I explained my reasons."

"A few months back when the library received the shipment of computers, I asked if you had a connection with Daniel Keary. You never gave me an answer."

Smart man. And he could throw a wrench in the whole investigation. "I knew him years ago."

"While he was in the CIA?"

"Does that really have anything to do with our concern for who shot Walt?"

"Guess not." He walked past her several feet and bent to the ground, then straightened. Confidence emanated from his bearing—sort of a cross between Barney Fife and Wyatt Earp. "If you need help, Paige, just ask. I know you and Miles are close, but he's not trained in police work. But I imagine you are."

"I appreciate your concern for me. I'm okay. Maybe a little neurotic now and then."

He raised a brow. "Excuse me if I don't believe that. You have my number. I sure hate what happened to Walt, and I intend to find out who did it. My next stop is Ty Dalton." With those words he left her in the persona of a woman who didn't know what was going on.

Paige watched him pull away slowly as though absorbed in everything they'd discussed. When he ran out of questions, would he put more together and do a search on her? Paige Rogers was as phony as the measurements on a Barbie doll. She'd better let Palmer know.

Paige had arranged for Savannah to arrive at the library for her internship at four o'clock on Monday afternoon. As soon as Miles finished football practice, the two planned to drive to Pradmore for dinner and to visit Walt. It wasn't a date, just two hungry people who didn't want to cook.

Who was she trying to fool?

She stood on her front porch and watched the quarter horses grazing near the fence across the road and enjoyed the late afternoon sun. The horses formed a picturesque scene against a backdrop of brilliant yellows and oranges. She made her way across the road to get as close as possible to the pastoral setting. As soon as she had patted her share of horses, Miles drove up in his truck and joined her.

"This is my idea of perfection," she whispered, as though the sound of her own voice would break the beauty of the regal animals and the amber afternoon. "My idea of heaven is right here."

"This *can* be your life." Miles wrapped his arm around her waist, and she didn't protest. She welcomed it. Sometime in the last few days, she'd chosen to stop fighting her emotions for him. If it was wrong to bask in his love and to return those feelings, then she'd deal with it later. The desire to tell him about Nathan nearly overwhelmed her, but that must wait.

"So what's your real name?"

She hesitated. "Mikaela Olsson."

"You don't look Swedish. I'd expect a blonde, blue eyes, and white skin."

"Hair color, brown contacts, and spray-on tan."

"Do you have a picture of yourself as a blue-eyed blonde?" Miles asked.

Paige swung a sideways look at him. "What do you think?"

"Never hurts to ask. I can't imagine you any more beautiful than you already are, but—"

"When would I make this transformation? Then again, once Keary is exposed, I could wear purple hair and orange eyes. The citizens of Split Creek will never forgive me anyway."

"They have skeletons in their closets too."

"Government ones?"

"Maybe. Where do your folks live?"

Miles was prying, but it didn't anger her. "Wisconsin. A dairy farm. They're still there, but I don't know if Dad is still in the milking business."

"When was the last time you saw them?"

"Are you psychoanalyzing me?"

"That was a career path that lasted one weekend while I was in college. Ended when the keg was empty."

"You're great with kids. But you'd be treading treacherous waters with me. I'm brutal with shrinks." She cast an admiring glance at the dipping sun. "Eight and a half years ago."

"Was it a good visit?"

She paused and remembered their disappointment when she had refused to accompany them to a Thanksgiving Eve church service. "I had my moments. Never had the opportunity to apologize before I was killed in a plane crash."

"When you first told me about that, I thought it was cold, harsh. Then I understood you'd deceived them out of love. Your life must be tough."

She leaned into him, not wanting to think about how long it would last. "Dr. Freud, there's nothing I can do. Even when Keary is behind bars, I doubt if my parents will take me back with open arms. Would you?" The truth about her son bannered across her mind.

"Can't analyze love." His words may have been spoken about Paige's relationship with her parents, but she understood the intensity of his feelings. She had no answers either. "What causes a man to betray his country?"

She could tell him this part. "I'd worked with Keary on other missions. During one of them, his wife and two children were killed in a car accident. He never got over it. Things like that change people forever. Numbs them from caring. Miles, I've been involved in places you've never heard of. Done things that cause me to question my faith."

"And I doubt if we can solve the dilemma about world peace tonight. So let's get some dinner and check in on Walt." He planted another kiss on her cheek.

She had to seal these moments in her hard drive for when reality blue-screened her emotions.

Miles backed his truck out of the driveway and onto the road. "Are you ready for a big Harley ride?"

"I'd rather bridle a turkey."

"I'm sure you miss the excitement from your operative days."

"I don't do fast and dangerous, remember?"

He gave her a disapproving look, one that said he knew better.

"I do cook and help out football coaches who have a party to give on Sunday afternoon."

"Oh yeah. Nearly forgot about that. But the Harley ride is a big occasion."

"How big?"

"My opportunity to get the iron butt award."

"The what?" Paige stared at him incredulously. What would he come up with next?

"If a rider can accumulate a thousand miles on his bike in twenty-four hours, then he gets the iron butt award."

"Woo-hoo! Is it an iron-on patch?"

"Very funny."

"That will have to be a solo flight," she said.

"It would be nice to have you to talk to."

*I'll treasure this for as long as I can.* "Try your Bluetooth."

"Oh, Miss Rogers, you do make a man's heart weaken."

"You can sweet-talk all you want, darlin', but I'm not climbing onto the back of a Harley for a thousand miles."

"How about an hour?"

"Forget it."

"Did you train at the Farm in Virginia?"

She laughed, the first time in a long time. "Miles, you've been watching way too much TV. I can direct you to a book that has good, sound information. It's in the library."

She wondered if he thought her role in the CIA was all danger and excitement. The reality was she spent a lot of time waiting while other ops moved into position for the assignment. And nothing happened until those who were under surveillance revealed more and more about themselves and allowed the operatives to act.

He turned onto the interstate. "I've heard that if the average American knew what was really going on in our country, they wouldn't leave their homes." His serious tone inched her closer to reality.

"Possibly." *True, so very true.*

"Are you planning to stay in the CIA?"

He'd nailed her there—the perpetual prayer request. "Maybe. I don't know. It's a real . . . spiritual struggle. A real conflict of interests."

"What do you really want?"

She leaned against the headrest. "If the cobwebs of my past were woven into something that made sense, I might be able to answer your question."

"Fair enough."

A buck leaped across the road, and Miles swerved to miss it. "That deer may have escaped a hunter's shot, but he'll end up as roadkill if he doesn't mend his ways."

Roadkill Paige understood. She understood past pain might never vanish, but Miles seemed to have been able to forgive himself just as God had forgiven him. It seemed like she was holding on to a ragged rope in the pit of a deep, dry well, too tired to crawl out.

"Where are you?" Miles asked. "Bad memories?"

"Nightmares. But let's not talk about it. I'm in the mood for Italian food and ice cream."

"Why am I not surprised? Vanilla?"

"Is there any other? I hear the Dairy Whip in Pradmore has a fall special with lots of Reese's Pieces sprinkles." She reached over and touched his hand. "Just remember to keep all the tidbits of my life to yourself or—"

"I already know."

# CHAPTER 42

"FROM THE LOOK on your face, you must have heard about the latest polls," Sheila says. "Governor Daniel Keary has become a reality."

I smile at her. She has the poise and the looks for a public-pleasing first lady. Once we're in office, I'll get her to work on the ten pounds she needs to lose and encourage her to do something about the crow's-feet around her eyes.

I stand from my office chair and kiss her. "I'm so blessed to have you—for more reasons than you know." I take a deep breath.

"What's wrong?"

"When you walked into the office, I had momentarily forgotten the horrible news."

Her face registers alarm. "What, honey?"

"One of the vice presidents from WorldMarc was killed in Angola."

She gasps. "Who? What happened?"

"Joel Zuriel. Plane crash. He'd been checking on oil wells."

"Please send our condolences. I'll arrange flowers or a charity contribution." Sheila touches my face. "Did he have a wife and family?"

I hold her tightly. "No, he was single. Life is so fleeting, Sheila, and we have so little time to do what matters most."

# CHAPTER 43

MILES REALIZED how much he wanted Paige in his life for as long as he could draw breath. But the likelihood of that happening shadowed reality. No matter the outcome of the problem with Keary, Paige had most likely designed a plan for her life, and it most likely didn't include Miles. But he could think about it. No harm done there.

He should be strategizing Friday night's game. The opposing team this week had a defensive line that would give the Bobcats' offense a rough night. Poor Chris. He'd played quarterback at practice this week with the persistence of a . . . well, a cornered bobcat. Miles believed Chris's back was hurting him, but he'd denied it.

Walt would be dismissed from the hospital tomorrow, but the doctor had already said he couldn't attend the game. Maybe the next one. If he were able then, the Chickasaw Wonder would be seated on the bench with the other players, wearing bandages instead of his uniform. He didn't need *The Red Badge of Courage*; Walt had lived it.

This had been Miles's best coaching and teaching year since he'd started at Split Creek. Not only was his team moving closer to the state trophy, but his students were excelling scholastically. Ty Dalton had phoned him on Monday to say that he fully intended to "execute" his original plan to have Miles removed as the next season's coach. Dalton had also filed a complaint as to the inappropriateness of Miles tutoring some of the football players to keep up their grades. What a joke. Dalton was under suspicion for arson and shooting Walt. That man needed to suit up for a reality check—and not with his girlfriend.

His mind returned to Paige and the issues with Daniel Keary. Miles tried to imagine the life of a CIA operative. Did she go through the motions of living—getting ready for work, stopping for a Starbucks before heading into the office, enjoying holidays, and worshiping on Sunday? Or was Paige's life in a constant flux, ever alert and waiting for instructions for the next assignment? The more he thought about it, the more he realized her life had to be both. Could Miles live with

Paige's double role? Could he kiss her good-bye in the morning with the knowledge she might be killed when she stepped out of their house? Did she want children? And could he raise their children alone if she didn't survive a mission?

Paige leaned against the side of her car and watched the nurse push Walt's wheelchair out of the hospital and toward his dad's truck. She swallowed the emotion threatening to surface. Adults and teens from Split Creek High School lined both sides of the walkway, clapping and cheering. The two pastors who had counseled the kids at the hospital and the Greywolfs' priest stood among the well-wishers. Walt was beaming—and alive.

"We almost lost him last Saturday," Miles said, standing beside Paige. "Now look at him. Laughing, talking . . ."

She'd been thinking the same thing. "But the shooter is still out there."

"George says the investigation hasn't turned up a thing." Miles breathed in deeply. "I'm more than a little concerned about the other players."

Paige waved at Mrs. Greywolf. "George is a dogged cop. Won't rest until the shooter's found."

"What about you? How are you doing?" Miles's softened tone revealed his feelings for her. Where would they be when this was finished?

"I'm a survivor, and I've committed myself to the end."

Miles offered a half smile. He stood with his arms folded across his chest. What emotions was he attempting to conceal? Anger about the unresolved crime? His fear about loving her?

"You're a good man, Miles," Paige said. "This town is lucky to have you teaching and mentoring its youth."

"God makes me look good. I'm useless without Him."

"What's going on?" she asked.

"Are you reading me again?"

"Can't help it." Paige started to say because she loved him, but that would only make things worse. "I know how to make a man talk."

"Oh?" His eyes widened.

She realized the connotation and attempted to cover her tracks. "From a professional point of view."

"You're digging a deeper hole."

"From my experience in the spy world?"

"I see. What do you think is bothering me?" he asked.

"Me."

"Bull's-eye." Miles turned to her. "When this is over, will you leave?"

"I have to."

"There is no 'have-to' in the equation." Miles's frustration rose in his voice. "I want the opportunity for a relationship between us to work." He glanced at the crowd cheering on Walt and then back to her. "I want a family."

Paige caught her breath and turned toward the small crowd surrounding Walt. "Your home is here, and when this thing explodes, no one will want me to stay in Split Creek."

"You underestimate the people here. Unless you plan to take on your former role and work overseas. Would you pray about us?"

Paige forced down a lump in her throat. "I have, Miles. I've prayed about us since I realized how important you are to me."

"Someday I'd like to hear the words."

"Not until this is over . . . and maybe not then."

"Please, because loving you is driving me crazy."

Paige pressed her lips together. She'd revealed more to this man than to any other person in her entire life. "To me, love and marriage are holy, and that requires trust. What I do is not built on those values. Have you any idea what I did to make sure you weren't one of Keary's men?"

When his face blanched, she captured his gaze and refused to let it go. "I didn't think so. I lie to people, deceive them for the purpose of sucking out information. There are times I secure a witness's confidence, do my best to keep them guarded and safe, and then they still get killed. Is that what you want from a wife? It all comes down to a choice—us or my job. Because I refuse to make a lifelong commitment to someone when I won't be able to tell him what I'm doing when he's not around."

Before Miles had a chance to speak, Voleta walked their way, waving and smiling. "How come you two aren't with the rest of us?"

"We prefer to be fans on the sidelines." Paige gave her a hug.

"Isn't it wonderful the way people have turned out for Walt and his family?" Voleta asked. "Makes me love this town even more."

Voleta reached out seemingly to shake Miles's hand, but instead, she hugged him. He stiffened. Her jeans were a little snug—more like poured onto her—and so was her knit top. *Use your head, Voleta.*

"Good to see you." Miles patted Voleta's back.

Voleta smiled. "I need to head back to the salon for a late appointment. Eleanor was a real sweetheart to let me be here this afternoon."

"Tell her I said hello," Paige said. "And you're going to call me later about what we discussed this morning?"

"Sure thing." Voleta made her way back to the crowd and stopped to visit with the priest.

"Voleta and I are organizing women to prepare meals for Walt's family. We've contacted their priest, and we're working with others from their church," Paige said.

"I'm sure the Greywolfs will appreciate that."

"It was Voleta's idea. She'll make it yet."

"It's a great way to keep the community connected with what's happened." His response held no emotion, but should it? She'd dropped a bomb on his heart.

"But she needs to learn a little discretion about how she dresses." Paige shook her head. "One step at a time."

"Ready?"

When Paige nodded, he opened the truck door, and she climbed inside.

"Did I tell you that you look gorgeous today?" Miles gathered her hand into his.

Good. He'd veered away from the "us" topic. "Uh, twice. Once when you picked me up and again when we first stepped out of the truck at the hospital."

"When you expose Keary, it'll be over, and we'll have a chance at life together. Doesn't matter if you choose to stay here in Split Creek or you decide to stay with the CIA; I'm not letting you go."

Paige wished she could feel so self-assured. "Even after what I just said?"

"I've already had my own conversation with God."

# CHAPTER 44

MILES KNEW HIS PLAYERS were scared to play the sixth game of the season without Walt. The Bobcats were headed for the play-offs, but their star quarterback was out for the season. Instead of their usual joking and laughing, they acted as if they were about to attend a funeral. They almost had.

"I want to play my own position," Chris had said earlier while the team was suiting up. "I'm a receiver, not a quarterback. Makes me feel dirty, like I've betrayed Walt."

"You can do the job." Miles gripped Chris's shoulder. "What do you think Walt wants you to do?"

Chris blew out an exasperated breath. "To lead the team to a win."

"Then do it. And I think the rest of the team needs to hear that too. Gather around, guys." Miles motioned to his team. "We need to talk." Once he had their attention, he glanced at his watch. Time was running out, and he felt the same anxiety they did. "When we started practice last August, none of you were assigned positions. When I announced them, many of you were mad that a sophomore was going to play first-string quarterback. Some of you bullied him, messed with his car, blackened his eye, and a few other things I won't mention. Then Chris and Walt chose to help unite this team into a fighting force that brought us through win after win. Walt can't be here, and the same guys who once hated him aren't willing to head onto the field without him. Walt earned your respect each time he ignored the barbs and helped add points to the scoreboard. All of you care about him. I'm proud of how much you've grown this season. I'm proud of your accomplishments. But I ask you, what does Walt want you to do tonight?"

The boys glanced at each other without a word.

"Win," a linebacker said.

When the players agreed, Miles held up his hand. "Then win this game for Walt. Dedicate every play, every pass, every tackle, and every point to our player who can't be here with us."

"I will." Chris stood from the bench. "And after we win tonight, maybe we could visit him at home."

Those were not the sentiments of someone who was involved in Walt's shooting.

Miles clapped his hands. "All right. Those are the Bobcats I know. We have ten minutes before we head out onto the field. Ten minutes before we capture our sixth win of the season."

Shortly before ten o'clock that night, Miles knocked on the Greywolfs' door. He'd phoned earlier to see if the family approved of the team's paying Walt a visit. The boys were excited, more like little boys than near men. Walt was resting on the sofa when the Bobcats arrived.

"Don't you go to sleep when you have the whole team here to see you," Miles said.

Walt's eyes snapped open. "My parents won't tell me a thing about the game. We won, right? I mean, we had to win. Right?"

The players filled the room and responded to Walt's question by simply talking among themselves in an attempt to look defeated.

"Should we tell him?"

A defensive tackle shook his head.

"I don't know," the kicker said. "He doesn't look very good, and he *is* on painkillers. You know—drugs."

"We'd better go home and come back when he's feeling better," another said.

"Coach, you've got to tell me." Walt stuck his leg out from under the blanket, then grimaced. "We won? I know we did. What was the score?"

"Steady. No need to climb out of there." Miles rubbed his chin. "Do you think Walt here can take the news?" He nodded at Chris.

"We won tonight! Twelve to six," Chris said. "If you'd been there, it would've been twenty-four or thirty to six."

That was probably the closest thing to friendship Chris had ever attempted.

Walt relaxed against the pillow. He swiped at a tear. "Thanks, guys. I knew you could do it. Wow, we're headed into the play-offs for sure."

"Hey, bro, we did it for you." Chris reached out to shake Walt's hand. "We just believed you were there with us."

"Thanks, guys. I *will* be there next week. The doc is letting me go back to school on Monday. Next Friday night, I'm going to be at the game."

He glanced at Miles. "But I'll be there Sunday afternoon for the football party."

Miles stepped back so his players could crowd around Walt. The Chickasaw Wonder had more friends than anyone in school. He deserved it after what he'd been through. But Miles would feel a whole lot better when the shooter sat behind bars.

Paige stood outside Miles's farmhouse and admired the L-shaped porch and the old church pews on each side of the door. Miss Eleanor had told her that his house looked like a model home, and Paige had wanted to see it for a long time. The outdated double standard for men and women had hovered over them. For some reason, in this community, it was okay for Miles to call on Paige but vastly inappropriate for her to reciprocate.

She balanced the chocolate fudge half-sheet cake on her knee and knocked on the heavy oak door. Palmer had phoned her earlier with the news that Zuriel had been killed in Angola. No surprise. She'd analyze those details after the football party. Miles opened the door before she completed her two-knock routine. He wore a soft blue sweater and jeans.

"Hi, Coach. You look like quite the gentleman farmer." Paige stepped inside. She took in the winding staircase and rich hardwood floors. "This is gorgeous. You told me you'd remodeled a bit here and there, but I hadn't expected the detail and exquisite work."

"Thanks." Miles inhaled and sent an admiring, hungry-man look at the cake. "Mmm. Chocolate. Want a tour? I think we have a few extra minutes before everyone gets here."

"Absolutely. I might steal some ideas on how to spruce up my own house."

"Do I get a kiss first?"

She rolled her eyes and did her best imitation of a teenage girl. "Like, is that the only way I get to, like, check out your house?"

"Like, yeah."

She nodded at the cake while smells of food teased her nostrils. "You'd better set this somewhere first."

"Follow me." Miles took the cake and led her into a huge kitchen, where she nearly drooled over the room's design. Light oak cabinets, an island, and brown and black speckled granite countertops peeked from under finger foods and desserts. And the classic lighting fixtures . . .

"This looks like a page out of a decorator magazine."

"Page?"

"Photograph." She made her way to a huge stainless steel stove that must have set him back a chunk of change. "Your stove looks like it debuted on the cooking channel." She opened the oven door. "Miles Laird, you've never used this."

"A few times."

"If this is where the tour begins, then you should be charging admission."

"All I want is a kiss."

She laughed—one of the things she did best with him. "I nearly forgot."

"No, you didn't. I can see it in your eyes."

Paige wrapped her arms around his neck. "You've been reading too many spy novels again."

"I'm reading romance." He pulled her tighter to him and without hesitation claimed his admission for the evening's tour.

When at last they parted, she was glad he couldn't read her thoughts. "I'm selfish, but I wish I didn't have to share you with other guests tonight."

"There's a party here? I lied. You're the only one invited."

She gestured around the room. "And why all of this food?"

"Thought we might get hungry."

The doorbell rang before she had an opportunity to respond. Miles groaned. "Someone's early, so the tour will have to be postponed."

"I paid for my ticket."

"It expires." He winked before disappearing down the hallway to answer the door.

This afternoon, Paige refused to think about Keary. She'd been right in trying one more time to prove his lawlessness. She'd taken the actions of an operative, a Christian, and a mother who cared about innocent people. Keary would be found out and charged for his murdering, lowlife tricks. All she had to do was allow God to orchestrate the universe—a difficult course for a control freak. But confidence helped her keep her focus because Keary *would* spiral down and crash. And Nathan and her parents would be safe.

Hours later, Paige pulled a pan of little sausages wrapped in pastry from the oven and set them on a cooling rack on the kitchen counter. The guests had eaten a ton of food, and still it continued to vanish. Teenage boys were like vacuum cleaners, and their daddies were right behind them. Midway through scooping the sausages onto a serving tray, her cell phone rang. The number on the caller ID was unfamiliar. She started to ignore it and let the caller leave a message, but her curiosity took over.

"Check out the six o'clock news," a male voice said and hung up.

Her party spirit took a nosedive. Keary must have a new tactic, or he wanted to let her know about Zuriel in his own way. Hesitation left her staring at the phone. Without a doubt, Keary was nervous about the CIA investigation. Then why had he had Zuriel killed, unless he'd been assured that the death could be made to look like an accident?

Miles walked into the kitchen. "I looked around and saw you were gone."

"Food supply ran short."

"What's wrong?"

She needed to better hide her preoccupation. "I received a call telling me to watch the evening news."

"Who from?"

"One of them, I suppose." She picked up the tray of food. "Not sure if I want to see it or not."

Miles lifted the tray from her arms. "I think we should, or you'll be worrying about it all evening."

The kids had the TV on in the game room, where most of the people had gathered. Had something happened in Washington or overseas? Her mind raced with the possibilities. Miles used the remote to change channels, and she saw the promo for the upcoming evening news. Two minutes to six. Tension settled on her shoulders while impatience ground at her nerves.

"What's going on, Coach?" Walt asked.

"Oh, I just like to get a quick glimpse of the news before Monday morning."

A couple of the players moaned. "You mean we have a quiz tomorrow? You can't expect Walt to go through another traumatic experience."

Miles swung them a grin. "Never know."

Why was it necessary for her to view the news? Keary had succeeded in winning the people's support, and he obviously still planned to have her on board in his new regime. Miles knew the truth, but did he actually believe her? The broadcaster interrupted her musings.

"Tonight's news features a startling announcement made earlier today by Daniel Keary, who is ahead in the polls as Oklahoma's next governor. Stay tuned for this breaking news."

Again she waited while a gamut of commercials spun their enticement. The world's best truck. The world's best orange juice. The world's best cell phone deal. Then a news anchor gave the TV camera a sober look.

"This afternoon, Daniel Keary called a press conference regarding a woman who is stalking him and threatening his family."

*Who could this be? Has he been cheating on his wife?*

The footage flashed to Keary, who posed behind a podium with his wife. He managed the demeanor of a politician quite nicely. "Eight years ago, during the time I worked for the CIA and was not married, I had a relationship with a woman who was also employed by the CIA. When I ended the relationship, she had a mental breakdown. As a result the CIA dismissed her from her duties."

Paige's heart threatened to burst from her chest. She stiffened. Had Keary won the battle *and* the war?

Keary had not finished his announcement. "During the past several months, this woman has attempted to force herself back into my life. When I refused, she began to pursue me and frighten my family, making our lives miserable. She also stated her intentions of bringing our past affair to the attention of the media. My pledge to the citizens of Oklahoma is honesty. I will not have my campaign tainted with lies and secrets."

Paige's rage bubbled. *What else, Lord? How can this be for the cause of good?*

"Rather than be asked by the press about this unfortunate disturbance in my family's life and how it could affect my role as governor, my wife and I have chosen to publicly refute any accusations of marital infidelity."

"What is the woman's name?" a reporter asked.

"There is no reason to exploit this woman who obviously still suffers from mental instability."

*You jerk. You lying son of Satan.*

The footage ended and flashed back to the newscaster, who kept her face rigid. "Since this announcement, sources have learned that the woman, whose name is Mikaela Olsson, is living in Split Creek under the assumed name of Paige Rogers. She is the local librarian, where Keary donated computers for the town's youth." A recent photo of Paige filled the upper right-hand corner of the TV screen.

Paige tasted the acid of devastation. She stared into the TV while uncomfortable silence hovered around her. She refused to look at Miles. His players and friends had heard every word. How embarrassing for him. Anger and the anguish of disappointment rooted in her heart. This had not been one of the scenarios that she and Palmer had discussed.

Her cell rang again, and she knew the caller without answering. Paige quietly turned and left the room. She grabbed her purse from the kitchen and hurried down the hallway. Her heels clicked on the hardwood floors, keeping pace with her heartbeat. The smells of food sickened her. The only sounds were the TV in the background and her incessant cell phone. It stopped ringing the moment her hands turned the doorknob. A few seconds later, it began ringing again. Miles touched her arm, but she shook her head and gestured him to back off. She stepped outside and closed the door behind her before answering the phone.

"What did you think of the evening news?"

Paige reclaimed her true identity—that of an operative on a mission. She knew the script. "Keary, what do you want from me? You've killed my friends and threatened those I love."

"I'm not finished with you yet."

"What do you want from me? I've never understood why you thought I'd get in your way. If that was the case, why didn't I expose you when you announced your candidacy?"

"Lying doesn't become you, and playing innocent is not your style. I should have gotten rid of you after that business in Africa, but your demise would have raised doubts about my integrity."

"Integrity? You don't know the meaning of the word."

"You are a fine one to question what I do."

"I want it to end." In truth, she wanted him dead. "Let the voters decide the election."

"When were you planning to tell me about Nathan?"

Panic attempted to worm its way through her control. "Who is Nathan?"

"Doesn't matter." He chuckled. "Think about this: if I can eliminate Rosa and Gonsalvo and Zuriel in a matter of a few hours, then I can locate my son."

Rosa and Gonsalvo? She had no choice. "What do you want me to do?"

"So, you've come around to my way of thinking? Smart move. All I need for you to do is check yourself into a psychiatric hospital until after the election. To corroborate my version of the truth."

"And if I refuse?"

"A farmhouse in Wisconsin will get my attention, as well as Split Creek's football coach. And then there is Nathan. I assure you, you would never see him again."

Trapped.

"And you'll leave my friends and my parents alone?"

"As long as you keep your nose clean and leave the state once your little vacation is over, and you follow my directions. For insurance purposes, my men will be watching the coach and dear old Mom and Dad. Nathan is another matter. I have the means to adopt him. Ironic, don't you think? Thought about it ever since I learned the truth."

Her knees weakened. *Not my son. You'll never have him.* "Whatever it takes. I give up."

"Of course you do. I value family. It's been a pleasure doing business with you."

Paige snapped the phone shut and wrapped her fingers around her keys. She would not go back inside the house. Miles had faced humiliation, and she looked like a pathetic mental case who had deceived them all.

The door opened behind her.

"Paige."

She heard Miles, but she would not give in to her emotions and turn around. People were probably watching from the windows. Right now they were stunned. They had to believe that Miles had been duped too.

He whirled her around to face him. "You can't run from this."

"I'm doing what has to be done. For your own sake, go back to your guests."

"Can't you give them an explanation of what happened?" His eyes held the torment of bruised love and unanswered questions.

"Most of what Keary said was true." She hated the words flung at Miles, but she had to protect him. "I tried to warn you from the beginning, Miles. Deal with it."

"You can't leave until we talk about this." His eyes blazed with an anger she'd never seen in him.

"Watch me." She pulled his hands from her arms.

"If you leave, we have nothing."

"We never did."

Paige opened her car door. She fought the flood of tears burning her throat and searing her heart. *Nathan. I have to protect him.*

# CHAPTER 45

PAIGE THREW A FEW clothes into a suitcase for the trip to the psychiatric hospital while fighting the fury that made her want to stick a knife into Keary's black heart and twist it. He'd lit the fuse for this whole nasty thing to explode in her face. She felt so stupid that she hadn't seen this coming.

With Keary's high profile, the news would hit national media, which meant her parents would learn their daughter was still alive. That kind of shock needed to come from Paige, not an impassioned newscaster or reporter. And what about her mother's heart condition? Thoughts darted about her mind as to what she should say—an explanation that hovered in the proverbial gray area. Would Paige ever be able to recognize untainted truth? Her plan to protect them from Keary had failed, but not in the way she'd ever expected. God had to fit somewhere in all of this. She needed guidance, and she was all prayed out.

A glimpse back to home, when life was easy and problems centered on the farm. She remembered summer picnics spread on a tattered quilt with mismatched silverware and chipped dishes, horseback riding with blue ribbons and proud smiles. Fall ushered in hayrides and the sound of voices echoing across the night air, picking apples and biting into the sweetest crunch known to man. She recalled the thrill of ice-skating, sled rides in frosty snow, and the aroma of hot chocolate on a cold day. Spring was her favorite time of the year—new growth and animals born on the farm. Memories swirled through her mind. Each one was an invitation to venture back to a simpler time. But most of all, she remembered the love of her family.

She would not look back. Tomorrow morning, she'd contact the life insurance company and take care of repaying the monies paid to her mom and dad seven years ago.

The call to Wisconsin needed to be made. Paige's fingers trembled, and she dialed the wrong number twice. She steadied herself and used the mental techniques that had once kept her alive to focus on what must be done.

The phone rang once, twice, three times. A pause. A click. "This is the Olssons'." *Mom's voice.* "We aren't able to answer your call right now. Carl's doing something with the cows, and I'm cooking. Always cooking. Leave a message, and one of us will call you back. It'll probably be me. Carl's always too busy with the cows." A tear slipped down Paige's cheek. Mom hadn't lost her sense of humor.

Paige should be telling them this in person, at the very least over the phone, not via an impersonal message machine.

"Mom, Dad, this is Mikaela. I'm sorry for what you are about to learn. The media has released information that will shock and hurt you. I'm sorry. So sorry. It was never my intention to deceive you, but to protect you. I . . . I . . . Please forgive me."

She slumped to the floor and buried her face in her hands. The past had collided with the present and breached the dam that had held back her emotions for so long.

Keary's heart had long since turned to charcoal, ever since his family had been killed, and his habits and even his reasons for helping kids were birthed in his own loss. Did it even make any sense? Children had been killed in the bombing eight years ago, and children had been killed in the villages where WorldMarc now drilled for oil. He'd destroyed countless lives with his lust for money, and he'd activated a quest for revenge that mocked her faith. She didn't care if seeking revenge was wrong. The nightmare had to end.

But first she had to concentrate on calming her fury. She needed to force the vibrating hate from her body and revert to her operative training. She was a Christian waffling between the tenets of her faith and an operative role that called on her to bring down an unscrupulous man and to protect those she loved. What kind of ethics did she live by?

She tossed the suitcase to the floor and hurried outside to her front porch. In the darkness, she sat in the white rocker and stared across the road. The sound of cicadas and the creak of the rocker slowly caused the violence in her soul to subside. She prayed for guidance and wisdom instead of how she could kill Daniel Keary without leaving a mark.

Two hours later, Paige locked the door to her haven in Split Creek and tossed a few meager belongings into the trunk of her car. Keary had phoned again, and she'd given him the location of a psychiatric facility in Tulsa. Determination had given her hope and a plan. Before leaving, she contacted Palmer.

"I heard about the press conference," he said.

"Figured that. Keary hasn't won yet. His announcement may play right into our hands. I'm to check into a psychiatric hospital. Sorry to hear about Rosa and Gonsalvo."

"Mikaela, they're fine. In fact, as soon as the

news hit our door, we moved them and Nathan to a more secure safe house."

"He told me they were dead."

"He wishes."

Relief swept through her. "He's also on to Nathan."

"We knew that was only a matter of time. I learned that my assistant has taken an apartment in Virginia with a male friend. That might be Keary's link to our office. She's being brought in as we speak."

*And I need to know the mole in Split Creek.* "What about Ty Dalton?"

"He's a little low on the food chain for Keary. The answer there lies in Zuriel, but he's now in a box. Jason Stevens is connected somehow, and we have enough to arrest him, but he's worth more to us free to continue business."

Depression slithered in and attached its tentacles to her heart. "Zuriel would have cut a deal. I feel like I've accomplished nothing."

"You've drawn Keary out of his hole and forced his hand. We know more than before. Tell me what your plan is, other than for him to think he's got the election and his past right where he wants them."

"I want him to feel confident in arranging my death. With what I'm about to do, the media will take the story and run with it—a former CIA operative who had a breakdown during a mission and now stalks Daniel Keary has admitted herself into a psychiatric hospital. I'm going to stay there long enough for Keary to believe his past is safe; then I'll check out of the facility and open the door for him to do his worst. I think with what he's threatened and Zuriel gone, he'll loosen his ropes and slip."

"Time is not on our side, but I see your point. I have a few things to do on this end too."

"What I fear most is his finding Nathan. I don't want my son used as a pawn."

"Keary won't hurt him."

"I know, but his intel has let him know that Nathan is his son, and he'll be obsessed with establishing contact."

"I'll make sure we can keep in touch."

"No matter what happens in the next few days, I want your word that you will look out for Nathan, Miles Laird, and my parents."

"You got it."

## CHAPTER 46

MY PLANS HAVE all fallen into place. After the clever way I exposed Mikaela, any judge in the country will give the governor of Oklahoma custody of Nathan. She nailed her coffin closed by admitting herself into the psychiatric facility. Of course, I gave her no other choice.

Stevens is with his contact, and soon I'll know where the CIA has placed Rosa and Gonsalvo and Nathan.

Sheila appears in the doorway. "Your son is asking for his daddy to tuck him into bed. I thought you'd have time before we left for dinner."

*My son.* She has no idea what I'll do to have my son. "I'm on my way."

Plan B means giving up the governorship.

# CHAPTER 47

SHORTLY AFTER MIDNIGHT, Paige pulled off Interstate 35 for coffee and gas before taking the turnpike from Oklahoma City to Tulsa. She turned off the engine and hurried inside the gas station. The coffee tasted like it had been made the day before, but bitterness was a taste she'd grown to recognize. Before joining the company, she'd added cream and two sugars. Then she'd learned to drink it black and medicate herself with caffeine.

She and Voleta had had some great conversations over coffee—Paige's strong and black, Voleta's sweet and caramel colored. They'd laughed about fashion trends, all of which Voleta had a tendency to follow, and men, most of which Voleta had a tendency to follow after too. They usually met early in the morning at the doughnut shop before Voleta had appointments and Paige opened the library. Her zany friend had eased the pressures of what Paige could not forget and the hopelessness of a future stained with blood from the past. Even though her friend wasn't a Christian, she was definitely a blessing sent from God.

*Does God really send unbelievers as blessings?* Paige supposed so. She took another sip of coffee. He certainly did in Paige's case.

Years before in a coffeehouse near Berkeley, Paige had chosen the path of keeping America safe. Convinced that was her purpose, she'd wormed her way into the areas of the world where only demons survived. Maybe she'd failed there, too, because she'd crawled out smelling as evil as what she'd tried to destroy.

She buried the question in the black depths of her soul until she could work through it all again. Still the thoughts about Voleta persisted.

Paige reached for her cell phone to check in with Palmer. They needed a means for her to keep in contact with him. Her phone wasn't in the pocket in her shoulder bag. She searched through the other zipped compartments. Granted, her mind had raced with Keary and Miles and Nathan, but she wasn't that scattered. When her phone still didn't surface, she searched through her car.

Her last call had been to Palmer. Then she'd

anchored it in the console. No, she'd slipped it into her jeans pocket. Patting the empty pockets, she moaned. She must have lost it. Great. Maybe she *had* lost her mind.

# CHAPTER 48

ON MONDAY, Miles fought the urge to call and check on Paige. His stubbornness won out. Neither did he intend to head to the library. His mind raced with questions about the real truth. He hated to think that she'd lied to him about the CIA and Daniel Keary. As bizarre as her story had sounded at the time, Miles had believed every word. But everything Keary had said in his press conference ate at his gut. Paige and Keary involved? Mentally unstable people had a way of convincing others, and she'd lied for a living. Paige hadn't denied any of Keary's accusations. In fact, she'd walked away from Miles.

*"Deal with it."* That had been a harsh way to end their relationship—if there ever had been one.

He recalled the night Keary had ridden the Channel 6 helicopter to congratulate the Bobcats on their win and Paige's reaction to him. If what the politician had reported was accurate, then Paige's reaction could have been a part of her mental illness. But the bomb . . . Certainly she wouldn't have planted a bomb in her own car. Miles rubbed the chill bumps on his arm. He didn't want to doubt the woman he loved, but logic gave credence to Keary.

His mind refused to let go of last night's press conference. The wary looks from the students, the sympathetic looks from the other teachers, the ache in his chest, and the lump in his throat plagued him all day and into the early afternoon.

During his free period, Miles retreated to his office. He pulled out a multiple-choice quiz that he'd given the kids on Friday, but as he tried to grade it, his concentration failed him. Too many problems marched across his sleep-deprived mind. Chris's performance on the field had improved, but not to the caliber that it needed to be for them to continue winning. In addition, Miles worried about Chris's back injury. All of which Miles could have handled if Paige had not disappeared—cementing his fears that she was truly mentally unstable.

A knock on the window of his office startled him. Chris stood in the doorway. He shifted from one foot to the other. "Hey, Coach. Got a minute?"

*This is not a good time.* "A quick one."

"Uh, I want to tell you I'm sorry."

Miles relaxed. "Thanks. You and I have had our share of bad sacks lately."

"Can't trust anybody."

Miles should have jumped in about trusting God, but neither his mind nor his mouth could form the words.

"My dad moved back in last night."

Miles lifted a brow. "How do you feel about that?" Great, now he was beginning to sound like Dr. Phil.

"Like . . . home started to be good with just Mom and me. But they're going to start counseling today."

"Have you talked to either of them about what this means?"

Chris pressed his lips together, as though the words he wanted to say would give away his emotions. "Both of them did the parent thing. I mean, they came into my room and made the announcement. And Dad said he'd go to church with us." The bell rang, and he glanced at the door. "Anyway, Mom talked about forgiveness, but he didn't say anything about what I saw that night at the hotel."

"Give him time." Miles needed to take his own advice.

"Yeah, right. Well, I came to tell you about my parents and to say I'm sorry about Miss Rogers. I really liked her. She helped a bunch of us with school stuff."

"I appreciate it." The second bell rang and Chris cringed. Miles pulled a pass book from inside his desk drawer and scribbled out a note. "Here, you'll need this."

"Thanks, Coach. See you after school."

After Chris left, Miles tilted back in his chair. He'd like to see the Daltons put their lives back together. Ty Dalton bothered him worse than a bellyache, but Ginny Dalton loved her husband.

After football practice, Miles got into his truck feeling more miserable than he could remember in a long time. No point in following up on the latest Channel 6 news or attempting to phone Paige. He'd check on her and ease his conscience by making sure she'd not harmed herself. In her mental state, she might try something stupid. He considered phoning Voleta to meet him there, but no one answered at the salon.

Miles drove to Paige's house. Pride had stood in his way all day with the realization she'd lied to him, but nothing could change his love for her. If she needed psychiatric care, then she'd have the best. If she and Keary had once been involved, then who was Miles to throw stones? But she'd done irreparable damage to his heart, and he'd never get that close to her again.

But what about the bomb in her car? The puzzle had picked at him all day. How could a person with a mental disorder obtain a permit for a gun? And who shot Walt? None of it made sense. Just before Miles had left school, a reporter had left a message for him to call. Fat chance.

He drove through town and out the paved road leading to Paige's house. He noted the cloudless blue sky with no hint of rain, but the weatherman kept promising relief from the drought. Miles pulled into the familiar gravel driveway while a fistful of questions pummeled him. *One answer at a time.* He scanned the area, and yet he didn't know what to look for. The quiet did nothing to ease the fear that Paige might have given up on life. By now, the entire nation had heard the bizarre story. And what about her parents in Wisconsin, or was that another lie?

Miles stepped from his truck and leaned against the closed door while studying the front of Paige's home. The neat flower beds beside the porch steps, the white rocker, and her red, white, and blue milk can looked like a scene from one of Norman Rockwell's paintings—rural America—not the home of a mentally disturbed CIA operative, or maybe ex-CIA operative. Everything that had happened since he'd interrupted Paige and one of Keary's men that August night seemed incomprehensible.

The search for Paige brought back the nightmare of searching for his younger brother after he'd disappeared. Miles had resolutely followed trails and bits of information from other druggies until he stumbled onto the rusty abandoned car that Bill had called home. There, his brother's body lay sprawled out on the front seat—emaciated and covered in sores and scabs—scabs from selling the blood from his meth-infested body to other addicts. Miles had spent countless hours in his pastor's office weeping buckets for the loss . . . the guilt . . . and the shame. He'd ended up running from the misery under the guise of starting all over to make a difference in kids' lives. And until this moment, he'd believed he'd laid the bulk of it behind.

*God, I can't find her dead. You wouldn't bring me down this road again, would You?*

Miles craved answers about Paige and Keary. As far as he could tell, Keary didn't have a single blemish on his record. He stood for all the good things the citizens of Oklahoma longed for. No one had a reason to question his integrity. No one but Paige, and she'd disappeared—or rather she'd run like he'd done in dealing with his brother's death. Unless she was inside the house and not answering her door or her phone. He climbed the porch steps, noting the familiar creaks, the ones he and Paige used to laugh about. He knocked and listened for the turn of the dead bolt. A few moments later, he knocked a bit harder. For the first time in his life, he wished he had a lock-pick kit. Probably something Paige carried in her purse. When she still didn't appear, he tried the knob, but it refused to turn.

He walked around the house to the back door. They'd planted purple pansies two weeks ago, and she'd made a roast with potatoes and carrots. After dinner, they'd played Scrabble. She'd insisted upon using acronyms representing missions and committees from the CIA that meant nothing to him, and he'd objected enough times to win the game. She'd promised to teach him how to make his favorite oatmeal raisin cookies the next time they were together.

Neither of them had spoken a word about Keary, but Miles knew her thoughts were there. As he'd watched her go about mindless tasks, he'd tried to guess what ran through her mind. Did it flow in a steady stream of suspicions? Did she always have her brain focused on the unusual? The old cliché bannered across his mind that you could take the operative out of the CIA, but you couldn't take the CIA out of the operative. Or had it all been Paige's fabrication?

The back door was locked too. He peered in the kitchen window and saw nothing. Heaviness rested on his shoulders. What if she lay on the floor inside and needed help? Or worse? The windows around the house were latched. He could break one and set his mind at ease. His attention turned to the single attached garage at the side of the house. He jogged to the side door. Locked. He attempted to open the windowless garage door. Locked. He had no way of knowing if her car was inside.

On the left side of the driveway, directly in front of the garage, he saw her silver cell phone. He picked it up and turned it over in his hands. He understood the technology to eliminate the tracing of any incoming or outgoing phone calls. No doubt she had it. After turning on the phone, he checked the call history. But any calls had been deleted. Her address book was devoid of any numbers. Not even the library, Voleta's, or Miles's own number. He glanced back at the house. If he had access to her computer, he could check the incoming and outgoing calls online.

Paige's phone rang. How did he answer? He muffled a "hey" in hopes of sounding like Paige.

"Mikaela, how are your parents?" a male voice said.

"This is Miles Laird, not Mikaela. Wherever she is, she doesn't have her phone. Since you know her by name and apparently know where she is, I need answers."

The caller hung up. Was it Keary using a disguised voice . . . or her contact . . . or a new boyfriend?

Miles had read every word on the CIA Web site. He didn't know anyone with connections there. According to the online information, if someone had information that might be of interest to the CIA, then the person could complete a form or call. He stared at the screen. He'd do both. The process was obviously designed to weed through the phonies and idiots who contacted CIA headquarters every day. Miles wrote in the subject line of his e-mail "For Mikaela Olsson's contact" and prayed such a person existed and that someone would take Miles seriously. However, the problem in Oklahoma was a national concern, and it did involve two operatives who'd once worked for them. Let the CIA sort out the truth. Miles reviewed his online submission, then clicked Send. What else could he do?

Tuesday night, Miles paced his house. He didn't feel like doing anything or talking to anyone. All he wanted was word from Paige, that she'd found help for her problems. TV news had more coverage about Keary's integrity—nothing substantial, just more of the same glowing reports about Oklahoma's best candidate. Miles didn't know whom or what to believe, especially the report of Paige's admittance into a psychiatric hospital.

A pounding on the door caused him to jump. Maybe George had learned something about Paige. Maybe she'd returned and wanted to see him. He swung open the door to greet a silver-haired man dressed in jeans and a brown leather jacket.

"Miles Laird."

It was not a question. "Yes."

"I'd like to talk to you about Mikaela Olsson."

*Not another stinking reporter.* "Who are you?"

"An old friend of hers."

"That doesn't tell me anything. You look like a news reporter to me."

"Government security."

"CIA?"

The man pulled his wallet from his jacket and handed him a photo of himself and a gorgeous blonde who looked enough like Paige that Miles knew it was Mikaela Olsson. "This was taken nine years ago when she worked for the CIA."

Miles handed the photo back to him in an effort to appear confident. After all, he'd once owned a government security business. "How would I know?"

The man offered a tight-lipped smile. "This shouldn't take long. Can we talk?"

Did he really want him inside? "Do you have a name?"

"Greg Palmer."

Miles hesitated. If Paige had spoken the truth, Palmer could be CIA or a thug for Daniel Keary. His leather jacket had plenty of room for a gun. "I have no idea where she is, but I'd sure like to know."

Palmer stepped in without an invitation and closed the door behind him. Little late for second and third thoughts.

"This isn't a social call," Palmer said. "Neither will you need a Band-Aid."

Miles forced a grin. "In that case, have a seat. Would you like something? coffee?"

"No thanks." Palmer walked into the living room and sat in Miles's favorite chair. "Mikaela checked into a psychiatric facility in Tulsa on Sunday night, just like you've been hearing from the media."

"So she is mentally ill."

"That's where you come in."

This guy talked in riddles just like Paige did. "What are you talking about?"

"We'd like for you to pay her a little visit."

# CHAPTER 49

MILES GRABBED the pink teddy bear from his truck seat and a plastic container full of oatmeal raisin cookies. Inside his jacket pocket was a jumbo-size bag of Reese's Pieces. He shut the door, methodically hit the alarm button on his key ring, and walked toward the entrance of the Magnolia Life Center to see Paige. Or Mikaela. Or whatever he should call her. He'd done his homework and called the facility to make sure he could bring a gift and the cookies. Palmer had supplied the bear, but Miles had baked the cookies. He'd purchased frozen cookie dough from the dairy case at the Piggly Wiggly and followed the directions for perfect cookies in ten minutes. Much more of this peculiar behavior and he'd be ready to join the CIA himself. This "drop" role added a little excitement to his life.

Besides being a part of Palmer's plan, the cookies and teddy bear were part of Miles's cover. In case Keary was watching, they made him look like a lovesick redneck. The politician wouldn't see Split Creek's football coach as a threat, only as a man coming to pay his cowgirl a visit—no high-tech strategy to pull Paige from the facility nor any CIA professionals making an appearance.

Miles resisted the urge to scan the parking lot and look for suspicious characters. What did he know about spies and espionage? He'd had to look up a glossary on the CIA Web site to discover that Paige had been an operative rather than an agent.

She'd checked herself in as Mikaela Olsson, and the news vultures had gobbled it up. Miles was told he'd have to supply identification in addition to securing doctor and patient approval before he would be permitted to see her. He hadn't been able to think of her as Mikaela. She'd always be Paige the librarian to him: pies on Thursdays, cakes for his football team, and Miles's dream of a sweet life with her—which was over. She'd stolen his heart and shattered it. Miles tried to tell himself it was over between them, that his errand for Palmer was simply his national duty. Nothing else. The truth had become so distorted. What did he really feel about Paige? As she'd so aptly stated, love and marriage meant a commitment to trust. They didn't have it. In fact, they didn't have a thread of it.

The sprawling redbrick facility near Tulsa used biblical principles to counsel its patients. Despite the lack of luster on the grounds, a statue of Jesus carrying the lost lamb offered a sense of peace. Paige might not be insane, but she did carry a load of guilt and shame for some of what she'd done in her role in keeping the United States safe.

Ever since Palmer had convinced him to give government security a hand, Miles had sensed relief, and yet he had no clue about the future. He didn't know what he'd find inside, and every time he thought about it, his ulcer took a giant bite of his stomach. Even if Paige had suffered from a breakdown in Angola, Palmer obviously believed she was right.

Keary might be ahead in the polls, but he'd lose the war.

Miles strolled through the double glass doors to the foyer, trying to look confident with the container of cookies, the pink teddy bear, and a racing pulse. A plaque that read "Come to me, all you who are weary and burdened, and I will give you rest" was mounted on a wall in front of him. The entrance glistened with cleanliness and the scent of fresh flowers. The earth tones soothed him, even though he wasn't a patient. *But I am a sojourner on a quest for truth.* Odd how his mind worked on a higher plane during stress.

"Can I help you, sir?"

Miles smiled at a black woman behind the receptionist's desk. Her name tag read Janetta Scott. "Yes, ma'am. I called yesterday to see if I could visit one of your patients and to see if I could bring this teddy bear and cookies."

The woman had a sincere smile. "I think I took the call."

"The patient's name is Mikaela Olsson." He studied her face for any sign of condemnation, as if it mattered. He set his gifts on the counter and pulled his wallet from his pocket. "Her doctor has given his permission, and I have my ID."

She paused, as though searching for words. "As I mentioned yesterday, Miss Olsson's permission must also be obtained. I'm afraid she refused the request this morning, and her wishes must be honored."

"Would you please ask Mikaela again? I sure would like to give these things to her."

The woman stood from her chair. "I'll check again. I'll be back shortly."

After waiting at the desk for a while, he decided that Janetta Scott's "shortly" meant hours. He glanced around at an empty sofa and chairs. An open Bible lay on a table with a few appropriate magazines, mostly devotionals and periodicals with family-oriented themes. Miles moved to the seating area and eased down onto a straight-back chair. He searched for something to occupy his mind. At least there were no issues of *Time*. He'd already heard about the article soon to be released hailing the perseverance of Daniel Keary in the midst of extreme stress and fear for his family. The *Tulsa World* referred to Keary as a consummate professional. What a bunch of bull.

Miles, conscious of his faith-filled surroundings and the facility dedicated to love and good mental health for all those in need, realized his thoughts weren't exactly inspiring. But he couldn't deny their validity.

Janetta Scott returned. "I'm sorry, sir, but Miss

Olsson will not see you. She doesn't want any visitors. And she asked that you not return."

Miles frowned. Palmer had prepared him for this. "Would you tell her that I have news about Nathan?"

Miss Scott dampened her lips.

"I believe it will make a difference," he said. "Would you please try one more time?"

Palmer had mentioned the name Nathan as if he expected Miles to know who—or what—he was talking about. Miles had been too proud to ask for more information. He figured he'd find out from Paige, if it was something he needed to know.

In less than five minutes, Miss Scott met him with a smile. "Miss Olsson has agreed to see you. If she asks you to leave, then please do so."

"I have no intention of upsetting her." Miles stood from the chair. "Thank you for all you've done for me this afternoon."

"She will visit with you in the patient area." The woman gestured down the hallway. "It's on the right. There's a garden area outside if you choose to enjoy the beautiful day." She paused longer than he expected. "Miss Olsson needs compassion and understanding."

"I just want to be her friend."

"Jesus calls all of us to be friends to those who need love."

The nurse's words wrenched Miles's heart and renewed his devotion to help Paige with the problem that was bigger than both of them. As angry and hurt as he'd been, she was still his lady, and he wanted to believe her feelings were intact too. He should have stood and fought for her— trailed after her when her car sped out of his driveway after the press conference.

Keary's announcement had thrown poisoned darts at Miles's love for Paige and had nearly been successful. But Palmer's visit had helped him see that his lady was the real thing. Then guilt had set in. After all, she'd confided in him and then he'd believed the scum Keary.

The green and tan tiled floor lay before him like Paige's Green Mile. He shook himself for allowing despairing thoughts to control the mood before he met with her. She would survive this ordeal. Maybe *they'd* survive this ordeal, and they'd have a good life together. That hope kept him going.

The teddy bear and container of cookies looked rather pitiful when he'd rather have brought her ten dozen red roses. But they fit the role he needed to play.

Paige sat curled up on a leather chair with stocking feet tucked beneath her and her toes sticking out. Running shoes sat on the floor beneath her. She wore no makeup—not that she needed it—and her hair hung in greasy ringlets. And her eyes . . . They were light blue, like the sky. The pang of fear that had attacked him moments before now tackled him again. She looked the part of a raving lunatic.

She wore a pair of gray sweatpants and a gray Split Creek High sweatshirt. Did her choice of clothes reflect her mood or her desire for what the small town offered? Miles wished he had the answers. Right now, all he wanted to do was pull her into his arms and tell her he loved her, maybe offer her some of his own feeble strength.

Paige made brief eye contact with him, then turned to the window. Conscious of others in the waiting room, he took a seat beside her.

"Hi. I had a hard time finding you."

She picked at an invisible speck of something on her sweatshirt. "I'm where I'm supposed to be."

"You are the best judge of that."

"Am I?"

Her mocking glance sent chills up his spine, defeating his confidence. "I brought you something."

Her attention moved to the teddy bear and cookies.

He offered her the plastic container. "I baked them myself."

"What kind?"

"Oatmeal raisin."

"Your favorite."

He shrugged. "I kept a few." He hoped his crooked grin might put a light in her eyes. It didn't.

She took the cookies and lifted the plastic lid. "Yum. Is it safe to try one?" So she hadn't lost her sense of humor.

"Of course. I've had my share."

She reached for one and took a generous bite. "Miles, these are the frozen kind."

"I haven't advanced to a recipe yet."

Her lips turned upward. "You need lessons. And the bear is for me too?"

He handed her the pink, furry, white-sweatered toy and reached into his pocket for the bag of Reese's Pieces. "I thought you'd appreciate its feminine qualities. And here's some of your favorite candy."

She took the bear and cradled it in her arms. "This is hard," she whispered.

"I know," he whispered back. Did she mean being in the facility or seeing him there? "Would you like to go for a walk?"

"Sure. I'll take my things to my room and grab a jacket and shoes."

He pointed to the floor. "Your shoes are here." Was she okay or not?


Paige had no idea whether everything she said, did, and ate—or even her bathroom habits—were recorded, but she couldn't take any chances. She assumed the psychiatrist assigned to her had not been sent from the company, but she had no room in her life for assumptions. One of the nurses might be on the company's or Keary's payrolls too. Sanity. She had to keep hers intact.

She set the candy and cookies on her dresser and

grabbed her jacket. Miles must not visit her again, and once they were clear of the building, she'd make sure he understood the precarious path he took in loving her. So she hadn't destroyed that yet. Paige didn't know whether to be relieved or to dread what Keary could do to him. But foremost in her mind was Nathan and what Miles had learned about him.

She started to put the bear on the bed, then realized she'd need it to continue playing the part of poor, deranged Mikaela Olsson, who was once a CIA operative who felt no remorse at cutting a man's throat. Now she was a delusional woman and the topic of far too many media reports. Tucking the Pepto-Bismol teddy into her arms, she slumped out of the small room and back to Miles. For the short time they'd be together, she wanted to enjoy every moment of his presence.

His smile reminded her of the many times he'd leaned over the desk at the library and flirted with her. And she'd flirted back.

Miles stood at the glass door leading to the prayer garden. He pointed to her feet and held her shoes in his hand. A female worker observed them. *Good.*

"Do I need these? Isn't it warm outside?"

"The grass is brittle," he said. "And your feet might get cold."

She handed him Miss Pepto-Bismol and sat in the middle of the floor to twist her shoes onto her heels.

She gathered up the strings in both hands as though she couldn't remember how to tie them. Miles bent and tied both shoes. Paige could not look at him, for he'd see how very much she loved him.

"Thank you. I couldn't remember how to do it," she said.

"No problem. Sometimes I forget things too." Miles's normally jovial tone had a hint of sadness. How horrible to deceive him along with everyone else. He offered a hand to help her up from the floor and proceeded to open the door.

"I like coming out here." She drank in the air. "My room feels like a tomb."

"Are the doctors helping?"

Paige purposely gave the impression to those around them that she struggled for an answer. "I'm taking my meds and doing what they tell me. My doctor's nice." She shivered—on purpose. They walked several feet in silence.

"Do you have a favorite spot in the garden?"

She stopped and slowly turned completely around. "Guess not." She hesitated, then pointed to an area where three people were admiring the flowers. "Over there." The elderly man with the threesome had audibly expressed fear of her.

Paige led the way to a bench. "Hi," she said to the three. "Do you mind if we sit here?"

The elderly man and his companions immediately walked away, leaving Paige and Miles alone.

"They probably know who I am," she said. "I

tried to warn my parents about Keary's announcement, but they weren't home. Had to tell them on their answering machine. I should have hit the Delete key on my life when I had the chance." She studied the flowers a few more moments before sitting on the bench.

"I highly encourage you to keep your finger off that key. How can I help?"

"You brought me cookies and a bear." She held out Miss Pepto-Bismol.

"It's a special bear," he said.

She peered up at him. Curiosity mounted. "How so? Does it have a football sweater too?"

"Almost." Miles lifted the bear from her arms and pointed to the pink heart on the sweater. He placed it back in her arms.

Her fingers traced the heart. "Sometimes here is what hurts the most."

"And sometimes what helps goes even deeper. Palmer picked it out."

Paige slipped her fingers under the sweater and pressed into the bear's body. *A bug. A means of communicating.* Her heart sped, and she caught his attention. "I love you." Speaking the words caused her to nearly weep.

"And I love you." His face softened. If only they could have exchanged those heartfelt words somewhere other than a psychiatric hospital.

"I'm sorry to have dragged you into this."

"I'm where I want to be," Miles said. "Waiting

on you to get better. Voleta plans to visit you tomorrow."

That was a positive, especially in light of Paige's suspicions. "I'll play the part. I do miss her craziness."

"I pray it'll soon be over. I'm supposed to tell you that Nathan is fine."

She nodded and clutched the bear, hugging it as though it were a baby. *The role, always the role.* Miles deserved to know about Nathan. "I have to tell you about Nathan."

"I was hoping you would. Code word for something?"

"This all might be easier if he could be explained in that context." When Miles didn't respond, she studied his face. He did love her, but this last confession would be the test. "Nathan is my son."

Not a muscle moved on his face. Had he been practicing how to restrain shock? "I see. . . . Nathan doesn't change how I feel about you."

"There's more."

"There's always more with my girl."

Her stomach swirled. "He's Keary's son too. I hid it from him for seven years, but he found out about two weeks ago."

Miles moistened his lips. "Now I'm beginning to understand. But it still doesn't matter. We'll see this through to the end."

She wanted to believe him, but skepticism was a reality. "Don't be too quick to say that."

"My life hasn't been squeaky-clean either."

"He'll kill for Nathan."

Miles nodded, his typical way of processing his thoughts. "So would you, and I'm right there beside you."

"We don't sound very Christian."

"Honey, it's honest. You're the one who told me about Keary's family and how that accident is probably why he turned traitor. Nathan must be an obsession to him, a possession. The difference between you and Keary is that you understand love involves sacrifice. Your life for the past seven years has been based on love."

For the first time, Paige had met a person who understood her heart. She took a cleansing breath filled with relief and regret. "I don't know what else to say."

He chuckled. "'I do' comes to mind. But we'll talk about that later." He paused. "I'm flying to Wisconsin on Wednesday."

She swallowed hard. "Why?"

"Because you can't. Because I know how badly you wanted to talk to them yourself. I might be able to answer some of their questions, assure them that you're okay."

"I don't know, Miles. Keary is watching your every move. It might be too dangerous. And besides, how can you take a couple of days off?"

"Personal days." He grinned. "Besides, it gives Dalton more fuel to oust me."

She glanced about, making certain no one approached them. "Be careful. You're making a lot of people unhappy. But you're always on the side of the underdog." She wanted to touch him, but she couldn't take the chance that someone might be clicking pictures. "Before I forget, what happened at last night's game?"

"We won. Chris is playing hard."

A blessing for Miles, and he deserved every one that came his way. "Are you ready for *this* game to continue?"

"I am." Miles said more in one sad glance than if he'd spoken a hundred words.

"You can't see me until this season is over."

"I understand." His shoulders lifted and fell. "I love you, Paige. I'm behind you in this no matter how it turns out."

She hated the turmoil and the circumstances that kept them apart. This wasn't in her training manual. She turned back to Miles. "And I do love you. Never thought I deserved real love, but it has happened. I'm sorry about—"

"No problem. I understand now. Sorry I didn't then." He smiled. "Let the cameras roll."

She jumped from the bench. "Why are you here? I told them I didn't want to see anyone. You're out to get me, aren't you? You're working with them to lock me away forever."

"Paige, calm down." Miles stood and reached out to touch her, but she screamed.

"My name is not Paige. It's Mikaela. Stay away from me. I hate you. I hate all of you. Help me, please. Someone get this jerk away from me."

Miles stepped back about six feet and held out his hands. "It's all right. I'll leave. Are you okay alone?"

"I can kill you! I know how." Paige bent to a martial arts position. That would certainly label her as textbook insane.

"Sir, we have this situation under control." A young man with a military haircut and the build of a professional linebacker hurried past Miles toward Paige.

"Get him out of here." Paige sobbed and buried her face in her hands.

The young man tossed Miles a wary look. "Sir, would you leave now?"

Miles nodded. "Sorry to upset you, Mikaela."

"Here, take your stupid bear." Paige threw the pink teddy at him, hoping and praying he saw through her every utterance.

Miles picked up the bear and brushed off the dirt. "Please, keep it." He handed it to the attendant. "She might want this later."

Paige snatched it from the young man's hands and held it close, as though it were her dearest possession. "It's mine." She forced real tears. "I want to keep it."

She heard Miles leave and continued to sob. Suddenly it was no longer an act. Soon this would be over. But not soon enough.

# CHAPTER 50

WHEN MILES DECIDED to make the trip to Wisconsin to talk to the Olssons about their daughter, the idea seemed like something he could do to help them through the shock of learning their daughter was alive. Paige had allowed her parents to believe she was dead. Nearly eight years later, she calls them and leaves a message, not even coming to see them in person. Assault number three came with Daniel Keary's announcement about her involvement with the CIA and a supposed history of mental disorders. How much more could these people take? And here he was thinking he could be the great ambassador. He felt sorry for her parents and wanted God's best for all involved. What would be the Olssons' reaction? They'd been lied to and possibly humiliated, just as he'd been. But he loved Paige, and his commitment to her would carry him through the storm and onto the truth. That sounded noble and maybe cheesy, as the kids would say, and yet he believed it.

*I must have lost my mind.*

For the past few days, his focus had swung like a pendulum between his responsibility to his team and his love for Paige. But he could do this and be back on Thursday afternoon for practice. Correction: his commitment to the team and to Paige was about relationships, not a to-do list.

People had more meaning in his life than a list of projects, like building a patio or putting a roof on his garage. His players struggled with the loss of Walt as quarterback and guilt for the way most of them had treated him. They were afraid and angry, but they were strong and working together as a team. Walt's physical therapists were optimistic about his full recovery for next year. And Chris was involved with his own physical therapy—and counseling. The only good thing that had come out of Walt's shooting was that the two boys were no longer at each other's throat.

The news about Nathan had momentarily thrown Miles, but the revelation explained so much of Paige's behavior. He'd learn more about the boy when this was over. Kids, whether you gave birth to them or they were born of your heart, always needed love. Miles prayed Nathan would weather this storm and be stronger for it.

This brought Miles to the present, driving on a lonely stretch of two-lane highway at the pace of a ninety-year-old on a Sunday afternoon drive. Miles had a cup of cold coffee on one side of his drink holder and a warm chocolate milkshake on the other. Rotten ulcer. He needed the coffee to stay awake and the milkshake to coat his stomach. The sweet taste sure beat Maalox. He peered out over the picturesque countryside, pretty with its autumn leaves and the afternoon sun glistening like a finely cut diamond.

Miles had no regrets about the trip, but he wished the right words to talk to the Olssons would drop center stage. Paige's parents were entitled to a little of the truth, something she'd tried to give him. She craved their love and support. They all needed each other, and Miles had no clue whether or not he could help.

He turned onto a country road, the tires crunching the stones beneath the car, and his nerves easing into overdrive. Three miles later, the farmhouse that Paige had described came into view. It reminded him of a calendar picture, complete with a red barn and two silos. He pulled into the driveway, recalling the maple trees that she'd said "canopied the driveway" as though they were soldiers guarding the entrance to the Olsson dairy farm.

Once he parked, he noticed a milk can on the front porch in red, white, and blue, and a porch swing. All this held special memories for Paige. Her roots were here, and she'd never given them up.

A black and white dog bounded up to the car. Its tail wagged faster than a hummingbird's wings. Miles opened the door. "You must be Fred." He let the animal sniff him before patting its head. The wind had a bitter bite to it, and the clouds cast a shadowy gray over the landscape.

As Miles stared up at the two-story, turn-of-the-century farmhouse, it seemed to have lost a bit of its friendly luster in light of his mission. *I'd never have made it in the CIA. I'd have ended up with more ulcers and severe reflux.* Stuffing his ungloved hands into his coat pockets, he walked the swept-clean sidewalk leading to the front door. Paige should be with him. They'd bustle in from the cold and prepare to spend the next few days with an older couple who longed to recapture the past. Maybe the next time with Nathan.

Fred followed him to the front door. Miles hesitated and willed his knees to stop shaking. He knocked and breathed another prayer. The door opened, and a blonde woman who had the same incredible blue eyes as Paige stood before him.

"Can I help you?" she asked. "Are you lost?"

*What a question.* "I'm where I'm supposed to be if you're Anna Olsson."

She stepped back. "Are you another one of those newspaper people? Because if you are, you can get right back into your car and get out of here."

"No, ma'am. I'm not. I don't have any use for those people either. My name is Miles Laird. I'm a friend of your daughter's, and I'd like to talk to you and your husband."

She shook her head and swallowed. Emotion seemed to seize her, and she covered her mouth. Miles was helpless to comfort her.

"I didn't come to upset you, but as someone who might be able to help you and your husband through this crisis."

"Who's there?" a gravelly male voice called.

"It's a man who claims he's a friend of Mikaela's."

Anna Olsson stared at Miles until her husband stood beside her in the half-opened doorway, where the heat escaped and the cold air blew through their home. As if they hadn't experienced enough damage to their hearts and minds.

"How are we supposed to know you're telling the truth?" the man said.

"She told me once about the orange suspenders you wear in honor of the harvest. She told me strangers had to let old Fred here get a good sniff before they tried to pet him. She has a red, white, and blue milk can on her front porch like yours. Her bedroom was at the top of the stairs, second room on the right. There used to be a bulletin board on the left side of the bed that was bordered by the blue ribbons she'd won at the county fair for her horsemanship. She said you were strong Lutherans, and every Christmas you gave gener- ously to world missions according to your harvest that year. She said you'd taught her how to bake traditional Swedish fruit breads. She–"

"Please, stop." Mrs. Olsson buried her face in her husband's chest. "Oh, my dear Mikaela."

Mr. Olsson wrapped his arm around her shoulder and pressed his lips together. Paige had his chin. "Come in, but if I find you are a reporter, I'll run you off with my shotgun."

"Sir, I'm on a mission of mercy here. Nothing more."

Mr. Olsson opened the door, and Miles entered the world of Mikaela Olsson—the world she had known before the CIA. The steady click of a grandfather clock ushered him into yesterday, and the woodsy scent of a crackling fireplace beckoned him to its warmth. He took in the antique furnishings and sensed the middle-aged couple eyeing him with pain-filled interest. And everywhere there were pictures of a blonde baby . . . child . . . girl . . . woman.

He reached for a photograph on the fireplace mantel that must have been taken when Paige was in high school. One framed picture after another lined the six-foot mantel, a shrine to the daughter who they believed had died. He saw the same wide smile, the same eyes curtained in thick lashes—his lovely Paige in the time of innocence. His heart knocked against his chest, and he remembered the gorgeous blonde in Palmer's photo.

"I always wondered what she looked like as a girl." His words came out like a whisper.

"We didn't recognize the pictures on TV," Mr. Olsson said. "*Shocked* best describes it."

"Would you like some coffee to warm you up?" Mrs. Olsson wrung her hands.

"Yes, ma'am. That would be nice. I'm not used to the cold."

She tilted her head and smiled, as Paige so often did. "Have a seat, and I'll bring you a cup."

"Can we sit in the kitchen?" Miles braved forward. "Seems like a better place to talk."

"Mr. Laird, this is difficult for the missus and me." Mr. Olsson glanced at his wife. "We have so many questions, and we don't know where to begin or who to believe."

Miles remembered the stories circulating about his brother and how difficult it was for their parents. "Sir, I don't have all of the answers, but I will tell you what I can."

"Then come on back, and we'll sit at the table," the man said.

The kitchen with its old-world charm and cinnamon apple scents greeted him. "Whatever I smell is something that she bakes."

"You must love her." Mrs. Olsson reached into a cabinet for a large mug. "I saw it in your eyes when you were standing on the front porch."

"That obvious? Gives me hope as far as Paige is concerned." Immediately he caught his blunder. "I'm sorry. I should have said Mikaela."

She nodded and poured him coffee from a percolator pot. He hadn't seen one of those since before his grandmother had moved to an assisted-living center. He took a sip of the coffee. "This is wonderful. Thanks."

Anna Olsson slid into a chair at a round wooden table. The time had come for him to say his piece and hope that God would give him the right words.

"I don't know what you've read or heard about your daughter, but I'm going to tell you what I believe is the truth."

Mr. Olsson nodded and took his wife's hand. "I pray you are telling us the truth."

"I've asked God to pave the way for understanding. Paige—uh, Mikaela—prays for the same thing."

"Mikaela is a Christian?" Mrs. Olsson's voice rose.

"Yes. It happened while she was overseas."

"She was a good girl, but not interested in the ways of God." Her father took a moment to compose himself. Right then, Miles would have done about anything to take away their pain.

"Your daughter did work for the CIA. I don't know the details, because that's classified information. The part she told me is that while on an assignment, all of her team members were killed except for her and another operative. She was injured and required a lengthy hospital stay." He took another sip of coffee. "She'd discovered something about the mission that led her to believe that the other surviving operative had betrayed them. It was her word against his, and she couldn't secure the evidence needed to have him brought to justice. She resigned from the CIA and established a new identity."

"But why couldn't she have come home?" Mrs. Olsson's eyes brimmed with tears.

"The other operative threatened to kill you unless she disappeared. He blackmailed her into changing her identity and allowing you to think she was dead. She did it to protect you, or so she thought."

"Mikaela chose to live her life alone . . . to save us?" Mrs. Olsson could barely choke out the words. "My poor little girl did that for us?"

"I . . . I want to believe you." Mr. Olsson wrapped his arm around his wife's shoulder.

"Sir, has the phone ever rung during the past eight years and when you answered it, no one was there? Did you ever wonder who it could be?"

"That's not really fair to ask. Those calls happen to everyone. But in the beginning, I used to wish it were her." He glanced down at his folded hands on the table. "My little girl in the CIA. . . . I shouldn't be surprised when I think back at her shenanigans. That girl whitened my hair. Why, I nearly went bald over some of the trouble she got into. But I never doubted her love for us." He took a breath. "Those news reporters say she's mentally unstable . . . and in a psychiatric hospital."

"I don't believe she has mental problems, and you shouldn't either."

"But the fella running for governor of Oklahoma confirmed it. He said he'd worked with her."

"I believe if we let her and the CIA continue their investigation, not only you but also the whole nation will learn the truth."

"What's your role in all of this?" Carl Olsson asked.

Miles studied the older man and his wife. "I'm a football coach and a teacher at Split Creek's high school. I met your daughter at the public library where she's worked ever since coming to Oklahoma. Circumstances brought me into this, or Mikaela would still be trying to figure things out on her own." He took a deep breath. "She's a brilliant woman, but I'd like to think I can help in a small way."

"It looks to me like you're helping in a big way," the man said.

"She had a minor in library science," Mrs. Olsson said. "She always loved books."

"I have a purpose in coming here today." Miles warmed his hands with the coffee mug. "I'm asking if you will pray for Mikaela."

Sincerity deepened in Mr. Olsson's eyes. "I wish we could have talked to her the day she called, but she didn't leave a number. What else can we do but pray?"

"Thank you. She loves both of you very much."

"We could go see her at the hospital," Mr. Olsson said.

Miles shook his head. "That's not a good idea. She wouldn't be able to talk to you candidly, and it might put you in danger. This is the safest place for you to be. I understand it's easier to keep you guarded here."

Mrs. Olsson gasped. "Guarded? Us?"

"Yes, ma'am. I've probably told you more than I should. Protection has been in place for you since sometime in August."

Mrs. Olsson touched her heart. "Out here? On our farm? We've always lived here with no problems at all. And . . . and Fred alerts us to folks driving up and down the road." She turned to her husband. "Oh, Carl. I'm frightened."

Mr. Olsson drew his wife close to him. "Now, don't you worry, honey. I'm right here, and according to Miles here, important people are protecting us." He hesitated. "Is it Chet? He came to us in August. Said he had a family to support about twenty-five miles from here. I gave him a job, and he's a hard worker. Comes real early and stays late. Most nights he sleeps in one of the spare rooms."

"I wouldn't know, sir. But it is vitally important for you and your wife to keep to yourself what I've told you about your daughter."

"Nothing will be said." He glanced at his wife, and she nodded.

"When can we see Mikaela?" Mrs. Olsson asked. "I want to tell her I love her." Her voice broke, and she grabbed a tissue.

"I don't know when it'll be safe," Miles said. The kitchen was overly quiet. Afternoon sunlight streamed through the window. "But I do know she will want to see you as soon as she can."

"Maybe Thanksgiving?" Mr. Olsson asked.

Miles caught himself wanting to build up their hopes, but reality might be disappointing. "Let's just say that when it happens, we'll all feel like it's a holiday."

"We've waited this long," the older man said. "You've given us hope, and that's all we have left." The older man snatched up a tissue and squeezed his wife's hand. "I need a cup of your coffee, sweetheart."

"But the doctor said you weren't supposed to have caffeine after breakfast."

"I'm . . . celebrating that we have another chance at being parents to our Mikaela."

Their familiarity relaxed Miles. "My dad is always on to my mom about drinking caffeinated coffee." He scooted his chair back from the table. "I guess I've taken enough of your afternoon."

"Nonsense, you're staying for supper," Mrs. Olsson said. "And you can stay the night, too. I don't imagine you're used to driving on these roads, and once it gets dark, they can be treacherous."

"I appreciate your hospitality. Are you sure about this?"

"Normally I have a suspicious nature," Anna Olsson said. "But I see the love of Jesus in your eyes, and I hear love for Mikaela in your voice."

"Then can I help with chores?"

"My kind of man," Mr. Olsson said. "I'll find you a warm coat. That dress jacket won't keep out the cold, and the cows don't care how you look. I'll dig up some boots and gloves. Oh, and you can meet Chet. That man may be my bodyguard."

Miles hadn't done farm chores since he was in high school. A combination of the cold and the work helped release all of the built-up tension. He learned how to hook up automatic milkers, how much feed to give the cows, and the importance of proper sanitation and cleanliness. During the evening hours and after Chet retired to his room, the three talked about Paige. Miles listened to stories of her girlhood pranks and leafed through old school yearbooks. He did his best to tell them about the woman he'd grown to love. How he desperately wanted all of the missing pieces to form a complete picture. He chose not to tell them about Nathan. That was Paige's job.

Miles stirred in his sleep. Had he heard something, or was he dreaming? He listened, but all that met his ears was the stillness of the farmhouse. Lately his sleeping hours centered on the CIA—high-suspense drama, the product of an overactive imagination and a juggling of what was reality. This whole thing with Paige needed to be over so they could get on with their lives. He turned on his side and started to drift back to sleep. A door slammed. A rifle shot shattered glass. He threw back the quilts and bolted from the bed. A woman screamed. Then another sharp crack. *The Olssons!*

At the door, he anchored chest to chest with someone. "Laird, stop right there," Chet said. "On the floor and stay there until I tell you to get up." No doubt who was guarding the Olssons. Miles didn't think twice about obeying.

Footsteps pounded down the stairs. "Carl, Anna, you two all right?" Chet's voice boomed.

"Yes," Carl said. "I have a rifle in here, and it's loaded."

"On the floor and stay there until I come after you. Hold on to that rifle. Got it?"

"Yes, sir."

The back door squeaked open and rattled shut. Four more shots fired. Miles waited for something else—voices or an exchange of fire—anything to alert him to what was happening. Lying on the cold wooden floor, he felt more like a twelve-year-old kid than a grown man. He couldn't handle the helplessness any longer. Crawling on his belly, he made it out of the bedroom and down the stairs. As soon as he touched the floor, another shot pierced the air. His eardrums rang, and his heart thumped like a scared animal.

Miles inched across the living room toward the older couple. "You two okay?" He heard sobbing. "Anna? Carl?"

A bullet sailed through the Olssons' bedroom window, sending a splattering of glass. Anna sobbed louder.

"Miles, we're fine," Carl said, but he didn't sound very good.

"What's wrong?" Sweat-drenched, Miles was glad he crouched in the dark because he wouldn't have wanted the Olssons to see his gut-wrenching fear.

"Carl's shot in the side," Anna's voice brimmed near hysteria.

"Hush, woman. I got hurt worse peeling potatoes in Vietnam."

Miles crawled to their side. Seemed like he'd bandaged enough victims lately, and he didn't like the slimy feel of blood. From the shadows, it looked as though Anna was holding Carl's hand. Miles pulled a sheet from the bed. "Help me wrap this around the bleeding."

Two more shots fired. Each time Anna gasped. Then it grew quiet.

"Take the rifle," Carl said. "You might need it."

Miles grabbed the weapon and waited.

The back door opened. Miles cocked the rifle and sucked in a breath.

"Carl, it's over," Chet called. "You two can relax."

"Not quite," Miles said. "Carl's been shot. Not too bad, but it needs attention."

Chet swore loud enough to echo through the house. "I'll call an ambulance, and you two are moving to another location."

Carl moaned. "What about my cows?"

Miles wanted to smack him.

# CHAPTER 51

FRIDAY MORNING, Miles stood at the window of his classroom and stared out at the gray October day. If absence made the heart grow fonder, then his heart would soon burst. His life seemed to be a constant search for diversion from thinking about Paige and the danger looming over her. Wednesday night's encounter with Keary's thugs had shaken him worse than he'd let on. How did Paige deal with it? Two men had been involved; both were dead.

Miles had worked at teaching today with a fervor that surprised even him, but his thoughts were on Paige. Her blue eyes stayed fixed in his mind, and her words of love kept his spirit alive. They would find a way to make their relationship permanent. He refused to consider anything less.

Principal O'Connor cleared his throat behind him. *Now what?* The principal didn't make social calls. Ty Dalton had not given up on his crusade to end Miles's teaching and coaching days at Split Creek. Miles greeted O'Connor.

"Can I have a word with you?" O'Connor asked.

"I'm free until the end of the period."

"First of all, I want to wish you success in tonight's game. It's been a tough season."

"Thank you. They're a good team, and I'm proud of them."

O'Connor closed the door. "Ty Dalton has a new concern."

"Why am I not surprised? What is it now?"

O'Connor shifted uncomfortably. The man looked to have aged ten years since the start of the school year. Retirement could not come soon enough. "He has added to his list of reasons to dismiss you that you are not a good moral example to the students."

"And where did he get this?"

"He claims you knew all along about Miss Rogers or whatever her name is. He fears our youth will use you as a model for immoral behavior."

Miles thought he would explode with the new accusation. "My response to the school board is this," he said. "I have never involved myself in any immoral behavior with Paige Rogers or Mikaela Olsson. At the next school board meeting, I would like to give my response to all of Ty Dalton's accusations."

O'Connor studied him. A slow smile spread over his lined face. "All right. I like a good showdown."

"Shall I bring my attorney, or simply invite all of the parents?"

"Miles, I don't care who you bring. It'll be the best school board meeting we've seen in a long time."

O'Connor shook his hand and left the classroom. One more diversion until Paige was released.

Miles jammed his hands into his jeans pockets and tried to ignore the churning in his stomach. The second quarter of the eighth game of the season, and the Bobcats were exhausted. No wonder. They were playing a tough team. Miles's players had determination written on their faces but defeat in their passes and plays. Pep talks and *attaboy*s hadn't done a bit of good.

"Get your head out of the clouds and do something with those guys."

Ty Dalton's grating voice didn't help the situation on the field. It wouldn't take much for Miles to punch that arrogant, wife-cheating, poor excuse of a man.

"Excuse me?" Miles delivered all of his frustration into a fiery glare.

"If the Bobcats lose, it's your fault." Dalton stood beside Miles and crossed his arms over his chest.

Miles saw no reason to waste his energy in responding.

"So your girlfriend is a mental case and slept with a politician. Deal with it."

Miles *really* wanted to level him. Especially since those had been Paige's parting words.

"You're interfering with the game. Get off the field before I get someone to escort you."

Dalton chuckled. "Doesn't matter. This is your last year coaching football, and from the way you're coaching tonight, it's probably your last game."

Miles threw him another seething look. A dozen retorts slammed against his brain, but why stoop to Dalton's level? Instead, he focused on a play going sour. Chris had hesitated a moment too long, and a linebacker headed straight for him. The sound of body smacking body and the crash of helmets alerted Miles to a hard sack. Chris lay sprawled on the ground. The ref blew his whistle. Chris didn't move.

*His back.* Miles took off at a run. Maybe he just had the wind knocked out of him. Miles knelt beside his injured quarterback. "Hey. How are you doing?"

Chris opened his eyes and licked his lips. "I'm okay. Just help me up."

"What about your back?"

"It's fine." Chris attempted to move, but pain pushed him back down, its effects evident in his pinched face. "Give me a minute to catch my breath. It's not bad. I just hit hard."

"Do your part!" Ty Dalton raised his fist to the black sky. "The team's depending on you."

Chris closed his eyes. "Coach, get him off the field."

With that statement, Miles no longer had any doubts about the seriousness of Chris's back. "Off the field," he said to Dalton.

"You can't keep me from my son."

"I don't want you here," Chris said through pain-filled eyes.

"Why? I'm your dad. I have rights—"

Chris's eyes clamped shut. "Do you want me to answer that in front of everybody? You haven't been a dad since you came back from Angola."

Miles inhaled sharply.

"Mind your mouth," Ty said.

Chris attempted to lift himself on his elbows, but Miles held his shoulders down. "Stay still. Help is coming."

"Did you try to kill Walt?" Chris asked. "Or were you with that woman?"

Dalton stood and stepped back as though he'd taken a hard tackle. "Guess I had that coming."

"And the coach's barn. Did you set fire to it?"

"Easy, Chris. The stretcher's right here," Miles said.

Tears rolled down the boy's face. "I can't do this to the team. I'm sure I can get up if you help me. If we don't win, we lose our chances for the play-offs."

"You've done your best. Listen, Chris, you're worth more than any game. I'm proud of you sticking through the season when I know you hurt every time you suited up."

The tears continued to flow down the boy's face, and Miles had to blink back his own. Within moments, a doctor and EMS team with a stretcher carried Chris off the field. The crowd stood and applauded. Miles caught a glimpse of Walt as he grabbed his crutches and hurried toward Chris. Two fine men had given their best to a team that Miles would never forget.

"I've said it before, and I'll say it again. You are all winners," Miles said. He'd been consoling his players in the field house for more than an hour. With both Walt and Chris sidelined, the team had been unable to rally. "Nothing's changed. You're the best. Winners understand the importance of teamwork and helping each other. The play-offs were important to us, but they will be next year too. For those of you who are seniors, your lives are forever changed by how far we went this year. You have the potential of success in whatever you choose because you know how to fight for what you want and believe in. Those of you who will be back with the team next year realize how your skills will help you have a proud season."

"You'll be with us, won't you, Coach?" Walt asked, staring at his leg.

"God willing. But it doesn't matter who coaches the Bobcats. You have the desire and the discipline to make any coach proud." Miles sat on a bench beside a 250-pound tackle who was sobbing like a child. Sometimes words weren't enough. Sometimes the best comfort came in the form of tears.

Hours later, as he stared at the ceiling and tried

to get his body to wind down, Miles kept reliving the week. How could he ever get used to the trauma of Paige's life? It was all he could do to comfort a team of good kids who'd lost a football game.

Poor Chris. Miles had stayed at the hospital until the doctor assured those who waited that the boy was resting. Ty didn't bother to show. That's when Miles realized that Chris had seen his dad's girlfriend. Maybe she knew something about all that had been going on with Daniel Keary.

Miles rose from the bed and dialed the number Palmer had given him.

## CHAPTER 52

PAIGE FLUSHED another pill down the toilet in her room. As had become her habit, she'd allowed the nurse to think she'd swallowed her meds. Dulling her mind with sedatives and antidepressants didn't accomplish her goal at Magnolia Life Center, which was to placate Keary. However, the days proved endless, with little to do but read and make polite conversations with the staff—and carry on her role as the unstable ex-CIA operative. The old mind-training resources rolled into place and kept her alert. From Paige's point of view, she was playing defense instead of offense. And that had left her in a defeated—and sour—mood.

TV news carried snippets of her past role in the

CIA, all according to Keary's interpretation. The director of the CIA had no comment. But the reporting had grown old. A photo of her before and after the identity change hit the news for three days. No one at the facility said a word, but the whispers and curious stares were constant.

Regrets assaulted her about many of the good people of Split Creek. George had nearly figured her out before Keary's press conference. When this mission ended, she hoped he'd allow her to explain a few things. He and Naomi had been good friends, the kind she valued and respected. No point in ruminating about Mr. Shafer, Miss Eleanor, Miss Alma, the faithful book club group . . . and Voleta.

The confinement had forced her to take an honest look at her life and her relationship with God. When she'd been with the CIA years before, her work had become an addiction. She'd lusted after missions and taken chances, inviting danger and defying life. But with her faith had come a change in the way she viewed herself and those around her. She now worked for God, a pretty good boss in her estimation. The danger still gave her an adrenaline rush, but the success of her mission was not in her hands. For certain, she'd never again gauge her worth on performance. She would never again be a marionette too preoccupied with herself to see who held the strings. She was Mikaela Olsson, CIA operative and, more importantly, a child of God.

Mikaela's longed-for promised land would be a place where she could find peace about her responsibilities to the CIA. And finally it became clear that she'd find it only with a return to dignity. Monday morning she planned to leave Magnolia Life Center and see what Keary would do in retaliation. She was cutting it close with the election on Tuesday, but the time element was her ace.

The long hours had given her time to consider Keary's next move. Most likely, he was planning her suicide. That would keep his hands clean and would eliminate all the dangerous information she possessed. Her committing suicide would also create sympathy for him among his supporters—the nightmare for his family would be over. He'd claim to have regrets for a life lost to mental illness. As governor, he might even initiate legislation to better assist those suffering from mental disorders. What a joke.

But Keary's confidence would be his downfall. Mikaela's concern for Nathan *could* be her downfall unless she proceeded as an operative and not as a panic-stricken mother.

The narrow span of time left to prove Keary's guilt made her plan risky, but it gave her the edge. He wouldn't see the bulldozer knocking over the campaign signs.

Saturday morning before breakfast, Miles decided to pull a tree stump from his side yard. It had been there since last May. Didn't matter that the ground was rock hard. He simply needed physical work that didn't call for much thinking, and spending an hour on a tractor with some chains would help relieve the frustrations anchored in his life.

The team's loss last night still weighed heavily on his mind, but what his boys had learned was far more valuable than the satisfaction of a perfect season—they'd learned how to be men.

At ten thirty, his stomach growled and the stump hadn't budged. He readjusted the chain fastened around it and picked up a thermos of coffee in one hand and a bottle of water in the other. After a long cold drink and several hot gulps of the other, he sized up his problems—all of them—and realized the only one he had any control over was the stump.

George pulled into the driveway and stepped out of his car. Fearing something might have happened to Walt, Chris, Paige, or any of a dozen other folks, Miles switched off the tractor's engine.

"Hey, George. What brings you out here?"

"I made an arrest this morning at Denim's, and I wanted to tell you about it."

"Hope it's decent news, 'cause I'm in a bad mood."

George gave him a grim smile. "Ty Dalton. I arrested him for shooting the Greywolf kid and burning your barn."

"Did he confess?"

"He refused to tell me where he was during the shooting. Enough evidence for me. And the fire marshal found his fingerprints at your barn's site."

"He and Chris had a few words at last night's game."

"Heard about it from one of the refs. Ty was drunk at seven thirty this morning. Drinking coffee and swearing up a blue streak about how you'd put his boy in the hospital. He didn't even know the ER released Chris shortly after midnight." George shook his head. "Before Dalton took that stint for WorldMarc Oil in Africa, he was a decent man. Not sure what happened there, but he's been a horse's . . . well, a pain ever since. He asked me not to tell his wife. Wanted her to find out like the other folks, I guess."

*Is this closer to being over?* "Possibly."

George rubbed his jaw. "Been to see Paige?"

Miles nodded. "Just once. She didn't want me to come back." That much was true.

"I sure hate what's happened. Sure do. I suspected something with Paige, but nothing like this. Voleta couldn't bring herself to go see her. I'm real sorry. Heard she—"

"George, I don't want to talk about it." Miles wanted to tell him to mind his own business and get on down the road. But he had a strong feeling that the truth about Daniel Keary was about to . . . get uprooted. "Guess I'll get on back to this stump."

"That's what I do when I have a lot of stuff on my mind."

"Does it help?"

"Nah. Just makes me so tired, I don't care."

George left and Miles continued to brood. He didn't want to see or talk to anyone. Within thirty minutes, with the stump still refusing to move an inch and his stomach growling even more, Miles saw Ginny Dalton drive up. Chris climbed awkwardly out of the car.

"How you feelin'?"

"On pain pills. Can't drive." He pointed to the stump. "If I could, I'd give you a hand."

"Oh, this is a solo project." Miles stared at the kid. "Sorry about your dad."

"Yeah. I'm sorry too. Mom's . . . pretty upset." Chris blew out an exasperated breath. "Life sure can be a mess."

Miles wished the young didn't have to grow up so fast. "I'll be praying for all of you."

A mockingbird broke through the silence.

"Thanks, Coach. I had my mom drive me over to Walt's house. I apologized for all the stuff I started. I owe you one for slicing your tire."

"I figured it was you. All I ever needed was an apology."

"I . . . I took a tire to Walt when I went to see him. Wasn't easy."

Miles squinted with a little liquid emotion that slipped from the corner of one eye.

"Walt's parents treated me like I was their long-lost kid. His little brothers and sisters acted like Walt and I were heroes. Mom and I stayed for breakfast, and man, his mom is some cook."

"I ate breakfast there once. I know what you mean."

Chris looked at his mom sitting in the car. "Well, I just wanted to tell you what happened and stuff."

"You're a good man, Chris Dalton."

"Thanks. See ya on Monday."

Miles waved again at Ginny and Chris. A peanut butter and mayo sandwich sounded good before he pulled out the stump.

# CHAPTER 53

"GOOD JOB in finding out where they're holding Nathan," I say to Stevens over the phone. "All three in the same place. The CIA made it easy for us after the problem in Wisconsin."

"Yeah, but my contact's finished. She got a call from Palmer saying he needed to see her right away. I didn't like the sound of it. So while she showered, I removed the bug. Once she left, I cleaned up the place."

That means it will take some time to find Mikaela's parents, but there is no longer any reason to eliminate them. I am disappointed about not killing the coach—I have a personal grudge against him. I glance at my watch. Need to cut this call short. "And you're sure that woman won't be able to recognize you later?"

"Positive." Stevens chuckles. "The next time, I'd prefer a woman who isn't ugly and a hundred pounds overweight."

I laugh with him. "Hazards of the job."

"I will be at the helicopter pad within the hour."

"See you then." I have a passport for Nathan . . . and a change of identity for both of us.

"Are you regretting the election?"

"I won what mattered most." I end the call and glance around the office that has served me well over the past seven years. I can work just as well in France. Perhaps better.

## CHAPTER 54

EARLY MONDAY MORNING, Mikaela packed up her belongings and announced her intentions to leave Magnolia Life Center. A nurse, the one she suspected was working for Keary, tried to convince her to prolong her therapy.

"A while longer will help you work through your problems and obtain the tools to maintain a positive outlook on life," the dark-haired nurse said. "Our programs work the best when the patient participates for a full month."

Mikaela used her best calm demeanor. "I can manage life. If I have problems, then I'll be back. Thank you for helping me."

"You're welcome." The head nurse smiled as though she understood. "The doctor wants to see you in a week and strongly urges you to find a counselor. Are you returning to your home in Split Creek?"

"I'm not sure."

The woman stood, chart in hand. "The doctor wrote you a couple of prescriptions. Follow the directions carefully."

Mikaela took them and left the facility. She had no phone, and her guns were hidden at home. But she knew Palmer and Keary were alert to her every move. She stopped at a gas station off of I-44, grabbed her shoulder bag with the pink teddy bear, and called Palmer from a pay phone.

"I left Magnolia Life Center," Mikaela said. "What's happened?"

"My assistant admitted to an affair. Said she'd just been with him and agreed to a test. We have proof it's Jason Stevens. He's not answering her calls, and his belongings are gone from their apartment in Virginia—swept clean."

"He must have planted a bug."

"And had sense enough to retrieve it. I sent her back to the apartment in case he shows up."

Mikaela remembered the woman—midforties and devoted to her job. "I bet he's taking Zuriel's place."

"Are you headed home?"

"Yes. I'm going to get my prescriptions filled in Split Creek to make my presence known. I think the mole will show up unannounced."

"I'm sure of it."

"Why?"

"Voleta Graft."

Mikaela's senses numbed—all but the sound of Palmer's voice. "You've got to be kidding."

"She used to date Jason Stevens."

Voleta? The woman who had weaseled her way into Mikaela's life under the premise of needing a friend? The woman who'd asked for Mikaela's help to budget money? The woman who'd helped Mikaela organize a fund-raiser dinner for the Greywolfs? "Are you sure?"

"She's been on Keary's payroll for almost five years. Her real name is Janelle Webster."

Anger burned in her chest. "Why didn't I see that coming?"

"You weren't the only one she had fooled. We didn't figure her out until we dug deeper into Stevens."

At last, the mole. "That sure answers a lot of

questions." She closed her eyes and forced herself to focus. "What about Nathan?"

"He's all right. His new location is a little north of Dallas, about an hour and a half from Split Creek. We're working on a tight schedule, so don't do anything stupid and contact him before this is over."

She longed to hear Nathan's voice, reassure him that soon they'd be together. But every moment was precious. "Okay. I'll pick up a new cell phone and contact you as soon as I get home."

Two customers were ahead of Mikaela at the pharmacy, two more people shopped—and all of them stared. Good. The word would get out soon. Her one concern was Miles learning she'd returned and showing up at her front door.

She paid for the meds and a prepaid cell phone and walked across the street to the doughnut shop for coffee. Voleta usually faced the window looking out into the street. Inside the coffee shop, enticing smells that beat the food at Magnolia Life Center competed against customers gawking at her. More talk. Grabbing a cup of black coffee and a chocolate peanut butter doughnut, she climbed into the car. *Take the bait, Voleta.*

After the first bite of doughnut, she called Palmer and gave him her new cell number. In midafternoon, Mikaela opened the door to the little bungalow that had offered so much peace and contentment. She'd miss the warmth . . . the time spent here with Miles . . . and the hours of laughter with Voleta. She and Nathan would have a future together, or she'd die trying. If Miles chose to be a part of it, she'd be one happy lady.

No doubt Keary planned to spend the upcoming election in an unholy smugness neatly tied with a spectacular gold bow. He'd be furious that she'd left Magnolia Life Center ahead of time, possibly angry enough to slip. That was *her* ace. Mikaela stood in the middle of her kitchen and scolded herself. God held the reins, not her or the CIA. She finished her coffee and doughnut . . . and waited.

A knock at the door alerted her to the next step in Keary's plan. She tucked her automatic into the back of her jeans and pulled her loose shirt over it. The knocking continued. Mikaela grabbed Miss Pepto-Bismol and set the bear on the sofa.

"Coming," she called and glanced through the blinds to see Voleta standing on the welcome mat.

Mikaela opened the door and went into sad and mad mode—the same facade that had given her national acclaim.

"Hey, girl." Voleta reached out to hug her. Her hair now had purple and pink streaks, and she'd added another eyebrow ring. "Good to see you."

"How did you know I was home?"

"I saw you get into your car from my window. I wanted to chase you down then, but I was brushing on color. I'm really sorry about everything. I wanted to visit you, but—" Voleta brushed a tear from her cheek—"I didn't know what I'd say, and—"

"You were hurt that I'd betrayed you too?" Mikaela fought the urge to confront her treachery, but she needed Voleta to make incriminating statements.

Voleta nodded. "It hit me so hard. Can I come in?"

Mikaela purposely hesitated and then stepped aside for Voleta to walk in. They sat on the sofa, the same spots where they'd always talked about life and watched movies.

Voleta shifted as though uncomfortable. "I didn't really expect you home this soon. Are you better?"

"A lot of things are still a blur, but I think I can manage with a counselor and meds."

"I'm here for you. You can trust me with anything." Voleta shook her head. "I never had any idea you were anything but a librarian. You must be real smart."

*You're the smart one.* Mikaela took in a deep breath. "I lied to people."

"Doesn't matter. Best friends are there for each other." Voleta had become a new animal, a cross between a rat and a snake.

"You're sweet. But I don't want you to lose customers because of me. In fact, if anyone sees you're here, they might cancel their appointment."

Voleta's eyes widened. "Then I don't need them."

How long did Voleta plan to continue the charade? "Yes, you do. Bills, remember?"

Her friend swiped at another tear. "You mean more to me than money. So what are you going to do?"

Bingo. "I'm taking the next couple of days to figure that out."

"Let's go to Pradmore for dinner. My treat. I'm sure the food at Magnolia Life Center was horrible."

"I'd rather cook." *You're not dumping my body along some back road.* "Had enough, Voleta? Why are you really here?" Mikaela reached for her weapon tucked into the back of her jeans, but Voleta was faster and pulled a Glock from her purse.

"Your choice."

*Showdown.* "I hope Keary paid you well."

"Pays my bills. With your left hand remove that gun from your jeans."

Mikaela obeyed and studied the woman who wore the red badge of betrayal. "What you're doing will only get you killed or the rest of your life in jail."

Voleta slipped Mikaela's gun into her purse. "The eternal optimist. I'm way ahead of you." Her cell phone rang, and she answered it. "I got her. Sure, I'll pass on the news."

"What news?"

"He wants you to know that he has Nathan, and

in a few moments they'll be heading out of the country."

Mikaela tried to fight the trembling. She had to think fast. Whether Keary had nabbed Nathan or not, she had to delay any plans. "Please tell him not to forget Nathan's inhaler. He has severe asthma." She banked her lie on the hope that Keary didn't have Nathan's medical records.

Voleta tossed a disbelieving stare before she called Keary back and relayed the message.

Mikaela played the part of the distraught mother and took the phone when Voleta handed it to her. "Daniel, he must have his inhaler!"

"He looks fine to me."

"Can I talk to him?" If Nathan was with Keary, no doubt he'd be upset.

"I don't think so. You lost, Mikaela. One more time." The call disconnected.

Voleta peered at Mikaela as though examining her soul, which was a whole lot cleaner than Voleta's charred heart. "If you're stalling, it won't do any good."

"My son's health is what's important."

"His father is quite capable of taking care of him. At least he didn't knowingly desert his own son in the toilet bowl of Africa."

# CHAPTER 55

"SIR, THE HELICOPTER IS READY," Stevens says.

With the sound of the whirling blades in my ears, I grab my briefcase and climb into the chopper with Stevens and two of my men. We have plenty of weaponry to take care of the operatives and Rosa and Gonsalvo. Two more men are on the ground en route to the CIA safe house north of Dallas. By now Mikaela is dead. No traces of Daniel Keary or Jason Stevens will have been left behind, only the new identities . . . along with my son. Soon all that I've ever wanted will be with me, and we'll have a wonderful life together. I can continue to make plenty of money from southern France without U.S. restrictions—even expand my businesses. Politics no longer holds my interest.

A moment of regret touches me when I think of Sheila. But her family will be a strong support for her. She'll do fine. Although the initial flurry of love or lust—whatever attracted me to her besides money and ambition—has long since vanished, I still want her to find happiness. She loves the little Korean kid. He'll help her through this.

Mikaela's plea for Nathan's inhaler demonstrated she's lost her skills as an op. France has plenty of doctors, and once we land, I'll take Nathan to the finest one in Paris. Rather pathetic for a woman who once held a promising future. All of her efforts in trying to prove me guilty are about to fade into oblivion.

In a little over two hours I'll have my son. The company's jet is fueled up and ready for me at DFW.

## CHAPTER 56

"DO YOU HONESTLY think you'll get away with this?" Mikaela shook her head. "Real clever. You did a good job. You were behind all of it—working for Keary as his yes-girl."

Voleta laughed. "And you thought you were a good op. Had you fooled."

"Do you know who shot Walt?"

"I did."

*Miss Pepto-Bismol has your confession recorded.* "Why? He's a sixteen-year-old kid."

"Ty Dalton needed to learn who was in control."

"You shot Walt to show Ty that his son or wife could be next?"

"Smart girl. It worked, too. He tried to break it off with me, and I wasn't finished with him yet. I have Dalton right where I need him—in jail. He should never have told me what he saw in Angola. Spineless redneck. But I will give him credit for setting Miles's barn on fire."

For once Mikaela felt sorry for the town's chief mechanic. "The library shooting?"

"Oh yeah, had to keep my Harley in Pradmore, along with the Camry I used for the chase that day on the road. Thought you might scare down, but you surprised me."

"And you planted the bomb in my car?"

She nodded. "I figured you'd find it, and Keary needed to throw a little more cash into my account to keep you alive awhile longer."

Voleta wouldn't live long enough to spend any of it. Keary would make sure she was dead as soon as she outlived her usefulness. "I heard Jason Stevens gave you orders."

"Jason is none of your business."

"A sore topic?"

"I'm getting bored with this. Sit down." She motioned to the chair and Mikaela complied. Voleta opened the door and fired a shot into the left front tire of Mikaela's car.

Mikaela needed to buy time. Let Voleta play all the games she wanted. "What's the plan?"

"A megadose from the prescriptions you just had filled and a bullet to your head." Intelligence sparked in Voleta's eyes, but she was overly confident. Just like Keary. She reached into her purse and pulled out a bottle of water. "Down them."

"You don't want to add murder to your list."

"Nothing new." She waved the gun toward the pharmacy bag. "Take them. You can't hold a whole bottle of pills in your mouth. And if you refuse, I always have another plan."

A little more time and help would arrive—complete with a recorded confession. An engine roared outside—a motorcycle. Voleta kept the Glock aimed at Mikaela and made her way to the window. She cursed. "It's Miles."

Mikaela listened to Miles climb the steps and knock on the door. Could she deter him? refuse to answer?

"Bring him in," Voleta said, "or I'll bloody your porch."

Mikaela stood from the chair and slowly opened the door. Palmer's men needed to get there fast before it was too late. The sight of Miles, his smile, and the warm glow of love in his eyes made her physically ill. This was going down badly.

"Hey, I was driving by and saw you were home."

"This isn't a good time." She sent him a silent warning. "I'll call you later."

"Mikaela, I have your gun aimed at him."

Mikaela met his eyes. Too late to save Miles from this. She widened the door, and he joined her and Voleta.

"How cozy," Voleta said. "Both of you can have a seat on the sofa here."

"What's going on?" Miles asked.

"This is my welcoming committee," Mikaela said. "Voleta seems to think I'm a threat."

Voleta's laugh scraped at Mikaela's nerves. "Your sweet librarian is about to shoot you and blow a hole through her own head."

"Is Keary paying you enough for murder?" Miles asked.

Voleta shook her head. "You're smarter than I gave you credit for."

A car door slammed. Then another.

"What the—?" Voleta swore.

Miles stood. "You've been caught."

Mikaela took her place beside him. "Give it up. The CIA's here, and your confession has been recorded."

"Liar." Voleta stole a look out the window. "I have no problem getting rid of you two."

Mikaela took a quick step forward and swung her hand against the Glock. It fired once, twice, then went flying across the room. Miles went after the gun, but Voleta reached it first and fired. White-hot pain seared Mikaela's shoulder just before she lunged at Voleta. The door opened and Miles shouted for the team's assistance.

The first operative in the door was the fellow who had sat beside her at the football games, the same man who had struck up a conversation with her the day at the convenience store. A woman operative stood on Mikaela's porch—the supposed wife who had supported her "husband's" obnoxious comments about the football team. What a great support system. The pain persisted in her shoulder like she'd angered a whole hive of bees.

"She needs a doctor." Miles bent to her side.

Mikaela grimaced and swiped at the blood dripping down her arm. The bullet had taken some flesh and exited without doing too much damage. She pointed to the bear. "The bug's in there. You'll need it."

Mikaela reached for her cell phone despite Miles's protests. She punched in Palmer's number. "I think Keary may have Nathan or be heading for him. I'm going after my son."

"You're hurt," Miles said. "Let these people do their job."

"Listen to him," Palmer agreed. "You're in no shape to travel. I talked to Raif about thirty minutes ago, and everything is fine. But I can get backup on the road."

Mikaela struggled to her feet—annoyed with Palmer and Miles and the pain in her arm. "I'm going after Nathan." She closed her phone.

"You don't have a car," Miles said.

Mikaela moaned, not out of pain but in memory of the flat tire. "I'll take yours."

"I rode my bike."

She took a deep breath. "Let's go. Nathan is

about an hour and a half from here." She made her way into the kitchen and grabbed a towel. Miles snatched it from her and wrapped it around her arm. "You need a man to take care of you." Granitelike lines deepened around his eyes. He reached into the upper cabinet and pulled out her Beretta. "This one's for me."

Despite the circumstances, she offered a quick smile before hurrying out the door with her cell phone in her pocket and her Smith in her left hand.

# CHAPTER 57

MIKAELA'S SHOULDER THROBBED to the hum of the Harley flying down the highway. She concentrated on getting to Nathan before Keary and playing out all of the possibilities. Her phony pleas for him to bring Nathan's inhaler probably didn't hold solid ground, but it might give him something to think about.

Miles increased their speed. "You sure we're heading in the right direction?"

"Palmer gave me the directions."

"And your arm?"

Later she'd tell him how she'd nearly fallen off his he-man Harley. Dizzy with pain best described it. "I'm good."

"And that's why you're holding on so tight. I'm thinking Palmer has men in Dallas who will get there before us."

Mikaela hoped so, but she also knew rush-hour traffic. Miles drove against the flow, which evened the odds. She glanced at her watch: ETA for them was twenty-two minutes and counting down. Her mind flooded with unanswered questions. When had Keary left Oklahoma City? Was he driving? Who was with him? How would he explain snatching Nathan and the election tomorrow?

*God, I don't care what happens to me, but don't let him take my son.*

Ten minutes later, they drove into bone-chilling rain. Wet, slippery pavement set them up to lay the bike down, but Miles sped even faster. Mikaela squeezed his waist with a mixture of gratitude and an attempt to endure her wounded shoulder.

"Exit the feeder and take a right at the cross-road," Mikaela said. "Two miles down the road, take a left for another three and a quarter miles. It'll be a small bungalow-type house on the left."

Miles didn't question her. Perhaps he understood she needed to think through the urgency of getting Nathan safely away from Keary. When they swung into the quarter-mile-long driveway leading to the bungalow, no vehicles were in sight. She refused to subdue the flow of adrenaline.

Raif met her on the front porch as Miles pulled the motorcycle around to the back. "Backup got caught in traffic."

"I'm taking Nathan," Mikaela said. "Toss me your keys."

"The last time I gave you my keys, you and Nathan were nearly killed." He pointed to her shoulder. "The blood on your arm indicates another problem."

She was in no mood to argue—only to get Nathan safely away from the house. "Then you get him out of here."

A vehicle sped down the narrow driveway toward them. Mikaela held her breath, hoping and praying it was filled with CIA and not Keary's men. Miles appeared around the corner of the house, and the three of them hurried inside while two other operatives moved to the back of the house. A moment later, the whirling blades of a helicopter gathered their attention.

"Miss Paige!" Nathan sprung from the kitchen table covered in books, papers, and a checker-board. Rosa and a young man who must be Gonsalvo sat with him. Anissa moved to the window to see what was happening outside. "You came to see me," Nathan said.

She caught him, nearly toppling with the fire in her arm and her desire to hold her son. His face paled.

"What happened?" He took a step back.

"I'm all right, honey."

"Maybe you need some Band-Aids."

She wanted to kiss his precious face and keep him safe forever. "I—"

"Great." Raif's voice broke her thoughts. "Those aren't ours."

Mikaela shut down her emotions. *Later I'll be second mommy.* "He won't risk firing with Nathan in here."

Miles studied the men outside. "Looks like they brought a small arsenal."

Mikaela nodded to Rosa and silently apologized for endangering her life and Gonsalvo's. "The three of you need to get on the floor in the middle of the house." Rosa looked older, but she was still the same lady who had befriended Mikaela years before.

"Send out the boy," Keary called. "And no one will get hurt. You have my word."

"Your word? *I'm* not that big a fool," Raif said. "And we're about to have company."

"And I'm not that big a fool," Keary called back.

The other four men took cover. Stevens lifted an automatic. "I bet that boy is on the floor and away from any windows. And so are the Ngoimgos."

Keary stopped Stevens. No doubt concerned for Nathan. Looked like a stalemate until help arrived. "It works both ways," Keary said. "We start shooting, and you'll release the boy so he won't get hurt."

Mikaela's insides twisted. She tossed a look at Miles. He should be in the other room too.

Raif pulled out his cell phone and punched in a number. He swore. "Backup's still caught in traffic." He snapped it shut. "You're not getting the boy or the Ngoimgos," he shouted. "You're an idiot, Keary. Big risk on your end, considering Nathan . . ."

"Then you'll all die for a cause that has nothing to do with any of you."

Mikaela bit her tongue to keep from verbally tearing into Keary. It struck her that he would rather see Nathan dead than not with him. "We've got to get Nathan out of here."

"I'm thinking the same thing," Miles said. "I'm afraid Keary will get desperate and Nathan will get hurt."

Two men guarded Raif's SUV.

"Cover me, and I'll use the bike," Miles said.

She wanted to scream at the so-called coach. He could get himself killed, and she doubted he knew how to handle the gun in his hand. "I'm ready to give this all I have," she said. "Are you?"

"Since the first time you hitched a ride."

A bullet sailed through a window. Then several more. She made her way to the shattered glass and shot out two of the tires to their SUV. "Now we're even," she whispered. "They think I'm dead. Seems like I do my best work then."

She made her way to Nathan. Everything within her cried *no* to Miles's plan, but none of them had a choice. She held her son to her, desperately ignoring the fire in her arm and clinging to the fire in her heart. "I love you, Nathan."

"I love you too." His little body quivered. "Why are those men trying to hurt us?"

"They think we have something of theirs. But they're wrong." She swallowed the lump in her throat. Lifting his chin, she peered into his blue eyes. "Have you ever ridden on a motorcycle?"

"No, ma'am."

"You will now. A friend of mine is going to take you on a fast ride away from the men who are shooting at us. Do whatever he says."

"Aren't you coming?" He blinked back the tears.

Tears nearly blinded her. "I'll join up with you after the police get here."

"Promise?"

Oh, how she wanted to keep this promise. "Yes. God willing. I pray this is the last time we will be separated."

Miles appeared in the doorway. "Cover me while I go out the back." He tousled Nathan's hair. "Once I pick you up, we're traveling fast."

"Okay, but I'm a little scared."

"Just pray, brave boy," Miles said. "Just pray."

Mikaela caught one last glimpse of her men and nodded. Miles scooped Nathan up into his arms and darted out the back door toward his bike. Raif, Anissa, Mikaela, and the other two operatives poured a wall of gunfire into Keary and his men. Two fell.

The motorcycle's engine roared into action, but Keary broke from behind the SUV and raced toward Miles. Mikaela pulled open the door, firing as she stumbled toward Keary. He would not stop Miles and her son. He would not.

Keary turned, long enough to give Miles a few seconds to speed away. Rage filled Keary's face as he unleashed his weapon's fury on her. A sharp pain, then another, attacked her leg. Blackness threatened to overtake her. But it didn't matter. Miles and Nathan had gotten away.

Hours later, Miles sat at Paige's bedside, one hand in hers and the other wrapped around Nathan's shoulders. She'd gone through surgery to remove three bullets, and now they were waiting for her to wake up.

He'd been afraid he'd lost her. When he'd ridden back to the operatives, all he could see was blood. Paige's blood. He told Nathan to close his eyes, but he knew the boy had seen far too much.

That's why he was keeping Nathan with him. For once, something had to go right in the little boy's life. With Keary, Stevens, and Voleta in custody, Miles wanted to believe Nathan and Paige had a chance for life. Together. Safe.

Paige opened her eyes. She smiled—that county-fair smile that got him every time.

"Hey," she whispered. "How are my guys?"

"We're good," Miles said. "Aren't we, pal?"

Nathan nodded. "You have lots of Band-Aids now."

"I do." She seemed to fight for every word.

"Why don't you rest, and we'll be here when you wake up."

"We promise," Nathan said.

"No, I want to enjoy every minute with you. I'm okay . . . really."

Miles had so much to say . . . so much was unknown about the future.

"You handled yourself like a pro," she finally said.

"I had good reasons."

"How good?"

He leaned over and kissed her lightly. "My motives are selfish. I love you, Paige, and this little man beside me. We've gotten to know each other pretty well over the past several hours."

Moisture welled her eyes. "I'm so lucky. Hey, I have a request for you two guys."

"What's that?" Miles stroked her cheek.

"Call me by my real name—Mikaela."

Miles wrapped his arm around the little boy's shoulder. "We can do that, can't we?"

Nathan peered up at Miles, then to Mikaela, and nodded. So trusting. Miles wanted to always be there for them. "Today I proved to myself that faith can see us through anything. Whether you want to work for the CIA or shelve books or stay home to rear our babies, we'll do it together."

"Yes."

"Yes?"

"You're stuck with me."

He kissed her again, a slow, lingering promise for the future. "A couple of people from Wisconsin are waiting to see you."

"They're here?"

"Yes, and half the town of Split Creek, waiting to see how Mikaela Olsson is doing."

The next morning, Miles flipped on the Channel 6 news. "I want to hear good news for a change."

Mikaela raised her bed. "You think? Keary has some powerful attorneys." She glanced at Nathan curled up on the other bed. He'd fallen asleep shortly after two that morning.

Miles took her hand. "I believe the system is on the side of justice."

". . . CIA operative Mikaela Olsson has lived undercover in Split Creek, Oklahoma, for seven years gathering information to prove allegations that Daniel Keary betrayed his countrymen eight years ago in Angola and has been involved in illegal practices since then. Olsson faced persecution and threats to her family from Keary in an effort to keep her quiet. However, yesterday, through a well-organized sting operation, Olsson exposed Daniel Keary and others who attempted to kill her. . . ."

Miles clicked off the news. "What do you think?"

"It wasn't completely accurate, but it sounded good."

"I like the ending. The mission's completed."

Uneasiness swept through her. Tomorrow held so many uncertainties. "It may not be happily ever after." She studied Nathan's face, so peaceful despite the turmoil in his young life. What a perfect little boy. What a gift from God. "He'll need years of counseling to work through all of this," she whispered. "And someday I'll have to tell him the truth. I have no idea how or where to begin."

"Honey, God is bigger than all of our problems."

"I know, but I don't want Nathan to ever hurt again—or you." She closed her eyes and bit back a surge of pain in her leg. She hated to use the morphine drip.

"We can't prevent our loved ones from hurting any more than you can wish away the pain in your leg." He kissed her cheek. "So use the drip and trust God to lead us where we need to go."

Another tear trickled from her eye. "I love you, Miles Laird. I hope I can someday give back to you what you've done for me."

"Oh, you have." He squeezed her hand. "Now let's talk about our next Harley road trip."

# A NOTE FROM THE AUTHOR

*Dear reader,*
My goal in writing *Breach of Trust* was to provide you with adventure and suspense through the lives of unforgettable characters from the first page to the last.

Exploring the life of Mikaela Olsson and the sacrifices she made to protect those she loved provided an opportunity to examine the emotions involved in the work of the CIA. I am grateful to the CIA for its research recommendations in helping me portray as accurately as possible the responsibilities of an operative. My understanding of this highly respected organization was guided by its mission statement: "The Central Intelligence Agency (CIA) is an independent U.S. government agency responsible for providing national security intelligence to senior U.S. policymakers."

I have often wondered how a Christian operative views faith juxtaposed with a commitment to safeguard our country, for their dangerous missions often involve activities that believers may question. My character resolved that issue by acknowledging that she could use her God-given talents and abilities to secure necessary information yet still live out her faith.

I hope you enjoyed Mikaela's journey, because this story was written for you. Every word is for you—to inspire, to entertain, and to challenge all of us to be better people.

Expect an Adventure
DiAnn Mills
www.diannmills.com

# ABOUT THE AUTHOR

AWARD-WINNING AUTHOR DIANN MILLS is a fiction writer who combines an adventuresome spirit with unforgettable characters to create action-packed novels. DiAnn's first book was published in 1998, and she currently has more than forty books in print, with combined sales of over a million copies.

Six of her anthologies have appeared on the CBA best-seller list. Eight of her books have been nominated for the American Christian Fiction Writers' book of the year contest, and she is the recipient of the Inspirational Reader's Choice award for 2005 and 2007. *Lightning and Lace* was a 2008 Christy Award finalist.

DiAnn is a founding board member for American Christian Fiction Writers and a member of Inspirational Writers Alive; Romance Writers of America's Faith, Hope, and Love chapter; and the Advanced Writers and Speakers Association. She speaks to various groups and teaches writing workshops around the country. DiAnn is also a mentor for Jerry B. Jenkins's Christian Writers Guild.

Her latest releases are the Texas Legacy series, *When the Nile Runs Red*, and *Awaken my Heart*.

# DISCUSSION QUESTIONS

1. Mikaela Olsson, aka Paige Rogers, has lied to her friends and family about her life. How do you feel about that decision?

2. Do you think Miles was right in choosing a sophomore to play the coveted quarterback position?

3. What Bible story (or stories) do you see reflected in Mikaela's life?

4. The life of a CIA operative is controversial. Do you think a Christian can live out his or her faith while performing the tasks necessary to keep our country safe?

5. Mikaela had to make some tough decisions regarding Nathan. Would you have made the same choices?

6. Was Mikaela right or wrong in keeping her identity from Miles for so long?

7. At times, Miles was frustrated with the lack of knowledge about Mikaela's past. Do you

feel he would have been justified to abandon the relationship?

8. Real love means one makes sacrifices for the good of the other. What sacrifices did Miles make for Mikaela?

9. Do you think Keary would have hurt Nathan? Why or why not?

10. If you were the prosecutor in Keary's subsequent trial, whom would you select as your prime witness?

11. If you were Keary's defense attorney, how would you build a case for his innocence?

12. Do you think Mikaela will resume her role with the CIA?

13. If you were a resident of Split Creek, would you accept Miles, Mikaela, and Nathan Laird into your circle of friends?

**Center Point Publishing**
600 Brooks Road • PO Box 1
Thorndike ME 04986-0001 USA

(207) 568-3717

US & Canada:
1 800 929-9108
www.centerpointlargeprint.com